ETERNAL PEOPLE

ETERNAL PEOPLE

by

David Milofsky

For Bruce,
An old friend of mine—and of literature. With thanks for having me back in Northampton.
David 4/14/99

University Press of Colorado

International Standard Book Number 0-87081-502-4

Published by the University Press of Colorado
P.O. Box 849
Niwot, Colorado 80544

Printed in the United States of America.

The University Press of Colorado is a cooperative publishing enterprise supported, in part, by Adams State College, Colorado State University, Fort Lewis College, Mesa State College, Metropolitan State College of Denver, University of Colorado, University of Northern Colorado, University of Southern Colorado, and Western State College of Colorado.

The paper used in this publication meets the minimum requirements of the American National Standard for Information Sciences—Permanence of Paper for Printed Library Materials. ANSI Z39.48-1984

Portions of this work were published originally in a slightly different form in the *Madison Review* and *Prairie Schooner.*

Library of Congress Cataloging-in-Publication Data

Milofsky, David.
Eternal people : a novel / David Milofsky.
p. cm.
ISBN 0-87081-502-4 (cloth : alk. paper)
1. Jews—Wisconsin—History—19th century—Fiction. 2. Religious communities—Wisconsin—Fiction. 3. Jews—Persecutions—Ukraine—Fiction. I. Title.
PS3563.I444E74 1998
813' .54—dc21 98-24620
CIP

07 06 05 04 03 02 01 00 99 98 10 9 8 7 6 5 4 3 2 1

For Jean,
and to the memory of my parents

preface

Eternal People is a work of the imagination rather than a scholarly treatise on Jewish immigration in the nineteenth century, yet it has historical underpinnings. There was a socialist agrarian movement of Russian Jews in the United States known as Am Olam, and its members did establish a number of idealistic communities throughout the West, though the most successful of them lasted only a few years. My interest in the Am Olamniks was piqued by a passing reference to the movement in Irving Howe's masterful work on Jewish immigration, *World of Our Fathers.* Yet when I tried to find more on the subject, I found that very little had been written. Howe's source was an article by Abraham Menes in a YIVO annual entitled "The Am Oylam Movement," and there were one or two other articles in such obscure periodicals as *The Jewish Messenger, The Overland Quarterly,* and *The Reflex.* Though Am Olam had clearly been important in nineteenth-century Russia, it was nearly forgotten to contemporary America, even among Jewish scholars.

Far more useful for my purposes were original documents from settlers who had actually participated in the movement. Of course, everyone interested in the subject should simply be grateful for the existence of YIVO, the Institute for Jewish Research, and I am. I also deeply appreciate the assistance of Fannie Zelcer, archivist of the American Jewish Archives in Cincinnati, who graciously supplied me with copies of journals of early settlers in agricultural colonies in the West. The Oregon Historical Society very kindly sent me a copy of Helen E. Blumenthal's unpublished thesis on New Odessa, the most successful of the Am Olam colonies, and Mrs. Blumenthal was very generous in answering my many questions about the colony, both by mail and over the telephone. The late Joe Sinaiko shared his memories of immigration from Russia in the early years of the twentieth century, as well as his extensive knowledge of farming in the upper Midwest.

Perhaps the most curious and intriguing member of New Odessa was its leader, a Russian positivist named William Frey. The most important work on this mysterious visionary is Avraham Yarmolinsky's *A Russian's American Dream,* though Abraham Cahan, who knew Frey, discusses him at some length in his autobiography, *The Education of Abraham Cahan.* The largest collection of material relating to Frey is in the New York Public Library. I am grateful to the research librarians of that remarkable institution for generously allowing me free run of the Frey Collection during the long, hot summer of 1981. In addition, Lewis Greenberg's exhaustive *The Jews in Russia* allowed me to understand precisely what the Jewish settlers had undergone in their native land and why they were willing to leave.

Like Joseph Abrams, I was fortunate enough to matriculate at one of the world's great universities, the University of Wisconsin. While there, I studied with Merton M. Sealts, Jr., a distinguished scholar in American literature who, probably without knowing it, kindled in me a lifelong interest in the American idealistic movements of the nineteenth century. My friend Robert D. Richardson, Jr., generously shared his knowledge of Thoreau and Emerson during several long nocturnal conversations and in the process answered many naive questions that nevertheless needed to be answered. James Nelson and Richard Knowles allowed me to serve them as research assistant and in the process taught me all I have needed to know about methods of scholarly research. Yechiel Lander, Hillel Rabbi at Smith College in Northampton, Massachusetts, patiently instructed me in Yiddish literature and culture, something as fascinating as it was foreign to me at the time. I am grateful to all of my teachers. Any mistakes in this material are, of course, due to my imperfect understanding rather than to their instruction.

Similarly, I am indebted to the librarians of the State Historical Society of Wisconsin, where I have studied for thirty years. Their pamphlet *The Great Peshtigo Fire* by Reverend Peter Pernin is an eyewitness account of what was perhaps the greatest catastrophe in Wisconsin's history, though because it occurred on October 8, 1871, it has been overshadowed by another conflagration on that same day, the Great Chicago Fire. I drew upon Reverend Pernin's account for much of the material on forest fires in *Eternal People.*

Jo Reitman, librarian of *The Milwaukee Journal* for many years, was generous in sharing the resources of that distinguished newspaper. Through Ms. Reitman, I became aware of the Jewish agricultural settlement of Arpin, Wisconsin. Arpin was not a socialist colony, but it was of great interest to me all the same. I have placed my fictitious colony, New Zion, near a real town, Gays Mills, Wisconsin, and next to an existing river, the Kickapoo. During several visits to the area, I informed various citizens of that community that I was planning to write a novel about the area, and they were unfailingly cooperative and amused by my project.

For ten years I have had the good fortune to work in the English Department of Colorado State University in Fort Collins. I want particularly to acknowledge the two remarkable women who have served as chair during that period, both distinguished Americanists: Dr. Rosemary Whitaker, who had the courage to hire me, and Dr. Pattie Cowell, who has carried on brilliantly since Dr. Whitaker's resignation. Dr. Loren Crabtree, dean of the College of Liberal Arts, and Dr. Robert Hoffert, associate dean of the College, have both supported my work financially and given me their friendship, which is of greater importance. Professors Charles Smith, Steven Schwartz, Leslee Becker, SueEllen Campbell, and John Calderazzo have all in different ways—and often, I suspect, without knowing it—offered encouragement at crucial times. Similarly, Professor Gerald Chapman of the University of Denver and Professor Loring Silet of Iowa State University have given generously of their time and knowledge, often at some cost to projects of their own.

During the long gestation period of this novel, I received grants from the National Endowment for the Arts, the Colorado Council on the Arts and Humanities, the Bread Loaf Writers' Conference, Iowa State University, the University of Denver, and Colorado State

University. The MacDowell Colony in Peterborough, New Hampshire, possibly the best place in the world for a writer to work, twice granted me fellowships at important times. This book was completed there.

As a writer, I am lucky to have had loyal friends who are also unstinting in their honesty. George Cuomo, mentor and friend, read many versions of this novel and, thankfully, never tired of it. Elizabeth Cullinan and the late Stanley Elkin not only offered illuminating criticism but also shared their lives with me, in the process giving a young writer an image of what a writer's life should be. I am grateful to Steve Smith, Jay Neugeboren, Carole Oles, Clint McCown, Margaret Robinson, and the late John Williams for their insight and friendship. Of course, any writer would be lost without such perceptive editors as Anne Mollegen Smith, Mimi Jones, and Fred Hills. The late Leslie Cross, books editor of *The Milwaukee Journal* taught me, among other things, that politics and journalism can, and often should, mix. Howard Morton Ziff served as a larger-than-life model of a newspaper editor at the top of his game, and Elizabeth Steinberg exemplifies all that is best in literary publishing.

I also want to acknowledge Luther Wilson, who is forging new directions in publishing at the University Press of Colorado, as well as his able staff, especially Laura Furney and Darrin Pratt.

Finally, I must thank friends and family who supported me in ways too numerous to mention and too important to ignore. I am grateful to Jaque Milofsky, whose belief in me was all the more remarkable because there was no reason for it. I am grateful to Teresa Harbaugh, a true patron of the arts, who provided shelter in every sense of the word. Joyce Meskis's commitment to writers and writing must inspire all of us; it has certainly inspired me. My children, Jennie, Mimi, and Sam, cheerfully accepted the oddities of a sometimes absent and often absentminded father. My greatest debt is expressed in the Dedication.

ETERNAL PEOPLE

Book One

I must die in this land, I
must not go over the Jordan;
but ye are to go over and possess
that good land.

—Deuteronomy 4:22

one

The train stopped only briefly in Gays Mills, and almost before Yosl could get his satchel and climb down, it was moving slowly away in a dignified rain of dust and cinders, at once decorous and violent. Even the train seemed in a hurry to leave Wisconsin, cross the Mississippi, and get to the Great Plains.

For a moment, Yosl stood expectantly, looking at other passengers who had gotten off, the stationmaster, the carts and wagons that were being loaded with grain and dry goods. The dusty air tickled his nose and made his eyes water. Then he understood: there was no one to meet him. He hadn't wired his time of arrival. He wouldn't have known whom to wire. Suddenly, he felt more alone than ever. Before, he had a destination, and the long trip took on its own rhythm, making him feel a part of something, even if it was only a train full of strangers. Now he had arrived, but he had no idea where he was. He picked up his suitcase and followed the hanging dust of a wagon into town.

Gays Mills spread away from the Kickapoo River, meandering as the river did, its blocks marching in oblong patterns until they petered out into prairie that stretched away in all directions. As many people were walking as riding, and Yosl enjoyed the hot summer sun on his bare head and back. Brick buildings alternated with stone of a pale, sandy color; raw pine tenements marked the boundaries between them.

Wood sidewalks ran the length of the three-block Main Street, and now the dirt road became crowded with horses, wagons, and pedestrians, all jostling each other for position.

The town was no bigger than a large shtetl, but though Yosl saw no Jews, here, unlike Russia, the gentiles did not seem threatening. They moved past him on the sidewalk as if he weren't there, and that made Yosl feel wonderfully, limitlessly free to do as he liked, to be whatever he would become.

It seemed remarkable that at the age of nineteen, when he should have been at university, he could get on a train in New York and ride a thousand miles across the country to a small town without having anyone demand anything of him. There were no internal passports or identification papers, no suspicious guards or physical examinations, not even unfriendly passengers. Was it possible that this was at last a world free of anti-Semitism? Here, it was possible to think so. Loneliness would be a small price to pay. Yosl shouldered his pack and asked directions of a man sweeping the steps of a dry goods store.

"New Zion?" the man repeated, querulous at first, then comprehending. "You must mean the Russians. Just walk outside town five miles. It'll be on your right."

Yosl smiled and thanked the man. Only in America, he thought, could a Jew be confused with a Russian.

two

Beyond the last shanties on the fringe of town, the road hooked sharply to the right and narrowed, becoming little more than a country lane. The river was nearly hidden now by high grass and was, in any case, only a trickle of dirty water. Rising to Yosl's left was a succession of rocky bluffs, but the landscape otherwise did not vary from the sandy hills on the horizon. Everywhere he looked, Yosl saw vast empty fields with only a scrim of trees as a border and the road running through them like a thin dun ribbon. There seemed to be no one else in the world this morning, only himself in the space between the muddy river and the distant hills.

As he walked, Yosl tried to record his impressions, but the farther he went, the more difficult this became. His shoes were hot and stiff, more suitable to city pavement than a rutted country road. He felt blisters forming beneath his heels, and sweat ran freely down his back. The suit he had been so proud of an hour before now felt like chain mail. The satchel was an anchor threatening to pull his arm from its socket. Before he had walked two miles, his trousers were caked to the knees with dust. Finally, Yosl wrapped a handkerchief around his throat and mouth, hoisted the satchel to his shoulders, took off the hard leather shoes, and tied his suit coat around his waist. Feeling more like an itinerant peasant than an adventurer, he continued to New Zion in relative comfort.

Several miles farther on, the road ended in a clearing. Facing Yosl was a dense thicket of pine trees on one side and unbroken prairie on the other. Beyond the open space, he saw some shacks, and past them a large, rectangular building, open on one side. A garden flanked the main structure and stretched toward the river. Above it all, a flag waved in the wind, inscribed with the Torah scrolls. On it was written "Am Olam." Eternal People, Yosl thought. Next to the scrolls were a crudely drawn plow and anvil.

Because of the weathered wood, low buildings, and dense underbrush, New Zion was practically invisible from the road. Moreover, it seemed to be deserted. It was only as he moved closer that he began to see signs of life. Chickens picked at the dirt and shook their beaks in the sun as they ate; a thin spiral of smoke issued from one of the houses. On the porch of the large building, which Yosl now saw had a long table and chairs as its only furniture, a girl sat watching him. She appeared from a distance to be little more than a child, but as Yosl came closer, he saw that she was close to his own age. She had blond hair, blue eyes, and an open, attractive face. But her drab brown dress hung off her shoulders and concealed her figure. Yosl was about to attempt English when she addressed him in Yiddish.

"You must be from Russia."

Yosl was put off by this. In his weeks in New York, he had grown contemptuous of new arrivals. Now this girl had labeled him immediately. "How did you know?"

"They all look like you when they come," the girl said. "No one here wears a suit." She walked across the porch to examine Yosl more closely. "I'm Elzbeta, but call me Lizzie. What's your name?"

"Yosl. I've come to find my uncle, Shmuel Abramovitz."

The girl's face registered something between anger and disappointment. "Over there," she said dully, and pointed to a small outbuilding.

Yosl picked up his pack. "I suppose we'll be neighbors," he said. "It's good to meet you."

But Lizzie seemed to have lost interest. She picked up a bag of seed and started feeding the chickens, her arm describing a long, regular arc in the sunlight as the birds ran first one way then the other after the sheets of grain that were raining down upon them.

Shmuel's home was little more than a shed and seemed on the verge of collapse. Rather than knock and risk this destruction, Yosl boldly pushed the door open. When he looked in, he could see nothing in the blackness, but as his eyes adjusted, he saw slats of light coming from a shuttered window and then indistinct shapes. Finally, he was able to make out an enormous body dwarfing the narrow pallet upon which it lay. His uncle, snoring loudly in the close, fetid air, was unaware of Yosl's arrival or anything else in the moving world. The room smelled of yeast, and Yosl took shallow breaths to keep from gagging. He dropped his satchel and swept his arm in a circle, searching for a chair. Behind the door, he found a small deal table and a three-legged stool, where he sat to consider his situation.

He had not expected New Zion to be a nondescript collection of shacks populated by bad-tempered girls and drunks. How could the great editor Abraham Cahan consider this a socialistic outpost worthy of the name? It occurred to him that he could retrace his steps, return to New York, to the newspaper, and forget about New Zion. Who would know or care? He would be embarrassed to return this way, to have to explain to Cahan that his desire to join his uncle had not even survived the trip west. But it was no crime to make mistakes, only to refuse to accept them for what they were and change.

Shmuel belched, and Yosl felt his gorge rise as he smelled his uncle's stale breath. Gritting his teeth, he moved his stool closer to the bed. The knowledge that this was his only surviving relative brought tears of anger and exhaustion to his eyes. He reached over and touched Shmuel's shoulder.

"Uncle, it is your nephew. I have come to live with you. Wake up."

Shmuel grunted and expelled air through his nose. Then one small, black eye opened to examine the intruder. "Who?"

Yosl stood now. "Uncle. I have come from Russia to see you."

Shmuel sat up and stretched, his arms seeming to crowd the ceiling. Yosl saw he was wearing a hat with the visor turned around, a leather vest, and a pair of voluminous stained trousers. Now Shmuel put his arms through his suspenders and stood to look at Yosl. He was a big man, larger even than Yosl had imagined from his father's description, over six feet tall and weighing more than two hundred pounds.

His face was flushed except where it was covered by a spiky black beard that encircled his jaw. His pendulous stomach was barely circumscribed by his pants, and the small hat looked comic perched on his forehead like a birdcage.

"Uncle?"

"I heard you. For God's sake give me peace first thing in the morning." Shmuel's voice was not loud; it had instead a scratchy quality, as if it had been used infrequently.

"I'm sorry," Yosl said. "I wasn't sure you heard me."

"I should be deaf in addition to fat and drunk?" He was peering into the corners of the room. Finally, he extracted a pitcher from beneath a ledge. He offered the jug to Yosl. "Here, drink. It's only cider beer, it won't hurt you. The Indians make it."

The walk from town had made Yosl thirsty. He took the flask and drank deeply, feeling the warm liquid run down his shirt front. Then he gagged, spitting and coughing up everything he had swallowed, feeling the bitter drink in his nostrils.

Amused, Shmuel patted Yosl on the back. "At least you tried it," he said. "Now tell me, what are you doing out here?"

Yosl felt his disappointment turn to anger, and once again his eyes filled. He wiped them with his sleeve and blew his nose. "Uncle," he began, his voice a croak. Then he was crying, and though he didn't wish to be seen like this, it was not in his power to stop. He bent over in his chair, his thin body racked with sobs, and finally Shmuel put his arm around him.

Yosl embraced his uncle, feeling his strong warm body and the rush of his own tears hot on his cheeks. He buried his face in Shmuel's chest, imagining it was his father, that they were all together again, and that nothing had changed, that there had been no pogrom and no one had died. Yosl was grateful for the freedom of America, but it would be worth living a life in bondage to have his parents and sisters alive again. Shmuel held Yosl so tight Yosl thought he would lose consciousness, yet he did not complain, for he knew that in this mute gesture Shmuel was admitting guilt and sorrow, saying what would be impossible in words. Finally, Shmuel released him, and Yosl, shaken, sat on the edge of the small table, his hands still trembling. When Shmuel spoke, it was in a soft, kind voice.

"It is a hard thing to be alone at your age."

Yosl nodded. "Yes. I miss my family."

"It may sound odd," Shmuel said. "But I miss them, too. Twenty years ago it was impossible for me to admit I needed anybody; now that I can, they are all gone."

"So you know about the pogrom, Uncle?"

"Cahan, the famous editor, wrote me. He knows everything, even what isn't worth knowing." Shmuel shook his head. "We used to be friends. He said you would be coming and told me what happened. Before that, I read of such things in the *Forward,* like everyone else, but I never thought there would be trouble in White Russia. Always it was in the south, but we had been safe. Now, no one is safe. I even wonder if we are here."

Yosl was seeing a new side of his uncle. He had always thought of him as strong and fearless. Never as reflective or doubting himself. But Yosl couldn't imagine any danger in America. Here Jews could not only own land, but the people left them alone and seemed friendly. Not wanting to contradict his uncle, Yosl said, "Mr. Cahan was kind to me. He rescued me from Castle Garden and gave me work when I knew no one in New York. I had no idea America was so big, that I would have so much trouble finding you."

"So now you are a journalist?" Shmuel said.

"Hardly that. Widows and orphans would bring me their letters and I would correct their spelling," Yosl said.

"Your modesty is becoming," Shmuel said. "But you can read and write?"

"I was a student in Minsk before all this happened. In New York, Mr. Cahan made me study English. It was inevitable that I would learn something."

"You make light of it, but it's no small thing," Shmuel said. "How long have the Jews been in Russia? Five hundred years. And how many have even bothered to learn the language? It's no different here. A Jew can live his whole life on the East Side and not know enough English to order breakfast. This makes sense?"

"I suppose many people are too busy working to learn the language or go to school," Yosl said.

Shmuel grunted, as if he might accept the point. He inhaled deeply and opened and shut his eyes a few times. “And why were you so anxious to find me?”

Yosl was surprised. “You are my father’s brother. Where else would I go?”

“America is very different from Russia, Yosl,” Shmuel said gently. “Your father knew that, God rest his soul.”

“Father said that when Jews became farmers, the world would starve.”

Shmuel laughed now. “Yes, there is something to that, though we haven’t starved yet. But who would have thought there would be ten different ways to plant corn and that our comrades would have to debate each one before getting on with it?”

Yosl remembered hearing his uncle described as a young rebel, the black sheep in the family who would not be controlled by his grandfather but chose instead to run off to America. He hadn’t been prepared for his soft voice and gentle humor. He had expected to admire and fear his uncle; instead, to his surprise, he liked him.

Shmuel shook his head again and now Yosl saw deep lines in his forehead. “I told your father to leave, I begged him. But I was the younger brother, the *luftmensch,* what did I know? He said he understood the Russians, that they were animals. Vodka and money were all that mattered to them, and he had plenty of that. When Cahan wrote about the massacre, I felt like going back and fighting myself, even if they would kill me,” Shmuel said bitterly. “Then I considered living a better life, even becoming a rabbi as Father wanted. But what good would it do? Would one death have been prevented if I gave up drinking or studied the Torah every day?” He paused, raising his eyebrows, though Yosl had the feeling Shmuel wasn’t really talking to him. “Pah, it would have done no good at all,” he finished.

Shmuel was right, but his logic angered Yosl. “Uncle, you are the oldest surviving man in our family and you deserve my respect. But you make it hard. My mother and father lie in shallow graves and you sit here arguing philosophy.”

Shmuel seemed impressed. He took off his hat and ran his fingers through his hair. Then he removed his glasses and polished them with his shirtsleeve. "A regular tiger," he said at last. "And, of course, you are right. I feel guilty, so I explain things to make myself feel better. I apologize." He offered Yosl his hand.

Yosl turned away. "You owe me no explanations."

"Yes, yes, I do. Even if there is no good reason for it, I am alive, and your father, a much better man, is dead. And simply because I had the good fortune to leave before the Tsar sent his men north."

"Why did you leave, Uncle?"

"Ach, who knows," Shmuel said, running his fingers through his hair. "I remember why I thought I left. I was going to save the world. But even that was only half the truth. I was a communist; sometimes I still am." He stood and squinted out the small window at the garden. The summer foliage pressed flat against the glass, but Yosl could see the corn, high and yellow against the dark green background. Shmuel turned to face Yosl, hands in his pockets. "But I was also tired of living the way we did in Russia. You know what I mean, Yosl. I was sick of hunching my shoulders so I wouldn't look so tall. I was disgusted with myself for trying to disappear whenever a goy looked my way. I was tired of the moronic peasants and petty bureaucrats who could decide my fate on a whim simply because of the accident of my birth. I was sick of it all."

Yosl wondered whether his father had felt this way. If so, he had never let on; instead, he'd taken pride in outwitting the peasants, letting them think they were getting the upper hand and then succeeding in spite of it all. Still, his great passion in life had been Yosl's education. Even as a small child, Yosl remembered his father's telling him about the great universities in Germany where Jews could study anything they wanted, side by side with the gentiles. What Shmuel said made sense, but looking around the room, Yosl saw little evidence of his high ideals.

"And here you have found such a paradise, Uncle? In this place with wine bottles on the table and a dirt floor? You haven't even a real bed to sleep on."

Shmuel seemed amused. "What does all that matter? Am I such a dandy that I need a fresh suit every day? These things aren't important, Yosl. In Russia, I felt like a fish on a line. I was sick of having that hook in my lip. But I will be honest with you. Even that was not the main reason. I was tired of being a Jew. I couldn't stand the stench of the prayer house on winter mornings, the old men in their moth-eaten capotes, the cringing women shuffling off to the *mikva* each month to wash sex from their bodies." He paused and breathed deeply at the memory. "I hated the Russians, but I hated the Jews, too. I hated myself. I wanted to live a different kind of life. To stretch to my full height, speak as loudly and arrogantly as I pleased, to love many women, gentile women. Everything."

"And you've done this?"

"Not all of it. But tell me, my father and grandfather were pious men. They spent their days and nights studying the Gemara and Mishnah and what did it get them? Are they less dead than the others?"

The question made Yosl uncomfortable, for he had had the same thoughts, especially in New York, where he had seen women without wigs for the first time, women in expensive silk dresses and lipstick. "That is not for me to say, Uncle. I hardly knew my grandfather."

"Yes, very well," Shmuel said, nodding his head. "But you see, I did, and that is why I left. I don't blame you for being disgusted with the way you find me, Yosl. I congratulate you on your anger. It is good for young men to be mad at their elders—God knows I was. Each generation discovers for itself what a mess the world has become and decides to change everything. I wish you good luck. But I haven't lived my life to inspire you or set an example. That was never my idea."

Shmuel's humility made Yosl feel presumptuous. In fact, he had no idea what he would do differently than his elders, no plan at all. It was absurd for him to pass judgment on his uncle when he had done nothing in his own life. "I'm sorry, Uncle. I didn't mean to sound so foolish. It's just not what I expected."

Shmuel patted Yosl on the shoulder. "Of course. I understand. I wrote Cahan about New Zion, but how could he know how things really are? Our life here is no paradise. But we are free, that's the main thing. Anyway, I'm glad you've come—for my sake, not yours. As you say, I'm your only surviving relative. Perhaps now that your father is gone, I can stop being his little brother."

Yosl remembered his father as being fond of Shmuel but also contemptuous. He used to joke that he was the only Jew in Russia "with a poor relative in America." Now Yosl saw that it wouldn't have been easy being the youngest in the family. But all he said was, "I've always wanted to be a farmer."

Shmuel seemed pleased by this and smiled. But when he spoke, his voice was brisk, even stern. "One thing you must know, however it appears—everyone in New Zion works hard or they must leave. Men, women, children, everyone."

"I'm not afraid of work, Uncle."

"Good. Most of the men spend their days in the forest cutting trees and clearing land. The women do the gardening and much of the cooking, though we all take turns in the kitchen. There is no surplus, but we manage to eat enough to stay alive and even sell some cheese. The other thing is that we are Jews, but not as your father was. When I came here, I cut my earlocks and changed my name. Here, I'm called Sam. Sam Abrams. It will take some time for you to adjust, but I'd like you to try to remember this for the future."

"Who should I be, then?"

"You are my nephew, so the last name is the same. And in America, they will call you Joseph, or Joe."

Yosl tried the unfamiliar name on his tongue. It seemed strong and firm after the sibilance of his given name. He thought he liked it. Then he remembered Lizzie. "I met a girl outside who showed me your house. A blond girl. Thin. Is she Jewish?"

Shmuel seemed to know whom he meant. "Ah," he breathed deeply. "You've met her, then."

"She spoke to me in Yiddish."

Shmuel nodded. "Her father is an idiot who calls himself Edward Liberty. He is a Russian, an aristocrat, who was an officer in the army before he found God. Six months ago, he dropped among us and proceeded to take over the camp. If you talk to some of my comrades, they will tell you it is a good thing, that he is the Messiah himself. As you may have guessed, I am of a slightly different opinion. But you'll make up your own mind. Liberty is one person you can't avoid." Shmuel rose and hiked up his pants. "You've come a long way. You're hungry?"

"I could eat, Uncle."

"Spoken like a judge. Come with me."

Shmuel pushed open the door, letting in a brilliant shower of sun. Then he gestured toward the yard. Leaving his pack behind, Joe Abrams entered the bright midday light of New Zion.

three

He awoke sweating, with his father's voice harsh in his ear: "Run, run, my son. Survive!" Yosl sat straight up in his bed, uncertain for a moment where he was and terrified. Then, slowly, the ghostly outlines of the empty beds of the dormitory took shape, comforting him.

The dream had been the same: always it was his father screaming in torment, always he was running away. Unlike Lot's wife, he never looked back. Despite the persistence of the dream, however, Yosl remembered almost nothing of the pogrom. There had been little warning, no one running ahead to tell them of the soldiers' approach, no hoofbeats outside their door. Only a sudden commotion in the hallway and then his father's face, red as fire, telling him to run.

Yosl had—out the back door, through the mill, and into the forest. In his panic, he had been oddly aware of details: he remembered the softness of the pine needles underfoot, the sweet smell of wildflowers contrasting with the tumult all around, the odd sense of calm in the midst of destruction. Then the river was spread out before him like a prayer shawl. Stealthily, he waded through the muck until he was almost submerged in the torpid water, lilies soft as poultices wreathing his chin, a large rock between him and the riverbank.

Even after the cold had numbed his feet, Yosl kept down, his nose barely clearing the surface of the river. In the distance he heard the shrill yells of battle, though he didn't know what resistance the Jews could possibly make. Once, he thought he heard his mother cry out in agony and involuntarily rose from his hiding place before shrinking back into the water.

Toward dusk, the noise faded away until there was only the shush-shushing of the ancient fir trees overhead. This forest had sheltered his family for generations, but now the solitude was palpable. Yosl climbed dripping from the river and then retreated apprehensively to what remained of his village.

From a distance, it seemed essentially unchanged. Smoke rose from the roofs of several houses, and the shacks looked a little more decrepit than usual, but that was all. What was most noticeable was the silence. No dogs, no people standing in the small square in front of the well, nothing.

In the center of their yard, Yosl found his father, a knife sticking out of his chest, a thin smear of blood outlining his pale lips. He knelt by his father's side and looked into his pale eyes. Was death ever any more painful than this? His father had been a simple man who wanted only to live as best he could and feed his family. Now he lay dead on a dusty road, in a forgotten shtetl, at the age of forty-nine. Yosl lay his face against his father's, letting his lips brush the cold stubble. Then he shut his eyes and looked for the others.

His mother was not far away, modest, as always, in repose. Her expression seemed peaceful despite her ordeal, and her skirts had not been disturbed. No wound was visible. The Russians had demanded nothing more than her life, and Yosl was grateful. Flanking her were the two girls, so small that they might have been errant piles of clothes. Nothing moved in the entire village. Only he had survived.

Now Yosl felt sick and retched fruitlessly. He hadn't eaten since morning, but his stomach was churning in anger and grief. Dumbly, he wandered around the clearing, tears running freely down his face. Somewhere, thousands of miles away, in St. Petersburg or Moscow, an official had put a pin in a map and issued the ukase that had made him an orphan. Then they had sent the soldiers, who had directed the peasants to kill and burn the village. Yosl realized they had shown restraint. At Kishinev, women's stomachs had been slit open and their breasts cut off with sabres. Cossacks had broken into the shul and impaled the rabbi on a Russian flag. The Torah scrolls had been defiled. Here, there was none of that. No one had driven nails through the eyes of the Jews; no one threw babies out of second-story windows. The peasants had only done as they were told and left.

Still, Yosl wanted to take up his father's ax and storm the governor's mansion. Even to be killed trying would be a relief. He felt guilty for even partially excusing his parents' killers, for understanding and crediting them with restraint. It was his reasonable habit of mind, the way he had been taught to think at university. He shivered with disgust at his own impotence. A peasant he had known all his life might have pulled the trigger that ended his father's life, a man who brought him candy when he came to the mill with his grain. But how could he take revenge for this? Who would he even be looking for? It was hopeless. All Yosl could do was bury his family and leave this place behind him.

There was a shovel in the shed behind the house. In the half-light, a brisk wind moved through the clearing, plastering his wet pants to his legs. Yosl shivered and rubbed his hands together. Behind the cottage, he dug four graves to discourage the wolves he knew were waiting in the forest. He wrapped his parents and the girls in blankets and covered them with dirt. Then he sank to his knees, covering his head with his shirt, and sang the Kaddish. He prayed to God to forgive him for deserting his family, for not fighting and dying as they had. For surviving.

When he arose, Yosl was disoriented. It was dark and cold, and he was wearing only his blue student uniform. He found a dry shirt and his father's long leather coat in the house. In the darkness, he tried to make out the borders of his village, though calling it a village was a bit grand. A collection of shacks, that was all. There was no real road, for there was nowhere to go. He searched for the hovel where he had attended cheder, but it was too dark to see clearly. It was as if none of it had really existed, as if he were imagining his life.

He wandered up and down, trying to identify the dead, but the bodies were indistinct lumps on the ground, no longer friends and neighbors, no longer anything. He wanted to stay till morning, to bury everyone properly, but who could tell when the peasants would return? Praying that the souls of those who lay unsheltered in the clearing would be protected, he dovened in the direction of his parents' graves. He felt sick when he thought of the wolves, but his first responsibility was to stay alive. Once more Yosl looked at the deserted village disappearing before his eyes into the darkness. Then he hoisted his father's ax to his shoulder and walked into the forest.

Ten miles south, the slow stream in back of the mill connected with the Neman River. This would be his way out. Before that, however, Yosl would have to find his father's cache. He had just come home for vacation when Isaac suggested a walk in the woods. They went deep into the forest, the river at their side, until finally his father stopped and indicated a tree. "It is better that we talk here," he had said. "There is no reason to alarm your mother and sisters."

"You are alarming me, Father."

Isaac smiled slightly. "You are nineteen, a man, as tall as I am and blond as a Russian. It is your lot to sometimes be scared. It might save your life."

Then his father had pointed at the tree. About three feet from the ground, the bark was peeled away from the trunk. "Here, Yosl, if you dig a hole, you will find a passport and enough money to get across the border and into Germany."

"But I can't go without you."

"I pray God you won't have to, but things are very bad for us right now. Always before I have felt secure. The village is small and easily ignored, and the officials have expensive mistresses. This is White Russia, after all. Not the Ukraine."

Yosl understood. What Jew had not heard of the pogroms of the '80s and '90s in the south? Who did not know about Kirova and Kishinev? But here, the governor was more lenient. Unlike his colleagues elsewhere, he had never cooperated with the Sacred League in their mission to drive the Jews out of Russia or invited the Black Hundred to send in the Barefoot Brigades to loot Jewish homes and rape Jewish women. "And now, Father? Has something changed?"

Isaac sighed. "The Tsar is at war with Japan, and it is always easiest to blame the Jews for the nation's sacrifice. Let a Jew find a way to make his life less miserable, and they will pass a law to frustrate him. Yes, much has changed."

In the moonlight, Yosl kept his eyes to the ground, and after an hour of searching, he found the tree with the hash mark on it and dug up the metal box. In it were some rubles and papers. Yosl took them and walked toward the Neman.

The river was fast and cold, and the sight of it made Yosl sad. Wet rocks gleamed like skulls in the moonlight and the water throbbed a steady hymn to the night. Yosl tried to think of his father, up to his waist in the roiling water, dragging logs off the riverbank and pushing them downstream, red-faced and jubilant with the work. But it was impossible. Tree branches drooped over the water like tentacles and the current seemed malevolent in the darkness.

Each summer Isaac had taken logs down the river on a raft, with a bottle of vodka between his knees. Sometimes he had joked that he might miss Germany altogether, just keep going through Lithuania and into the Baltic. Now Yosl decided this would be his escape route. Most emigrants went south, through Galicia, to Brody, where they waited months for papers allowing them passage west. Yosl did not intend to spend his money on bribes. He would bypass Brody and take his chances.

The summer before, they had left their raft submerged beneath the water. After wading a hundred yards in each direction, Yosl found it and was surprised to see it had held together through the winter. He had helped his father bind the logs with thick leather thongs. He discarded the anchor of rocks and pushed off into the cool water. The raft moved swiftly, purposefully, in the night, and Yosl felt the logs shift under him, rubbing his legs raw like harsh soap.

He lay back on Isaac's coat and studied the sky. As he floated downstream, he saw occasional lights on the riverbank. A peasant's hut or a hunter's cooking fire. In the distance, they seemed benign, even welcoming. He wondered if he could find his mother's relatives in Kiev or Odessa, but lonely as he was, he didn't really consider stopping for a moment. He was leaving forever. Russia was dead for him.

All the hope the *maskils* had inspired, all the brave talk he had heard at university of a new age in which Jews would take their rightful places in the world now seemed foolish. They had been led to hope and that hope had nearly killed them. Of course, there would be explanations for what had happened, and Jews would give them. Things will be better; we must be patient. Yosl had heard it all before. This time he would take the warning and leave. But where to go? That was a question. He had no clear sense of geography, no compass, not even much food.

He looked again at the stars. In America, they would be guiding pioneers. Perhaps his uncle would be looking at the heavens also for guidance. Yosl felt small and insignificant, alone on the river, buried in his father's coat, a tiny spot of life in the eternal blackness. His fate lay with the Neman; it would decide if he would be delivered into freedom. Overcome with exhaustion, he closed his eyes and slept.

During the night, the raft started to come apart. By holding it together with his hands and then by floating himself on one of the logs, Yosl was able to pass over the border into Lithuania. Then he journeyed north, traveling only at night and stealing food from farmers' barns. He had heard rumors of gangs that roamed the border area and haunted train stations looking for immigrants, but he couldn't walk to America.

One evening he ventured into a station, where he waited timidly for the clerk to recognize him. On the train to Hamburg, safe at last, he relaxed, thinking the worst was over. A kind of euphoria came over him. Single-handed, he had escaped death and made it past the Russians. Soon he would be in Germany, birthplace of the Haskalah, where Jews were free to study at the great universities and enter the professions. He leaned back on the plush seat and allowed himself to dream.

At three A.M., the train stopped in Germany and everyone was ordered out. Yosl and the others stood like statues in the pale moonlight outside an imposing white stone building. Husbands comforted their wives, mothers their children. Huge piles of bedding, suitcases, and other belongings littered the field. Then men came out of the buildings, enormous in white coats and carrying leather briefcases. They moved among the passengers, separating men from women, shouting, "Quick, quick." Then the passengers were herded into the white building.

Everyone was directed to examining rooms smelling of antiseptic and told to undress. Their belongings were confiscated and they were left, naked, to wait. All around, Yosl heard men and women calling to each other, and babies crying. A cacophony of fear. Next to him sat a wizened little man whose face was twisted into a sneer. His body was thin and brown; wrinkles moved up his ribs like chevrons. Then Yosl saw he had been noticed. The man winked and shrugged his shoulders.

"Wait until you have something to cry about," he said, indicating the others. "Here," he gestured toward the floor. "Have a seat."

Yosl sat down, but the man said nothing more. He seemed ancient, his eyes sad and rheumy, despite his strong, youthful voice. His skin hung in folds, as though he had lost a great deal of weight. "How long will they hold us?" Yosl asked.

"A day, a night, another day. Long enough to look up every *toches* on the train. The Germans leave nothing to chance when it comes to cleanliness."

"But why are we here?"

The man looked amused. He licked his lips as if he were trying to think of an explanation. "Don't you know Jews carry diseases?" he said. "Like dogs and cats. The Germans worry that if they don't look out, they'll catch poverty from us." Then he smiled and patted Yosl on the back. "Don't look so scared. You got nothing to fear, a strong, healthy boy like you. Me, that's another story."

Soon they were taken to a large room where huge women with biceps flapping rubbed a slippery soap over their bodies. Then steaming water from an immense cauldron was poured over them. Prayers were offered to the Almighty, children cried, while above it all, the men screamed for order, but Yosl felt calm. No one here seemed to care who they were, only what they smelled like.

After the showers, they were given muslin gowns and told to assemble in a large hall. Light was coming in through the windows when Yosl finally reached the front of the line. The doctor peered into Yosl's eyes and ears and stuck a stick into his mouth far enough to make him gag. The doctor passed him on with a bored shrug. Yosl felt sorry for him. Being up in the middle of the night examining a trainload of terrified Jews would not be a pleasant assignment for anyone.

Back on the train, clean and warm for the first time in days, Yosl stretched out to relax. But no sooner had he closed his eyes than he heard the rasping voice again. "How many seats you'll take up, then?"

Yosl looked up to see his friend from the examining room and realized he hadn't expected the older man to make it out. "I'm sorry," he said automatically.

"You apologize too much," the man said. "It's a Jewish disease." Then he thrust out his hand. "I'm Hayim Goldman."

"My name is Yosl Abramovitz." He offered the other man his hand. Goldman looked skeptical, but he took it in his.

As the train began to roll, the older man produced cigarette paper and a pouch of tobacco from his pocket. He took what seemed like an hour to prepare a smoke, then, when he had finally lubricated the brown paper with saliva and lighted it, he turned to Yosl. "So, where's your family?"

"Dead. Except for my uncle in America."

Goldman nodded, his face grim for a moment. Then his expression softened and became almost wistful. "And you're what, seventeen?"

"Nineteen. I was a student in Minsk."

"And now? Well, now you'll go to America to live with your rich uncle. Where will that be?"

Yosl didn't bother to correct him about Shmuel's finances. It had just occurred to him that he had no idea of his uncle's whereabouts. "I don't know."

"East or west?"

The words meant nothing. Yosl could only think of America as an entity, not as something with sections, regions, even cities, like other countries. It was America, that was all. A state of mind, not really a place. "I have no idea."

Goldman put his hand on Yosl's knee. "Yosl, you're alone in the world and I have no wish to make your life more difficult. But you are in some situation. Your mother and father are gone. You've got an uncle somewhere in America, but you don't know where. So maybe you have a little money and you get on a boat and you even survive the trip. Fine. What will you do once you get to America?"

Goldman's questions made Yosl uncomfortable. He felt exposed and vulnerable. "You don't have to worry," he said. "That's *my* problem, Mr. Goldman."

"You're right about that," Goldman said, undeterred by Yosl's sarcasm. "But listen to me. America's not like Russia. They ain't got shtetls there. The police don't keep track of where everyone is all the time. You can't just walk into the study house and someone will know your uncle. There's no study house and practically no Jews. All they got is Indians and soldiers shooting each other out there. Now, how are you going to find your uncle, will you tell me that, please? You don't speak the language, and you're practically a yeshiva *bucher*."

"I studied English in Minsk," Yosl said stiffly.

"And if your tutor understood you, you were lucky."

"How do you know so much about it?"

Goldman spread his hands before him like a map. "Know? I got to know something to ask questions? I know nothing, that much I know."

Yosl turned to the window and watched Germany speed by. The train stopped briefly at a town and he was tempted to get off and seek his fortune there. Goldman was right. He would never be able to find Shmuel in America, so what sense did it make to go there? But though he didn't move, the idea that he had a choice lessened the tension. He turned to look at his companion. "What about your family?"

The other man looked uncomfortable. He twisted his cigarette in his lips and hunched his shoulders, though it wasn't cold in the car. "It's been a long time since I thought that way," he said in a whisper. "But once, yes, I had a wife, a son."

"Was there a pogrom in your town?"

"In a way, it was worse than that. I left my family to save the world."

Yosl had only recently begun to think of a world beyond the borders of his village. He couldn't imagine a man having such aspirations. He had known radicals in Minsk, but he'd never understood them. "How?" was all he could manage.

Goldman grimaced. "A good question. But at the time, it didn't even occur to me." He puffed his cheeks with smoke, then let it out with a sigh. "I had this passion for freedom," he said. "Not just for me, to do as I pleased, live where I liked. No, I wanted freedom for the whole human race. I went away to make revolution."

This idea presented itself to Yosl as something concrete, akin to building a house, say, something his father might have done. "And how is such a thing made?"

Goldman looked amused, as if he had never met anyone quite so stupid. "You must go away to live among the people and instruct the peasants."

Yosl nodded, though he couldn't see what Goldman could teach peasants. The man seemed too delicate for hard work; his hands were too soft.

"The funny thing is I was the one who ended up being taught," Goldman continued. But he wasn't laughing. "Everyone knows about Kishinev, but maybe you never heard about my town, Gomel?" He leaned forward now and tapped Yosl's knee. "It was in Gomel that the Jews realized for the first time that not only would the army not save them, but that they were actually helping the barbarians."

"They didn't know this before?"

"Not everyone is so smart as you. Besides, we're not a violent people by nature. We were prepared to reason with the Russians, or bribe them. Remember, the pogroms of the '80s and '90s were different. There were beatings, even rapes, but few murders. It was mostly luck, where you happened to be, not life and death."

Yosl thought of his father, of his success in bribing the town officials. He wouldn't have gone to university if his father hadn't known who needed money. "I'm not so smart," Yosl said. "I didn't mean that."

Goldman brushed him off. "Don't be so sensitive. It's only my manner of speaking. What I meant was that things changed once the Tsar started this crazy war. Before, he used the Jews as scapegoats when times were bad or when it seemed the revolution might actually succeed. But now Russian boys were being killed, slaughtered by the Japanese, both on the land and at sea. And war is very expensive. Something had to be done to make up for that."

"Jews had to die, too?"

"Congratulations. But with one difference. From the time they heard the Black Hundred was planning a raid, the people of Gomel started to prepare. Instead of waiting passively to be slaughtered, they gathered together every kind of weapon they could lay their hands on. Rakes, hoes, hammers, and axes were put into a central store. Men were given knives and clubs; nails were driven into logs; women boiled water to throw from upper windows and they sharpened their knitting needles in case all else failed. Barricades were erected at all entrances to the ghetto."

"And what happened?" Yosl asked, excited now. "Did they win, did they kill the Black Hundred?"

Goldman smiled ruefully, but his eyes were sad. He shook his head and looked at the floor. "How could they? They held out for nearly two days, which was remarkable enough. But there were terrible losses.

At last the soldiers who had been waiting outside town rode in and opened fire. Then there was no hope. If the Jews had been allowed to fight on, even with things as unequal as they were, who knows? But they couldn't fight the army's guns with rakes and scythes."

"And your wife and son?"

"Dead, both of them." Goldman nodded and looked out the window, his eyes glazed with tears. "But the worst thing is how stupid we were—the revolutionaries, I mean. When the first pogroms broke out, we all congratulated each other and offered toasts. This is the beginning of the revolution, we thought. At last the peasants are rising up against their masters. That the oppressors happened to be our people was only a coincidence. Sacrifices needed to be made." Goldman smiled ironically. "Some must die in order for justice to be won. God, what fools we were."

He took a handkerchief from his pocket and dabbed at his eyes. Then, to break the tension, Yosl said, "You were a *maskil,* then, an intellectual?"

"What I was then was a fool," Goldman replied sharply. "I am still a fool. The difference is that now I know it. After Gomel, I realized that nothing had changed in twenty years, nothing for the peasants and nothing for the Jews. And nothing would change. We were still being slaughtered to make up for the Tsar's blunders."

There was a general roar of conversation in the car, but Yosl had no difficulty hearing Goldman's hoarse voice. It was as if an envelope of loss had been placed around them, isolating them from the others. He believed what Goldman had said—that nothing had changed—yet guilt and anger remained mixed in his mind. Why must the Jews always suffer? Why were they never able to feel safe in the world?

"And are you still a revolutionary?"

Goldman's thin, white lips stretched over large, yellow teeth. "It would be nice to feel part of something. But it is hopeless. I went back to Gomel to say good-bye to my past. I sang Kaddish for my wife, for my son. That was all."

"And now?"

"I have a friend in Hamburg—friend, I haven't seen him in twenty years. But he was smarter than I; he left to make a life when he was still young."

"How will you find your friend?"

"The same way you will find your uncle. Except for me it will be easier. I will go to a shul and ask a rabbi."

"And if no one knows him or if he moved away?"

Goldman's expression brightened. He turned to Yosl and smiled. "What if, what if? You should be a Talmudist. If all else fails, I'll get on a boat and go to America with you. What do you think of that?"

The wind had picked up outside, rattling the leaves in the trees, sounding like rain. Joe shivered in the drafty dormitory and pulled the thin blanket around him. He wondered what had become of Hayim. They had become separated in Hamburg and were reunited only by chance the week before Joe was to leave. Hayim had tried to convince Joe to stay, to continue his studies in Hamburg. What was the point in going off into the wilderness when he had friends here to guide him? In Hamburg, Joe could have a real future, perhaps enter one of the professions after his studies were through. What was there to match this in America, where the future was, to say the least, uncertain? But not knowing exactly why, Joe had remained adamant.

Joe remembered the port, immense and seeming almost to move itself, like the enormous ships in its harbor, on a wave of immigrants, peddlers, agents, and curious bystanders, all pushing and shoving, eager to be somewhere else. Yosl had hesitated, unsure where to go, but Goldman pushed him ahead. "Stay here and they'll pick you dry," he said.

Goldman's friend had arranged passage for Yosl on the *Kaiser Wilhelm,* but before going on board, he was forced to strip to the waist and submit to another examination by a doctor in a dirty white smock. This time there were no baths, and no clean clothes, but the result was the same. The doctor waved him through.

Then they were standing together before the gangplank. Four months had passed, and now Goldman's face was red and sweating in the August sun. Yosl noticed wisps of gray in his tightly coiled hair and wrinkles around his eyes, but he seemed at peace with himself. Yosl imagined the wrinkles on his stomach had been filled in by regular meals. He felt better knowing that Goldman was settled, that his past was behind him, and that now his life would proceed as it should.

"This is a good ship," Goldman said. "Fortunately, you won't have to travel in steerage. Let's hope you are lucky in America. Keep to yourself, don't gamble, and don't get in fights."

"I'm not a fighter," Yosl said.

"In a way you are. Otherwise you wouldn't be doing this, going off to America." Goldman nodded in agreement with himself and looked away, embarrassed. "You're a good boy, Yosl. Too young to be on your own, but you have it in you to be a good man. Work hard and you'll do well."

"I will. And I'll repay you for this."

"Don't worry about that. My friend has plenty of money. This is a *mitzva,* a good deed. Let him have that; he has everything else." Yosl thought he would say something more, but instead the older man put his arms around him, holding so tight Yosl could hardly breathe. Then, as quickly as he had embraced him, Goldman released him. "Now, go," he said. "It's time."

Yosl stood watching Goldman walk away. Hayim had sheltered Yosl from thieves and provided a future, which was what his own father would have done. He knew he should stay, that he owed Goldman that much, but he felt powerless to change his plans. America was vast, energetic, and wild. Having lost his family, he wanted to leave everything familiar behind and start clean in a new place.

Halfway up the gangplank, Yosl stopped to look down at the crowd. It was only a mass of color, the people indistinguishable from one another. Far below, he saw Hayim waving his arms and calling out. In the uproar, Yosl couldn't make out the words, but he imagined Goldman saying, "We will meet again."

Yosl nodded his head vigorously and waved back. "In America, Father," he called out. Then the line of immigrants heaved again, pushing him up and away, into the maw of the *Kaiser Wilhelm.*

four

Joe awoke the next morning in a large drafty room flooded with sunlight. He heard sounds from the kitchen, a meal being prepared, people moving around, and he knew he should volunteer to help; he remembered what Shmuel had said about shared work. But the trip and the strangeness of his surroundings had exhausted him. He lay back and closed his eyes.

Shmuel had insisted on showing him the land, and despite his initial reservations, Joe had been impressed. An orchard with robust young trees hid behind the dusty sheds and garden. Deep in the forest that lined the riverbank, men worked cutting wood, which they sold under contract to the railroad. Shmuel said they had taken 150 cords out of the forest in the last year. Joe had no idea what a cord was, but he understood that this had put the commune on solid financial footing. In addition, fifty acres had been cleared for crops; besides the garden, they planned to build a mill and dairy barn.

Shmuel had taken him to an empty shed where feed and equipment were kept. Twenty hoes and a small plow were lined against one wall with military precision. Shmuel ran his hand lovingly over the blade of one and smiled at Joe in the darkness. "Your father and the others thought we'd starve, that we were helpless visionaries. But look at all this. We have built a community and we have no problem feeding ourselves. Getting along is another matter, of course."

Now Joe sat up and threw the covers back. He was about to go downstairs when he heard a slight rustling noise. He looked around, but saw nothing. He thought he must be imagining things, but then he heard the noises again, accompanied by sobbing. It sounded like a child. But where? Bookshelves lined the walls; in the middle of the room stood a library table. His uncle had shown him the "library" with pride, emphasizing the community's belief in the importance of continual study. Except for his months at university, these were the first secular volumes Joe had ever seen at close range, the first books he could actually take down and read himself. In Russia only a wealthy man could have collected such a library, but here books were available for all. Joe could understand why Shmuel was proud. There were Kant, Spinoza, and Marx, but also a Frenchman he'd never heard of: Comte. There were books on agriculture, astronomy, and even a small atlas. On the bottom shelf, nearly buried by the intellectual weight of the other books, was a translation of the Torah.

Joe heard the sobbing for a third time and scanned the hall again. It seemed to be coming from an area adjacent to the bookcases, where an oriental screen covered with shawls bordered the room. From his bed, it looked like part of the back wall, but at closer range, Joe saw the screen concealed a small alcove in which he discovered a girl of seventeen or eighteen lying on a cot. Joe stood silent, reluctant to invade her privacy. Then, embarrassed lest she should turn and see him watching, he said, "May I help, miss?"

The girl turned quickly, startled by Joe's voice. Then she looked back at the wall. "Go away," she said.

Her quick dismissal made Joe more determined to help. Besides, she was very young and also beautiful, with rich, dark hair that hung in a single braid below her shoulder blades. In contrast to her broad shoulders, she had a tiny waist. Joe wanted to see her face again. "Why are you crying?"

The girl's shoulders heaved. Then she straightened decisively and turned to look at him. "There's nothing for you to worry about," she said. "It's only that my sister is getting married today." Then her face came apart again.

Joe sat next to her. "It's all right. So your sister is getting married. That's nothing to cry about. That's good news. She will still be in the community, won't she? And you'll get a new brother, and soon, nieces or nephews." He felt foolish talking this way, as if he'd been part of New Zion for months or years, but he wanted to reassure the girl.

She shook her head. "It's not the same. We've always been together. Since we left Kiev. Now, I'll be alone."

"In the midst of so many people? Have you no other friends?"

"It's not the same," she repeated, and Joe knew she was right. "Who will I talk to, share my secrets with? There is no one else."

"You can talk to me." Oddly, the girl had made Joe feel lonely, too.

"I don't even know you," she said dismissively. Then curiosity seemed to get the better of sorrow. She looked frankly at him. "Where did you come from, anyway? I haven't seen you before."

"My name is Joseph Abrams. I arrived yesterday to be with my uncle, from Russia, like you."

The girl shivered at the memory. "I thought I would never emerge from that ship alive," she said. "Sometimes I wished I wouldn't. They could threaten to shoot me and I wouldn't get back on that boat. It even made me dislike water."

In New York, Joe had heard unbelievable stories about traveling in steerage. The inedible food, the filth and crowding of people like cattle belowships, the brutality of the stewards who carried bludgeons to punish those who disobeyed. If you survived that, there was the noise, the constant rocking, the swaying cots, and on and on. His informants were eloquent on the subject, making him feel guilty for the comfort in which he had crossed. His passage had been pleasant, if bittersweet. A chance for introspection in the midst of his chaotic rush into the future. Each night, he walked the decks for hours, but he preferred to stand in the stern, looking back in the direction of his native land.

"At least we don't have to go back to Russia," was all he said now.

"My name is Annuta," the girl said, ignoring this. She had stopped crying, but dark spots remained beneath her eyes. "Thank you for looking after me."

Joe was being dismissed, but he didn't want to go. "Who will stand with you at the wedding?" he asked.

The girl looked surprised, as if she hadn't considered this. "I'm the maid of honor," she said. "I will stand by myself."

"I see," Joe said. "And is the wedding to be held here?"

"Of course. Everyone will be there," she said.

"Then I am invited, too?"

"Yes. If you are one of us, you are welcome."

"You are too kind," Joe said.

Annuta's lips were small and dainty, her posture stiff and correct. "Mr. Liberty says it is impossible to be too kind. Now you must leave. I have to dress."

The kitchen was crowded with men and women moving back and forth. Shmuel presided over all in an enormous white apron, shouting instructions in a deep voice. He waved a wooden spoon back and forth, though he seemed to be cooking nothing. "Yosl, here," he called out, gesturing to Joe with the spoon.

"Yes, Uncle. I just woke up."

Shmuel pointed out the door. "We need water," he said.

"From the river?" Joe asked.

"There is a fresh stream just past those trees." Shmuel waved toward a thicket a hundred yards in the distance.

"And what will I carry the water in?" Joe asked, feeling stupid.

"There," Shmuel said, pointing at two wooden buckets joined together by a yoke leaning against the side of the building.

Balancing the contraption on his shoulders, Joe trudged off in search of water. The stream ran swift and clear, and it took Joe no time to fill the two buckets. He washed his face in the cold water and drank his fill. Then he hoisted the yoke onto his shoulders and began his trip back to the kitchen. The leather cut into his shoulders under the weight of the full buckets, and Joe hadn't gone ten yards before his legs started to shake. Pride made him continue another few yards before stopping. He tried to contrive a way to cushion the wooden yoke, but he hadn't walked far before the leather was again cutting through his shirt. His arms felt like lead, but he forced himself to walk on until, near collapse, he had to stop. After a half hour, he reached the kitchen with his load. His shoulders were bleeding and his hands were raw from the wood, but his uncle offered no sympathy.

"It's a good thing we didn't need that water for cooking," Shmuel said. Then he looked in the half-empty buckets. "Is there anything left in there?"

A young woman in a long brown dress rang a bell to announce the meal, and Joe followed the others into the dining hall. Perhaps twenty people were gathered there, and what appeared to be the bridal party occupied the table at the front of the room: there was a young woman dressed in white with a veil hiding her face; next to her was an ascetic-looking man in a dark suit and boutonniere. Several older people sat with them at the table. Annuta, looking forlorn, was by herself, at the end. A tall man with a high forehead, gray-blond hair brushed straight back, and an erect posture seemed to be in charge. Joe looked for his uncle, but Shmuel had vanished. Joe took the first vacant seat that he saw.

"I thought you'd sit with Annuta," Lizzie said. "Weren't you together upstairs?"

Embarrassed, Joe looked around, but no one seemed to have heard. He felt suddenly transparent, as if his every move were being scrutinized. "I only met her this morning," Joe said.

Lizzie nodded, but said nothing. She was watching the man on the dais. Joe looked at her carefully. She was wearing a faded smock, and she was older than he had first thought, perhaps nineteen or twenty. Her hair was pulled back and she had pinned a sprig of violets to her bodice. Her expression was open, noncommittal, and this made him like her more.

They sat silently through the meal, but afterward, as they were clearing the tables, Joe asked, "Is that man your father?"

Lizzie smiled. "Is it so obvious?"

"I just noticed you looking at him."

"Perhaps he's my lover," she said.

Joe flushed. He was not used to girls speaking so openly. Now Lizzie laughed. "Yes, that is Father. Would you like to meet him?"

"Later, perhaps," Joe said. He didn't know how to talk to the daughter, how could he hope to engage the father?

Lizzie put down the plate she was holding and rested her hand on her waist. Now her expression was serious. "I must tell you something. Your uncle probably warned you about Father, but he couldn't have told you everything, because he doesn't know what we've been through."

"Actually, he told me very little," Joe said. "Only that he and your father don't get along."

Lizzie seemed impressed with Shmuel's restraint. "You could say that. I don't get along with my father all the time either. No one does."

"Of course."

"It's just that we can't go on pretending that they aren't enemies."

"Enemies?" Joe hadn't known it was that serious.

"There are some people who think your uncle should be banished from the community." She hesitated. "Of course, there are others who would like Father to go."

"What if neither will leave?"

Lizzie smiled. "Then things will continue as they are, I guess."

After dinner, everyone walked to the banks of the Kickapoo. It was midafternoon, but under the trees the heat seemed less oppressive. A slight breeze blew off the river and Joe felt languorous, at ease with his new surroundings. His muscles ached pleasantly from his labors, and Lizzie had given him some cream to rub on his blisters. While he didn't know the people who walked alongside him, he knew they were all united, dedicated to a common cause. It seemed remarkable that a group of Russian students and intellectuals with no training had been able to forge a life for themselves in the wilderness. He was proud to be part of it.

Boys from the study houses of Vilna and Odessa had been transplanted here in Wisconsin, where they spent their days chopping down trees. Men and women who had grown up in the ghettos of Kiev and Lwow, the sons and daughters of peddlers and tailors, canned sugar beets from their own gardens and pruned their apple orchard in hopes of a future harvest. Most striking of all was the freedom of the place; it was in the air, and infected everything. The way the settlers walked and held their heads, their willingness to examine every question, their confidence in their work. There was no fear in this place, and that was intoxicating. Here, people were free to buy and cultivate land and then live on it as best they could with no interference from anyone. They were also free to fail and die, of course, but that seemed a small consideration on such a beautiful afternoon.

"You look happy," Lizzie said.

"Why shouldn't I be?" Joe said. "I love to listen to the wind, to walk on soft ground. Aren't you happy?" But she had walked ahead and didn't hear him.

Liberty called the group together where the river arched around a bend. Cottonwood trees floated overhead and a slight breeze carried puffs of white downstream. The leader now wore a white fringed surplice. The large sleeves opened and shut like mouths in the wind as he waited for the others to quiet down.

Joe caught up with Lizzie and stood beside her. Two yellow birds chased one another, dipping low over the rapids, then climbing back to the limbs of the trees. No one seemed to notice; all attention was fixed on Liberty, as if the beauty surrounding them didn't exist. "Is your father a minister?" he whispered. He had never witnessed a Christian service before.

"Not exactly."

"My uncle says there is no religion here, that it's all superstition, that he stopped being a Jew when he came to America."

"We were never Jewish."

"But you're religious?"

"That's hard to say. Father's a positivist, but that's not an ordinary religion."

They had been speaking Yiddish, but there was no word for Liberty's religion. Joe tried it in English. "Positivist?"

Lizzie nodded. "Father calls it the Religion of Humanity. They think you can figure everything out logically, like mathematics. It's one of the things your uncle and my father disagree about."

Lizzie's answer did not completely satisfy Joe, but Liberty was about to begin. He looked around for his uncle but couldn't find him. He wondered if Shmuel disliked ceremony, or simply refused to recognize Liberty's authority. As if he intuited Joe's thoughts, the leader began by addressing this question.

"Some of you might ask," he said in a high-pitched voice, "how we as a socialistic community can participate in a wedding? How we can even accept the existence of such an institution as marriage? We might say Ben and Rebecca are already married in our community, bound inextricably through our common labor to our dream of a revolution in human relationships.

"Raise these objections, and I will congratulate you. Traditional marriage is only a transfer of property—a woman is given by her father to her husband, who is then paid a bounty for taking on this responsibility. It is little different from the sale of livestock or a piece of land. The woman is seldom consulted."

He paused and looked out over the heads of his congregation, his blue eyes piercing in the afternoon sunlight. "But of course, I speak of marriage as we knew it in Russia, especially among the Hebrew people who employ skilled matchmakers, people trained to join together young people who often have never even met before they are called to the marriage bed. Women are seen by Jew and gentile alike as chattel, with neither the ability to think nor the means to support themselves. They are considered helpless without the strong arm of a man. That we think differently is manifest in the community we have built, and this is why we gather here today.

"We neither pretend nor intend to join Ben and Rebecca in marriage—they have accomplished that on their own. We seek only to celebrate their love. In this, we are honored by the presence of Ben's father and mother, who have journeyed from Chicago to be with us, and by several of our friends from the village of Gays Mills."

Joe looked around. Ben's father wore a yarmulke and stood to his son's right. His wife, short and stout, looked disgusted with the proceedings. Perhaps she had expected a rabbi. Certainly, she had no idea a priest—or whatever Liberty was—would perform her son's wedding ceremony. To the right of Ben's mother, apart from the other guests, stood a young man in a dark suit and glasses. He held a notebook, and occasionally he would jot something down. Joe wondered if this was Liberty's friend from town, and what he was writing about. It made him feel guilty, as if he should be recording the day's events as well, to send to Cahan in New York. But he had neither paper nor pencil. He set himself to try to remember everything.

Liberty licked his lips. "But if we do not accept the suzerainty of any political unit greater than ours, we do recognize a higher authority in spiritual matters." Here, the groom's mother seemed to attend, and even smiled slightly. Liberty paused. "I speak, of course, of the faith of Comte, Fourier, and Spencer, which far from merely rebutting any single religion, incorporates them all into a mighty whole, greater than any single God. I speak of course, of the Religion of Humanity."

The audience responded, "Amen." Lizzie, however, seemed restless. When Joe glanced over at her, she rolled her eyes and sighed loudly.

Joe looked out at the muddy river and remembered the stream behind his father's mill. What would his parents have thought of a wedding in an open field with no Torah scrolls, no *chuppa* to shelter the bridal party, and no rabbi? Just this visionary dressed like a Russian priest. Momentarily, Joe felt guilty, as if by coming to America, he and the others had dealt a blow against Judaism more potent than any pogrom. Brutality had never changed a Jew's faith; only reason could do that. He tried to concentrate on the trees, the sunshine, to forget such things.

But Liberty brought him back to the present. The leader was reciting poetry, which Joe took to be a substitute for formal vows. His lips pursed, birdlike, Liberty extended his arms to the sky, exposing ragged cuffs as he exclaimed:

"What day is it; dark or fair?
Brings it future joy or care?
What ray this morn broke through the night?
Did the ray herald Black or White?
Who knows, who knows save only Fate?
It is too late, it is too late
To ask. Today it will be done.
May it end as sweetly as it's begun.
The moment's here,
Too near; too near!
They wait; they wait;
It is too late!
The Youth, the Maid!
They must be said
Those words of Fate;
To wedded state,
They quickly go,
Their love to sow."

Most of the guests nodded in vague comprehension, guessing at Liberty's English. But a few seemed deeply moved. Annuta dabbed at her eyes with a small lace handkerchief. Lizzie was unaffected by her father's eloquence. "God," she muttered. Then Liberty cleared his throat significantly, signaling that he hadn't finished, despite the reference to sowing. He went on:

"Youths and Maidens, gather, gather;
Come old mother; come old father.
Maidens bring the blushing bride;
Lead her to the Bridegroom's side."

Now Lizzie laughed out loud. The others, assuming Edward Liberty's daughter must understand the poem more completely than they, smiled encouragement. Liberty looked annoyed, but Lizzie couldn't stop laughing. The other guests seemed to awaken, and even the bridegroom's mother showed new interest. Finally, Lizzie managed to control herself. "Sorry," she whispered.

Despite his daughter's interruption, Liberty had maintained his erect posture and outward show of dignity. But now he pulled anxiously at his beard and put his notes aside. "Life is a never-ending search," he said. "For peace, freedom, brotherhood, and love. Above all, love. I congratulate you, Ben and Rebecca, on this marriage consummated in the spiritual life of New Zion. You are man and wife."

Joe found the short speech moving and felt intensely the lack of love in his life. All around him men and women were kissing each other loudly, and quite naturally, he would recall later, he took Lizzie in his arms and kissed her, feeling her tongue, subtle as tissue, brush his teeth before retreating discreetly. Then without discussing it, they walked away, heads down, content to be together.

They wandered vaguely upstream and found themselves in a small clearing. Lizzie produced a loaf of bread from her apron, tore it apart, and offered half to Joe. "Sit down," she said, setting off waves in the tiny blue flowers that dotted the grass.

Lizzie was chewing contentedly, looking off into the distance. In profile, her features were classic, her nose straight, her cheekbones giving off faint shadows on the planes of her face, her lips full but not gross. Her eyebrows were so fine and white that it seemed she had none at all. Wisps of hair floated in the breeze. Unaccustomed to being with women, Joe wasn't prepared for a girl who spoke so openly. He had no idea how to act with her. Her skin was soft and white. Joe smelled the flowers in her hair and for a moment felt slightly dizzy. They were discussing religion, but something else was happening. "I've never heard of a religion like this," he said. "I'm afraid I still don't understand positivism."

Lizzie smiled. "No one does. That's why they're so impressed with Father. Basically, he thinks everything is divine."

"Everything?" Joe had a sudden image of the Black Hundred sweeping down the streets of his village, of his parents and sisters lying dead on the ground.

"Father knows there's evil in the world," Lizzie said quickly. "He's not stupid. It's just that he thinks even those people can be made better. That they're bad because they don't know enough to be good." She raised her eyebrows. "I know, it's pretty hard for me sometimes. And I've been listening to him all my life."

The ultimate perfectibility of man was a Jewish idea, Joe thought. Perhaps Liberty and Shmuel had more in common than they knew. "Your whole life?"

"As far back as I can remember. I was born in Kansas, in a place like this, except there weren't any Jews. Some Russians started it. It wasn't very different."

It had never occurred to Joe that gentiles would find Russia anything less than paradise. "Why did they leave?" he asked.

This seemed to irritate Lizzie. She put down her bread. "I suppose you think the Jews were the only ones who hated the Tsar, who suffered under his rule?"

Joe did think this, but he didn't admit it. "Of course not," he said.

Lizzie wasn't persuaded. "But you do," she said. "You're so self-centered. God's Chosen People, so no one else matters, is that it?"

"No," Joe said. "But surely gentiles had better lives than we did."

"Better, perhaps," Lizzie said, "but not good. Siberia is full of gentiles who resisted the Tsar. Even among the nobility, those who had the most to lose, there were resisters. Father was in the Geodetic Corps with a brilliant career before him, but he couldn't stay in Russia. I don't say you didn't suffer, but in a sense the choice was made for you. Leave or die. It wasn't that simple for us."

Death was simple, there was no denying that. Still, there was no point in arguing. "Why did your father leave, then?"

"Because he was a communist," Lizzie said.

"Many communists are still there, fighting for the revolution."

"Father and his friends don't believe in violence. The other revolutionists thought they were cowards. The Tsar thought they were crazy."

For the first time in his life, Joe felt some spiritual kinship with the ruler of Russia. "But the Tsar blamed the Jews for all the assassinations, for the attack on the Winter Palace. That's why he ordered the pogroms. Gentiles were safe, weren't they?"

"Compared to the Jews, maybe. But Father was a mathematician. He sacrificed everything for this." There was regret in her voice, as if she were thinking of the life she might have lived if Liberty had stayed in Russia. "That's why he takes everything so seriously. In Russia, he says he was a nobleman but a slave. Here, he's an aristocrat of the spirit."

"Your father is a poet."

Lizzie smiled. "He used to be wonderful. When he was younger, women would come up after his speeches and ask to come live with us." She smiled at the memory. "He's still wonderful, sometimes. He'll forget about positivism and talk about the world that's coming, the new life we'll make. Then his face will be as red as a lover's. But then he'll become self-conscious and start preaching again." She was quiet for a moment, then she seemed to forget about her father. "What about you?" she asked abruptly.

The question caught Joe off balance. "Me?" he said.

"Yes. What were you studying in Russia?"

He remembered that he had been reading the Zohar when he left Minsk. "I just studied," Joe said. "Spinoza, Kant, anything I wanted to, really. My father had decided I would be a scholar, and he wasn't a man to argue with."

"He sounds like my father," Lizzie said.

The suggestion made Joe smile. "Not exactly," he said. "But he had his own way of thinking about things. I was supposed to go to university and be a great man. He never told me any more than that, just be a great man."

"Can you do this in America?"

Joe ducked his head modestly. "I never think of myself that way."

Lizzie nodded. "Well, then, what were you interested in?"

"Many things," Joe said, giving himself time to think. "Science, and I like reading very much. History. Agronomy, though as you can see, I have never held a spade in my hands. In New York, I worked for a Yiddish newspaper."

"Then Father will want to meet you," Lizzie said without any real conviction. Her face had turned sad, with small blue half-circles shading her eyes. "Father used to talk all the time about going back to St. Petersburg. He said we were only preparing here for the revolution and that once we'd learned to live communally, we could go back home. I always think of Russia as my home, though I've never been there." She sounded wistful now. "He would tell me stories about the peasants, red-faced men, and women with large bosoms. He said Russia would be the first communist country because of them, that they were natural communists because they had always shared their land."

This didn't sound like the peasants Joe had known, but he said only, "Your father came to America to live like a peasant?"

Lizzie smiled. "I know, it seems ridiculous. What you have to understand is that Father is terribly sincere."

So were the anti-Semites, Joe thought. A sincere enemy was the worst kind. They were the committed ones, the ones that couldn't be persuaded or bribed. Liberty sounded like a lost man to him. "And how long has he been here?" he asked.

"Twenty years. But the wonderful thing is that time means nothing to Father. He wants to write a book about Comte and show the world. He has so many plans." She sighed. "He'll never do any of these things, but he doesn't know that, so he isn't sad. He still thinks he's preparing for some great act."

Joe stared into the distance, following the river to the last bend and then letting his eyes lose focus. A slight wind had come up and the leaves rustled in the trees like paper. It was pleasant to sit with a pretty girl and talk about great ideas. "It would be nice if your father could succeed," he said.

Lizzie looked down and pulled at a few strands of grass before letting them go in the wind. "He won't," she said. "Any more than he did in Kansas. They wouldn't even let him into Oneida. A perfect life just isn't as important to most people as it is to him." She smiled. "Of course, he has kind of a strange idea of perfection."

Her sense of humor was her saving grace, Joe decided. But it was strange to hear a daughter explain her father so carefully, so lovingly. It was as if she were his wife. "His life doesn't have to be yours, does it?"

"I know," Lizzie said slowly. "Father does, too. But he pretends he doesn't know what I do, what I think, and I allow him to pretend."

"That must be hard in such a small place," Joe said.

"We're getting along so far." Lizzie sighed and got to her feet.

Joe put his arm around her shoulders and they started back. Now he could see smoke from the cooking fire and people crossing the clearing in front of the dining hall. Before they separated, Lizzie said, "There's a dance later. Are you coming?"

"I don't know how to dance," Joe said. He had an image of a circle of Jews dancing the hora and shouting loudly to the music.

Lizzie smiled. "In a new country, you have to learn new things." Then without waiting for an answer, she kissed Joe on the cheek and walked off.

five

Joe walked along the riverbank, thinking about the wedding, Liberty, and Lizzie. The wind had blown in clouds, and the light was diffused; the grass was blue-gray, and whitecaps were visible at the rapids. Cahan would want to know his impressions of New Zion, but Joe didn't know where to begin. Still, he must write something. Cahan was not a patient man.

Joe remembered their first meeting. After arriving in America, he had been held for two weeks at Castle Garden. Sitting alone in a small room, with only a cot and a table for furniture, he had been terrified that he would be sent back to Russia. Finally, in desperation, he'd written to the *Forward,* inquiring as to Shmuel's whereabouts. A few days later, Cahan had sent for him. Standing in the soft moss of the riverbank, Joe thought the rattle of the leaves overhead suggested paper being run into a dozen typewriters. Joe could almost smell the ink of the newsroom.

He had been shown into Cahan's office, but the editor was nowhere to be seen. Yosl looked down into East Broadway, where the unending mass of immigrants flowed back and forth. He had been in America only a short time, but he knew the legend of Abraham Cahan. Having escaped the Tsar's police, he arrived penniless as a boy in the '80s, only to succeed spectacularly. Cahan now advised mayors and senators. Wealthy and respected, he was a speechmaker, socialist theoretician, and Jewish public figure. Yet still, somehow, a friend of the workers.

Yiddish newspapers had existed before Cahan, but he had made the *Forward* the most influential journal among the newly arrived Jews of lower Manhattan. Cahan told them how to dress, what proper American manners were, what subjects they should study in school, even how to blow their noses. Childless himself, Cahan had understood instinctively that settlers in a strange land needed a father. Authority was more appreciated than a shoulder to cry on. Beyond that, Yosl knew Cahan had written novels in English that were printed by the great gentile publishing houses and discussed in the leading literary journals. While never shrinking from being a Jew, Cahan had succeeded in becoming an American. And now this man had called him. Not knowing what to do with his trembling hands, Yosl jammed them in his pockets and retreated from the window to wait.

Outside, in the newsroom, two editors read copy, hunched over a long table. Young boys carried the finished work upstairs. Elderly Jewish men wearing yarmulkes moved through the room at a leisurely pace, stopping periodically to schmooze with colleagues. They seemed to be in no hurry. There was, in fact, a scholarly, distracted air about the place, as if the staff were rabbis rather than newspapermen. In tiny open cubicles at the rear of the room, writers worked on their articles for the next edition. Then, without warning, the door to the hall flew open and the editor entered the room, bringing with him a force that drove the newsroom into a frenzy. Cahan looked quickly left and right, then strode into the office. He flipped through the papers lying on his desk. Now he turned abruptly and looked at Yosl. "Well?" Cahan said.

The editor was of medium height with fair coloring. His eyes were intense, crowded together behind wire-rimmed spectacles. He wore a pin-striped suit and his wavy hair was combed in a pompadour. For a moment, Yosl was speechless. Then, in a voice he hardly recognized, he said, "You sent for me, Your Honor."

Cahan looked quizzically at Yosl and smiled thinly. "Russian," he said. "I hardly hear it anymore. Everywhere I go, it's English or, here, Yiddish, and sometimes both at the same time. Yinglish, they call it.

But an elegant Russian, literary Russian, never." He shook his head. "You're still in your student's uniform."

Yosl felt self-conscious. He hadn't changed since leaving Russia and still wore his father's heavy coat. "Yes, Your Honor. I was at university in Minsk."

Cahan gestured toward a chair. "Sit," he said, and settled himself behind his large desk. "I was a student myself before I came here. In Kiev." He shook his head in wonder. "It was quite unusual then, a gift from the Tsar, to let a Jew study at university. Only a few were permitted for fear we'd contaminate the others. Of course, we did." He smiled, bemused. "I never knew how I would eat from one day to the next. Then I would get a crust of bread and some soup, and I'd forget how it felt to be hungry—until the next day, when I would face the same problem again. Everything then seemed uncertain, dangerous, but also anything was possible, or so I thought."

Cahan's reflective tone made Joe bold. "And now?"

"Now?" Cahan seemed surprised. "Well, I'm certainly not hungry, you can see that for yourself." He pinched a small roll of fat around his waist. "Sometimes I wish I was. It was more interesting." He shook his head as if to drive away the memories. He picked up a piece of paper that Yosl recognized as his letter. "So you have come here from Minsk. For what?"

"I'm looking for my uncle," Yosl said.

"Ah," Cahan said, looking again at the letter. "You are young Abramovitz. Forgive me, I have a great deal on my mind. But I knew your uncle long ago. We came over on the same boat. A big man with a loud voice and a temper. Also a drinker, unusual for a Jew. Still, he was a socialist, a good man."

"You are a socialist, then, Your Honor?"

"I?" Cahan said. "My critics don't see it that way. I got a letter from one who asked me what handkerchiefs had to do with socialism, and I said, 'Even socialists have nothing against clean noses.' " He laughed shortly, but his expression seemed more like a grimace. "Sometimes I think they're right."

Yosl changed the subject. "You've seen my uncle, then?"

"Not in fifteen years," Cahan said. "I have friends who might know where he is. He used to send me letters to print in the paper from time to time. He was in Kansas, then Oregon. The last I heard, he was living with some group in Wisconsin."

The strange names swam in Yosl's head; not daring to say them, he tried to remember for the future how Cahan had pronounced them. "How far is this place?"

Cahan smiled. "Too far to send a greenhorn who can't make change. Besides, we don't know if Shmuel is still there. He used to move around a lot."

Yosl looked around him. Books lined the walls, and papers sat in piles on the floor. For the first time, the idea that he might not find his uncle didn't frighten him. Since Cahan had summoned him, he wouldn't be sent back to Russia. The newspaper office seemed like a congenial place.

Cahan broke in on his thoughts. "You were a student. I presume you can read and write, unlike most of the illiterates that come over on the boat?"

"Of course," Yosl said, suddenly angry. Who was Cahan to question him or call others illiterate who didn't have offices in tall buildings or wear expensive suits? His father could not write books in English, but he read his Torah portion each morning. Still, Yosl was aware of his precarious position. In a more measured tone, he said, "I know German, Russian, and Polish. And I have studied a little English."

Cahan seemed impatient with his answer. "I don't care about any of that," he said. "Can you read and write Yiddish?"

"The jargon? What educated person writes in Yiddish?"

Now Cahan was scornful. "My young friend, I am not interested in educated people. I am trying to publish a newspaper that will speak to the common man; a paper that he will want to look at when he comes home at night with swollen feet and an aching head; a paper that he will read because he enjoys it, but also one that will inspire him to dream of better things for himself and his children."

"A paper, then, for the illiterates?" Yosl said.

Cahan didn't seem offended by this. "Exactly," he said. "No point in fooling ourselves. There are too many fine revolutionists who have been to universities and give beautiful speeches in elegant Russian that no one in the audience understands."

"I'm no revolutionist," Yosl said. "I want to find my uncle and get a job."

"I am offering you a job," Cahan said.

"I'm not a writer, either."

"Who is, to begin with? It is a vocation that finds you, not one that a person may seek. You can write, that's all that matters to me. People come to us who can't. They need someone to compose their letters for them. Letters like the one you sent us for the *Bintel Brief.* They have problems, but they're too poor to hire lawyers. We're all they have. The job doesn't pay much, but we'll give you your meals and enough money to buy a suit. You can sleep upstairs in the compositors' room."

"Why should you do all this for me?" Yosl asked.

"Perhaps I have a soft heart," Cahan replied ironically. "I knew your uncle. We were friends when we were young, which is the best time to have friends."

After weeks of traveling, Yosl was tempted. The chance to work at a job and earn some money was appealing. But he hadn't come to America to be a clerk. "I'm grateful for your kindness," he said. "But I came here to find my uncle. Until I do, I'll gladly work for you. Then I must go."

"Good," Cahan said. He rose and came from behind his desk. Taking Yosl's arm, he guided him to the door. Then he pointed to a gray-haired man at a desk near the window. "Mr. Greenberg will help you get started."

Yosl turned to leave, but Cahan called him back into the office. "I wonder if your uncle ever mentioned an organization called Am Olam? Perhaps in a letter."

The words were Hebrew. Eternal People. But Yosl had hardly seen his uncle since childhood and could recall no specific conversations with him. "No," he said. "I don't remember. Should I?"

Cahan shrugged. "You were a baby. They were a group of young people who came here in the '80s, hoping to establish agricultural colonies in the West."

"My uncle was a farmer," Yosl said quickly. "My father thought it was ridiculous. He made fun of him."

"Your father was right," Cahan said. "Idealism is sometimes foolishness disguised as principle. They died out after a few years, or nearly so. One colony remains. In Wisconsin. That's where I heard your uncle was staying."

Cahan suggested Yosl study English, so three evenings a week he sat at a child's desk, trying to penetrate the mysteries of a language he had only seen in books. The teacher was German and disdained his newly arrived students, who sat on windowsills and radiators because there were not enough seats.

Though most of the scholars were rough men with torn shirts and callused hands, there was never a disturbance, and a palpable yearning for knowledge permeated the room. Despite his contempt for them, they held the teacher—or professor, as he was called—in reverence. They leaned forward in an attitude not unlike prayer, craning their necks, hoping that improved hearing would yield understanding.

Yosl knew little more than the others, but he had acquired the habit of learning and was not discouraged. He attended class regularly, mimicking the teacher's tortured expressions, and in time, his speech improved. One evening after class, he tried to engage the teacher in conversation. "I am at university in Minsk," he began.

The teacher was gathering up his books and seemed uninterested, remote. "This is not Minsk," he said curtly.

"I know that, Your Honor," Yosl said.

"If you want to study here, you should learn the English past tense."

The teacher's rudeness did not so much intimidate Yosl as anger him. Sweat beaded the man's thin upper lip. This dandy was not going to condescend to him. In German, Yosl said, "I will learn the past tense, and I will write it better than you, Your Honor. That is a promise."

Now the teacher looked at him with some interest. "You will, will you? Then for next time, prepare an additional exercise for me and read it to your classmates." He clicked his heels and walked out of the classroom.

When he was not studying, Yosl would go to Cooper Union or visit the Astor Library, where he would sit alone at the large tables, contemplating the red and green spines of the books that lined the walls. Eventually, he got up the nerve to take them down from the shelves. Though he couldn't read very well, he loved the illustrations. There were pictures of exotic birds and others of the sere landscapes of the deserts. Yosl would put himself in the picture, imagining he was a wind-burnt Arab in robe and burnoose, looking for an oasis, or an explorer in darkest Africa. Yet it was only in the library that he truly felt like an explorer; at all other times, the reality of the Lower East Side intruded too readily, driving the romance away.

After the reading room, he would stand in the lower hall, looking up at the statues of the Greeks and Romans watching grandly over everything. He studied the heads of Sophocles, Socrates, and Julius Caesar, but Demosthenes was his favorite. He could see himself standing on the seashore, his feet bathed in foam, his mouth filled with pebbles, shouting English verbs at the surf. Then he would leave and walk the streets until late at night, feeling less American than before but more himself.

One night, as he was returning to the *Forward* along Hester Street, he noticed bright lights and a man standing outside one of the tenements that lined the street. "Here, you, come along now," the man said.

Yosl looked around. "Me?"

"Who else is standing there? Don't you want to learn to dance?"

Yosl looked at his feet to see if he had betrayed some sign of this unlikely talent. "I have never done any dancing," he said carefully.

"Of course not," the man said scornfully. "Who had time in the old country? But this is America. Here, even Jews can dance. Come in." He gestured with his right arm while continuing to look down the street. When Yosl came closer, the man propelled him down the stairs and into the smoky basement with a shove. The room was filled with men and women shuffling in time to a tinny phonograph. Yosl blinked in the darkness, but then he saw a woman in a green gown coming toward him. She was auburn-haired, and the dress fit tightly over her body, exposing her breasts. Yosl thought he had never seen such a beautiful creature in his life.

"What's your name?" she asked.

Yosl told her, but could say nothing more. This didn't seem to bother the woman. "Your first lesson costs one dollar," she said, putting a perfumed arm on his shoulder. She moved closer and stroked his neck with one finger, making Yosl shiver involuntarily. "Come," she said. "It's only a dollar."

Numbly, Yosl reached in his pocket and found the money. They embraced and made a giddy circuit of the floor. He had never been so close to a woman, certainly not to such a woman as this. Could she be Jewish, he wondered. She wore no wig, and yet she spoke Yiddish. He tried to look at her face, but she pulled him close, rubbing against his groin until Yosl felt himself growing hard. He tried to pull away, embarrassed at his lack of control. But she continued her gyrations, holding him now around the neck and caressing his cheek with her lips. Then, suddenly, the music stopped and the dance was over. Yosl stood alone, exposed to the world.

The girl smirked at him. "Another dollar for another lesson," she said knowingly. The host had reappeared, and he was smiling, too. Yosl tried to cover his embarrassment with indignation. "I didn't ask to come here, I was kidnapped," he said.

The girl ignored him. "If you want to go upstairs, it's two dollars," she said.

"I haven't got any more money," Yosl said helplessly.

"Then it's time to leave, greenie," the host said, grabbing him by the coat and pushing him out the door. On the street, Yosl turned to protest, but the host was already walking down the block, looking for new customers. He swept his hand in a dismissive motion at Yosl. "Get lost," he said. "And next time, don't wet your pants."

As the first red light was moving across Manhattan, Yosl would take cheese and bread and climb to the roof of the *Forward* building. Though there were many taller buildings in New York, Yosl had never lived in one that was even two stories high. From his seat on an old milk crate next to the soot-blackened chimney, he imagined he could see all the corners of the earth, understanding everything, missing nothing. Then, as dawn spread across the city, he would descend to begin his day's work.

On the street floor of the building, the words "Jewish Daily Forward" were printed in ornate letters in English on the glass, and then, larger, on the door. The same legend was repeated in Hebrew at the top of the building, for God to see. From the time the *Forward* opened until closing, masses of people crowded into Yosl's small anteroom. Sitting at a tiny table with a pad of paper before him, he enjoyed the bustle of a newspaper that spoke not only to the whole Jewish world but was the voice of a million immigrants in New York. Yet the stories he heard were so heartbreaking that it was all he could do to write them down.

A woman had been abandoned by her husband two weeks after arriving in New York. She had three small ones and no training for a job. Could he help? How could he not try? All day long, they came: young men looking for guidance, girls anxious to find a husband, parents uncertain about the strange customs of America. Men unhappy with their "greenhorn" wives and wondering if a marriage arranged in the old country could be annulled in the new. Desperate as life had been in Russia, there had been means to handle these problems, rabbinical courts, a system that at least made sense to those living within it. Here, all was chaos and uncertainty. The immigrants feared the police, American lawyers, even venturing above Twenty-third Street. All they had was *The Forward,* and everyone wanted to see the great editor, to put his problem before Cahan, which was impossible. Before Cahan would respond, their questions had to be cleaned up, or composed, as Cahan put it.

At first, Yosl was overwhelmed and sickened by his responsibilities, but in time he became the advocate of the downtrodden, counselor to the confused, composer of the universal plaints of lower Broadway. He would listen carefully, head cocked to one side, and then ask questions, trying to refine the problem, to get to the heart of it. To see where the pain really lay. That was Yosl's job as he saw it. The way something was presented to the editor often determined his response, so Yosl spent as much time trying to imagine Cahan's frame of mind as actually writing the letters. Soon Yosl became nearly as popular as the editor. Lines would form around his desk even before he arrived in the morning, and more than one widow left after talking with him, not even bothering to have her letter composed and set in type.

Yosl's colleagues in the newsroom made fun of his sentimentality and took to calling him Mozart, but he made no apologies. He was genuinely moved by his clients' courage. People who had nothing yet asked only to be given a chance to make their way in the New World. In his fascination with the work, Yosl began to forget his own problems. He attended the Yiddish theater, ate at cafeterias, and walked the streets with greater confidence. But Cahan still puzzled him. The editor was by turns avuncular and tyrannical, praising Yosl's writing but then telling him not to get involved, that people made their own problems and must make their own solutions.

"What socialist believes that?" Yosl asked. "These people are victims of the system. The Tsar oppressed them and now America ignores them."

Cahan shrugged. "Tears never made a revolution," he said. "If they did, the Jews would rule the world."

One *shabbos* night, Yosl was invited to Cahan's home and sat through a long meal at the heavy mahogany table, marveling at the nearly complete lack of conversation. Yosl had hoped Cahan would tell him how to become a writer, a great man. But if the editor taught at all, it was by example, giving little away. Yosl had imagined Cahan's home being full of interesting people with lively stories to tell, but Cahan's wife excused herself, and Yosl sat alone in the large room while the editor smoked a cigar. There was no music or conversation beyond the merely perfunctory, and the evening ended early. There were no further invitations, though Cahan did not appear unfriendly at the office.

Six months after Yosl's arrival, Cahan called him to his office. As always, the editor was wearing coat, tie, and vest. He stood behind his desk, shifting from foot to foot. Yosl had bought a jacket striped in red, blue, and yellow off a pushcart to replace his father's coat, and a pair of blue gabardine trousers.

"Ah, the coat of many colors," Cahan remarked sardonically.

Yosl ducked his head, embarrassed. Now he wished he hadn't thrown away his student's uniform. "You wanted to see me?"

"Yes," Cahan said. "Sit." He pointed to a chair, though he made no move himself. "I've heard from your uncle."

Yosl sat forward, eager for news. "Yes?" he said.

Cahan seemed bored. He didn't offer to show Yosl the letter, but merely jabbed at it with a pencil. "So, you still want to go to Wisconsin?"

"I want to see my uncle, but I'm happy here. I've been traveling a long time and it's nice to have a home."

Cahan seemed pleased by this. "Greenberg says you're doing well. That the illiterates line up at your desk early in the morning to tell their sad tales."

"It isn't hard to understand their misery," Yosl said simply.

The editor looked around, as if someone might be surreptitiously listening, then leaned forward, his voice a hoarse whisper. "Yosl," he said. "I'm about to tell you something private. I want to make you a proposition, but promise me that if this doesn't interest you, you'll forget this conversation ever took place. Agreed?"

Yosl was bewildered. What confidential business could he have with Cahan? "Of course," he said. "I'll tell no one."

"Good," the editor said and lapsed into a prolonged silence. Finally, he looked up. "You remember when you first came here, I asked you about Am Olam?"

Yosl nodded. "Farmers. You said my uncle was among them."

"Exactly. And his is the only colony still in existence. But in his letter, Shmuel intimated that all is not well there. That the comrades are divided."

"Over what?"

Cahan shrugged. "Who knows. Jews have never needed a reason to quarrel before, why should they now? I have my suspicions, however."

Yosl waited, but again the editor seemed to have lapsed into a stupor. Finally, Yosl broke into his thoughts. "What are these suspicions, then?"

Cahan looked up and smiled. "Forgive me. This has been much on my mind. The original principles of Am Olam were both foolhardy and noble. The original members of Am Olam were not made to be farmers, and they knew it. But they also believed that the answer to anti-Semitism was for Jews to learn to live independently. Some hoped to establish their own countries, or cantons, with diplomatic ties to other governments. Fools, visionaries—take your pick, but who can live without the examples of people willing to suffer and die for their dreams? It makes our lives possible. Am Olam is important for this reason. I wouldn't like to see the Wisconsin colony die, like all the others."

"Did my uncle say it would fail?" Yosl asked.

"Shmuel is inscrutable. He only says that there's trouble. I'd like to have my own report." Now he looked meaningfully at Yosl. "You see?"

"But what can I do? I know nothing of this community."

Cahan spread his hands before him. "You are my employee and you are doing an excellent job. Therefore, I've decided to promote you. As of this moment, you are no longer a composer. Now, you are a correspondent."

Yosl had a sinking feeling in his stomach. "But I only write what others tell me," he protested.

"Is reporting any more than that?" Cahan replied. "Anyway, a letter is a letter. Go to Wisconsin and write to me about the community. There are Jews scattered all over America, even in Europe, who are eager to know of the efforts of their brothers on the frontier. But don't limit your reports to the Jews. Meet the gentiles, too, the people in the towns and villages. Give me the smell and feel of the place in your letters. I want it to be as if I were there myself. You understand?"

Yosl didn't want to contradict the editor. Besides, the idea of Wisconsin had begun to excite him again. "I think so," he said.

"Good." Cahan put his arm around Yosl's shoulders. "You came here a scared boy, but I've seen you grow into a mensch. You've traveled halfway around the world. Now, you'll go still farther. That's more than most people accomplish."

"Riding on a boat is no accomplishment," Yosl said.

"It's something," Cahan said benignly. He stepped back and looked at Yosl critically. "I think you've gained a little weight? You seem taller."

"It comes from eating regularly, Your Honor."

Cahan laughed. "I believe you're right," he said. Then he handed Yosl a book. "Take this with you," he said. "It will help you understand America."

On the dust jacket was printed *Leaves of Grass.* "Is it about nature?"

"Yes," Cahan said. "Human nature. Now, go, your work is waiting for you."

The memories of New York were like a dream. Joe lay back and let the wind blow across him, feeling the weeds against his face like a lover's caress. Now, he took Cahan's book out, and it fell open at a page the editor had marked:

> You whoever you are!
> You daughter or son of England!
> You of the mighty Slavic tribes and empires! You Russ in
> Russia!
> You dim-descended, black, divine-soul'd African, large fine-
> headed, nobly-form'd, superbly destin'd, on

equal terms with me!
You Jew journeying in your old age through every risk to
stand once on Syrian ground!
You other Jews waiting in all lands for your Messiah!
. . . .

Health to you! good will to you all, from me and America
sent!
Each of us is inevitable,
Each of us limitless—each of us with his or her right upon
the earth,
Each of us allow'd the eternal purports of the earth,
Each of us here as divinely as any is here.

Joe closed the book. They were all inevitable, all waiting for the Messiah. He rose to his feet and started back toward the commune. He wanted to talk to his uncle about Cahan.

six

You tell yourself you are a man, but you feel like a boy. You are among comrades, yet you are alone. Each day you rise and go to the fields, where you work harder than you believed possible. You come home too exhausted to eat, but you cannot sleep. Your eyes itch and your forehead pulses with anxious blood. Despite this, you are unaccountably happy. At last your life has purpose. You stride out in the morning with the men and spend your days on your knees, but say prayers to no one. Everywhere, there is a high, brilliant glow, and the sky is pink long into the night.

You are fascinated by the women. By their long, free-flowing hair, their smells, and by the hint of license they carry with them. You want to be closer to them, but you can think of nothing to say, no questions to ask. Surreptitiously, you watch them bend over as they work, haunches straining to break free of the fabric, and at times it is so painful you must immerse yourself in the cold, fast water of the river.

You have never been so aware of your own body. A small ridge of muscle has risen on your chest. You measure it with your finger, watching it pass from one knuckle to another, moving as slowly as a glacier across your ribs. Veins pop like rope from your arms when you carry water for dinner, and you hold the bucket an instant longer than necessary, hoping the girls will notice. You have new power in your legs. You could walk forever, if only you had someplace to go. You believe you have some great task to perform, but no one tells you what it is, and you are too embarrassed to ask. For now, it is enough to feel it inside without betraying your secret to others.

Lost on the great plain of America, you remember the pine forests of Russia, but as time goes by, there is less and less to recall, less to regret. You feel at once poised on the edge of accomplishment, and pointless. The trees have also been scattered at random across this country, planted by nameless pioneers who have moved on. For nothing grows naturally in this place; everything must be planted. But the trees demand no explanation for their existence. You envy the trees, the river, for their placidity, but this does not help.

Alone in your bed, you lie awake and ask the great question—Why? Then a cloud moves across the moon and darkness obscures everything. You sleep.

Book Two

Would that we had died by the hand of the Lord in the land of Egypt . . . for ye have brought us forth into the wilderness, to kill this whole assembly with hunger.

—Exodus 16:3

seven

July 26, 1905

Dear Mr. Cahan,

Greetings from New Zion, from Wisconsin, from the West. I have been here scarcely a month, and already I am indistinguishable from the natives. I wear denim overalls, a straw hat to shield me from the sun, high black boots, and my hands are rough and callused. I have even been issued a gun, but thus far I have been unable to hit anything. Some of the men go forth with "shoot irons" every day, but mine is too heavy and awkward. Besides, it is only a .38-calibre, while a .44 is standard. I may be an American now, but I am still a pacifist at heart.

The sky is enormous, like a great starred hand that holds the earth gently in its palm, rotating it daily for diversion. Living here, where the most common means of transport is one's feet and paved roads are nonexistent, it is hard to believe New York can exist. The prairie stretches endlessly around us, dotted by occasional clumps of trees, and people are less numerous than cattle. Yet if I close my eyes, I can see the cheerful chaos of Houston Street and hear the rumble of trains through the night.

Our life would seem as rough to you as our shelters. We live on five hundred acres, of which nearly seventy-five are under cultivation. Our community is just outside the small village of Gays Mills, on the Kickapoo River, though the Indians for whom the river is named have been gone for more than a hundred years. We have two main buildings—a large dining hall and dormitory, where I sleep, and a community building, which houses our meeting hall. In addition, there are several shanties for those who for one reason or another don't live elsewhere. Our common buildings are not elegant, but they are adequate. From my bed, I can see the sky through the ceiling, and when it rains, I sleep with a slicker over me. In winter I will have to seek protection, but now I'm so tired at night that it is hard to be disturbed about this.

Trees shelter our community. We have planted box elders and white ash to go with the oaks and maples that grow here naturally. We also have a grape arbor and a small apple orchard. In time, we shall harvest our own fruit. Perhaps because of the orchard, our community is frequently visited by small birds, and hawks who prey on the smaller animals. With the aid of a guide, I've managed to identify several species, including jays, orioles, cardinals, the red-tailed hawk, and a large barn owl, who is more secretive than the others, but who seems to live in an abandoned shanty near the river and ventures out only at night, when his screams awaken everyone and bring the men out in nightshirts with their guns, looking for interlopers.

Because of the abundance of trees, everything here is constructed of wood and mud plaster. It is a matter of local pride that we have not had to resort to mud huts like our neighbors to the west in Nebraska and Iowa. Wood is seen to be evidence of sophistication, and thus we are very sophisticated indeed.

You will want to know something of our neighbors, the gentiles. Gays Mills is a pleasant village which serves as a port for farmers who wish to ship their wares downriver. There is a large hotel and a few stores that sell general merchandise. A train station serves the region, and there are four or five saloons on the main street, each of which employs a piano player to entertain its patrons. Sometimes a woman will stand and sing with abandon of lost love, and the customers enjoy this immoderately, calling out to the women and sometimes throwing money at them. Gambling is carried on openly, and while I know nothing of these games, I am told that the saloons have faro tables and that their patrons also play something called poker and another game called *rouge et noir,* which must be of French origin. Piles of greenbacks are wagered in these games, yet arguments are few, and losers, though naturally disgruntled, seem to bear their victors no ill will.

Life on the commune bears little resemblance to that in town. As you know, the fundamental philosophy of New Zion is Marxist—each man works according to his ability, each receives according to his needs—yet here, women are equal to the men and share the considerable tasks which take most of our time. To give just one example, simply providing clothes for everyone is a major undertaking. Needless to say, the clothes one brings to the wilderness do not last forever, and though there is a dry goods store in town, we do not have adequate money to buy ready-made. Thus, we must make our own, and this is no small chore.

We trade milk or cheese for shearing rights at a nearby farm, where a large woman called Hattie does the shearing. She is able to catch a sheep, tie it, then throw in on the shearing table with an ease that astounds me. After this, the wool must be washed in the river before it can be treated. This process is a great entertainment for the children, who splash and play in the water while their elders work.

When the wool is dry, we "pick" it, removing all the trash and burrs the sheep have accumulated in their travels. It is arranged in rolls the size of a chalk pencil but a yard long, and then it is sent to the carding machine. Here again, Hattie takes charge. She has both a very large spinning wheel and a loom for weaving. But first she must spin the rolls into thread and then coil it into skeins for weaving.

Finally, the yarn must be colored. The women work together, comparing their dyes for brilliance. Reds and browns are made from walnut bark, and sometimes dyestuffs such as logwood for black and madder powder for red are purchased from itinerant peddlers. Often, rusted iron—or iron filings—are used to make colors "set." All this, of course, is mere preparation to actually sewing the garments, which takes much time on its own, and this, in turn, is only one of the many chores which fill our lives. You may imagine that we endeavor to make our clothes last and that we appreciate fully the labor that goes into their manufacture.

As you are aware, Edward Liberty is the leader of our group. Liberty did not start the commune, but right now he is its soul. He is not a Jew, but then most of those here are Jews in name only. The comrades think of themselves, first and always, as socialists and are disdainful of religion, though as far as I can tell, they are nearly ignorant of our faith. Some are budding positivists, in deference to our leader, and most of us at least listen to his lectures out of respect. My uncle and a few friends are the angry exception. All of us adhere, more or less, to a daily schedule, as follows:

6:00 A.M.	Rise
6:00–8:00	Study mathematics, the first science in Comte's classification
8:00	Breakfast
8:00–11:30	Work in fields, forest, or dining hall
11:30–l:30	Rest and study
l:30–4:00	Work again
4:00–5:00	Recreation
5:00	Supper
6:00–9:00	Study

Several nights a week, Mr. Liberty gives lectures—on positivism, vegetarianism, or whatever strikes his fancy. On Wednesday, we discuss current events, and on Sundays we hear mutual criticism. On Sunday mornings, Mr. Liberty chants hymns to the accompaniment of a battered hand organ and offers prayers, which are followed by fraternal kisses all around.

Liberty believes Jews are, by their birthright—that is, he doesn't hold it against us—narrow-minded. We are self-centered, clannish, and suspicious, he says. He offers no evidence to support these theories and at the same time flatters us by saying that no movement can survive without our support. Yet no one seems insulted; few even question the truth of his assertions. While people die in Russia for the sin of being Jews, here it is not even worth arguing about.

Liberty's religious ideas, I must confess, bewilder me, but the man himself is fascinating. Often he appears at meetings wearing what appear to be clerical vestments, and he has about him the ill-fed glow of the martyr. Whether this is inspiration or mere hunger—you may have noticed that we eat only two small meals a day—I cannot say.

Our diet, like everything else, follows from Liberty's teachings. In Wisconsin, food is plentiful; still our leader preaches a kind of voluntary starvation. He believes that meat befouls the digestive system and that hunger is an act of contrition in a world where many must suffer it daily. Our food budget is fifteen cents a day per person, and often our meals consist only of a watery soup and those inedible Graham crackers that taste like plaster and fall to pieces in your hands. The others accept this regimentation without complaint, but I have already done my starving in Russia, so I eat with a clear conscience whatever I can get my hands on. Nuts and vegetables grow wild in the fields, and I make periodic trips there on my own. Thus I stay in good health and in favor with Liberty, who often cites me as an example of the rightness of his nutritional philosophy.

I feel impossibly older than before. Even the children here seem grown-up, bending beneath heavy loads in the fields, helping uncomplainingly with the chores until late in the evening. Liberty does not believe in childhood, yet I find myself admiring him. Whatever he may demand of us, he ask ten times that of himself. His clothes hang from his shoulders and his personal belongings would not fill a cigar box. Tall and muscular, his voice is strong and warm. When he addresses you, there is the absolute sensation that the world we know has ceased to exist, and that you and he inhabit another, adjacent universe that he has just created for the express purpose of talking privately with you.

Looking back over this report, I realize that my description may make our life seem cheerless, but in truth the forest and fields often ring with laughter, and good fellowship characterizes our daily intercourse. The children laugh and play and swim in the river, and we have a large library to stimulate our minds. There is the excitement of conquering a new land, of meeting challenges daily that would have defeated us in our former lives. And there is the prairie, vast and brooding all around, to inspire and terrify us with its power. Rising like an endless sea of sandy waves, it nourishes, resists, and goads us to be strong and resilient. The oppression of my former life is still in my mind, but in the act of clearing land or felling trees, worry washes off me like mud in the bath, and then I feel freer than I ever imagined was possible. For all this, I do not know whom I should thank but Liberty. He is either a saint or a madman. I will study him and perhaps be able to decide.

Your friend and employee,
Joseph Abrams

eight

Joe was halfway to the woodlot when he remembered his hat and started back. He had neglected to cover his head one day and suffered with a fiery sunburn for a week. The commandment made sense not only in the synagogue but at New Zion as well. The clearing was empty except for the omnipresent chickens pecking hopefully in the dust, but when he entered the dining hall, he heard voices. Hesitating lest he should intrude where he was not wanted, Joe let his eyes adjust to the light and at last made out Edward Liberty at one of the long tables with a small girl in a red pinafore, her hair done up in elaborate braids. Liberty was conducting a lesson, but the girl shook her head back and forth violently, causing the braids to slap against her back like tiny whips. "I can't do it," she wailed. "I tried and tried, but I can't."

Joe couldn't see Liberty's face, but the leader didn't seem sympathetic. "You must, Bella," he said in a monotone. "Now, thirty-six times twenty-four equals what?"

The girl said nothing for a moment, then cried, "I don't know. I didn't know before, I still don't know. It's too big."

"It is not too big," Liberty insisted. "Today you pay no attention to the rules of multiplication, and you make mistakes in mathematics; when you grow up, you will pay no attention to the rules of life, and you will surely go wrong. Now you smudge your notebook, tomorrow you will blacken your soul."

It seemed ridiculous to compare failure in mathematics with mortal sin, but Joe said nothing. Bella started to cry, wiping her tears on her sleeve. "Stop it, Bella," Liberty said evenly. "I am not angry, but you must finish before you can go into the fields." He said this as if working in the broiling sun was to be the child's reward. "Go on. Or here, I'll give you another: fourteen times twenty-two. That's easier."

Bella's cries were painful sobs as she continued shaking her head. Joe's heart went out to the child, but he was fascinated by the clinical tone of Liberty's commands, his obsession with mathematics, and his insensitivity to the little girl.

"Bella," Liberty repeated. "If you don't stop crying and finish your lesson, I'll have to pour a bucket of water over you. I mean it."

Bella's cries reached a crescendo of misery and fear at this, but before Joe could move, Liberty dumped a pail of water over the girl's head, drenching himself in the process. Too late, Joe ran to Bella's rescue. "What's the matter with you," he shouted. "Are you a madman or what?"

Water dripped off Liberty's beard. "I have only kept my word," he said calmly. "The child would not respect me otherwise. I would not respect myself."

"No one respects such cruelty." Joe said angrily. "Why should a little one need to remember such large sums? Of what earthly good is this?"

Liberty ignored these questions. He dabbed idly at his forehead with a sodden handkerchief that he had pulled from a vest pocket and looked at the ceiling. He patted Bella on the arm and said gently. "That will be all for now. I will see you tomorrow. Don't forget to study." The child smiled shyly at Joe and ran out the door.

"You are the nephew of Samuel Abrams?"

Joe felt his anger receding, draining out of him. The cool curiosity of Liberty's question was rhetorical, of course. The leader knew perfectly well who he was. But Joe wondered what he wanted from him. "I'm Joseph Abrams," he said.

Liberty turned to examine him, and Joe noticed that the bone in his nose was a sickly white, accentuating the skeletal quality of the man's face. The skin seemed taut enough to split, and so dry that in places it was flaking like a rash. Liberty was ill, Joe decided. It was nowhere so evident as in his eyes, which glowed with interest. "I have been wanting to speak to you," Liberty said, "but what I have to say is confidential. Could I trouble you to come to my quarters for a few minutes?"

Joe was not used to being treated with such respect by his elders. "Come with me," his father would have said. Even Shmuel ordered him around. But this man, whom he had insulted in front of Bella a few moments before, was different. He seemed to have forgotten the whole thing. "I am supposed to be in the forest," Joe said. "I only came back for my hat."

"Yes," Liberty said. "Of course. But they will not miss you for a short time. Come." He held out his arm now as if it were both an invitation and a command.

The leader occupied a shanty like Shmuel's, but Liberty's was nearly bare, with white pine floors that were dry and bleached from scrubbing. Liberty stood aside to let Joe enter, then took his place behind a small wooden table stacked with books and papers. There was no other furniture. "I cannot offer you a seat," he said. "I prefer to stand while I work; it improves circulation to the brain."

Joe wondered if Liberty slept on his feet. Then he saw a mattress filled with corn husks in the corner. "I don't mind standing," he said.

"Ah," Liberty said, as if Joe had revealed something important. He brought his hands together and peered at Joe over his steepled fingers. "I wonder," he said at last, "to what extent you share your uncle's opinions?"

Liberty's Russian was formal, which made Joe want to mimic him. "Which of his opinions do you mean, Your Honor? My uncle has a great many."

This amused Liberty. "Excellent. Which, indeed? A man without opinions is like a book without pages. I meant you must know of Shmuel's animosity toward me."

Suddenly, Joe felt vulnerable in the hot little room. "I don't think my uncle dislikes you," he said, knowing it wasn't true.

Liberty brushed this aside with a majestic sweep of his arm. "Perhaps not personally, though I'm not sure. But we have important disagreements, isn't this so?"

There was no point in denying it. Joe nodded and looked at the floor.

"I only mention this because I'm interested in you," Liberty said quickly. "I don't expect you to betray your uncle."

"He is the only family I have in the world," Joe said. "I would never do anything to harm him."

"Who would ask you to?" Liberty said innocently. He shrugged his shoulders and puffed his cheeks. "It would be like questioning my devotion to my daughter." Liberty looked through his bushy eyebrows at Joe. "You've met, I believe?"

Joe blushed. He wondered if Lizzie had told her father everything, though what made him blush was not what had happened but what he had felt. "I admire your daughter," he said stiffly.

Liberty nodded, pleased by this. "Yes. Actually, we have discussed you at some length. Elzbeta tells me that you're a journalist."

"Oh, no," Joe said quickly. "When I arrived in New York, Mr. Cahan guaranteed my employment, is all."

Liberty nodded. "Exactly. So you worked for his newspaper, the *Forward*?"

"My job was not important. I was little more than a stenographer."

Liberty ignored this. "So. A journalist, experienced, and probably able to take shorthand as well?"

Things were getting out of control. Next he would claim Joe had been the editor himself. "No one else could read my notes, and sometimes I can't either."

Liberty shrugged. "You also read and write English, I believe?"

"I do both imperfectly," Joe said. He remembered the crowded classroom, the disdainful German teacher, and his struggles with English grammar. "Not very well."

"Who in this world can be said to be perfect?" Liberty said. "Perfection is the goad that drives us, not the possession of a single man that breathes."

Liberty floated on the strength of his own words, and Joe waited for him to return to earth. He thought of his work, the clean sweep of the blade in the moment before it bit into the tree. He was eager to get back to the forest.

"What I mean is that here we can't be so particular. I am a Russian like all the rest, but I am also a man carrying a message for America, one so important that, like medicine, it must be administered whether or not the patient wishes to swallow it."

"I'm afraid I don't see what this has to do with me," Joe said.

"Everything," Liberty snapped. "I want you to become my amanuensis."

"Amanuensis?" Joe said. Even pronouncing the word was a challenge. He had no idea what it meant.

"Secretary, assistant—make up your own title. What do you think?"

Joe thought he would have trouble getting used to Liberty's changes of mood. Now Joe smiled hopefully, trying to ingratiate himself, like a suitor visiting his fiancée. He thought a secretary would at least need a chair. "What would I do?"

Liberty shrugged. "I receive many letters, but my English is abominable. I can make my needs known in a shop, but in my correspondence, I want to persuade, to inform, if possible to be eloquent. This is impossible for me now."

"I'm not sure I can help," Joe said. He did not think of himself as being eloquent.

"Whatever you can do would be an improvement," Liberty said. "So. I need assistance with my correspondence and also with the newsletter."

"I didn't know there was one," Joe said. He had been impressed with the library, but few seemed to use it. If they didn't read Spinoza and Kant, why should they care about a newsletter? "Everyone seems too busy to write," he said.

Liberty shook his head sadly. "It is the unfortunate truth, but starvation would be preferable to failing to alert the world to the results of our experiment."

Joe was going to ask, "What experiment?" but thought better of it. Liberty had his own view of things. "Could I see a copy?" he asked.

"Publication has yet to begin," the leader said. "I am arranging for a small printing press to be sent, and I hope a comrade in Kansas, a printer by trade, will come to operate it. In the meantime, we will do it ourselves. You will be the writer."

"The only writer? But I have no ideas," Joe protested.

"Such modesty is appealing," Liberty said. "At first, you will write as I and the others direct you."

Joe wondered what Shmuel would think of this, but there seemed no way to extricate himself from the situation. Beyond that, he wasn't sure he wanted to reject Liberty. Cahan had told him to get to know the leader, and Joe's curiosity had been aroused. Then there was Lizzie, though he wasn't sure his working for the leader would please her. "What about my work in the forest?" Joe asked.

Liberty's hands were clenched in fists so tight his knuckles seemed to gleam. "It is my responsibility to evaluate each comrade's contribution. You are hardly more than a boy. Your arms are like twigs. How could anyone think chopping down trees could be as valuable as working here with me in this office?"

Joe wanted to roll up his sleeves and show the leader the progress he had made. "I do my share," he said stiffly. "I am stronger than I look."

"I don't mean to insult you." Liberty said. "The question is what work is best for you? You are an educated man. We would be foolish to waste your education."

Liberty's logic was irrefutable, but Joe hesitated. "I must talk to my uncle."

"Of course. Only remember that your uncle has as much right as anyone to contribute to the newsletter. It is to be the record of our collective life, not the organ of a single propagandist."

Liberty's voice resonated in the empty room. "I'm sure my uncle will be glad to hear that," Joe said. But he knew Shmuel would not like the idea of his nephew's working for Liberty. He turned to leave, then remembered something. "The newsletter," he said. "Does it have a name?"

Liberty's eyes lit up. He inhaled as if he were nourished by the wonder of it all. "We shall call it the *Positivist Investigator*," he said.

Joe was both touched and dismayed by Liberty's enthusiasm, wondering how he could live up to the leader's expectations. "And what shall we investigate?" he asked.

Liberty laughed silently, as if he were humoring Joe because the answer was so obvious. "Everything!" he crowed. "Everything."

nine

Shmuel listened silently while Joe told him of Liberty's offer, his huge right hand resting on his pendulous stomach. Periodically, he would reach for the cider. After drinking, he wiped his beard with his fingers and belched softly.

Finally, Joe finished. "What do you think, Uncle?" he asked.

Shmuel rose to his feet, towering over his nephew, and jabbed Joe's chest with a thick forefinger. "Wait here," he said, and went outside.

Joe closed his eyes. The fruity smell of malt was overwhelming in the close, dark room. For the first time in his life, he felt the urge to drink, to forget himself and New Zion. He hadn't invited this controversy, had wanted only to do his work quietly without annoying anyone. But as hard as he tried to order his life, it kept spinning out of control. He knew that this was the way of the world. Had his parents asked the Cossacks to invade their village? Still, he felt persecuted. Was it his fault he was literate? And it was Cahan who had made him take the English classes. Yet he knew Cahan had done him no wrong. He just disliked being caught between Shmuel and Liberty.

Outside the window, Annuta was carrying a pail of water toward the kitchen. Joe rose to go help her, realizing they hadn't spoken since her sister's wedding. But then he heard his uncle at the door.

Abe Rosenfeld and Morris Held were with him. Abe was tall, like Shmuel, but thin, with a ruff of black beard encircling his jaw and a solid line of hair running above his eyes like a pencil. Held was something else. Small and wiry, with burning blue eyes, he was the only clean-shaven man in New Zion, and a bitter enemy of Liberty. When the leader closed his eyes at the Sunday meetings and chanted, "Humanity, humanity, the soul of perfectibility," Held grinned like a madman, his lips drawn over his gums, a soft hissing sound like a burning fuse the only sound he made.

Shmuel motioned Abe and Held to seats. Then he pointed at Joe. "Gentlemen," he said theatrically. "This is my nephew. Only nineteen years old, gone from his mother's breast for less than a year, and already he has conquered New York City and Edward Liberty. As you can see, he is quite a mensch."

Shmuel laughed disdainfully, then sprawled on his cot. Joe looked at Abe, who shrugged and raised his eyebrows. He was not a man to waste emotion and consequently had great influence among the comrades. Held sat motionless, his chin resting on raised fingers, tension radiating from him like heat. Occasionally, he rotated his jaw, as if cleaning his teeth, but even then, his face reflected a struggle to contain the anger he felt toward the world. He licked his lips and spoke in a strained voice.

"Shmuel says you're employed by the great Cahan, that you're a journalist."

It was so nearly what Liberty had said that Joe had to stop himself from smiling. "Mr. Cahan was my sponsor and I am grateful to him," he said. "If it weren't for his generosity, I wouldn't be here." Joe looked at his uncle for support, but Shmuel's eyes were closed and he was breathing deeply.

"He gave me a job, a place to sleep," Joe went on. "In return I helped poor people publish their misery in the paper in hopes of finding a soul who would understand their pain. I would not claim to be a journalist." He realized that this was the second time in an hour he had made this assertion. He wondered if it was really true.

Held's forehead was creased by deep horizontal grooves that banded his face from his hairline to his eyes. When he lifted his eyebrows, his face was a washboard. "But isn't it true that you are still working for Cahan? And there are no such people here in need of your services."

Joe felt no obligation to share his secrets with Held. In fact, Shmuel's little inquisition had begun to irritate him. "The people I worked with are not so different from the rest of us, but Mr. Cahan was kind enough to pay for my ticket here and I'm grateful for that, too."

Held seemed to wait for further amplification, but when Joe said nothing, he didn't press him. Shmuel was examining the ceiling. Abe looked embarrassed.

"Did Cahan mention me?" Held asked suddenly.

"I beg your pardon?"

"When you said you were coming to New Zion, did he say his friend Mo from the old country, from the boat, from the past, was here? Did he mention me?"

Joe felt unexpected sympathy for the man. He had spoken in a wistful tone of afterthought with only the suggestion of anger, but Joe knew this was the question he had wanted to ask all along. "I'm not sure he knew," he said at last.

Held grimaced and looked down. "But he knew where Shmuel was. That's how you got here in the first place. He'd know." He laughed bitterly. "Cahan knows everything, everyone. I hear he's even a great thing with the goy writers—William Dean Howells and the Boston aristocrats. They've taken him up, invited him to dinner and praised his books in their newspapers to people who don't know the difference between Hebrew and Yiddish." He spat in the dirt. "Abe always knew everything. He looked like a bar mitzvah boy when the rest of us were shaving, but young as he was, Abe was always thinking, planning ahead. Smart. He was so smart he looked stupid sometimes, so no one thought anything of it. And now look at him and look at us."

Rosenfeld's low voice broke in. "We're not here to talk about Cahan, Mo. That ain't the boy's fault." He turned to Joe, his brown eyes gentle but questioning. "Shmuel says Liberty wants you to help him with a newspaper or something. Can you tell us about that, Joe?"

"He wants me to be his secretary because he can't read or write English."

Abe's large head seemed to dwarf his body. He turned to Shmuel. "What's so terrible about that?" he asked quietly. "Joe is going to answer Liberty's mail, so we all come running in here like a bunch of rabbis?

Maybe I'm missing something, but what's the problem, Shmuel? Don't waste my time. I got work to do."

But it was Held, not Shmuel, who answered. "It's important because Liberty is not just a fool with grandiose ideas—it's worse than that. He's meshuggah, crazy, out of his mind. He thinks he's God, the new Messiah." Since this vision didn't clash with Joe's own impression of the leader, he attended more closely to what Held was saying. It was the first time he'd been able to make any sense out of the man.

"If he were only an opportunist, I wouldn't care," Held said. "He'd take our money, then leave us in peace. What bothers me is that he's serious about this; he really believes starving and studying multiplication will bring on revolution. And he's convincing enough to persuade the others of this lunacy. That's why he's dangerous."

"Okay," Abe said. "For a change, you're right. I agree with you about Liberty. But we're talking about Joe." He put his large hand on Joe's shoulder. "Tell me," he said. "Are you a positivist, a believer, like Liberty?"

Joe was insulted by the question and felt himself go red. "Of course not," he said. "I am a Jew, nothing else."

Abe nodded pleasantly. "There, Mo, you see? The boy has not been misled."

"Maybe not," Held admitted. "But is he a Marxist?"

Abe smiled. "To tell the truth, I'm not much of one myself anymore. I'm too tired at the end of the day to study philosophy. But this, too, is beside the point. If Liberty is going to have a newspaper—and we can't stop him from doing that—then it's better that one of ours is working with him than someone else, isn't that so?"

Joe disliked being spoken of as if he weren't there. He hadn't come to ask their permission to accept Liberty's offer, exactly. Yet now they were deciding whether or not he should work on the paper.

Held had been deep in thought, and now he turned back to Joe. "Well, what about it," he snapped. "Will you keep us informed?"

"Of what?" Joe asked.

"The newsletter, Liberty's rag, of course, what else?"

"You can read it yourself," Joe said. "You can even contribute. Mr. Liberty said it won't be his organ but for everyone."

Held laughed, showing blackened gums and yellow teeth. "He would say that. The question is what will he do?"

"Why don't you give him a chance before you judge him?" Joe said, surprised at his own arrogance.

Held was about to reply when Abe inserted himself into the conversation, canceling Held out. "What we would like, Joe, is just to meet with you every so often, to talk things over. Would you mind doing that?"

Put so reasonably, Joe could hardly refuse, and he was grateful to Abe for quieting Held. "I always enjoy talking to you," he said.

Abe rose and patted Joe on the shoulder. "I am satisfied," he said, bringing the questioning to a close. "Shmuel, where is the cider you promised us? All this talk has made me thirsty."

Yet even after the flask had been passed around the room twice, Held remained silent, his small white hands still clenched into fists. The man was a mystery to Joe, as enigmatic as Liberty but somehow more malignant. Though Held was smaller and older than Joe, he frightened him because anger made Held heedless. Such men were the most dangerous. Joe decided to stay clear of Morris Held.

ten

Before Joe could begin his new job, he became ill. He was working in the fields when a sudden chill came upon him. Thinking only that he had been sweating too much, he kept on working. Next, his eyelids became unbearably heavy; it was all he could do to hold them open, and his eyes itched from a dryness that he blamed on the sun. Then the weight seemed to spread downward to his drooping shoulders, and even his abdomen. Finally, his bones seemed incapable of supporting his body. For an hour, Joe struggled on, but at last he went to find Shmuel.

"Uncle, I don't feel well," he said.

Shmuel looked at him appraisingly, opened his eyes with a dirty finger, then clapped him on the shoulder, almost knocking him into the underbrush. "You've got the ague," he announced.

"Ague?"

"Malaria, the shakes, call it what you want. Everybody here gets it, sooner or later. Put the water together with the newly turned earth, and you can't avoid it."

Joe had no interest in his diagnosis. "Can't work," he said, and collapsed.

When he awoke, Annuta was sitting beside his bed reading. It was light outside, but the sun was higher than he remembered. "Is it morning?" he asked.

Annuta smiled. "Several mornings, by now. You've had a good long sleep."

"I slept for three days?"

"Not all the time. For a while, it was all we could do to keep you in bed. Then you had some bad dreams; after that, you slept."

"Dreams?" He was immediately embarrassed for what he might have revealed. It surprised him how much he cared what Annuta thought; he wanted to appear strong and self-possessed to her, not vulnerable and weak.

She nodded and put down her book. "You thought you were in Russia, that the Black Hundred had found you."

Joe shivered involuntarily at the thought. "God forbid," he said. He tried to rise to his elbows, but a wave of dizziness drove him back onto the pillows.

"Not so fast," Annuta said. "You're still weak. Here, I made this for you." She held a spoonful of liquid to his lips.

Joe tasted it and made a face. "What is it?"

"Herb tea," Annuta smiled. Joe's reaction didn't discourage her. She held out another spoonful. "It will help you get well."

Joe nodded and took another sip. It wasn't as bad the second time. He drained the cup, and then he did feel stronger. The room was empty and quiet. The fact that she had watched him sleep, heard his dreams, made him both bold and shy, as if she had seen into his soul and learned his secrets. She had tied her hair into a bun that made her look older and less innocent. "This is very kind of you," Joe said.

Annuta blushed. "It's nothing," she said. "I was glad to help."

"It's nice to see you smile," Joe said. "The first time I saw you, you were crying, and you have such a pretty smile."

Annuta made a show of preparing to leave, but she didn't budge from her chair after shifting her book and sewing from one arm to the other. "I haven't felt really happy since leaving Russia," she said. "Since we left Mama and Papa behind."

Joe wondered if she would cry, but her eyes were dry. "And your sister?"

"It's different now," Annuta said. "We don't sleep in the same place, and when we meet in the kitchen, there's no time to talk. After all, she has a husband to care for." Annuta looked down into her lap, then directly at Joe. "And what about you, Yosl, are you happy in America?"

The question caught Joe by surprise. He had been thinking about her, playing the big brother. "I don't know," he said. Happiness hadn't been his reason for coming. Adventure, excitement, even security, he had hoped for. He wanted to be free to make his own way, be a man like all other men. If he could achieve that, he supposed he would be happy. "I miss my parents, too," he said simply.

Annuta nodded. "I also miss other things. I miss the brick streets in Kiev and going shopping on Shabbat. We were always late and had to rush before the stores closed. Then we would have to hurry to dress before Papa came home." She smiled at the memory. "I miss the heat of the candles on my forehead and sitting and listening to Papa pray. I remember thinking that the table in our dining room was as solid as a rock, immovable. That its legs must go all the way to the center of the earth. Then one day some soldiers broke down our door and smashed the table to splinters. They took my parents, and I never saw them again. But in a way, losing the table was the worst. It was like the destruction of the Temple. Nothing was ever the same."

"How did you escape?" Joe asked.

"We ran, of course—first to the neighbors and then to relatives. They passed us from one friend to another until finally we were on a boat to America."

Annuta's hand was resting on the coverlet, and now Joe covered it and stroked her palm. He wanted to say something, but he knew reassurances were not always reassuring. Sometimes it was better to listen. She dabbed her eyes with a handkerchief and blew her nose. Then an enormous exhaustion invaded his body, and the heaviness in his eyes returned. Still holding Annuta's hand, he gave way to sleep.

In the middle of the night, though what night he could not have said, Joe awoke, his right arm tingling, but for once his mind was lucid. He looked for Annuta, but instead it was his mother seated in the chair to the side of the bed. She was looking away, not at the window but into and beyond the wall. Joe was surprised not so much at her presence, for he had always believed in spirits, but that she seemed exactly the same.

Neither the pogrom nor her sojourn in the afterlife seemed to have affected Hannah. Her long French nose was the same in profile, and she was as solid as before, wearing her brown matron's wig and a voluminous gray dress. Her sewing, as always, sat benignly in her lap. Now she saw Joe examining her.

"So you've awakened at last. At home I could never get you to sleep, even as a baby. I doubt you closed your eyes the first six months of your life."

"I've been ill," Joe said. It seemed odd to talk about such things with someone who, after all, was dead. But then, what should you properly discuss with the dead? He changed the subject. "And you?" He stopped, uncertain how to phrase the question exactly. "How is it where you are?"

Hannah shrugged. "You know, Yosl, except for the Chasids, Jews never talk about what happens afterward. Now, to tell you the truth, I can see why. You do nothing, forever." She sighed. "On the other hand, there is no pain, no hardship or sorrow. I haven't been hungry since the day I died," she said with some wonder. "But your father and sisters don't complain, so why should I?" She passed her hand across her face, to change the subject, and Joe was touched by the familiar gesture. "I did not come here to talk about myself, Yossele," she said. "I am worried about you."

"Me?" Joe said. "I'll be fine. This isn't serious. Shmuel says everyone gets it. After a few days, a week, I'll be back at work."

Hannah smiled patiently, as if being misunderstood was a longstanding habit. "That wasn't what I meant," she said. "You were always such a sensitive boy. Those big eyes used to look at me with questions I had no idea how to answer. Even as a little child, you worried about things rabbis couldn't explain. Why is there suffering in the world, Mama? Who invented hunger?" She looked at the ceiling. "You needed a smarter mother, Yossele, but God in His wisdom gave me to you. I did my best, but I never thought you'd be here, in the wilderness, on your own at such an age. You should still be in school, studying books with your professors to guide you."

Joe reached to touch his mother's arm. Then he remembered she would have no substance and rested his hand on the bedspread. "I have Shmuel to help me."

Hannah laughed involuntarily, then covered her mouth. Though he knew it was impossible, Joe thought he saw her blush. "Ah, Shmuel," Hannah said in a voice Joe did not recognize. "How is he?"

Joe didn't remember his mother ever mentioning his uncle's name before. "He's fine," he said. He didn't know if he should mention Shmuel's drinking.

Hannah seemed not to hear. She was smiling wistfully. "I remember before he left," she said. "What a mensch. All the girls used to talk about how big and strong he was, his face, his hair. To us, he was a god, a giant. Does he ever mention me?"

"You?" Joe's voice was louder than he intended, and he backtracked, afraid his mother would be insulted. Did you send regards to a ghost? He had no idea of the proper protocol in this situation. "He was sorry to hear what happened, of course."

"Yes, yes, he would care. Shmuel felt things more deeply than the other men. You know, Yossele, I was supposed to marry your uncle."

"Shmuel?"

She nodded. "My father and your grandfather had agreed that their oldest children would marry. There was a *shadchen* to draw up the contract. It was all very legal. Then Shmuel ran away, which meant they considered him dead. That made your father the oldest boy. But originally it was Shmuel."

His mother's matter-of-fact tone annoyed Joe. Shmuel should have been his father, and Hannah pretended it made no difference. It was as if they were discussing guests for the seder. "And you didn't care?"

"Care? Who asked what a girl felt, or if she felt anything at all? I cried for days, but even my mother said it was all romantic foolishness, that I could learn to love someone else as well as I ever loved Shmuel." Now she said earnestly, "Yossele, you must know, your father is a fine man. I say nothing against him."

Joe nodded dumbly. Now his mother stuffed her needles and yarn into a cloth bag. "I have stayed too long," she said. "I only wanted to see you with my own eyes. Now rest." For a moment, she looked at him with a mother's concern, then she bent over the bed and Joe felt a light breeze caress his forehead. But when he opened his eyes, it was only the night rain blowing in at the window.

As Joe slowly regained his strength, Shmuel began to visit in the afternoons, his shirt still wet from work. Without any signal, Annuta would quietly retreat and Shmuel would take her seat. Now he looked doubtfully at the glass on Joe's bedside table, sniffed, and took a sip before spitting it out. "What is this crap?"

"Butternut tea," Joe replied.

Shmuel looked skeptical. "We used to give quinine, or maybe a shot of whiskey." He made a face. "You like drinking it?"

"Sometimes she gives me sassafras tea instead, and there's another with herbs I can't even name." He shrugged. "She's very kind to take such care of me."

Shmuel nodded. Joe thought acknowledging kindness made Shmuel feel guilty, as if accepting help constituted a debt. "Have you heard from our leader?"

"Mr. Liberty is very busy," Joe said. "He may have come when I was sleeping." Shmuel nodded again but seemed interested. Thinking of his mother, Joe asked, "Uncle, why did you leave Russia? Why didn't you stay at home with Father?"

Shmuel turned suddenly, as if he were angry, but instead his eyes were bright with interest. "I told you," he said. "I wanted to see the world."

"I know," Joe said. "Every boy in cheder wanted the same thing, but few made it as far as Minsk, not to mention America. I left because I had to, but not even pogroms were enough to convince some people to go. 'Maybe this will be the last one,' they thought. 'Now the Tsar will be kind to us.' But you went before all this madness began. You were part of the generation of hope, when for the first time Jews began to go to university. So why leave?"

Shmuel smiled broadly. "You're a smart boy, Yosl, smarter than I thought. Very different from your father."

"Not so much, I hope," Joe said.

But Shmuel said, "Oh, yes. Very different." Then he sat back, and for the first time, Joe saw memory take over his face. "You're right," Shmuel said. "I didn't have to go. In fact, my father wanted me to go to university, perhaps to become a doctor. But I wasn't interested. I wanted to be a soldier, live a life of adventure."

"My grandfather objected to this?"

"If only it had been that civilized. First, he beat me with a belt until my back looked like beet borscht. Then I was locked in a shed behind our house for two days with only a thin soup for nourishment. Your father would sneak out at night after everyone was asleep and give me whatever morsels he had been able to save from the table. I never forgot that kindness, Yosl. Your father was only fourteen. If he had been caught, he would have been whipped as badly. It was a brave thing to do."

Joe had always thought of his grandfather as a saint whose only desire was to study Torah until God called him. A man without earthly concerns, who hated impiety and was gentle and kind to all. But he knew only what his father had told him, and now he wondered why Isaac had concealed the truth and portrayed Shmuel's flight as frivolous. It troubled him to question his father, and this showed on his face.

"Your father was a good son," Shmuel said. "He was also a good brother, but his main duty was to his father. Besides, he had seen what trouble I got into. Who would wish that upon himself?"

This didn't explain things, but Joe wanted to move on. "What happened after Grandfather let you out of the shed?"

"I had been in there all day, under the hot summer sun, and was too weak to walk. Isaac brought water, and my mother washed my back with a sponge, crying the whole time. That night I slept in the pasture, and when morning came, I realized I could never go in that house again. I took some eggs from the henhouse and left with the coins in my pockets. I was seventeen."

"But how could you just leave for America without money or friends?"

Shmuel laughed and put his hand on Joe's shoulder. "Didn't you do the same thing?" he asked, and despite himself, Joe smiled.

"That was different," he protested. "I was very lucky."

"Isn't it time a Jew had some luck?" Shmuel said. "Here, drink your tea. I'm hoping you'll be well tomorrow."

"Why tomorrow?" Joe said.

Shmuel towered over Joe's bed. "I'd like you to come to a meeting."

It seemed to Joe that meetings were being held constantly at New Zion. "Is there something special about this one?"

Shmuel shrugged. "Maybe. Maybe not. We'll see." Then he did a peculiar thing. Kneeling at Joe's bedside, Shmuel held Joe by his shoulders and brushed his beard against both cheeks. "Get well," he said, rising. "I'll see you tomorrow."

Evening meetings were held in the dining room, empty now of tables, with the chairs and stools arranged neatly in rows of five or six. The large side doors were open, and people stood outside, occasionally venturing in like moths drawn by the light, then retreating shyly. Finally, Edward Liberty took his place at the front, and the loiterers rushed inside, anxious to find seats.

Liberty stood patiently, waiting for the noise to subside. The leader did not call the meeting to order by banging a gavel, nor did he make any attempt to direct attention to himself. He was quiet, relaxed in his frock coat, head inclined slightly to the right, tall and blond amidst the crowd of short, dark Jews. Then, without any preamble, as if he had simply been interrupted and was now continuing a conversation begun sometime before, he began to speak.

"Before we can think of other things," Liberty said, "we must consider our basic needs. Before we can have poetry, we must have bread. I am happy to report that we now have ten additional acres under cultivation, and this increases our chances of becoming entirely self-supporting in the next year."

There was no more talking in the room. Every seat was taken and men stood in the doorway, all attentive. Liberty's voice was soft but insistent in the crowded room, and those in the back strained to hear.

"I don't need to tell you," Liberty went on, "that self-sufficiency was the original aim of our comrades who came here nearly twenty years ago from Russia and formed the van of our movement. For too long we have been dependent on gifts and givers, on others who may look leniently upon us but do not really share our convictions. This is good neither for them nor for us. Now we produce our own cheese, butter, bread, and most vegetables. We have cows, chickens, and a few hogs, and we are able to sell logs to the railroad and barter our services with our neighbors in Gays Mills. Much has been accomplished, but more remains to be done."

"Father!"

Liberty had been speaking in a monotone, his gaze fixed on the ceiling joists. He jerked convulsively now, as if someone had tied a rope to his neck and pulled. Lizzie was standing against the side doors. They were tall and fair, and the two of them seemed like natural allies rather than adversaries. But Lizzie was angry. "Father," she said. "We know all this. You told us the same things last week and the week before. It is as though we are poor students who will never learn unless you repeat it into eternity. We don't need meetings to tell us what is common knowledge."

Liberty seemed amused by Lizzie's outburst, but the others turned away from her, embarrassed. Even in New Zion, a daughter should respect her father. "We learn mathematics by repetition," Liberty said mildly. "Why not communism?"

Lizzie ignored this logic. "We're tired from working all day; we don't need to be drilled at night. We have more important issues to discuss."

Liberty looked benignly at Lizzie, as if he were indulging a small child, yet Joe remembered how he had kept after Bella. "And what are these important matters, Elzbeta, since you have appointed yourself as a spokesman."

"Oh, Father," Lizzie said, and beat her fists against her sides. She stared at him, shaking her head but saying nothing more.

"Come, Elzbeta," he said. "If we must quarrel, and apparently we must, let it be openly, in front of the community. I have no secrets from my comrades."

Joe wondered if this was what Shmuel had meant, why he had wanted him at the meeting. But why should Lizzie have confided in him? It didn't make sense. Lizzie muttered something that Joe couldn't make out. "I didn't hear you, Elzbeta," Liberty said, still patronizing her. "Please, speak up."

"It's so easy for you," Lizzie said angrily.

"What, Elzbeta, what is easy for me?"

"All of it," Lizzie said, her voice strangled with emotion. "The starvation, the discipline, the holy goals, all of it. Not everyone is so happy, you know."

The comrades sat obediently, looking at Liberty. "Is this true?" he asked.

"I support Sister Elzbeta," Morris Held screamed. "Even your daughter realizes what a maniac you are." He looked around the room for support, but no one else spoke. "What have you to say to that?" he added.

"I?" Liberty said, looking behind himself, as if Held's question might have been addressed to someone else. "How can I respond without knowing the charges?"

"Oh, Father," Lizzie said wearily. "You men talk about communism, but you don't practice it. You talk about women's equality, but it means nothing to you."

"Have I treated you unfairly, Elzbeta?" Liberty said.

Lizzie stood, hands on hips, then she walked to the front of the room. "Not just me, Father, but yes, me, and the others as well. I'm taller than most of the men and nearly as strong. Why shouldn't I swing an ax or push a plow? Why should I be left behind to wash and cook?"

"Sister Elzbeta is right," Morris Held shouted, his narrow torso shaking with righteous anger. "We must all be comrades, treated equally. Revolution is not a game that a few may play."

Joe looked at Annuta, sitting quietly at his side, but she had the same peaceful half smile on her face that Joe had seen when she was caring for him. It was hard to imagine her chopping down trees. Now a man with red hair stood. "Of course, Brother Held is right. Communism does not exist where there is inequality. But I'd like to hear from the other women. Do they agree with Sister Elzbeta?"

There was an undercurrent of conversation as the women discussed this, then Liberty's high voice carried over. "Perhaps this is not the best time to make a decision. We can think about this for a week and then revisit the question."

"No, Father," Lizzie said. "We must decide this now."

"I support Sister Elzbeta," Held shouted again.

"That has been established," Liberty said dryly. He faced his daughter, arms hanging limp at his sides, his face sad. "You know very well, Elzbeta, that we tried to involve the women in heavy labor in the Progressive Community in Kansas. We failed because the women weren't strong enough to do farm work day after day. I cannot think you wish to have your sisters here also collapse from exhaustion."

Lizzie took a deep breath and looked down at the floor. Then she turned to face the room. "No, Father, that is not what I want. What I want is freedom."

"But how could you be any freer?" Liberty protested.

"We are not so free. Not so long as we do not choose the way we will spend our lives but have those choices made for us because of our bodies. Women should have the same freedom of choice that you men have. I suggest equality!"

There was scattered applause in the room. "Very well, Elzbeta," Liberty said. "I was not aware of your frustration; now, I am. But how do you propose to achieve this freedom you talk about."

Lizzie continued speaking to the group and ignoring her father. "Saul is right when he says the opinions of other women are important. And you are right, Father, when you say that most of us are not yet strong enough to work in the forest. All I ask is that we make preparation toward the time when those of us who wish to leave the kitchen may do so. I propose to have time set aside in the daily schedule for women to strengthen their bodies."

"Time for calisthenics?" Liberty said, bewildered. Exercise was not in the Comtean taxonomy.

"Why not?" Lizzie said. "Some people prefer fresh air to studying columns of numbers. Some men might even prefer doing domestic work. We will see. One's sex should not be tyrannical. I do not propose freedom only for other women."

There was general laughter at this, but Liberty was not amused. "Men are assigned to kitchen duty on Sundays and everyone helps at the evening meal," he said.

"That's not the same as cooking all day, as you would know if you had ever done it, Father."

"Perhaps the community should vote," Morris Held put in gleefully.

But Lizzie wasn't interested in Held's support. She wanted to help Liberty save face. "We don't need to vote, do we, Father? After all, do we even disagree?"

Liberty did not like losing control of the meeting, but he was a realist. "If there are no objections to this plan from others, I have none," he said. "Let the women exercise all they want, whether for recreation or in preparation for field work. If in a month or two, they are sufficiently improved, they may take their places in the forest."

Joe thought he was going to say more, but already people were on their feet, crowding to the back to speak to Lizzie. Held's head bobbed up and down in agreement with whatever she was saying, but Lizzie's expression was sad, as if she had been drawn into the fight against her will. Beneath this reluctance, however, Joe had seen anger. He wondered at the freedom Lizzie enjoyed but didn't appreciate. To speak out this way in public against her father and not suffer for it seemed remarkable to him. How inevitable and tragic fatherhood must be, he thought, to raise such a daughter only to lose her this way.

Lizzie was talking intensely to a large circle of admirers. A strand of blond hair kept falling in her face, only to be swept away in an impatient gesture, after which it would fall again, and once more be swept away. Anger suited her, Joe decided. He thought she had never looked so beautiful.

eleven

The first issue of the *Positivist Investigator* bore on its masthead the motto "Justice and Fraternity." Farther down the page, it was noted that the editorial board consisted of "the men and women of New Zion, Wisconsin, working in love and solidarity," but most of it had been written by Liberty with assistance from Joe, who had run off the paper on the small novelty press that sat in a corner of the office. Liberty had justified the expense by saying the community could fill printing orders from their neighbors in Gays Mills, but to Joe he had confided, "I would prefer to live on bread and water rather than go on without publishing the results of our work."

The *Investigator* ran to only four pages and was largely devoted to a call for fresh blood. "We are a various community," Liberty wrote, "committed to the principle that all men are brothers. Here, Hebrew and gentile live side by side, man and woman work together, united for the Good of Mankind, not riven apart by petty jealousies. We make no distinctions between hard labor and study that develops the mind and spirit. Our community is our family, and members cooperate and hold property in common. "Each for all and all for each" is our motto. From each according to his ability, to each according to his needs. Liberty, equality, fraternity."

In a black-bordered box, the requirements of membership were listed: "We want persons who are kind, tolerant, and devoted to communism as the best means of benefiting mankind. They must be actuated by principles and not merely selfish purposes. The community claims the right to veto the reproduction of undesirable children. Neither will anyone be accepted who is grossly sensuous, seeking only gratification without regard to the good of others."

"That should bring them in," Shmuel snorted when Joe showed him the paper. "Where does it say that everything can be forgiven if they bring money?"

But Morris Held was outraged. "We need our own organ," he shouted.

"How many newspapers can a community of sixty have?" Abe asked. "Besides, who could possibly believe this nonsense?"

But to Joe's surprise, response to the first issue was substantial. Communities in Arkansas, Missouri, and Utah wrote to wish Liberty success. Contributions were received from a clairvoyant in Pierpont, Nebraska, who foresaw peace and freedom along with the death of tyranny in the coming year and also from a Dr. Spencer in Bryant, Kentucky, who specialized in "afflictions both spiritual and physical" and welcomed inquiries. The doctor enclosed ten dollars to cover the costs of forwarding mail.

"How do we know if he's actually a doctor?" Joe asked, but Liberty seemed bored by the question.

"I believe in a free press. I cannot and will not question the credentials of every good person who wishes to appear in our pages."

"Dear Sir," wrote one correspondent,

> My name is Anson A. Reed and I reside in Union, Connecticut. I have been a communist for several years and am desirous of putting these theoretical principles into practice. I am thirty-nine years old and 5'6" high. I weigh 140 pounds. My wife is ten years younger, and we have two boys, Thomas Paine, three years, and Volney Voltaire, ten months. I studied phrenology with Lezer and Wells in Yonkers, New York, in 1888 and have lectured throughout the East. I make no use of strong drink or tobacco and have spent considerable of my own money to advance liberal causes.

Joe wrote to inquire as to Mr. Reed's current financial situation and turned to other matters. Every letter had to be answered, and correspondence now took up much of Joe's time. He still held the most important letters, but often Liberty returned even these, saying, "By now you know my mind as well as I do myself."

One morning, a homely, balding man in his mid-thirties arrived looking for Liberty. He wasn't from New Zion and Joe doubted he had come from Gays Mills. The man carried a leather satchel and a walking stick. "Tell him Dr. J. G. Briggs, leader of the God-men has arrived," he instructed Joe.

Small, with a pockmarked face and shapeless body, Briggs didn't seem like the physical representation of any deity, but Joe remembered the name. Liberty had told him to invite Briggs to New Zion because he had studied phrenology and also boasted experience as a printer. The doctor had apparently attended a seminary in Indiana, where he was now living, and had recently denounced Christianity for communism. He claimed to have read the complete works of Comte by the age of eight and to have set his life's pattern after that of the great man.

"I'll see if Mr. Liberty is in," Joe said. After searching the grounds, he found the leader, who came immediately. When they returned, however, Dr. Briggs had taken a chair and removed his dusty boots in order to aerate his toes. Liberty flinched involuntarily at this and seemed to steel himself before offering his hand.

"Dr. Briggs," he said. "We meet at last. It is an honor, sir."

Briggs shook Liberty's hand and then settled into his chair. "Nice little place you have here. To tell the truth, I expected more from the write-up, but it's fine."

Liberty's nostrils flared. He took a deep breath and held it before releasing it slowly. He removed his hat and shook his gray-blond hair into place. Joe could see he was still annoyed, but when Liberty spoke, it was in a monotone. "With the addition of more communists like yourself, we shall become larger," he said.

Briggs nodded vigorously and wriggled his bare feet. "Yes, well, I wanted to discuss that with you. Yes, that very thing: growth."

"I beg your pardon?" Liberty said. He wasn't used to sharing his long-range plans for the community with every rank newcomer.

Briggs extended his legs, causing Liberty to move as far away as possible. "What I mean is, I didn't tell you everything in my letter."

"I see."

Now Briggs shook his head and puffed his cheeks. "No, Mr. Liberty. With all due and given respect, sir, you don't. You couldn't possibly see."

Liberty looked as if he had been shot. "Then kindly instruct me, sir," he rasped, "that my vision might improve to rival yours."

But Briggs was in no hurry. He seemed unaware of any tension in the room and now patted the soles of his feet dry with the rags that served him as stockings and discarded them. Then, slowly, he pulled his boots on again. Finally, he took a pouch from his vest and started to prepare a pipe. At this, Liberty could contain himself no longer.

"Sir," he thundered. "Noxious weeds are not burned in this shelter. If you must smoke, do so elsewhere, and we shall continue this interview at another time."

Briggs was surprised but didn't seem offended by Liberty's outburst. He pursed his lips, then nodded at Joe. "Can we talk in front of this boy?"

Joe stood to leave but Liberty halted him with his hand. "Mr. Abrams is my amanuensis and a literary man," he said. "He is privy to my private thoughts and all the affairs of this community. I have no secrets from him."

Briggs seemed impressed. "That covers it, then," he said. "Okay, I said in my letter that I was a printer by trade, which is true. But that was all I told you."

"Dr. Briggs, I am a busy man," Liberty interrupted. "The well-being of an entire community—small as it may seem by your lights—depends upon me. Would you make your point clear?"

Chastened, Briggs went on. "Well," he said, "I didn't tell you anything about my background—where I grew up, who my parents were, things like that."

He paused and Liberty smiled in a condescending manner. "This information, of course, is interesting, Dr. Briggs. But hardly crucial to our work here."

Now Briggs grinned, as if Liberty had been caught in an elaborate trap. "Ordinarily, that might be true, Mr. Liberty," he said. "Sure. An outfit like this would be filled with characters anxious to forget the past, who don't want to remember or be remembered by Mom and Dad or Sister Sue. Every town on the frontier is full of convicts, or worse. And, of course, a lot of perfectly decent folks who just couldn't stay put back East and came out here to find a new way to starve or go broke. Sure, for ninety-nine percent of the comrades you'd be right. But in my case, you're dead wrong." Briggs accentuated the word "dead," which sent a tremor through Joe's body. He wondered if this man could be a dybbuk sent to haunt them in the pagan wilderness.

Liberty was insensitive to these nuances. His voice rose out of control, shrill in its anger. "Dr. Briggs, I fail to see the point of this slur on our people, all of whom are courageous beyond the powers of your feeble imagination and who have overcome tyranny and oppression in another land to dedicate their lives to a glorious experiment that can only benefit mankind and not themselves in any material way."

Briggs enjoyed Liberty's outrage. He smiled slightly and patted the tobacco pouch. "Good. Good for them, then," he said. "Nothing wrong with that. But tell me, how many of those fine people could say their very conception, the sweat and straining of the marriage bed and the delivery table, was given over to the betterment of mankind?" Briggs stood, his arm tracing a pattern in the air. He seemed taller, more statesmanlike; even Liberty was impressed by this oratorical flourish.

"My colleagues would call you a Talmudist, Dr. Briggs. You seem to specialize in unanswerable questions, in weaving an air of mystery around the most common things."

Joe agreed. He had no idea what Briggs was talking about.

"Then I will, as you ask, make myself plain, sir, though I'm not certain that you are the man of vision your newsletter led me to expect. Clarity has its place, but it is precisely the unknowableness of existence that makes it sweet." He hesitated for dramatic effect. Then: "You see, I spent my childhood in Oneida, New York."

Involuntarily, Liberty took a quick step forward. "You mean—"

"Yes," Briggs interrupted. "The circumstances of my birth were dictated by science, the whole of my personality determined, as far as was humanly possible, right down to the color of my eyes and the texture of my hair." He licked his lips and looked modestly at the floor.

"You see, sir, I am one of the famous stirpicults of John Humphrey Noyes, one of that small group others have chosen to call God-men."

Liberty was stunned. He staggered backward until a chair buckled his knees and he sat. He rested his head on his hand and gazed out the window for a long time before turning back to Briggs. Still he was too overcome to speak. Liberty had described Oneida to Joe as the paradigm upon which he modeled New Zion. The austere, scientific John Humphrey Noyes had always been his master, and Liberty had especially admired Noyes's plan to create an exemplary race by selecting out the finest qualities among his communards and then breeding for them as one did with bulls. Ironically, it was stirpiculture that finally destroyed Oneida, for the reports of immorality enraged their neighbors and brought out, Liberty said, "the mossy editorialists in the small towns, smug in their allegations of promiscuity, nauseating in their gratuitous, leering assault on others more moral than they could ever be."

In his youth, Liberty had hoped to go to Oneida, but Noyes's Christian piety had discouraged him. Joe remembered Lizzie's remarking that her father had been turned down for membership. Whichever account was true, Liberty had remained an admirer of the Oneida experiment. He found in it the perfect balance of body and spirit, for while he loathed sex himself, he knew it was necessary. One had only to look at the Shakers, pure in their injunction of celibacy, slowly committing collective suicide, to know that. Now he sighed and shook his head. "Dr. Briggs, I confess you are right. It is a greater honor than I knew. I have always stood in awe of Dr. Noyes."

Briggs nodded, pleased, but Joe was not impressed. He had not expected God-men to look like J. G. Briggs. God-men would not sit in shanties with their bare backsides visible through their braces; God-men would not have large warts on their foreheads or small pig's eyes or what might only charitably be described as a widow's peak; most of all, God-men would not be grinning, perspiring egotists laboring to hold sway over the leader of a forgotten commune in the Middle West. God-men, Joe thought, would have bigger things in mind than this, but he didn't interrupt to give Liberty the benefit of his doubts.

And even as he was running Briggs down in his mind, Joe remembered that God—or what he remembered from the woebegone cheder where he had studied Torah—worked in strange ways that were not only inexplicable but often purposely so. The idea that mortals might understand God's ways was seen as the height of arrogance. "You're supposed to be confused, Yosl," the rabbi had shouted. "If everything was clear, what would be the point of study?"

Joe thought of tongue-tied Moses—a stutterer who had to enlist his brother's aid to pass on the word of God, an unwilling Messiah whom even the Jews refused to believe without plagues of flies and locusts. Was it possible that a fat phrenologist from Fort Wayne was the one they had been waiting for? It seemed unlikely, but the unlikely was just what you should expect in such matters.

Now Briggs stood and began pacing. At length, he stopped and looked at Liberty. Liberty had been euphoric, but he saw Briggs was troubled. "What is it, Dr. Briggs?" he said. "You are among friends. You must allow us to help, if we can."

Briggs's face was clouded with doubt. "I just don't know, Mr. Liberty," Briggs sighed. "You're a fine man, I can see that. But we have differences. I have to be honest. You see, there are still some things I haven't told you."

Joe thought Briggs was like one of those boxes you saw at fairs: when you opened one, there was another inside, and inside that, still another, and another. Briggs was both more and less complex than he appeared, open and friendly one moment, wily the next. But Liberty was unconcerned. "Of course," he said. "I would expect there are many things a man like you could tell us."

Encouraged, Briggs said, "Mr. Liberty, I'm not alone." He paused and an involuntary "Ah" escaped Liberty's lips, as if this revelation was the most satisfying.

Briggs licked his lips. "When Oneida fell apart, and bigotry drove us from our homes, I realized I would never be content to live a conventional life, to spend my days stuffed into some other man's idea of how to live. Better to die than to be so regimented. Some of my brethren, it is true, chose to remain, living the truncated existence allowed by the supposed Christians of New York state. But that wasn't enough for John Humphrey Noyes, and I vowed it would never be enough for me.

"With a small group of brothers and sisters, I set out to replicate as nearly as possible Oneida, to create what my birthright gave me the right to expect from life: a community of peace and goodwill where men live in spiritual concordance with nature and one another. Because this is so crucial, I have left my colleagues and traveled independently as I could, looking for like-minded idealists." He stopped and looked seriously at Liberty. "The search has not been easy because I am unwilling to compromise my principles."

Liberty nodded emphatically in agreement. Joe knew he was a man with no fondness for compromise. But Liberty and Briggs were completely different: Liberty tall and ascetic, Briggs a squat man of the flesh. Yet in the heat of Liberty's shack they nodded and exchanged grimaced smiles like bedouins, each intent on outwitting the other. And if both felt victorious, perhaps they could be happy together. "Yes," Liberty said into the silence. "One's principles cannot be compromised."

Briggs nodded, satisfied. "That's why I am alone. I am an advance scout of sorts. If New Zion proves to be fertile soil, the others will join me shortly."

"How many are you?" Liberty asked.

"Our number varies. At present, ten are living together on a farm in New York, awaiting word from me. Naturally, we would expect to contribute our resources to the common good."

"Without being indelicate, may I ask what those resources might be?"

Briggs didn't seem put off by this. "Between us, we have three cows, some fowl, a hand press, and five hundred dollars," he said.

Liberty looked at the ceiling as if calculating what growth this would represent. But elaborate calculations were unnecessary. The common fund currently stood at $16.50, and the printer's bill was due. Despite this, Liberty feigned indifference. "Dr. Briggs," he said, "if you and your colleagues should decide it is in your interest, my comrades would welcome you enthusiastically."

Briggs smiled, a tight ring of white skin banding his teeth. "There's just one other thing," he said. Liberty nodded, patient as always where money was involved. "I told you we aren't anxious to leave behind our principles."

"Absolutely," Liberty said, a faint trace of irritation coloring his voice.

"Well, Mr. Noyes believed in a number of things that, for various reasons, were suppressed. I told you about stirpiculture," Briggs said, hesitating.

"Yes, yes, just now," Liberty replied. "Is there something else?"

Briggs looked directly into the leader's eyes. "I'm afraid so. You see, Dr. Noyes also believed in the philosophical purity of nudity."

The silence in the shack was so complete that Joe thought he could hear dust motes falling from the rafters. Liberty stared straight ahead, his eyes glazed, not speaking. Finally, Joe cleared his throat in embarrassment. "Nudity," Liberty croaked. "You said the *philosophical* purity of nudity? Oh, no, Dr. Briggs, that can't be. We have nothing further to discuss. I regret that you were inconvenienced in making such a long journey to so little purpose." He stood, head averted, expecting Briggs to leave.

"Now, now," Briggs said, "hear me out." His ruddy face was beaming and he rubbed his hands together. This is what the man wants, Joe thought: conflict, disagreement. "There is nudity," Briggs said, "and then there is *philosophical* nudity."

In the pause that followed, Joe's imagination ran free. He saw himself walking in a pasture with Lizzie and Annuta, then the three of them tumbling down the banks of the Kickapoo, coming to rest finally in the shallow rapids, where icy water washed their bare bodies, free and clean in the summer sunshine. The vision was so vivid that he became embarrassed, certain that his desire was clear to everyone, but Liberty and Briggs stood frozen in a tableau, unaware of anything except each other.

"What is nudity?" Briggs began again, but he was interrupted.

"Please, Dr. Briggs," Liberty said derisively. "If you must ask, I assume we are discussing different topics. What is nudity, indeed! You will say it is a return to our native state, to our most ideal selves, and I will reply that this is sophistic nonsense. I have no desire to descend to the level of my more primitive forebears. Nudity is little more than systematized depravity, the lusting after that which is unattainable. Why should the members of our community be content to while away their time ogling one another when important work remains to be done? Why should man, the one animal capable of complex thought, be reduced to the most basic mode of existence? It is, as I said, unthinkable. There is nothing more to say."

But such comments were little more than a challenge to Briggs. He looked at Liberty with new respect, as if he had underestimated his adversary. "Mr. Liberty, you're right. I was going to say those things, or an approximation of them, for that is what I believe. What animal spends his life confined in ill-fitting garments, trying to hide that which is most divine in him?"

This argument would have had more effect on a stone wall. "I have no wish to emulate the beasts in the forest, and I cannot believe this is your real purpose. Unfortunately, man is weak, malleable. Therefore, he must be properly formed. Your own Bible should have convinced you that precious little is divine in nudity."

"John Humphrey Noyes was a Biblical scholar of some repute," Briggs said thoughtfully, playing his trump card. "All we want is to carry forward his ideas."

But Liberty was unyielding. "I am and will remain an admirer of Dr. Noyes, regardless of the outcome of this interview. It is true that some of our comrades have confused communism with eating off the same plate and sleeping in the same bed, but they, thankfully, have departed us, and few tears were shed. I am sorry," he repeated, and this time Joe thought he detected real regret on the leader's face.

Briggs remained seated though he had twice been dismissed. "Mr. Liberty," he said, "you're a man of culture and refinement. I happen to know you gave up a place in the Russian aristocracy to come to freedom in America. I understand how important New Zion is to you. But this is all an unfortunate misunderstanding."

"Misunderstanding, Dr. Briggs?" Liberty said, his lower lip rolled back to reveal strong white teeth. "How could that be?" Now Joe imagined Lizzie, breasts swinging free from her lithe young body, blond hair dark from the water, running smiling beside him, her sex dizzying in its propinquity. But the vision faded instantly as her father continued talking. "After all," Liberty said, "what philosophical basis can there be for going about naked in the woods?" He sank back in his chair, satisfied with his erudition, as Annuta, shy but surprisingly sensuous, rushed in to join Lizzie. Shorter and more fully endowed, Annuta was also darker, with traces of auburn running through the black ruff below her waist. Her breasts were full and round, yet also firm, riding high on her chest and inviting his lips. Her neck was, paradoxically, long and thin, and Joe felt himself drawn by her mysterious brown eyes. She looked at him inquisitively, then she was gone, and Joe was back in the maddening inconsequence of Liberty's speech. He felt a new benevolence toward

Briggs and imagined Lizzie and Annuta, their strong bodies conditioned by weeks of calisthenics, swimming around him in the clear water. If this image was not divine, it was close enough for Joe.

"Dr. Noyes used to say that our bodies are the only artifacts of that better time before we left the Lord's embrace and entered this world," said Briggs. "That's what stirpiculture was all about: the perfection of the human body. But Dr. Noyes was no flesh peddler, Mr. Liberty. It's principle I'm talking about, and only principle."

Liberty seemed to come alive at this. "Well and good," he said. "But how do you intend to translate this principle, as you call it, into practice if not by turning our settlement into a nudist camp?"

"Oh, sir," Briggs thundered. "Don't patronize me. I am not a young man. I've lived a hard life, and my body is the record of the scars and humiliations of my existence. For me to appear naked in public, feeling as I do, would be a sacrilege, a defilement of God's holy temple on earth."

"Then I can't see what you are proposing," Liberty said. "Simply that we agree, philosophically, that the human form is a representation of the Deity?"

"That, yes," Briggs said. "That certainly." He sat for a moment before continuing in a softer, more intense voice. "Mr. Liberty, what would you say if a new race were to grow up here on the prairies? A race incorporating in its very blood and marrow the sweep and courage of the pioneers, together with the wisdom of the ages. Now, while there is still time, let us put the future on its proper course by combining the best of your hardy band of adventurers and scholars with my God-men. Let us continue the work begun by Dr. Noyes but do so in conjunction with the scientific genius of Comte and thus produce a spiritual inheritor of those two great minds."

Joe could see Liberty was tempted. But sex had cost him his wife, and he was slow to forgive. Lizzie had told Joe that early on, Liberty's wife, Marusia, had been as fanatical as Liberty. She had poured most of her small inheritance into that first commune in Kansas, only to see the community turn on them, forcing Liberty to seek shelter in a bemused farmer's vacant henhouse. Marusia had gone on lecture tours, raised money, and then come home to live and work in the squalor produced by people and animals living under the same roof through a hard Midwestern winter.

None of that had discouraged her. But one day a young Russian arrived, directed there by mutual friends. Within a week, Marusia and the young man were lovers; in two, they were gone. Eventually, Liberty's natural prudishness grew into a wide-ranging suspicion of all things sensual. Lizzie said he even disliked ripe fruit. But it was hard to find fault with stirpiculture. Reproduction as the handmaiden of science. Clean. Impersonal. The sexual antidote to sex.

"Who would administer such a program?"

"I have some experience in these matters," Briggs said modestly. "During my phrenological training, I also developed an interest in marital counseling."

Joe wondered what had become of the nudity. Perhaps Briggs had just used that to soften Liberty up, to make the leader think he had won in the end.

"Yes," Liberty said solemnly. "I have heard of the experiments of the Fowler brothers at Amherst. But I would not like to see my people dictated to, even by such a scientist as yourself. They would not stand for it."

"Of course not," Briggs said, the fingers of his right hand teasing his forehead as though he were trying to extract the solution to the problem. Then, struck by inspiration, he sat upright. "Let us do it together," he said. "I will, of course, utilize my phrenological charts. But science is nothing without humanity. In your wisdom, you will advise me as to the particulars of how to proceed."

"I shall counsel prudence always," Liberty warned.

Briggs grinned and shook his head. "I must remind you again, sir, that I am a *philosophical* nudist only. I would never countenance a school for scandal."

Joe felt disappointed, but Liberty stood and smiled broadly. For the first time, he appeared to be truly happy. Now he offered his hand. "Dr. Briggs," he said. "It is a pleasure to welcome you and your followers to New Zion."

twelve

Joe arched his shoulders and sank back in his chair with a satisfied sigh. The second issue of the *Positivist Investigator* lay on the desk before him, ready to mail. The typeface had been improved thanks to Briggs, and Liberty was pleased with the answer Joe had written to the Chicago journalist. A Rosicrucian from Kentucky had sent a sheaf of poems with a twenty-five-dollar donation, and Liberty had printed them with a border of lilies of the valley he had borrowed from a seed catalogue.

Joe glanced out the window and felt the edge of despair begin to color his good mood. Seeing the comrades moving back and forth with their sense of mission always made him lonely. Lately, he had been thinking more about his mother and father, wondering if he had done the right thing in coming to New Zion, wondering if they would have approved.

Mostly, he knew, he missed their companionship. He remembered cold winter evenings when they had sat hunched together in coats and blankets, their feet nearly in the fire, drinking his mother's soup and eating bread. At night, they brought the chickens, hogs, and even the milch cow into the house because packs of wolves from the lord's forest wandered freely through the village. Killing one of them would have been considered poaching, a crime punished at best by prison, at worst by death.

Joe remembered hearing the wolves howl in the distance and then tracking them by their barks and growls as they moved closer and closer. When they smelled the chickens, their howls reached a ferocious peak, and the wolves would throw themselves against the wooden door, making it shake and rattle loudly, though it never gave way. Often they tried to burrow through the soft dirt under the door. Once, when Isaac was away, Joe had seen the long white teeth and red snout of a wolf actually penetrate their doorway, and he had used an ax handle to drive the beast away. There had been no sleep that night, and in the morning Hannah found Joe shaking with cold and fear, sitting in the doorway, the ax handle still held tightly in his hands.

Wolves, hunger, freezing nights were all part of that life. But Joe's memories were mostly peaceful, ordinary. He recalled sitting outside with his father on a spring afternoon, eating radishes and black bread. And he remembered Hannah as a young woman, with her angular face and beautiful brown eyes.

His son's life would be different, Isaac had always insisted. Better. Joe would go to university and live in Minsk, read great books and meet important people. Isaac believed in secular education for Jews; he had never lost faith in the enlightenment movement of the '80s. "Torah is the basis of our lives," he said, "but we must also live in the world." Someday Joe would be a lawyer perhaps, or a doctor.

And now? His parents lay in shallow graves, and Joe spent his time writing Liberty's newsletter. Was this the better life his father had wanted for him? Perhaps he should return to New York. At least Cahan was a learned man, a teacher and writer. And at his age, changing paths wouldn't constitute failure. But he had come to like New Zion. He was even fond of Liberty. He would stay a while longer.

Shmuel stuck his head in the door, looking first right then left for Liberty. When he saw the room was empty except for Joe, he stepped inside. "Where's our leader?"

Joe nodded out the window toward the river. "Ah," Shmuel smiled. "Consulting with his banker?"

Dr. Briggs and his followers had set up camp on the banks of the Kickapoo, where they swam nude in the river and tried to catch fish with their bare hands. Joe had expected Liberty to protest, but so far he had accepted the newcomers with equanimity, and the God-men were always properly clothed at community meetings. One of the things Joe liked about Liberty was his unpredictability. Who would have guessed he'd save the commune from bankruptcy by forging an alliance with a group of nudists?

"He took Dr. Briggs a copy of the paper," Joe said, handing one to his uncle.

Shmuel glanced at the newsletter, then put it in his pocket. He wiped his forehead with a handkerchief and looked out the window. "Hot," he said.

Joe nodded, but he hadn't noticed. He had been at work since six in the morning, and then it had been cool enough for a light jacket.

"The crops are starting to burn," Shmuel said now.

"Burn?" Joe said, not understanding.

"In the sun. It's been five weeks since we've had rain, and the river's too low to do much good. We've been carrying water for the garden, but pretty soon it'll be all we can do to fill a bucket."

Joe felt his throat tighten with anxiety. "What will we do?" Suddenly, he felt magnificently irrelevant, with his paper and printing press.

Shmuel shrugged. "We could harvest now, but some of the crops aren't ready. Or we can hope things change, that we get some rain, something."

"We have milk, cheese," Joe said hopefully.

"Sure, but the sun is burning off the pastures, too, and it won't be long until the cows dry up. They're already thin."

Joe looked outside at the insistent sun riding high in the noontime sky. How could he have been unaware of this? "What will we do, Uncle?" he asked again.

Shmuel produced a flask of ginger beer and took a long swallow. "For now, we'll wait and see." He unrolled the paper and looked at the first page. "Rosicrucians, eh?" he said, and winked at Joe.

"All God's children," Joe said.

Shmuel laughed and patted his nephew on the shoulder. "Don't worry so much," he said. "It's not good for the digestion."

The heat continued, shriveling the beans and baking the tomatoes. The corn was harvested and stored for winter, and the women were sent into the woods to look for wild berries, acorns, nuts, and grasses while the men set off daily on hunting expeditions. In the evening, bucket brigades were set up to bring muddy water from the river in a final attempt to irrigate the garden and keep the fruit trees from dying.

"It won't work," Shmuel said one night. "We usually get thirty inches of rain in a year, and we've gotten less than fifteen. It's not enough. The crops must die."

"It could still rain," Joe said, but Shmuel brushed this aside and Joe knew he was right. Most of the crops were beyond salvation, and they had used up their surplus. Furthermore, they had no money to buy food from the merchants in town and little left to barter.

Though he listened politely when Joe told him these things, Liberty seemed unconcerned. He ate almost nothing anyway, and seemed to think it would be an interesting discipline to try to survive the winter without food. He was involved in soliciting contributions for the next issue of the *Investigator* and really had little time to worry about agriculture.

Liberty's indifference infuriated Shmuel. "Moron," he yelled. "Coward, fool. What does he think—the Lord will provide, or maybe that idiot Frenchman he's always chanting about? Does he think our children can live through the winter on bark and nuts?"

Joe started to speak, then thought better of it. His uncle was right. But there was no point in trying to change Edward Liberty.

"We'll have to pack a wagon and go over to Minnesota," Shmuel said finally.

"Has it rained there?"

"I don't know, but there are Jews in Minneapolis. If they give us money, we can buy some food."

"Why should they give us money?" Joe asked.

Shmuel shrugged. "Why not? Isn't it worth trying?"

In the morning, Shmuel took some chickens and what cheese the community had left and drove away. The farewell party included Joe and Annuta. "How long will you be gone, Uncle?"

"Two, maybe three weeks. If I don't come back, at least there will be one less mouth to feed."

"Why wouldn't you come back?" Annuta asked.

"Maybe I'll meet a woman like you. Someone who will feed me and bind my wounds." He raised his arm in farewell, and the wagon rumbled off down the road toward Gays Mills.

"Your uncle was joking, wasn't he?" Annuta said.

"About us?" Joe said. "He's right. I don't know what I would have done without you when I was sick."

Annuta blushed. "No, I meant about staying in Minnesota." But she smiled gratefully at Joe.

"I think so," Joe said. But in a way, he wished Shmuel would find someone and make another life for himself. He was getting too old to be a communist.

It was five weeks before Shmuel returned, but when he did, the wagon was full. He had corn and flour, beef and cheese. Most important, the Jewish community of Minneapolis had donated $250 to the cause. Shmuel stood proudly by while the wagon was unloaded.

"A *mitzva,* Uncle," Joe said. "Maybe the Lord will provide after all."

Shmuel shook his head and smiled knowingly. "If only it were true," he said. "I would have saved a lot of time. Do you have any idea how many yentas I had to listen to to get all this?" Then he winked at Joe. "Don't worry," he said. "It wasn't all torture. There were a few young widows, too."

"It's good to have you back."

"I'm glad you appreciate me. They're tearing their hair out in Minnesota."

It was good to see Shmuel so pleased with himself, Joe thought. He had a right to be. When the wagon was unloaded, they drank a toast with some wine the rabbi had included for sacramental purposes. Shmuel drank liberally to cover all the members of the commune, past and present, and Joe didn't see his uncle anymore that day.

thirteen

"Mr. Abrams, this is a surprise," Dr. Briggs said, extending his hand. Joe felt uncomfortable. He had resisted what Shmuel called the seances before this, but had decided to come over to see what the excitement was about. Since the arrival of the God-men, lines had begun forming early for consultations, and Mr. Liberty had finally permitted the phrenologist use of the meeting hall two nights a week.

Now Joe looked at the doctor's oily forehead and felt queasy. "I thought I should observe your technique," he said. "I've heard so much about it."

Briggs seemed to wink, but Joe couldn't tell if it was only a nervous mannerism. He felt people squeezing in behind him, and the rain beating on the roof added to his sense of oppression. Yet no one had forced him to come.

"As a journalist, I imagine your powers of observation are already unusually acute. But I hope you will not limit yourself to that. I would welcome the chance to examine you," Briggs said, smiling. There were black holes in his gums where teeth should have been, and Joe looked away. The idea of Briggs's hands describing the variations in his skull made him cold as death.

"For now, I wish only to observe," he said stiffly.

"Of course," the doctor said, and motioned him to a chair against the wall.

For all Joe's reluctance, the other comrades accepted Briggs's recommendations with the utmost seriousness. Ben and Rebecca credited him with helping Rebecca to become pregnant and thus solve the first crisis in their marriage. He had relieved neuralgia in one of the brothers. An older woman's arthritis had vanished under Briggs's ministrations. Headaches, indigestion, even depression could not compete with his therapeutic techniques.

Now Joe saw Annuta, small and shy among the others. He wondered what she was doing there but stopped himself from asking. The process was dramatic, almost stagy. Each patient was directed to a chair where the doctor's assistants directed a harsh light on the compliant skull. Briggs brought his hands down quickly on the bare necks, caressing them until he found what he was looking for, whereupon he would draw back and look heavenward as if to thank God. Briggs would stand, hands thrust forward, deep in concentration, and after careful thought prescribe a set of exercises to right whatever imbalance he had found. All this was accompanied by careful note-taking in large black notebooks, presumably for future counseling.

Annuta took her seat. Briggs untied the ribbons in her hair and let it fall loose like thick, luxuriant yarn. Drawing close, he examined her scalp, carefully separating the thick strands with his fingers, breathing deeply as he peered down her spine. His attention angered Joe, and he knew it was because he didn't like another man's handling Annuta so intimately, but there was nothing he could do about it. Now Briggs massaged Annuta's back and neck. Eyes closed, the doctor seemed to be in some private rapture, and Annuta was enjoying it, too. Finally, Joe could stand it no more. "Why don't you take your hands off her?" he said.

Briggs's eyes snapped open, surprised, but when he saw who had spoken, he relaxed. "Through observing, Mr. Abrams?" he said easily.

Joe ignored him and walked over to Annuta. "You're embarrassing the girl," he said. "You must have examined her enough already."

Briggs nodded his head, then looked up, his face calm but tough. "Are you an expert in my profession as well as in your own, Mr. Abrams?"

"I claim to be expert at nothing, but you've gone too far." Joe put his hand on Annuta's shoulder and felt her respond.

"Perhaps you'd like to take Miss Silvers's place," Briggs suggested. "You seem very fond of her."

Joe didn't answer. Holding Briggs's stare, he took Annuta's hand and led her outside. They hesitated at the entry. Joe had forgotten it was raining. "What were you doing in there?" he asked, embarrassed now by his protectiveness.

"Rebecca wanted me to go. I didn't know he would touch me like that."

"You didn't seem to mind," Joe said.

Annuta smiled. "Why, Yosl, you're jealous."

"Don't be ridiculous. I just didn't like to see that fraud manhandling you." Annuta continued smiling. "Come," he said. "Take my coat, or you'll get wet. I have to go." Without saying anything more, he ran for the office.

Once a week someone went to town to pick up mail and provisions. Liberty found himself too busy with the newsletter, and Joe, who was the only person he trusted, didn't know the merchants. Therefore, Liberty decided, Lizzie should accompany him. "The blind leading the blind," Lizzie said, but she didn't object.

When Joe called for her, however, Lizzie seemed inward, shy. Her blond hair was tied in braids, and she avoided his eyes. "Is something wrong?" Joe asked.

"Nothing," Lizzie said, but she wouldn't look at him. Joe helped her onto the wagon and spoke to the horse, whereupon the animal wandered off leisurely.

In early September, the winds had shifted from west to northwest, bringing with them warnings of autumn. Now Lizzie moved closer to him on the seat, and Joe was grateful for the change in season.

"What are you thinking?" Lizzie asked.

"Of how far I have come," Joe lied. "Last year, I was a student."

"I heard you argued with Dr. Briggs," Lizzie said.

"I lost my temper," Joe admitted, not mentioning Annuta.

"Father was pleased," Lizzie said.

This irritated Joe. "Why should he care?"

"I think he's worried about Dr. Briggs. He doesn't want anyone to be more popular than he is."

"By now he's looked at most of the heads in New Zion," Joe said, not sure of the significance of this, but feeling it had some.

Lizzie laughed, showing dimples on either side of her mouth. "Father's afraid he's looking into them as well," she said.

"Well, he's a mystic," Joe said.

Lizzie nodded, still laughing. "Has he examined yours yet?" she asked.

"Knowing Dr. Briggs, I'd think he'd be more interested in you than me. Pretty girls seem to have the most interesting heads, don't you agree?"

Lizzie gave him a knowing look. "That was what the argument was about? Pretty girls?"

"Not exactly," Joe said. But he smiled, relieved that he had told her about Annuta, even if indirectly. Lizzie laughed again, her voice echoing young and musical in the clear morning air as the wagon made the final turn into Gays Mills.

When Joe had arrived three months before, Gays Mills had impressed him as being pleasantly busy yet unhurried, the people friendly and not pushy. Emerging from the wilderness now, the village seemed to have all the speed and guile of Manhattan, and he put his hand on the pocket where he kept his money.

There was hardly space to stand on the wooden sidewalks, so after leaving Lizzie at the general store, Joe took a position in the muddy street to try to get his bearings. Horses and wagons filled with goods fought for space while men loitered in front of the shops. Children chased one another through their parents' legs. To his right, sprawled beneath the wooden ledge of the walk, Joe noticed an Indian lying unconscious, an empty glass jar at his side. The Indian's jaw was slack and his mouth hung open, revealing swollen red gums and a few yellow stubs.

He was dressed like a white man in denim pants and a filthy cotton shirt, but his black hair was tied in mud-caked braids that wrapped around his neck like water snakes. Joe looked up, expecting to enlist help from the passersby, but no one even glanced in his direction. Joe knelt at the Indian's side and cradled his head in his hands like a jewel. "Wake up," he whispered. "It's time to go home." But the Indian only groaned and then belched, his breath strong and fruity in Joe's face.

Joe lowered the Indian's head to the ground and looked more closely at his face. Scars pitted his cheeks, and his nose had evidently been broken, but the man was not much older than he was. He pushed him farther beneath the boardwalk, as protection from the sun and horses, then covered him with his jacket. He would check again later to make sure the Indian was all right.

The post office was as crowded as the rest of the town, and Joe waited forty-five minutes for the mail. In it, however, was a letter addressed to him, which he opened eagerly.

> Joseph,
>
> I have yours in hand. Details of your daily life, interesting and disturbing as they are, have aroused great controversy among our readers, who wish to know more of this important social experiment. Henceforth, you will be a regular correspondent of the *Forward.* I will hold your salary in escrow until you instruct me otherwise. My regards to your uncle.
>
> Cahan

It was hardly personal, but Joe was pleased that Cahan had published his letter. It seemed impossible that news of New Zion could be of interest in New York, not to mention Europe, but there it was: he had received a promotion. And the editor wasn't foolishly generous. With a new sense of himself, he walked into the street.

Within minutes, however, Joe had lost his feeling of mastery. He had no idea how to find Lizzie in the tangle of people or where he had left the Indian and his coat. Finally, he bought a loaf of bread and some cheese and walked onto a grassy area where people sat, eating, sleeping, or simply resting from the ardors of market day.

The morning's chill was gone, and Joe lay back, enjoying the warmth of the sun and his freedom from responsibility. It was wonderful to escape the office, to simply lie anonymous amidst these farmers, thinking of nothing. It occurred to him that today was the Sabbath, a day when pious men did nothing except pray, but the comrades recognized no Sabbath, no day of rest. Liberty despised holidays, and so Joe had broken the habit of a lifetime.

He slept, woke, then slept again. When he came awake the second time, he was disoriented. Now the park was full of people of a different sort. Many wore black coats instead of overalls, and they were bigger and broader, too. A platform had been erected in the shade of two giant elms, and men circulated, passing out handbills. Joe accepted one and sat up. Printed in heavy black letters was the simple admonition:

HEAR THE GREAT HEALER
MOSES OF THE MENOMONEE
GAYS MILLS FAIRGROUNDS
SATURDAY, SEPTEMBER 10, 1:00 P.M.

"Are you a believer?" A small man with ginger hair and a bow tie smiled at him.

"I'm sorry?"

The man nodded and sat on his haunches. "Didn't mean to startle you," he said, and winked. "You probably thought I meant another Moses?"

Joe had forgotten his accent; at New Zion he was indistinguishable from the others. But here, he felt naked, exposed, the man's strange, flat vowels cutting away his pretensions of anonymity like a knife. Yet the man's own speech was distinct from the farmers and shopkeepers, with a lilt that reminded Joe of the Irish politicians he had heard in Madison Square on Sunday afternoons. And while the remark about Moses made him suspicious, the man seemed friendly enough. "I was just taking a nap," Joe said. "I have no idea who these people are."

"I wouldn't think so," the man said. Now he offered his hand. "Sorry to interrupt you. I'm Bryan Dorsey. I run the print shop in town and edit the newspaper. Anyone gets born, married, or dies, I'd like to know about it."

Joe glanced at the handbill in his lap again, but Dorsey took it out of his hand. "That ain't my work. Stuff like this gives printers a bad name. Look at that lettering." His lip curled under in distaste. "What's your name then, boy?"

Joe didn't like being addressed this way, especially in light of Cahan's letter. He was a correspondent and deserved respect. "Joseph Abrams," he said stiffly.

"Down here for the day shopping are you, Joe?" Dorsey asked.

"I live here," Joe said. "Or nearby. I'm a farmer."

"Oh, are you now?" Dorsey said in a distracted tone. Then, suddenly interested, he turned to Joe. "Why, you must be out there along the river with the Russians. You one of them? Why, sure you are," he said, answering his own question. "Then this little gathering ought to interest you," he said, smiling but not letting Joe in on the joke. "Yes, indeed. It should be real interesting."

Joe feigned indifference, but he wished the man would leave. Joe began to eat his bread, looking off into the distance, but if Dorsey was affected by his rudeness, it didn't show. Without asking, he sat down, curling his legs beneath him, and unbuttoned his jacket. He wore high black boots and a leather vest, and beneath his clear blue eyes were white moons of skin. Thin blue veins were visible in his forehead, and he pushed his cap back, revealing a high forehead and an impressive mound of curly red hair. His looks suggested daintiness and good breeding, yet when he spoke, he was brusque and direct. Joe was both annoyed by Dorsey's patronizing manner and curious about his origins.

"Who is this Moses, then?" he asked.

"That's a good question," Dorsey said. "I've been trying to figure that out myself ever since I heard he was coming this way."

"You knew," Joe said, unable to conceal his surprise. It had been months since he had seen a newspaper and, in any case, he wouldn't have expected news of this Moses, whoever he was, to be reported widely.

"He's all over the Milwaukee papers," Dorsey said. "They even had a write-up in Chicago a while back. But mostly all I've got so far is what he ain't. For example, he's got nothing to do with any Indians—Menomonee, Blackfoot, none of them. And his name ain't Moses, which you could have guessed. It's Jacob Kleinschmidt. Kind of makes you understand why he'd change it, though. And if anyone ever got healed by him, they never mentioned it to anyone else, but it's a good story."

"Story?"

Dorsey looked surprised. "Sure, that's what these fellas are doing. It gets tiresome on the frontier, so every now and again someone comes through to tell us how he's going to change our lives, and that sounds pretty good, even if the chances of him doing it are slim. Well, that's old Kleinschmidt. He'll spend his time traveling around, preaching, healing, telling fortunes, leading crusades, whatever it takes."

"Takes for what?" Joe asked.

Dorsey looked concerned for Joe's sanity. "You might have been out in the woods too long, my friend," he said. "I'm worried about you, being here in town on your own. Got any money on you?"

Joe flushed. "I can take care of myself."

"Sure you can. I can see that," Dorsey shook his head. "Anyway, preachers have to live, just like the rest of us. But they got to keep moving, too. People get tired of the same show."

"If that's all there is to it, why bother about this Moses?" Joe said. He could tell he had hit on something, because Dorsey looked at him with new respect.

"It got to you too, didn't it?" he said. Then without waiting for an answer, "I just felt something wasn't right. All that talk about the big house on the river, the Indian stuff. That was different from the other drummers. And why Indians? You see what I mean? In Milwaukee you'd think he'd be after the Germans or the Swedes. And why's he coming out here? There's hardly enough people in Gays Mills to pay his way. Well," he gestured at the platform at the front. "It just didn't add up. But I couldn't find anything. Maybe there's nothing to find." He shrugged.

Joe waited for Dorsey to continue, but he remained silent. Joe still didn't know why Dorsey thought he would be especially interested in Kleinschmidt. Now Dorsey took out a small notebook and started writing. Joe waited as long as he could before interrupting.

"Excuse me," he said. "Is Gays Mills your home?"

For a moment, Dorsey said nothing. Then he closed the book and looked up. He was smiling but no longer seemed as self-assured. "It's been a long time since I thought of myself as having a home," he said quietly. "If I do, I guess it ain't here."

Now his face opened miraculously, and when he spoke, the tense, syncopated quality in his speech was replaced by an easy drawling familiarity that made Joe wonder who this man truly was. "I used to live in Boston," Dorsey began. "Then New York. But there were eight of us, and one day I forgot to go home and no one came after me. Since then, I've been on my own. For a while I lived in Chicago, running errands for a butcher, and then I caught on at a print shop. At night, I hung around newspaper offices and whorehouses. After a few years, I figured I knew as much as the reporters, which wasn't saying much. But

I had a little money saved, and somebody told me the man who owned the paper here was looking for a buyer. I came to see about it one day and never went back. Maybe I should have."

"But you have your own business."

Dorsey laughed. "I own the press and rent the office, but there ain't much business in a town three blocks long and getting smaller every day." He smiled ruefully. "So what's your story?"

Joe told him about leaving Russia and coming first to New York and then to Wisconsin to join his uncle. He mentioned New Zion but edited judiciously, omitting details about the God-men and Liberty's enthusiasm for stirpiculture. Dorsey listened patiently, interested but not pressing Joe, letting his eagerness to unburden himself carry the narrative. Occasionally, Dorsey would repeat a word, implying a question, and Joe would elaborate. He knew Dorsey was leading him, and suspected his new friend was a better journalist than he let on. But this didn't bother Joe. He wanted to trust Dorsey. Finally, he mentioned his promotion.

Dorsey nodded. "I remember your boss," he said.

"You know Mr. Cahan?" It seemed amazing.

"Not to talk to, but I guess everyone in New York knew about Abe Cahan. I'd see him at political meetings, and once or twice I passed him in the street, chin up the air, those eyes pressed tight together like black marbles behind the glasses." Dorsey imitated Cahan's posture and Joe had to laugh.

"You do know him," he said.

Dorsey winked. "Like I said, I saw him in the streets. Cahan was one Jew the Irish listened to, whether or not they liked him. They had no choice if they wanted the votes, and they did. I heard Cahan talk once, at a big labor rally—five hundred people and it was ninety degrees if it was above freezing. I thought the sun would burn a hole in my head. He talked for two hours and no one moved, and when he stopped, they all went crazy." Dorsey shook his head. "He was something."

Joe nodded in agreement. "He still is."

Dorsey smiled. "Maybe we can work something out? I could use help."

Joe was already dividing his time between Liberty's newsletter and the *Forward.* "I don't know," he said. "I'm very busy."

"Sure you are," Dorsey said in a voice that suggested he didn't believe it. "But with winter coming on, there won't be much work on the farm. I could use the company, and I'll pay you for what you do. Think it over."

Joe was about to reply when a drum roll interrupted him. A strange little procession was mounting the platform. First came the drummer, a short man in a checked vest and top hat, who circled the platform once then descended the stairs, the rat-tat-tat of his sticks echoing as he went. Left onstage were an Indian, a tall man dressed in a purple-and-gold brocade robe, and a young woman who stood timidly at the rear. Now the large man stepped forward and raised his arm. The crowd seemed momentarily unaware of him, intent instead on the fading cadences of the drummer, but in time they found places on the grass and the man onstage began to speak.

"Friends," he said in a voice both rough and intimate, which carried to the farthest reaches of the field without showing the slightest strain. "My friends." He held out his robed arms to the front rows, but his mouth hardly moved. It was as if the voice, like his arms, emanated from somewhere within the robe, separate from the man. "It is good to be here," he said, and now the voice, nearly narcotic in its effect, was the only sound in the meadow, soft but easily distinguishable from where Joe sat.

"It is good to be here today," the man repeated. "Good to share with you God's glorious sunshine, His plentiful bounty in this beautiful place." He spoke each word slowly, careful not to lose any of the associative power of a phrase or syllable, confident of his hold over his audience. He reminded Joe of the great rabbis he and his father had seen on past High Holy Days. He projected the same authority, the same emphasis on every word and gesture. For no reason, Joe suddenly felt frightened.

"Some of you know me," the speaker continued. "To others I am a stranger. My name is Jacob Kleinschmidt, the same whom some are pleased to call Moses for the work God has permitted me to do among our Indian brothers." As if on cue, the Indian stepped forward, his face expressionless, his body angry with red paint. Suddenly, Joe recognized him as the man he had seen unconscious in the street, completely transformed now into a fighting brave, tall and angry and proud.

Holding out his arm, Kleinschmidt said, "This is Crazy Dog, a Menomonee warrior responsible alone for the deaths of eight white men and their wives and children, a man who has collected fifteen scalps in his young life." This caused a stirring in the audience, and Kleinschmidt raised his arm for silence. "Through the beneficence of the Almighty, Crazy Dog has seen the errors of his former life and become a Christian, putting behind him forever alcohol and bloodshed, making repentance and good deeds his way of life."

"Too bad about those folks he already killed," someone called out. Joe shivered involuntarily as he examined the Indian's well-muscled arms and legs. He saw triumph rather than repentance on Crazy Dog's face and wondered at the way the dead eyes and slack posture had been transformed in such a short time.

The Indian stepped back, and Kleinschmidt was about to resume his speech, but some of the men moved closer to the stage. Crazy Dog seemed oblivious, but Kleinschmidt, aware that he had created a disturbance, waved his arms. "My friends, I have not come here today to speak of the successes God has granted me in the past, nor to tire you with Indian stories." The men stood directly in front of Kleinschmidt, looking menacingly at Crazy Dog, undecided about mounting the stage.

Smiling, Kleinschmidt drove them back with his hands. "No," he repeated. "The Red Man is not why I have come. The Red Man is the menace of the past, not the present, and certainly not the future. But," and here he raised his right arm to the skies, "that does not mean we can relax, for Satan does not—will not—and his representatives are working among us here today."

This caused a murmur in the crowd, and Kleinschmidt, smelling blood, added, "Yes, oh, yes. Right here today."

People looked around with anxiety and pride, for it seemed remarkable that their small community could harbor a threat to the God-fearing world. Kleinschmidt let the reaction build, then spoke so softly that the audience had to strain to hear. "Only recently did I learn of an evil so pernicious, so insidious, that it strikes at the foundations of Christian decency." The crowd seemed disappointed, and sensing this, Kleinschmidt rushed to the heart of his sermon.

"Friends," he said in a hushed whisper. "I am told that a mere five miles from this spot there exists a community of anarchistic Russians, most of them Hebrews, dedicated to a communistic way of life, people who deny God and live in a manner impossible to adequately describe with women and children present."

Joe had been daydreaming, but this mention of New Zion snapped him awake. Dorsey had a half smile on his face as if he had known what was coming. "What does he mean?" Joe asked. But Dorsey winked and held a finger to his lips.

Kleinschmidt held up his hands for caution. "Let me be clear," he said. "I do not mean to derogate the Hebrew race. As we are told in the Book, they are the Lord's Chosen People, a race almost miraculously gifted in commerce, a tribelike and pious people often unjustly persecuted in faraway lands for their beliefs. No, my friends, America was built on the principle of religious freedom, and Jacob Kleinschmidt would never say a word against the descendants of Abraham. But these communists are renegades. Their own co-religionists despair for their souls and accuse them of apostasy." The audience had been lulled by Kleinschmidt's defense of Judaism, though a few nodded in comprehension when he mentioned apostasy.

"These socialists are not Jews," Kleinschmidt thundered, bringing his fist down for emphasis. "They are the bastard offspring of that ancient and noble cast, who declare for no faith, no God, no morality. Who are despised by the pious rabbis for turning their backs on the ancient and martyred religion that nurtured them."

Despite Kleinschmidt's characterization, Joe admired the man's rhetoric. And he was right: there was no denying the rabbis would condemn them. "These are not the Jews with whom we are familiar," Kleinschmidt went on. "These are not the Jews who close their shops on the holy Sabbath and throng their temples in gabardine and skullcaps. Nor are these the rag peddlers who wander the West in search of a better life. No, these revolutionists are out to reform the world, which means the destruction of the American way of life, as it is written here in their hateful organ."

To Joe's horror, Kleinschmidt now held aloft a copy of the *Positivist Investigator.* How could he have gotten a copy? Joe had the list of subscribers, had sent the newsletter out himself. To make matters worse, Kleinschmidt began to read, and the audience was passive no more, laughing at Liberty's conditions of membership, disapproving of the constraints on childbirth. “Think of that,” a large woman with meaty biceps and a baby on her breast said aloud.

Kleinschmidt slapped the paper against his leg. “My first impulse was to ignore this. I was happy in the service of the Lord back in Mukwonago. Why bring a disturbing message to folks with trouble enough? But God caused this to come to me, and since I am His vessel, He wanted me to inform you. He will instruct me as to how I should proceed, and He will cause you to act through me.” His voice had gotten progressively softer until now, abruptly, he sank to his knees. “Let us pray,” he said.

The young woman started to play a dirge on a small hand organ she had produced from the back of the stage, and several men began moving through the audience with small wicker baskets for donations. Through it all, Kleinschmidt remained on his knees, eyes tightly closed, hands clasped before him, his lips reciting a private prayer.

fourteen

"Don't worry about Kleinschmidt." They were sitting in Dorsey's small print shop on Main Street. Dorsey was behind a cluttered desk, drinking coffee.

"How can I not worry?" Joe said gloomily.

"He won't do anything," Dorsey said. "At least not yet."

"How can you be so sure?" Joe had declined the coffee and now drank tepid water from a tumbler with dirty fingerprints on the glass.

"You're not thinking about it from his point of view. What does he stand to gain? So he goes out and destroys your commune, so what? To you, it's a tragedy, but in two days the whole thing is history and he goes back to Milwaukee empty-handed."

Joe was not used to analyzing destruction. What had murder and mayhem ever gotten the Cossacks? Well, he supposed they had been paid. The peasants, then? They took the Jews' property. But there was little of value at New Zion, so perhaps there was something to what Dorsey was saying. "Then why attack us?" Joe asked.

"Moses is nothing without an enemy. How can he take the faithful to the Promised Land without a devil to fight? He needs you too much to destroy you."

Joe ignored the irony of a Moses who wanted to fight Jews, not save them. "I come from Russia," he said.

Dorsey nodded. "Pogroms," he said seriously. "Sure. Terrible. But the situation was different. In Russia, you had centuries of Jew-hating. America's not perfect, but here the whole idea of religious freedom is written into the Constitution. There you had laws stopping you from doing things. Here, we've got laws that say do what you like. Even old Kleinschmidt didn't attack your religion, did he?"

Joe admitted he hadn't. But Dorsey's optimism bothered him. It was easy for the Irishman to feel at ease; he hadn't been singled out at a mass rally. Besides, Joe wasn't used to baring his soul to Christians. "You may be right about Kleinschmidt," he said. "But what about his followers?"

"What followers?" Dorsey said. "A few friends he brought along to help. The rest were farmers and townspeople. What have they got to gain by running you out? A few huts, some furniture maybe; whatever food or cash you might have on hand, which I'd bet ain't much. You see my point. Mind your own business, and you'll be all right. You buy supplies like everyone else, and no one's against customers."

Joe was not entirely convinced, but Dorsey's explanation was logical. Except for Kleinschmidt. "But why did he come *here*?" Joe said. "As you say, we're of little value, so why attack us? Surely there are other agents of Satan in Wisconsin?"

"Good question," Dorsey said. "Maybe to raise money. He might have squeezed his other sources dry. I hear he's got a large household, if you know what I mean."

"What about the newsletter? I sent them out. I know all the subscribers."

Dorsey smiled ruefully. "He was ahead of me on that one. I didn't know I had competition. I can't see Gays Mills as a two-paper town." The stream of pedestrians in the street had slowed, and the soft light gave Dorsey's face an amber glow. "We'll find out soon enough, I guess," the editor said. "But winter is coming. Don't expect a crusade before spring. Kleinschmidt was probably just getting a feel for the territory, and someone mentioned New Zion. There's a good chance he'll forget all about you by the time he gets back here."

No Jew would talk this way. Hope for the best? But perhaps Joe could learn optimism from this Irishman. Then he remembered Lizzie and stood abruptly. "I have to go. Someone's waiting for me."

"By the look on your face, I'd bet it's a woman."

Joe blushed. "Just a girl I came to town with. From our community."

Dorsey smiled. "Sure. Well, it was good to meet you anyway." He extended his hand.

Joe hesitated at the door. "Were you serious about my working here?" he said. "I don't have much real experience, but I've done some writing."

"Sure, I'm serious," Dorsey said. "I print the paper on Wednesdays, when there's anything to print—and sometimes even if there's not. Come in then. We'll have dinner and talk and put the sheet to bed."

Joe wasn't familiar with the American slang, but he got the idea. "Wednesday, then," he said.

Lizzie was sitting on a bench, eating an apple. For a moment, before she noticed him, Joe studied her, admiring her yellow hair, like pale gold in the late afternoon sun. She wore a faded plaid dress that clung to her waist, accentuating her curves, and lay as if painted on her long legs. Now she rose from the bench. "I thought you'd gotten lost," she said.

"I wish I had," Joe said. As they walked to the wagon, he told her about Kleinschmidt and the meeting in the park. But Lizzie seemed indifferent. When they reached the wagon, he helped her up and began driving out of town.

"Father always makes people angry," Lizzie said.

"Yes, but he wasn't attacking only Mr. Liberty. His name wasn't even mentioned. Kleinschmidt kept talking about the communistic Jews. Atheists, he call us. Us!"

"Did you expect to be loved for your revolutionary ideals?"

"I have none," Joe reminded her. "I came here because of my uncle."

Lizzie shrugged. "It doesn't matter. The point is, nothing will happen."

Joe felt as though he were talking to Dorsey. He envied the sangfroid of gentiles. "How can you be sure? You weren't even there."

"Because I've lived in America all my life," Lizzie said with certainty. "Americans love to argue, but they don't enjoy killing. Have you eaten?"

Joe looked at her in astonishment. "How can you think of food?"

Lizzie pulled a loaf of bread and a large piece of cheese from the satchel she was carrying. "Stop the wagon," she ordered, and Joe pulled off the road and tied the reins to a tree. "Come," Lizzie called out, and plunged into the underbrush.

Not knowing what else to do, Joe followed her into the forest and was surprised to see the dense thicket open into a clearing invisible from the outside. Lizzie sat beneath a tall linden with her dress spread out around her. "This is beautiful," he said. "Like a private room in the middle of the forest."

"There may be hope for you yet," Lizzie said. "Here," she said, patting the ground next to her. "At least we'll be massacred on a full stomach."

"That's nothing to joke about," Joe said.

"You're too serious," Lizzie said, handing him a piece of bread. "Eat."

Joe followed the loaf with cheese and sausage. Afterward, he enjoyed the quiet of the forest as Lizzie cleaned up the remains of their picnic. It was the first domestic work he had ever seen her do. Then he dozed off, and when he awoke, she was beside him, her eyes bluer than any he had ever seen, her hair gossamer, her skin pink and soft. On impulse he reached out, and she came willingly, as if in a dream.

When they kissed, Joe was submerged in a warm pool, the water cleansing and pure, washing over and under them. He was excited, but also more relaxed and at home with himself than ever before. Then they were lying on grass, legs wound around each other so tightly he could not imagine their ever being apart again. For an instant, an image of his mother made him pause, but Lizzie was too strong, too beautiful, to resist. Joe didn't recognize his feelings. His chest seemed inadequate to contain the pressure building within. The euphoria would surely take his head off. Then, in a moment he couldn't distinguish from the rest, it was over and they lay exhausted in each other's arms, looking at the trees that formed the ceiling of their forest room. Joe didn't trust himself to speak. He closed his eyes, and when he opened them, she was sitting cross-legged before him.

"That was your first time, wasn't it?"

Joe felt embarrassed, jealous of her other lovers. "Of course not," he said.

Lizzie laughed, her high voice echoing deep into the forest. "Oh, Yosl, there's nothing wrong with it. But how can we be friends if you're so sensitive?"

"Is this how you treat all your friends?"

She smiled widely, her eyes warm and intimate. "Of course not. You're not like anyone else I know. But then, I'm not like the girls in Russia, am I?"

Joe had known no girls in Russia or anywhere else, but he didn't admit this. "Not exactly."

"And you think this is wrong, immoral or something. How can we make love and not be married, isn't that so?"

"Maybe," Joe said.

"Oh, stop." Lizzie reached across and roughed up his hair. "Sometimes you talk as though you're forty. Are you so afraid to be young?"

"I haven't had much opportunity," Joe said.

"Well, you do now," she said with finality. "What we did was wonderful, so how can it be wrong?"

Wonderful was faint praise as far as Joe was concerned. It had been beyond words. "Your father wouldn't approve," he said, and immediately regretted it, for now Lizzie rose to leave.

"Then don't tell him," she said. "I won't. Come. We're late, and they'll wonder about us."

Joe rose unwillingly, surprised he was able to walk. Absentmindedly, Lizzie said, "Did you see Dr. Briggs?"

Immediately, Joe was alert. "Briggs?" he said.

"Yes," Lizzie said, as though it didn't matter. "In town. I thought he might have wandered over to hear the speech in the park."

Suddenly Joe felt cold. The sun had disappeared, and he had forgotten to look for Crazy Dog. "I didn't see him. Where was he?"

Lizzie didn't answer. She was striding away from Joe toward the wagon, her eyes intent on the bluff far ahead that towered over New Zion in the dusk.

fifteen

Liberty had called for him, and now Joe stood facing the leader in his shack. He had never seen Mr. Liberty as upset. His face was haggard and his shirttail was out, as though he had been tearing at his garments in the manner of Chasids. He leaned over the desk, hands welded to the wood, and looked into Joe's eyes. "Have you seen this?"

Liberty indicated a magazine opened to a feature article. "What is it?"

Liberty didn't answer. He sat heavily in his chair. "Just read it," he said, and looked gloomily out the window, ignoring Joe.

The magazine was called *The Comet* and was evidently published in Chicago, but it was the individual article, not the magazine as a whole, that had upset Liberty. Joe sat on the floor and began to read.

> **A Wedding Among the Communistic Jews of Wisconsin**
>
> Escaped from the depredations of bloodthirsty Cossacks, a handful of Jews from various districts in Russia have found shelter in a peaceful river valley in Wisconsin and have given this oasis the unlikely name of New Zion.
>
> That such a place should prove attractive to such people might at first glance seem strange, but then, the Russians are a strange people, and of them all, Russian Jews are perhaps the strangest. Thus it was with some trepidation that your corre-

spondent accepted an invitation to sojourn among these immigrants, to sit at their tables, eat their foods, participate in their rituals, and in general attempt to understand their customs, their beliefs, their lives.

Yet if this dislocation was upsetting to your correspondent, how small was this discomfort compared to the prior suffering of the people who so graciously welcomed him. For all civilized men and women know of the brutality and despotism of their native land. Anyone who dares to rise up against this injustice is driven with blows and in chains to the snows and mines of Siberia, or worse. Russia's only original novelist, Tchemicheffsky, for one romance, *What Is to Be Done?*, which had a socialistic signification, was sentenced to hard labor for sixteen years, and at the end of this time was refused his petition for exile. The works of Mill, of Huxley or Spencer, of indeed every author who dares to think of a possible change in the social order, are ruthlessly barred from libraries and thus the minds of all citizens of that hopeless country while the Imperial Family and their fawning court congratulate one another on their costumes and command of the French language.

The common people are very poor, good-hearted, and kind to their friends, but woefully ignorant and thus devoted to the very government that plunders its affluence from their grinding toil. It is these peasants who regularly kill and ravish the far more intelligent Jews, who are indeed only saved from utter destruction by the Tsar's soldiers, who know their value as collectors of wealth, taxpayers, and moneylenders.

And yet this savage country, with its immense expanse of land which seems to guarantee isolation and its laws which guard against every foreign idea or innovation is fertile soil for strange philosophies. Russian students, despite the constant surveillance of the police and the threat of exile, study with fervor the political doctrines of Karl Marx, the economical positions of Proudhon, and the harmonious fantasies of Fourier and Comte. And of the indifference of the masses to these innovative philosophies, our student cares nothing. "It is as if we had planted here the tropical banana, expecting it would fruit," one has written.

The Russian Jews are the aptest disciples of socialistic ideas. Jews, though, they are in name only, for eighteen centuries have gone by since the fall of Jerusalem, and no faith long survives the destruction of its temples. Judaism there is dead—the Jew survives not as the worshiper of the one God, Jehovah, but as the pure-blooded child of a singularly homogeneous and strongly marked race which formerly grew olives and grapes on the sunny hillsides of Palestine. Everywhere remarkable for acuteness of intellect and an extraordinary aptitude for the acquirement of riches, the Jew in Russia has also developed characteristics of great social sentimentality. There is in history nothing else which approaches the sentiment of the Sermon on the Mount, in which the heart of Jesus pulsates for every human being, friend or foe—and Jesus was a Jew.

I do not mean to say, however, that every Russian Jew is a humanitarian, that there are not those among them who are like Shakespeare's legendary Shylock, eager only to extract their daily pound of flesh from unsuspecting passersby. Only that in comparing Jews to the native Russians, we see that Jews present in proportion to population a much greater number of individuals who feel the stimulation of humanitarian sentiment, as expressed in the above-named socialistic doctrines, and thus are ready to risk fortune and even their lives in the service of purely humanitarian ideals. In a word, a very considerable part of nihilistic or socialistic Russia is Jewish.

It is, then, of these Jews that I write, particularly a small group of them, nearly all residents of Odessa and Kiev, who resolved to leave Russia and seek in our country a home where they would be free of the taxes and military service of despotism, and the brutality of Christian fanaticism, which they had seen more than once destroy their homes and dishonor their mothers and sisters. The band numbers about fifty, most unmarried young people, with a few older souls and married couples among them. Their hopes were vague, but passionate, their means so small that before they could journey to Wisconsin, they had to hire out as day laborers and maids for nearly a year to finance the trip. At last, however, they were able to buy four hundred acres along the Kickapoo River in Southwestern Wisconsin with the purpose of founding a social life very much like that which existed amongst the earliest Christians, when, after the day of Pentecost, they were filled with the Holy Spirit and were of one mind and one heart, and no man said that aught that he had was his own. This, then, is the Russian colony, near Gays Mills, Wisconsin, known as the New Zion Community.

To a visitor from the Metropolis, the commune cannot appear grand. The labors of this society have, for many reasons, been rude and inefficient; the improvements the settlers have made to the land are of the most limited character, and their gardens and outbuildings are noticeable only for their untidy appearance. Indeed, there could seem to be no point in noticing this community were it not for the singularity of its social life. The members have no religion; they have hardly a political organization and say they want to have as little as humanly possible. They have no defined code of morals, unless it is to be good. One of their young women once replied when I remonstrated with her for an unusual act of courtesy by exclaiming, "You are too good," "Why, we *cannot* be too good." In their favor is the fact that they seem to be entirely free of those extraordinary eccentricities of behavior which characterize many American reformers and those Russian come-outers who are not Jewish.

Yesterday was Sunday and there was a marriage. Nearly all the members eat and sleep and stagnate—I can hardly speak of it as living—in a large hall of their own construction: a wretched edifice built of rough boards and unplaned planks, and containing only two apartments, the lower story being the dining hall and kitchen in one, and the upper story a large sleeping room without partitions, except for a motheaten curtain hanging precariously from a clothesline that serves to separate the sexes. In the sleeping room, the community, with the exception of those who live in separate small shanties in the woods, not only sleeps, but lounges, reads, and debates. The bedsteads, which are of boards nailed together in the flimsiest manner, are placed under the eaves, and the center is furnished with a rough table for writing. As for reading, the Russian always reads stretched prone upon his bed.

We had been lounging thus on our beds most of the morning, taking a late breakfast and then going back upstairs to lounge again, or to read the previously mentioned philosophers. At about two, I descended to inquire about dinner and found several women busy making dried apple pies and custards—great novelties at New Zion, where the normal meal is made of bean soup and hard-backed biscuits of unbolted flour called after the name of that wretched dyspeptic Graham.

My first thought was that it must be some arcane Jewish holiday of which I would necessarily be ignorant. Or better, a birthday, for on his birthday a Russian must eat his pie, this being as necessary to his happiness as is a christening to salvation for an old-time believer in the Church. Be this as it might, I was delighted to smell the fresh-baked aromas and grateful to the unknown brother who had brought them forth. "Who is the good man?" I asked, and was told to my surprise that something even more important was being celebrated: the community's first wedding. A young man and woman had decided to enter into matrimony and with the impetuousness of youth had determined that it must be done at once.

There was of course an immediate bustle and hurry while every man in the community tried to find the suit in which he had left Russia and the women gathered flowers and baked. The rafters were soon hung with flowers, and on this great occasion, white sheets instead of oilcloths were spread upon the dining tables. The pies, now inscribed with the initials of bride and groom, were produced and set in places of honor, and the members of the community took their places at the common board.

As I had come only recently among these people and, save for a select few, did not fully understand their language but had to make do with my own feeble attempts at German and frantic gesticulations, I did not know the community sentiments toward marriage. Without having any evidence for my beliefs, I assumed they would disapprove, but plainly I was wrong. Now, however, a scene I had witnessed the previous evening made sense.

I had been returning from a walk along the banks of the river when I heard pitiful sobbing. On investigation, I found a young girl sitting alone beneath a tree, her shoulders shaking with emotion. Gentle as the men of New Zion are in speech and deportment, they look rough as woodsmen or farmhands, which in their labors they are. In the midst of this, the girl—her name, I was to learn, is Annuta—appeared like a charming flower which had somehow blossomed amongst the rude growth of the commune fields. It would take a stronger temperament than mine to resist comforting such a creature, and thus I did not, sitting instead and talking to her for a full hour. Yet I cannot claim any success, as Annuta never revealed to me the source of her grief but only repeated continually that her life must now be over, something that in itself seemed tragic.

Now, at last, I understood, as it was Annuta's sister who was to be married. Composed yet not happy, Annuta sat at a long table braiding wildflowers into a wreath for the bride and bouquets for the table. I should hurry on to the wedding, but bear with me for a moment.

Imagine this child who is a charming woman, or a charming woman with the freshness and abandon of youth. Just eighteen, Annuta is both. If your being is Arcadian, if your emotions are sensitive to loveliness and innocence, you hesitate, if you meet her in the grassy lands of the blooming orchard, whether to kneel at her feet and kiss her hand in homage to her womanly charms, or gather her in your arms as you would a dear little girl.

She is a brunette: dark olive skin, hair of that darkest brown which is so much richer and warmer a tone than pure black. Very large, dark brown eyes, with soft but passionate glances; a small but shapely head; features indeed not Jewish at all, but of a more softened, refined, and brightened Tartar type; her face rather wide, and lips a bit thick; and her expression, under any circumstances, that of quick intelligence and good nature; with a figure singularly graceful—robustly so; and well-formed hands and a firm step. This, then, is Annuta to whom the flowers were brought.

Today she is attired in a close-fitting black dress without even a ribbon as ornament, as if she were attending a funeral rather than a wedding, and her expression is somber. When I greet her, she looks up and her eyes are warm, but she does not speak. When she finishes the wreaths, she ties a thick Russian towel, embroidered with red, around her waist as an apron, and helps make the pies—a busy, and brave, little maiden, I tell myself, and the reader will undoubtedly agree.

The brothers and sisters had been gathered a few moments on the dining room benches when the bridegroom and his bride appeared. Both were young, perhaps twenty-two. The young man, well educated, had read philosophy at university. He was rather good-looking, with a shock of unruly hair and a Jewish profile. The bride is known in the community for her kind disposition and willingness to help others, as well as for what might be called her womanliness. But having cut her hair short for this occasion, her aspect struck your correspondent as being athletic, that of a strong-minded Diana rather than Venus. She was, however, very nicely dressed, in a plain white sheath, and wore a wreath of white flowers.

The very appearance of the bride and groom seemed to constitute an announcement, and immediately the members of the community gathered round, kissing both of them loudly in congratulation. As this kissing is distinct from that done by Americans, it is worth departing from the narrative to describe it. Each brother or sister in turn took the groom and bride in his or her arms and looked at them earnestly; then the lips were pressed together again and again, with a long, deep, and almost solemn emotion accompanied by deep sighs. Such kisses, I believe, are exchanged among English-speaking people only at moments of direst tragedy or the most passionate exaltation. These kisses, I think, are peculiar to the Russian Jews; at least, I have seen no other races kiss with equal effusion, such total abandonment.

After the embraces, dinner was served, along with the marriage pies bearing the initials of the bridal couple. The cook had been lucky, for he had dispatched a jackrabbit shortly after breakfast, affording us a rare taste of meat. Though deer are plentiful in the forest and fish are in the river, little time is left for hunting after the day's labors in New Zion, and thus game is seldom tasted. In any event, the rabbit made up into a capital ragout, which was a nobler ending for him—to be thus a means to philanthropic evolution by passing into the organisms of philosophers—than to fall prey, perhaps, to a sneaking coyote in the field.

The ending of the dinner completed this part of the ceremony and, I would have thought, the ceremony itself. But immediately after washing the dishes—for the entire community participates in such chores, including the bride and bridegroom—we all gathered together outdoors, where, in an extravagantly beautiful setting, we were held hostage to the leader of the community, who chanted bad poetry for more than an hour. At last, we were set free on the dubious mission of finding our individual identities with the aid of pocket mirrors. If the reader finds this unlikely, I can assure him that most of the assemblage was similarly incredulous. It is, in fact, a measure of the community's devotion to its shared ideals that the members persisted in this futile endeavor until the sun was low in the sky, at which time the leader called us all together again and dismissed us to other pursuits.

Though their respect for this man—who for his own reasons has cast aside his given name in favor of the *nom de guerre* Liberty—was too great to allow them to cheer, the young men and women set off for the community hall with alacrity. For now that the serious business was concluded, the ball was to begin. Sad to say, this society has no instrumental music, not even the poorest squeak of a fiddle. In this strait, the toughest throats amongst the brothers are called to fill the vacuum. Four good-hearted fellows were summarily arranged against the wall to chant for hours on end the strains of "la,la,la" with all the necessary changes of time and air necessary to guide the steps of the waltz, the polka, or the quadrille, and though this must have been a burden, none complained. Indeed, they laughed and seemed to enjoy the dance as much as any participant.

Of the dances, the favorite seemed to be the American country quadrille. This was danced again and again, with every possible variety of blunder and goodwill. The bridegroom, acting as leader of the dance and calling out the figure, tore at his hair like a Frenchman at the misdeeds of his friends, and shouted out his despairing instructions with a rolling Russian R, for all the world like an Irishman with a little whiskey in him. Altogether, the ball was a very rude affair, with hardly a graceful scene, except for a few steps performed by Annuta and her sister, the bride.

By rude, however, I do not mean rough, or that there was any breach of good manners, for the social courtesy of these people is remarkable. There is simply an almost universal lack of grace to their movements. Under such conditions, who could imagine a French community, for example, would do anything less than display all the charms of measured movement, music or not? On the other hand, the social bonds of the French would seem artificial when compared to the exuberant kissing and loud shouts of these people, whose enthusiasm for life must be contagious to the most jaded among us.

After the dancing, we were directed again to the tables, where miraculously vodka and sweets had appeared, and the celebration continued, fired anew by the presence of spirits. More dancing, more singing, until at last, your weary correspondent went off to his poor bed upstairs to sleep undis-

> turbed until the early hours of the morning, when the brothers and sisters stole gently to their rest on either side of the curtain dividing the dormitory.
>
> When I awoke in the morning, all was as it had been before the wedding. There was no hint of the festivities of the night before, nor would I have known positively that it had occurred were it not for the flower Annuta had pinned to my jacket. Now, I smelled its sweet, sad odor and wondered where that charming young woman could be. But rather than taint her image with reality, I stole away, as the memories of the evening had, choosing to make my farewell to that remarkable community silently and in private, but hoping somehow to return and partake once again of the hospitality of the communistic Jews of Wisconsin.

Joe finished reading and looked up, moved by the author's last words but jealous of the attention he had lavished on Annuta. Joe felt as if he had never really seen her, that the article was evidence of his insensitivity. After all, Annuta had nursed him back to health and catered to him in every way. Why should it take a journalist to open his eyes?

"Well?" Liberty was glaring at him.

"Who is the author?" Joe asked.

Liberty waved the question aside. "I was a fool," he said. "This man appeared, asking to live among us as an observer. He mentioned no magazine, no article. He was simply curious, or so he said. I had no idea he would publish his findings and make such sport of us. But I should have known better. I should have learned that much over the years."

Joe was puzzled. It seemed to him that the picture of the community was generally favorable. "I didn't feel insulted," he said.

"And why should you? It was not your speech that he derided as bad poetry, nor your name—laboriously chosen, I assure you—that he mocked. But that is not the worst of it. The problem is, if he attacks me, he attacks all of us."

Although Joe agreed with the writer's characterization of Liberty's service and doubted lasting harm could come to New Zion because of an article in an obscure journal, he said nothing. He picked up the magazine again. "Should I write them a letter?"

Liberty breathed deeply and paced the room. Finally, he said, "No, I shall not respond. We shall publish our own account of the wedding in the next *Investigator.* Needless to say, our friend will not be allowed to flaunt our goodwill again."

Liberty had gone to the window. Joe assumed the interview was over and rose to leave. He wondered where Annuta was working today. But as he opened the door, Liberty turned and said, "One more thing. Your uncle and the others must not know of this."

Liberty's face was white, his body stiff with anger. Joe wondered if it was vanity alone that had put him in such a state, but he knew better than to argue. His seriousness was impressive, even if the cause of it seemed foolish. "Of course," he said, and went out.

sixteen

Your love is a fist, but you are too weak to fight. You lie nauseous in your bed, and your head aches all day. One moment you are euphoric with the knowledge of love, the next you despair of ever seeing her again, but happy or sad, you think of little else. You remember her as she was, her strong supple legs, the thin line of sweat on her upper lip, the intensity of her eyes, lost in the act of love, her hands over your body, and the final interlocking of your legs, squeezing each other so tight that nothing but passion could escape. Yet now you are alone. You see her, but she acts as if nothing has happened. She smiles happily or sends a mock salute with a wave of her arm as she goes off with the other women to exercise in the forest. Nothing has happened, she seems to say, or rather, what happened has no special meaning, which is worse.

You exercise yourself, to take your mind off her. But every clearing reminds you of the thicket where you stopped. At meals, you cannot take your eyes from her. You are excited by the slight hills of her breasts pushing at her blouse, and at night you fantasize wild scenes of lovemaking. You tear at each other, sometimes even drawing blood, but you awake alone, the blankets damp from your passion.

What is worst is that you suspect everyone knows. They contrive to leave you alone with her, which is humiliating, for you know it is futile. You wonder if Liberty has arranged this, if your embarrassment is payment for some imagined slight. Yet you know this is nonsense, and because you do, you retreat from everyone, spending long afternoons alone on the river, hoping that distance will solve your problem, return you to the life you knew before love came between you and the ordinary.

You try to discipline yourself. You study English. You travel to the village and spend an afternoon with Dorsey. Borrowing from Liberty, you starve yourself, hoping the fast will drive his daughter from your mind. A kind of delirium takes over. You are lying on the riverbank, your head lost among the reeds, imagining yourself as the infant Moses being caressed by the Egyptian women. They change your linens, kiss your hot cheeks, but all of them are Lizzie. You beg her images to leave you in peace, but they all laugh, and the agony continues.

You hit on the idea of submersion and go into the river. There, sitting against a rock, you feel the force of the current moving through you. The water has a cleansing quality, as if it has taken everything and left you empty. You sit for hours, aware only of rushing water, of sound, of force. The damp cold invades you, cauterizes the open sore of love. When you finally rise, your legs cramp so you can barely walk to shore, but the absence of feeling is better than immobilizing pain. The forest dances before you, and with faltering steps you follow the mirage, embracing trees as you slowly make your way home.

seventeen

"What's the matter with you, anyway?" Shmuel sat at the foot of his bed.

Joe was confused. He couldn't remember sleeping. "What time is it?"

"Who cares?" his uncle said. "You look like a ghost."

Joe tried to sit up, failed, and sank back. "Uncle," he said. "I am in love."

"Others have survived; you will, too." Shmuel went to the chair for Joe's clothes. "Getting out of bed is the first step. Then we'll see about food."

Joe was too weak to argue. He followed his uncle downstairs, where Shmuel made him a breakfast of coffee and bread. "Have I made the lady's acquaintance?" Shmuel asked after Joe had eaten.

"To me, this is no joke," Joe said, surprised that the food had given him enough strength to be angry.

"Forgive me, then," Shmuel said, and he seemed to mean it. "I know what it is to be in love, but when it is not you who is afflicted, it is possible to laugh."

For the first time, Joe was interested in something other than his doomed love affair. "You, Uncle?"

"Why not me?" Shmuel said, suddenly indignant. "Yes, me. Many times, me." His voice changed, became softer, more intimate. "I don't blame you for being surprised. I used to study my parents and wonder how such old and shriveled husks could have generated enough passion to produce three boys. And though I've nothing for it, no wife or children to carry on my name, I've loved to such complete distraction that it ruined more lives than one."

"Here?"

"Does it matter?" Shmuel said softly. "But no, it was not here. It was long before New Zion. In fact, I first came here hoping to expel through hard work the anger love had planted in me. I wished to recover the innocent pleasure I once took in the open land and piney forests." Shmuel lapsed into an eloquent silence.

Joe waited until he could stand it no longer. "Where, then?"

For a moment, Joe thought he had intruded into areas that must remain private, at least to him. But then Shmuel resumed speaking in a hoarse monotone that Joe had to strain to hear, even in the empty dining hall. "It was in a place called Oregon, a thousand, two thousand miles from here, so far north and west that it was more nearly Canada than America. I was part of the only successful Am Olam community, sixty of us, the best of the boatload that came over in 1881. We were young, green as new corn, convinced that in time the world would be sitting at our feet, taking instruction in how to live. Our community would be a laboratory in which revolution and world peace would take shape.

"Such ideas, of course, can survive only in an atmosphere of complete ignorance. We lacked any sense of history and talked politics all day and into the night without the corruption of experience to sully the mixture. And it was exciting. God, Yosl, you have no idea how exciting it was. We used to pant, literally pant with our tongues hanging out, as we talked of the new world we would create. Sometimes, I would leave those discussions with an erection, and I'm sure the girls felt the same." Shmuel licked his lips and lapsed into silence once more.

"Was it like this?" Joe asked. "The place, I mean."

Shmuel looked around him. "Not so different, but larger, with solid log buildings, a library with many books, and a fireplace to read in front of on winter nights. Often, though, we were too excited, too full of ideas to even lie down."

The commune Shmuel described was what Joe had expected to find in Wisconsin. Looking around the shabby dining hall, he wondered if New Zion was a dream waiting to be born or the broken remains of a movement already dead. Shmuel wasn't bothered by such doubts. He went on suffering the privations of the frontier without asking why, or so it seemed. His uncle drank, but he didn't seem despairing. If he were, how could he oppose Liberty? One fought only when there was something to be gained, something of value. And Liberty's zeal seemed unaffected by twenty years of failure. The two of them made Joe feel like a superficial adventurer.

"Why did the community in Oregon fail, Uncle?" he asked.

Shmuel smiled. "It's interesting. Why, indeed, when we had everything we could have asked for? We were good farmers, and we even had money from the Baron de Hirsch Fund in England in case the crops should fail." Shmuel shook his head sadly. "We had no excuse, Yosl. But you see, we did have one problem, and we should have known it. We would have, if we had been older or smarter, or both. The problem was that while most of the men were young and single, there were almost no women, and those that were in the community were married. Portland was three days away, and except in winter, when travel was nearly impossible, every man was needed every minute." Shmuel sighed. "When I look back, I see it couldn't have gone any other way."

Joe was getting impatient. "What happened then, Uncle?"

Shmuel rubbed his eyes. "Ach, at the time, I was convinced I was being punished for disobeying my father and living a sinful life. But the odd thing was, I also believed I was the luckiest man alive. I was charmed and damned at the same time, unable to believe there was such ecstasy in the world, while hating myself for destroying the community I had dedicated my young life to building."

Joe was beginning to understand. "It was a woman, then?"

"Very good," Shmuel grunted. "You go to the head of the class. It was, as you say, a woman, but such a woman as you—as I—had never imagined. Her name was Miriam Gold, and though, of course, it was her husband's name, it described her perfectly. She had long yellow hair that hung to her waist and perfect white teeth. Unlike most Jewish women, she was fair, and everything about her that summer seemed light and pure. Her arms and legs were long and graceful, and she had a slim, muscular body that seemed made for love."

Joe was amazed and slightly shocked by Shmuel's poetry. But his uncle's eyes were focused on the distant wall, and he seemed only dimly aware of Joe's presence in the room. "What about her husband," Joe prompted him.

"We told him, of course. We were all comrades, remember. Neither owned the other, and women were not chattel. This was the law of our commune. I believe you've heard the same from our esteemed leader here." Shmuel laughed harshly. "Well, someone forgot to tell Ike Gold. Ike hadn't planned on a socially enlightened marriage, on sharing his wife equally with his brothers. He had antiquated ideas about these things, Yosl. You see what I mean."

A bitter tone had entered into Shmuel's voice now, one that spoke of old battles lost but not forgotten, and Joe regretted having urged his uncle on. But he was still curious. He said nothing; he waited.

Shmuel spoke as if it were an obligation. "Ike took the matter to the community, but first he came to see me. He brought a friend along, an ax." Shmuel shivered at the memory. "It was night, and I was returning to my room when somehow—God knows how—I felt him to my right. I turned and saw the ax coming at my head. I managed to take it on my hand and arm instead. It tore my shirt away, and my right arm was useless, but I fought—oh, how I fought—kicking Ike, and somehow I was able to knock him down. Then I stood over him, holding his goddamned ax in my hand while he spit at me. I wanted to split his head in two, but in the end I couldn't. I threw the ax away and left him there on the ground."

"And that was the end of it?"

"Such things don't end simply. In a meeting like the ones we have here, Ike told everyone what he thought had happened. He said I had seduced his wife. The truth was I hadn't approached Miriam. I was too innocent for such a thing, too naive, to imagine a married woman could have such feelings. She had pressed her body against mine in the forest and told me Ike didn't treat her like a woman. She begged me to make love to her, and I didn't resist. Not many men would have."

"And you told them this?"

Shmuel shook his head. "Who would have believed me? But I also had a sense of honor, God help me. It seemed important not to apologize. I wasn't ashamed." He paused and smiled ironically. "Not that it would have made any difference. They threw me out—me, a comrade and founder of the community. I had helped build the place, but that meant nothing. Gone. It was all gone." He shook his large head.

Joe tried to imagine Shmuel tall and young, strong and idealistic, but it was difficult now. His uncle's face was twisted into a grimace, and he wiped his eyes so often that they were a burning red. "What did you do then?"

"What could I do? I went to Portland and waited. Miriam had said she'd come. What a schmuck I was. I waited a week, ten days. I heard nothing, not even a letter. Finally, I left. I went to San Francisco, hoping to board a ship and lose myself at sea." He smiled ruefully. "I was romantic in those days. I figured my dying would show her something. A lot I knew about women, about life."

"Weren't there any ships?"

"I was no sailor. I hung around for a while, and then I drifted south, to Los Angeles. Then Mexico. Finally, I ended up in Oaxaca, hell on earth, but I was too sick to care. I tried to kill myself by drinking everything I could lay my hands on." Shmuel shook his head. "I must have a hell of a body, Yosl. I think those Mexicans even gave me horse piss to drink, but to me it was honey. The funny thing is that I wasn't even any good at suicide. It took me two years to figure that out. By then I'd lost thirty pounds and had a permanent case of dysentery. But I was still alive."

Listening, Joe felt guilty for having accepted his father's easy judgment of Shmuel. While his father had imagined Shmuel's exodus as being selfish frivolity, Joe understood that it had been animated by longing. And his uncle had been ennobled by suffering and exile. Sitting before him in his tattered wool coat and leather visor, Shmuel seemed to Joe more dignified, wiser and stronger than he had known.

"So you left Mexico?" Joe said.

"There was nothing for me there. This time I did find a boat and worked my way back to New York, where I heard another community was forming, and here I am." He hesitated. "So, you see, Nephew, I know something about love."

Joe had forgotten Lizzie in the rush of Shmuel's story. "I apologize, Uncle," he said. "I should have known that without being told."

"Nonsense," Shmuel said. "Who is the young lady?"

Joe was surprised. He had assumed it was common knowledge. But Shmuel seemed genuinely curious, so he told him about the trip to town, Kleinschmidt's speech, and finally, Lizzie. "I was afraid to say anything for fear you and Mr. Liberty wouldn't approve," he concluded.

"Who cares what we think?" Shmuel snorted. "What's important is whether you're happy. To me, you look miserable, but that's part of being in love. And Liberty was the one who sent you off together in the first place. To be fair, which is against my principles, he may have meant nothing. On the other hand, there were any number of people he could have sent along besides his daughter."

"How could he be so cold-blooded?" Joe asked.

Shmuel took off his visor and ran his fingers through his hair, then blinked his eyes. "Look at it another way. He likes you. After all, he made you his secretary, the editor of that ridiculous paper. Perhaps he was just trying to bring the two of you together and didn't know a graceful way of doing it. Liberty isn't much on etiquette. Anyway, would it be so different from your father going to a *shadchen* to find you a bride? In Russia, you wouldn't have thought anything of it."

"I suppose you're right," Joe admitted.

"Of course I am," Shmuel said. "In this country there are no matchmakers, and that's good, but you can't blame parents for trying to look after their children. Besides, knowing the young lady, even as little as I do, I doubt she'd do what her father told her if she wasn't interested herself."

The mention of Lizzie embarrassed Joe. "We haven't discussed marriage, Uncle," he said. "I'm not even sure she loves me. She believes in freedom."

"I see," Shmuel said, and Joe thought he did. "She's not sure she wants to marry at all, ever?"

"She says people shouldn't belong to other people."

Shmuel nodded. "Her father's daughter. But perhaps not. I sense that there's more passion in her than in the old man."

"Oh, she has passion," Joe said without thinking.

Shmuel smiled. “Then there’s hope.” He reached out and touched Joe’s knee. “But for now she has doubts?”

“Advanced ideas,” Joe corrected him.

“It comes to the same thing. So,” Shmuel said, puffing out his cheeks. “The problem is yours. Do you want to wait for her to come to her senses and realize what a mensch you are, or would you rather walk away and forget about her?”

“That’s impossible,” Joe said, but he felt better for Shmuel’s having put it the way he had. It was nice to think that even if he was miserable, it was because he had chosen to be. “I think about her day and night. It seems so obvious that I turn red whenever we’re in the same room, and so I try to avoid her. In a place like this, that’s not easy. I go for long walks near the river, but when I return, inevitably, she’s the first person I see. It would be impossible to avoid Liberty’s daughter anyway.”

“What does she say when you see her?”

Now it was Joe’s turn to be ironic. “She says hello. She asks how I am. Of course, I can’t even hint at how I feel, so I hate her for it. The odd thing, Uncle, is that this makes my love more intense. I am embarrassed to talk this way, but I don’t understand myself anymore.”

“Why be embarrassed? Having a soul is nothing to be ashamed of. Without it, you’d be a dried-up prune, like your employer. I envy your feelings, painful as they are. It’s better than feeling nothing. But now, I want you to tell me something about this Moses you’ve seen in Gays Mills. This new Messiah.”

Joe had nearly forgotten Kleinschmidt and had to think for a moment whom his uncle might mean. “I’ve told you what I know about Kleinschmidt, Uncle.”

“Yes, but I’m interested in your opinions. Do you think he’ll be back?”

“He said so, but Dorsey doubted anything would happen before spring.”

Shmuel nodded. “And this Dorsey, he’s offered you employment?”

“It amounts to almost nothing.”

“I wasn’t thinking of the money,” Shmuel said. “It would be valuable for us to have someone in town who might hear about Moses’s plans and alert us.”

"Dorsey says pogroms don't exist in America."

"Easy for an Irishman to say," Shmuel said. "It so happens, however, that he's right—so far. All the same, I want you to accept his offer." Now Shmuel smiled. "But can you work for three newspapers at once?"

"I think it's safe to say, Uncle, that I am the only man in America who reads them all regularly."

Shmuel laughed. "Maybe, but this Moses seems to have broad reading habits. We must keep our eye on him."

Miraculously, Joe's spirits lifted. He was still preoccupied by Lizzie, but he was no longer disabled by love. He attended to his work, performed his chores, and thought of other things. Now his love was a kite, not a millstone, a way to escape the routine, to experience adventure while sitting quietly at his desk. Somewhat to his surprise, he found he enjoyed thinking of the future, fantasizing about what would happen to him, where he would live his life, and with whom. At first as recreation, and later as a discipline, he developed the habit of planning ahead. He considered whether he should marry and have a family or live alone as Shmuel did. And he found that these thoughts existed independent of Lizzie. He might marry Annuta instead, or, more likely, someone he hadn't even met. There was no way to know. While his love remained constant, he began slowly to envision a future.

eighteen

Joe was not prepared for his visitor. He had been up late correcting copy, and his eyes burned in the morning light. A late November frost hung on the trees, turning the world white, and he had to hold up his hand against the glare. At first, he didn't recognize Annuta's sister. Rebecca was pregnant and bundled against the cold in a long brown cloak. She seemed to have aged, and small spidery lines radiated out from her eyes, which were more deep set than before.

"Marriage must be hard work," Joe thought. "Please," he said, rising and offering her the only chair. "Mr. Liberty is out, but he'll be back before long."

"I've come to see you," Rebecca said slowly. She continued to stand, ignoring Joe's outstretched hand and the chair.

"Me?" Joe had never even spoken to the woman before.

"I won't take much of your time," Rebecca said.

"Take all you want," Joe said. "I was only surprised. I assumed you wished to see Mr. Liberty."

Rebecca didn't respond. She kept her eyes trained on the window, intent, it seemed, on nothing. Joe began to feel uncomfortable. He knew little about pregnancy. He wondered if she was ill, if he should call one of the women to help. Finally, Rebecca broke the silence. "Why are you torturing my sister?"

The question was put so quietly, so reasonably, that it took a moment for Joe to understand what she had said. "I?" he said, astonished. He hadn't seen Annuta for some time, other than in passing. He couldn't remember when they'd last spoken. "I've done nothing to your sister. I wouldn't dream of hurting her in any way."

"And yet you are," Rebecca said. "As surely as if you were beating her daily. I just want to know why."

Joe couldn't hold her gaze and walked to the window to organize his thoughts. It was Lizzie who had been his obsession, not Annuta. He shook his head to clear it and rubbed his eyes. "I'm sorry," he said at last. "This is all new to me."

"Surely you know she has been in love with you since the day you met?" Rebecca said, exasperation coloring her tone.

Joe shook his head. "I had no idea. She hides her feelings very well."

Now Rebecca's voice rose. "Ah, yes," she said sarcastically. "The man is always innocent, the last to know. Even when she makes overtures, exhausts herself nursing you, still you are completely ignorant of her true feelings? Is this possible?"

Joe shrugged his shoulders helplessly. He could see Rebecca's point, but he couldn't admit that he hadn't considered her sister because of Lizzie. "It was very generous of Annuta to care for me, but she's a kind girl. Everyone knows this."

Rebecca wasn't satisfied. "She used to be a happy girl, too. Carefree, friendly. Now she walks around as if she was covered by the shroud of death. She deserves better. It may be that you're as innocent as you say, but I'm her only family in the world. It is my responsibility to ask what you mean to do about all this."

Joe was impressed that Rebecca had come and spoken to him, but he felt as if the situation concerned someone else entirely. He could see now that Annuta's care constituted more than simple compassion. And he knew that in Russia it would have been considered improper for a young girl to spend long hours alone with a man in his room, sick or not. This was America, but they were all Russians—whose rules should they follow? Lizzie wanted him to forget all his notions of propriety, while Rebecca accused him of humiliating her sister. "I'm sorry," he said. "You're right to be angry. Pain is pain, intentional or not."

"My anger means nothing, but Annuta is important. That's why I came."

"What would you like me to do?"

"Speak to her. If you don't love her, it is better for her to hear it from you. Otherwise, she imagines an idle remark or gesture has some hidden significance, and she continues to hope. When you helped her carry water to dinner last week, she was so happy it broke my heart."

Joe had completely forgotten the incident, and felt guilty for his inattention. "Of course I'll speak to her. I was insensitive." That much was true. Considering what Lizzie had put him through, he should have known better.

His apology didn't seem to touch Rebecca. She pulled her shawl closer and moved her feet as if preparing to leave. "This is all I came for," she said, and with no further pleasantries, she walked out the door.

Not wanting to speak of intimate things in the dining hall, Joe asked Annuta to go for a walk. It was growing colder each day, and people gathered in the common room as soon as chores were over, making privacy impossible. Yet Annuta's hopeful expression made Joe gloomy. How could he have been so blind to her infatuation, especially when, as he now realized, he had encouraged it all along?

She was thinner, but she had brushed her hair and put on a new dress before coming to meet him. Despite Rebecca's concern, Joe thought the weight loss had improved her appearance. The pudgy good looks of adolescence had been transformed; Annuta now seemed more like a woman who had yielded something to experience. Without his noticing, she had become very attractive, and this confused Joe.

In Russia, with a father and brothers to protect her, Annuta would have flourished. Men from other villages would have competed for her favors with the boys from her own community. A *shadchen* would have been hired, and her father would have mulled the offers carefully, considering this fellow's inherited wealth versus another's scholarship. Finally, Annuta would have been married in a fine ceremony by a famous rabbi and gone off to live with her new husband. Here, of course, things were entirely different. There was no father, no *shadchen,* and few available men. She was forced to fend for herself, with only Rebecca to help. Joe felt sorry for her.

Still, he was pleased to be walking beside her in the autumn sunlight. While she lacked Lizzie's force, Annuta had a serene and peaceful quality that calmed Joe. Pale and delicate as a fading summer flower, she was serious, but not aggressively so. Adrift in a democratic wilderness, she had been shunted aside, but her beauty remained. Joe didn't blame himself entirely for her predicament, but that changed nothing.

They walked upstream, neither daring to break the silence of the forest. The trees were bare now, the birches white as death but lovely against the dun-colored underbrush. Their feet rustled the leaves, and the wind whipped up the water. Finally, he said, "Your sister told me how you feel. I wanted to apologize for my selfishness." He felt lame and ridiculous.

"There's nothing to apologize for," Annuta said. "It's my own fault. I know Lizzie is far more interesting than I am, but I can't help how I feel. I love you. There, I have said it, so I should feel better." The statement, so simple, so unguarded, touched Joe. After Lizzie's elaborate explanation of the social realities surrounding their relationship, Annuta's declaration had the force of a knife cutting through cake. Annuta had pulled her scarf over her head, but Joe could see that she was crying.

"No," he said. "I should have spoken to you before things went this far."

"It wouldn't have mattered," Annuta said. "The first time I saw you, when you comforted me in the loft, I loved you. I had never met anyone like you."

Despite himself, Joe was flattered. "I didn't do anything unusual."

"But you are unusual!" Annuta cried. "You don't have to do anything. Americans are so confident, so sure of themselves, and you were shy and kept to yourself, not saying very much. But you were warm, you cared. Even when you ignored me, I was happy. I imagined I didn't see you because you were spending your time studying; Father wanted me to marry a scholar."

"But none of us here are Americans," Joe protested.

"They are trying madly to become so," Annuta replied. "Look around and you'll see." A small smile crossed her lips. "I imagined how we might have met in the old country, how my father might have arranged a match. That would have made me so happy, to be with you and with Papa."

She started to cry again, and Joe's heart went out to her. Freedom meant nothing to this girl; it could not ease the pain of losing her family. "Annuta, listen to me. I'm not the person for you. Perhaps you should return to New York. There are many young men there, newly arrived like me, and *shadchens* who arrange matches. That's what your father would have wanted, not this." He gestured toward the shacks of the commune and the ruined garden.

But Annuta just shook her head. And Joe didn't blame her. He might as well tell her to go to the North Pole. Where would she live in New York, and who would look after her? He put his hands on her shoulders, thinking to calm her. But the sight of her cheeks wet with tears caused him physical pain. He pulled her to his chest, then buried his head in her hair, smelling violets and thinking of spring, of renewal. Annuta tilted her head slightly and they kissed, at first tentatively, then with greater assurance. Joe had imagined she would have no experience, but her mouth was warm and soft, her body molded to his, her hands cradling his head and pulling him down to her. Perhaps, he thought, some people know about love instinctively.

Then they were on the ground, half sitting, half lying in the dry grass. The wind blew around them, isolating them from the world in its sound and bluster. He warmed his hands on Annuta's small round breasts, tasting the salt of her tears and feeling the heat rising within him. When she touched him, he thought he would explode, but the sensation subsided, only to be replaced by another even more intense. She was folded around him now, their bodies exposed to each other but protected from the wind. For a moment, Joe felt afraid. "We shouldn't," he whispered.

"It doesn't matter," she said.

How could it not, he wondered. But then he forgot his objections, forgot Lizzie, Rebecca, Shmuel, Liberty, everyone and everything except Annuta and the wind that howled in his ears, binding them together. They lay on their sides in the underbrush, holding each other tight, the rush of the river overpowering even the wind. They both knew there was safety here, protection. Hearing Annuta's ragged breathing, Joe fought to control himself, to hold back, but it was no use. In his moment of release, he felt a mixture of relief and despair, as if some vital connection with innocence had finally been cut for good. Looking up at the pale gray sky, he wondered aloud, "What have I done now?"

nineteen

Bryan Dorsey pulled a copy of the Gays Mills *Beacon-Call* from the press and spread it on the table. "There," he said. "Joseph Abrams, Assistant Editor" was printed neatly on the masthead, just below Dorsey's name. Joe knew they constituted the entire staff of the paper, which at the best of times ran to only four pages, including advertisements. Still, he was pleased. Cahan had not granted him a byline in the *Forward* as readily as Dorsey had awarded editorial rank.

"I don't deserve it," he said. "All I did was copy down a few births and deaths from the La Crosse paper and set type."

"Who cares?" Dorsey said. "If you didn't do it, it wouldn't have gotten done. Anyway, this makes up for the lousy pay."

"I appreciate it," Joe said, leaning back. And he did. But he was also grateful simply for having a place to escape to. He had been unable to face Rebecca, and though Lizzie said nothing, he was sure she knew about Annuta. He felt both proud and disloyal and didn't know whom to blame if not himself. It would have been easier if he didn't care for Annuta, if he could say, with Lizzie, that making love didn't tie them to each other. Joe's trouble was that he felt tied to both women.

Fortunately, it was a slack time of year. The harvest had long been completed, and the third issue of the *Positivist Investigator,* including a lengthy article in which Briggs compared New Zion favorably to Oneida, had been distributed. Aside from Liberty's correspondence and the infrequent inquiries from prospective comrades, Joe had few responsibilities, so he spent more time in town. He would walk the five miles to Gays Mills at noon, when the sun was warmest, and then have dinner with Dorsey before working late on the paper. One night, Dorsey had insisted that Joe stay overnight rather than walk home in the snow, and now it had become routine. The small woodstove in the *Beacon-Call* office provided more heat than the fire in the drafty dormitory, where the wind blew unimpeded through the timbered walls.

Dorsey pointed farther down the page to a small box in the classified section: "Dr. Jacob Kleinschmidt welcomes inquiries relative to his recent visit to the Kickapoo Region and volunteers for a planned summer Pilgrimage to the Western District." A box number in Milwaukee was listed below.

Joe looked at his friend. "What does it mean?"

"Who knows? Probably nothing. He wants money, that's for sure."

Joe nodded. He had learned to trust Dorsey's instincts. After all, nothing had come of the Moses's earlier visit. "But what about this pilgrimage?"

Dorsey puffed his cheeks and let the air out slowly. "If anyone answers the ad, which I doubt, he'll take everything they give him. If not, it doesn't hurt to say he's coming. He can always change his plans later if no one replies."

Joe had been feeling relaxed, self-assured, but now he shivered. It was impossible for him to share Dorsey's nonchalance. "Who took the ad?"

Dorsey looked around the office. "Who do you think? I can't go around refusing advertisers. No matter what we think, they've got a right to be in the paper."

"Of course," Joe said. But it still seemed strange. The Tsar didn't advertise for volunteers for the pogroms. Here, as Dorsey told him, there were no pogroms, but a man was allowed to use the public press for recruiting roughnecks. The thought depressed Joe, but he couldn't really argue with Dorsey.

"This one was odd, though," Dorsey continued thoughtfully. "It came in the front door."

"What's unusual about that?" Joe asked.

"Nothing, for locals. But the Moses is in Milwaukee or Mukwonago or God knows where. He's a traveling man. You'd think he'd write or wire the ad in. But no. Fella comes in with the copy all written out as neat as you'd like and pays cash on the spot. I'm supposed to run it twice, this week and next."

Joe was only half listening, his mind dully tracking Dorsey but taken up with an ancient fear. "Did you recognize the man?" he asked.

Dorsey shook his head. "Nope. And he wasn't an Indian."

"That means Kleinschmidt must have a representative in Gays Mills," Joe said. This idea made him even more uncomfortable than before.

"Maybe," Dorsey said. "But I know everyone in town. Unless this one lives in La Crosse or somewhere else and rides circuit up and down the Mississippi Valley. And if that's true, why bother with us? Why not put your ad in the La Crosse paper or go on up to Eau Claire or Black River Falls?"

Joe nodded. It didn't make sense to pick on New Zion. "It would be interesting to learn more about Mr. Kleinschmidt," he said.

Dorsey smiled. "I'm way ahead of you. A friend of mine works for one of the German dailies over to Milwaukee. He's a socialist, too, a real radical. I wrote and asked him about our Moses."

Something still bothered Joe. "The man who brought in the ad. You've seen him again in town?"

"Never saw him before—or since. I remember him, though. Short and fat and going bald on top. He tended to run on a bit, too—not about the Moses, just the town. He wanted to know how long I'd been here, where I was from. Offered to buy me a drink, but I told him I was busy." Dorsey winked. "I'd have one now, though. Come on, we forgot to eat dinner."

They put on their coats and started across the street. Dorsey walked straight ahead, face pointed directly into the wind, but Joe hesitated before going inside. He could hear the noise of the restaurant and felt the hard wind of December in his eyes. He stood for a long moment, letting it freeze his forehead, enjoying the cold deep into his brain before going inside. The street was empty, but he imagined Cossacks on horses thundering down upon him and instinctively moved under the awning for shelter.

Dorsey's description could have fit a hundred men, but the fact that he hadn't been familiar to Dorsey wasn't reassuring. Of course, he could be a farmer, or, as Dorsey said, live in La Crosse or one of the other towns. Yet the description fit J. G. Briggs, and now Joe wondered if the doctor could possibly be working for Kleinschmidt, and if so, why he had come to New Zion.

Joe held his hat with one hand and used the other as a rudder against the wind. It seemed as if he had been walking forever, yet he still had a mile to go. At times, he wanted to stay in Gays Mills until spring, talking late into the night with Dorsey and enjoying the camaraderie of the tavern before bunking down in front of the potbellied stove in the *Beacon-Call* office. He had learned a card game called sheepshead from some German farmers and had become proficient enough to win some of the time. He liked thinking of himself as a gambler and had taken to smoking cigars. Much as he liked the village, however, he always seemed to find himself walking back to New Zion after a day or so. He worried that he would miss something or that Liberty would discover he could get along very well without him.

Now the small gray shacks came into sight, hazy in the blowing snow, rising only slightly above the high banks that had already accumulated. Once, Joe had walked home in a blizzard so intense that he had missed the community completely, not realizing until the light had started to fade that he must be lost. He had backtracked in the darkness, fighting panic, and finally arrived home at midnight.

Smoke rose from the dining hall, and Joe imagined a cozy fire and a group of comrades sharing recollections of the old country, or more likely, debating life in the new. He thought of Lizzie. He wanted to seek her out and declare his love, but time was a bruise that would not heal. If he was going to say anything, it should have been weeks ago. Now he felt awkward, and there was Annuta to consider. He decided to concentrate on politics for a while; it was less confusing than love.

He was making his way, head down, toward the dining hall, when his path was suddenly illuminated and he heard his uncle's voice: "Nephew. Come in here."

Joe looked up to see Shmuel gesturing to him. He was hungry, but his uncle seemed agitated. Reluctantly, Joe pushed open the door of the shack. Inside, Abe Rosenfeld and Morris Held were sitting around the small table with a short, white-haired man whose spectacles and long nose lent an expression of perpetual surprise. "Close the door." Then Shmuel held out his arm to the stranger. "Nephew. I want you to meet Rabbi Isaacson, who comes to us from Minnesota."

"A rabbi?" Joe could not hide his astonishment. He had guessed there were none within a hundred miles, or if there were, that Shmuel wouldn't know them.

"Yes, of course, a rabbi. What did you think?" Shmuel said, annoyed now. "Show some respect, Yosl."

Chastened, Joe took off his hat and bowed slightly. "I'm sorry, Rabbi. I meant no disrespect."

Rabbi Isaacson smiled broadly. "I am too old to be insulted. Your uncle has been telling me about you, my boy," he said, standing now to shake hands.

The rabbi pronounced boy as "buoy," and Joe imagined a ship making its way to port in a storm. But Isaacson didn't look like a rabbi. Clean-shaven, he wore a dark businessman's suit and no yarmulke. His hair was combed neatly back over his ears, and a gleaming part divided his head into halves. His cheeks were red and glowed with health. Isaacson looked like a prosperous businessman, not a teacher or religious leader. It was confusing, like everything else. "He has?" Joe said at last.

Isaacson's eyes opened wide. "Yes, indeed. I know you were a scholar at university in Minsk, isn't this right? And I know of the tragedy of your dear parents and of your religious training in Russia. You were bar mitzvah?"

"Of course."

"Ah, my dear young friend, there you are wrong," Isaacson said. "Here it is by no means a matter of course, not even in New York or Chicago, and certainly not in the wilderness. Here, there are Jews in name only, Jews who have forgotten or never knew what it means to be Jewish, Jews who have made meaningless the sacrifices of their parents. Bar mitzvah is a sacrament with God, but sadly, many have forgotten God even exists and live barren lives of despair and pointlessness here."

The rabbi was short, but his voice boomed in the small room, inducing vertigo in Joe. He reached for a chair and put his other hand to his forehead. When he opened his eyes, the rabbi was studying him, concerned. "You are all right, my boy?"

"Yes, Rabbi, I'm fine. I just don't understand . . ."

"What I'm doing in this cauldron of apostasy?" the rabbi finished his sentence. "Very good. Your uncle told me you were a prodigy, intelligent beyond your years. We agree about very little, but I can see he was right in this."

Joe felt inadequate to the rabbi's intellectual force. The man's voice was immense, his presence indomitable. Certainly he was one of the Jews in name only that the rabbi had mentioned, yet he had been called to meet this great man. He looked over at Abe and Shmuel for help, but they said nothing. "I don't understand," he said again. He looked at the others. "Mr. Held, you're a Marxist. You don't believe in religion."

Held scowled, but the rabbi smiled benignly and nodded his head. "Yes, very good," he said. "What about it, Mr. Held?"

"I am a Marxist," Held said. "But it is ridiculous to deny the force of religion. Marx was born a Jew, after all. Anyway, who can live here and ignore it; that is what your friend Liberty is, after all—a preacher. If we are to have religion, it might as well be something we're familiar with. At least as Jews, we all know the prayers."

"And you, Uncle?" Joe said. He had never seen Held so uncomfortable.

Shmuel shifted his feet. "I haven't been to a shul since I left Russia," he said. "The rabbi knows this and is my friend anyway. He's an intellectual whom I met originally in New York and saw again when I traveled to Minneapolis. He has a unique understanding of these things and is able, through who knows what power, to see a way of my remaining a Jew. This is miraculous enough for me. Besides, he knows more about socialism than most of the so-called socialists here."

Joe was shocked. "Can a rabbi be a politician?"

Isaacson laughed shortly. "Many things are possible in America, my boy," he said. "Judaism is eclectic and embraces many beliefs, some of which may seem to be in opposition to each other. Often, they are. This is where we get our strength—from discord. The rationalist distrusts talk of an afterlife, while the Chasid celebrates mysticism and communicates with those who have passed from this world; some go to shul every day, while others do not pray at all. Jews speak in many voices, many languages. We are too few to insist on unanimity. I don't believe in it, anyway."

The rabbi looked at each of his listeners in turn. "Things are different here than in Russia. What was right there may not be right in America. How could I possibly claim to lead while refusing knowledge of the world in which my congregants live, or be unwilling to go to them wherever they choose to settle? Torah gives life; it is the one thing without which we can't exist. I do not say "live," notice, but "exist." Life is impossible without Torah. But early in my training in Vienna, I developed a passionate interest in literature and philosophy, in the problems of the world. Torah is my salvation; I suppose this is my curse." He gestured vaguely toward the dining hall.

Joe thought for a moment. Then he said, "But why visit us now?"

The rabbi shrugged. "As Shmuel said, we are friends, and he asked me to come. I'll look around, speak to your comrades, and we'll see. Probably nothing will change." The rabbi hesitated. "You are familiar with the phrase *Judischer selbst hast*?"

"Self-hate? Aren't there enough people who hate us as it is?"

The rabbi laughed. "Indeed there are. But it really is not funny. In a way, it is tragic. Jews are always finding new ways to hasten their own destruction; someday we will hand our enemies guns and direct them to shoot." He smiled thinly to show he was not entirely serious. "Even when there is no direct danger, we are reluctant to assert ourselves for fear the gentiles will disapprove. Thus, in the Jewish districts of the Lower East Side, the political leaders are all Irish. We imagine others will hate us less this way. And the same is true here, in your community."

"You mean Mr. Liberty?"

"Of course," Held exploded. "Who else could he mean, the president?"

"Easy, Mo," Abe said. "It's not the boy's fault."

Held turned away, but Joe spoke to the rabbi. "Mr. Liberty was invited here; the people wanted him to be their leader. Isn't this true, Uncle?"

Before Shmuel could speak, however, Held said, "Sure, originally, we asked him. What did we know? Now we'd like to invite him to leave. The situation is getting worse, now that he's got that damned head reader with him."

"Mo means that Liberty's more popular than ever," Abe put in.

"But isn't that democracy?" Joe asked.

"Democracy," Held spat out. "If you took a vote in Russia, the majority would want to butcher every Jew. Isn't that democracy?" His voice was a sneer. Joe was embarrassed for the rabbi, but Held had a point. They could all be in danger.

"This isn't Russia," he said quietly.

"Of course not," Held said. "And Liberty isn't the Tsar. But what he's doing is a perversion of our principles. Whatever positivism is, it isn't socialism, is it? Who cares if a majority approves their own demolition? If we can see what's happening, we have an obligation to act."

The rabbi put his hand on Joe's shoulder. "You must excuse my friend Mr. Held," he said. "He is brilliant, but easily frustrated. Your uncle believes that some of your comrades may be more likely to listen to a rabbi than a Marxist."

"And you are willing to do this?" Joe asked.

The rabbi smiled beatifically. "It is my duty to speak to whoever will listen. Moreover, I am an optimist. I do not consider even such a man as your uncle, who boasts about never going to shul, hopeless. Shmuel, Morris, Abe, and you are all my responsibility. Besides, I happen to agree with what's been said. If Edward Liberty, as he chooses to call himself, is not evil, he is profoundly misguided, and he may be mad. I hope to convince some others of that, for the good of all. That, you will agree, is a very Jewish idea."

Then the rabbi clapped his hands together, looking pleased with himself. "Shmuel," he cried out. "It's cold in here. I would like some tea."

Book Three

There is a noise of war in the camp.

—Exodus 32:17

twenty

January 10, 1906

Dear Mr. Cahan:

Greetings from your least faithful correspondent. When I left New York, I imagined I would be simplifying my life by coming to Wisconsin; now I yearn for the days when I slept in your office and walked the wild streets of Manhattan, alone and happy in my ignorance of the New World. I have written before of Dr. Briggs, the Oneida phrenologist who joined us last summer with his God-men. Now, however, I am less worried about him than about my uncle, who, with a group of his friends, seems determined to overthrow Mr. Liberty with no clear idea of what will follow.

I am not concerned that this revolution will succeed—there is almost no support for it—but rather for the effect the attempt will have on community morale. Shmuel and his friends have even enlisted a rabbi in their fight, a learned and distinguished man who came to our last meeting as a visitor but stayed to be insulted by Liberty, who declared that the Jewish religion is responsible for the oppression our people have suffered. Liberty claims Judaism teaches meekness in the face of tyranny, while the Religion of Humanity, or positivism, offers new life and liberation.

Why anyone would consider our life here liberation is a mystery to me. We subsist on turnips, a thin corn soup, and Graham crackers and are always a mouthful away from starvation. While it is true that we have more acres under cultivation than before, the drought would have wiped us out last summer had not the Jews of Minneapolis come to our rescue. Liberty is either unaware of this or simply ignores it. What is most remarkable, however, is the way the comrades hang on his every word, inhaling him as if he were some infinitely rare and precious perfume, nodding and smiling like Chasids in the presence of a legendary rebbe. Perhaps it is that words like "freedom" and "liberty," so rare for thousands of years among our people, have a narcotic effect.

In your last letter, you asked about Indians, and I must confess they play a small part in our life, though they are the true victims of oppression here. Those who have left their reservations live in unspeakable poverty on the fringes of town and salve their disappointment in liquor. The proud chiefs of the Indian wars are but a distant memory. Last week, however, I traveled with Shmuel to a small village a few miles away. The purpose of our visit was not political, but practical in the extreme—my uncle wished to replenish his supply of the hard cider the Indians produce. Nevertheless, I had a chance to observe them at close range. The Indians are Blackfeet, descended, I think, from the famous Chief Blackhawk, and live what seems a desperate existence. Yet they did not appear to be dissatisfied. They sell or barter beads and blankets along with their cider to the white settlers in the area; in return they are given various farming implements, liquor, and occasionally a horse.

The chief of the tribe is a tall man with long gray hair and a tragic face who greeted Shmuel like an old friend. They held each other in outstretched arms for what seemed like hours but was no doubt a minute or two and then performed a kind of slow dance in place. After this ritual was completed, we were taken inside the chief's tent, which turned out to be filled to the bursting point with men, women, and children, all sitting side by side around a smoldering fire.

The air was filled with smoke and grease, and the Indians glistened in the dim light. Carcasses of deer and rabbit hung from the lodge poles, and I found their dead faces to be a haunting reminder of the inability of our comrades to hunt or trap game. Initially, I was taken aback by the Indians' painted faces and fierce expressions, but because my uncle seems to be a favored customer—or perhaps merely a frequent one—we were given the best seats in front of the fire and generous samples of the Indians' brew from a clay pitcher. In time, I began to relax.

Despite the good will of our hosts, however, I found the cider to be almost undrinkable. The meal we were served also was not to my taste, as it consisted of smoked dog and a mush made of maize and dried beans. The smell in the tent was overpowering, the crush of humanity suffocating. Yet, I feel like an ingrate, for my uncle's friends could not have been kinder or more generous with their meager supply of food. When we eventually rose to leave, I noticed that neither the smell nor the smoke was as offensive. I shall visit again and report further.

Otherwise, life is uneventful. The snow makes travel difficult, so my trips to Gays Mills have become less frequent. Like the animals, I use the winter to hibernate. It is a time for re-examination, for renewal, for rest. We live on what we have put aside—string beans, corn, pumpkin squash, turnips, some wheat, and occasionally cheese—and this teaches us the lesson of thrift. We have the cows for milk and chickens for eggs, and we make bread. There is little to do in the office, and thus the bulk of my labor goes into organizing Mr. Liberty's correspondence. In the darkness of January, however, I've discovered a warmth in our community that was not present in July.

Unable now to go into the fields, we must look to one another for entertainment. Small groups congregate and reminisce about life in Russia. We maintain a small library, and in addition to political discussions, we sometimes read aloud from Pushkin, Lermontov, and Chekhov. Art gives hope, and in hope lies happiness. We grow stronger as a group daily, and spring moves closer.

I look forward to hearing from you soon; until then, I send my best wishes for the coming year to you and my colleagues on the *Forward.*

Your friend and employee,
Joseph Abrams

twenty-one

On a springlike morning in late January, Lizzie came to visit Joe in the office. Liberty had gone to talk to Briggs, and Joe was reading a draft of a long article on vegetarianism. She wore a brown tweed shawl over her blue dress, and her blond health radiated throughout the room. As determined as he was to be furious, Joe couldn't help smiling. Though he saw her constantly, they hadn't been alone for more than a few moments in months. Still, he despised his eagerness; he felt like a pet dog.

"May I come in?" Lizzie asked.

"Please," Joe said, rising to get a chair. "I'm honored."

Lizzie looked sharply at him, then softened. "Don't be sarcastic," she said. "I've been busy."

"Yes," Joe said. "There is much to do in winter. Still, I thought sometime in the last four months we might have met."

"We see each other every day."

"You know what I mean."

Lizzie removed her bonnet and sat down. "You could have come to me."

"I didn't feel welcome." Joe said hoarsely, the words tearing at his throat.

Lizzie looked away. "You are always welcome," she said softly. Joe was surprised at how subdued she was. Even her gestures seemed smaller;

her hands lay obediently in her lap and her expression was without animation. It was hard to believe she was the same girl who had confronted her father in front of the whole community. "I didn't come here to argue," she said.

"Why, then?"

Lizzie sucked in her cheeks and looked at the floor. "I'm concerned about Annuta. She eats nothing and cries all the time. You aren't a cruel person, I know that, but I don't understand this."

"I didn't know you were close friends."

"We're not. I don't have to be her friend to worry about her."

Joe had noticed Annuta's pallor in recent weeks, but there was no way to take back what he had done. "It really doesn't concern you," he said.

"I think it does," Lizzie said.

"Why?" Joe asked suddenly. "Why must you be everything to everyone? Who deputized you, made you the spokesman for mankind—your father?"

Lizzie's eyes flashed. "Of course not." She shifted uncomfortably in her seat. "The truth is I feel responsible."

"You mean you think I've done to Annuta what you did to me?"

"No," she said quickly. "Anyway, I did nothing to you. We both participated. We're adults, and we made love one day from mutual need. What of it?"

Joe smiled scornfully. "Answer your own question," he said.

Lizzie seemed to struggle with her composure, as if she were trying to remember scripted lines. She wrapped her shawl tightly around her shoulders and began to pace the small room. "There's no reason for two people not to make love if they're so inclined." She looked so stiff that Joe felt sorry for her, but he said nothing. "That doesn't mean we have claims on each other; we're free to do as we please, go where we like."

"And you say I'm innocent."

"What do you mean?" Lizzie said angrily.

"You're not talking about barnyard animals but human beings, with feelings, Lizzie. Everything you say is so intellectual and sensible. But we're not rational. We have these feelings, we can be hurt. Where does that fit into your equation?" He held up his hand to forestall her protests. "Yes, yes," he said. "I know. We're free." He shook his head. "I've tried to remember, chanted it at the ceiling like my Torah portion on long sleepless nights. It didn't help me forget the softness of your skin or the smell of your hair." He looked at her. "You say I'm free. How wonderful. Free to be miserable, to feel loneliness and rejection. This freedom has led me to the conclusion that nothing is really free. There's a price for every action one takes. Because of you, I'm willing to pay, Lizzie, but it's not free. Nothing is."

She started to speak, but Joe held up his hand again. "I've been waiting two months to tell you this," he said. "Let me finish." He paced the room and then turned to her again. "I've also been thinking about communism. Of course, I'm in favor of everyone having all they need, of equality. No one opposes that. But if being a good communist means ignoring our feelings and acting as if our bodies and minds aren't related, then I'll never be good enough for you."

He felt tears forming and wiped his eyes, angry at himself. He wasn't through and didn't want to lose control. Lizzie was twisting her shawl in her fingers, her shoulders tensed. "You don't understand," she whispered.

"I understand perfectly," Joe shouted. "And Annuta's misery is the result. I justified her pain, using the logic you taught me. 'We're adults,' I told myself. 'Therefore, nothing matters.' But it doesn't work, Lizzie. Not for Annuta, not for me, not even for you, really. You can't simply decide love doesn't exist because it isn't logical. I love you—and Annuta, God help her, loves me."

Lizzie seemed shrunken in her chair. "That's what I was afraid of."

"Is it so terrible?" Joe said. "Don't worry. It won't leave this room. No one will ever know your shame."

"You're such a gentleman, Yosl. Such a bourgeois gentleman."

"I am what I am."

Lizzie crossed the room and took his hands in hers. "It isn't that I don't love you," she said. "Maybe I do. But for so long I've protected myself against loving anyone that I don't know what I feel anymore."

"It's a great mystery," Joe said. "Love even has its own literature."

"Don't mock me."

"I've never been more serious. It's natural to be suspicious of something that dominates your thoughts day and night, makes you a stranger to yourself. I hate the way love makes me act; sometimes I hate you because you're responsible."

"If you didn't love me so much, you might kill me?"

Joe smiled. "The thought has crossed my mind."

"But how was I to know you'd react this way?" Lizzie said plaintively.

"The others didn't?"

She flushed. "There were no others. I just wanted you to think so, to impress you. Now I feel I should pay for what I've done, as you and Annuta have."

"Don't be silly," Joe said. "I'm the one who should be grateful."

"For all your suffering? Forgive me, Yosl, but that's so Jewish of you."

"You're wrong," Joe said. "Jews don't enjoy suffering; gentiles like to think we do. Important lessons can be learned through sorrow, but who wants pain in his life? No one I've met. Still, I'd rather be alone than have you feel obliged to me."

"Do you want to marry me?" Lizzie asked suddenly.

"Of course," Joe said. "I've always hoped to marry a woman I loved. But I'm not thinking about that."

Joe thought Lizzie looked relieved, as if, having made the offer, she could draw back again. "What, then?"

"I want the same things as you. I'm young. I want to go my own way and do what I can with my life. Love wasn't in my plans; you caught me by surprise."

Lizzie seemed delighted by this. "Oh, thank you, Yosl," she said, laughing. "That's the nicest thing you could say to me."

Joe said nothing to this. He didn't understand, but he was glad she was pleased. Then she looked soberly at him. "I don't believe in marriage," she said. "Father doesn't believe in it . . ." She hesitated, tears glistening in her eyes. "I don't know what to believe anymore. It's all so confusing."

Joe held her in his arms, and her shoulders shook with emotion. Finally, Lizzie stopped crying. She dried her eyes on her shawl and kissed Joe's neck gently.

"I must go," she said. "I've got to think about things."

Joe nodded. "I'll be here."

He was still watching the open door, memorizing her figure, when her blond head reappeared, the sun's light creating a halo. "Talk to Annuta," she said. "That's very important."

twenty-two

Joe watched the Kickapoo moving higher against its banks. Swollen from the January thaw, the river roiled and pushed against the land, occasionally running over and swamping the shore before retreating and taking with it a bounty of tree branches, leaves, boots, and stray boards from abandoned fires and trappers' shacks.

The river rolled south, a liquid junk heap, mud-brown and ugly among the verdant pines and white snow. Watching it, Joe thought of the Nile, flooding annually, and the farmers who abandoned then returned to the river like unrepentant lovers who couldn't stay away. He was used to thinking of rivers as sustainers of life. As a child he had gone to sleep with the sound of the rapids in his ears and played in the water all summer long. But the Kickapoo seemed angry, not benign. At least the Egyptians had the sense not to build towns in the lee of the Nile.

It was the American character, he decided, to risk everything, even in building a house. Americans were fast, self-confident, all-embracing and violent, but generous, too. They always moved forward, and they certainly wouldn't let a river tell them where to live. Water lapped at his boots, and Joe wondered if he would ever become an American.

Gays Mills was a sea of mud. Men stood in their wagons, whipping their exhausted horses, and slowly the protesting animals dragged their loads along the street, steam rushing from their nostrils. Joe scraped the mud from his feet on the porch of the post office. It had been three weeks, and among the many envelopes for Liberty, there was a letter addressed to him from Cahan. Joe was about to open it when he heard someone call out, "Hey, Ike."

He was surprised to hear Yiddish in town and turned to see a small man in a black hat looking him over. "Were you speaking to me?"

"Who else?" The man sat on his haunches in front of the feed store.

Joe looked around. They were alone. "My name is Joe," he said, and immediately felt foolish.

"Sure, but it could have been Ike, am I right?"

"It was my father's name," Joe admitted.

The man shrugged expressively, vindicated. "I thought so."

Joe rose to get a better look at this fellow who seemed to know everything about him. He was short and wizened, yet he seemed very young. He spoke a street dialect, not the literary Yiddish Joe was accustomed to. "What is it you want?"

The man spread his hands. "Want? Nothing. Just passing the time of day. I'm stuck between trains and I never seen you, that's all. I can usually spot greenies."

The man's confidence made Joe mad. "I've been here almost a year."

"Congratulations. Four more, and if you're lucky, you can vote." The man smiled, which made him look younger still. "I don't mean to give you a hard time. Actually, I haven't been here so long myself." He offered Joe his hand. "Ben Schwartz, from Madison," he said.

Schwartz appealed to Joe's good nature. Besides, he knew hardly anyone outside the community. "A year ago, I hadn't heard of Wisconsin," Joe said, shaking Schwartz's hand. "I certainly didn't know there were any Jews here."

"Jews are everywhere," Schwartz said complacently. "In China there are Jews, why not Wisconsin?"

"It makes sense," Joe said.

Schwartz smiled broadly, showing one gold tooth. "We agree it makes sense. But you talk like a *maskil,* an intellectual. What are you doing in this godforsaken place? That's what don't make so much sense."

"I suppose you're right," Joe said. He described his journey to find Shmuel and New Zion, but Schwartz still seemed skeptical. "It's terrible about your family," he said. "Awful. But you're an educated man," he said. "Why waste your time farming in the wilderness with a *luftmensch?* I mean no insult to your uncle."

Joe didn't really know the answer. No one had put it quite this way before. "I was just a student," Joe said. "I never graduated."

"So? Graduate here. In America, anyone can. I myself am presently a student in Madison."

"At the university?" In his baggy pants, dirty shirt, and boots, Schwartz didn't even vaguely resemble his classmates in Minsk.

"Sort of a student. In the winter I take a course or two and they forgive me my tuition. Then in the summer I work and pay them back. It's a good system."

The idea of a university that would actually give money to poor Jewish students seemed incredible, but Joe tried to hide his surprise. "Then you're a farmer?"

"Not exactly. My family owns some land, but mainly I buy farmers' crops and then sell them to someone else. I'm what they call a middleman. I work for myself, but also for the big companies in Chicago."

"We're entirely self-sufficient," Joe said proudly.

"It's a good way to stay broke," Schwartz said dismissively. "You take all the chances, and you're lucky to turn a profit every other year. Me, I'm protected. If there's a drought, it's not my crops that get ruined. To tell the truth, the farmers I buy from spend so much time growing their food and making cheese that they don't have time to make money. I feel sorry for them."

He patted his knees. "Take my advice and go to the university." He looked disapprovingly down Main Street. "This is no place for a smart boy like you."

"Even if I'm happy here?"

"You could be just as happy in Madison and learn something useful at the same time. You might even find a nice girl." Schwartz sighed at the thought, then tapped Joe on the shoulder. "If you ever decide to come, look me up. Ben Schwartz on Mound Street. Just ask for the Greenbush. Everyone there knows me."

"Greenbush?" Joe imagined an arboretum, lush and verdant.

Schwartz smiled ironically. "It's the Jewish section of town. There's not a tree in the place, but plenty of Jews. You'd like it." And he was gone.

Joe looked in at the newspaper office, but the door was locked. Finally, he found Dorsey in the cafe, deep in thought, a half-eaten plate of food in front of him. Normally, Dorsey had a group gathered round, and punctuated silences by shouting at the cook. But today he looked worried, and Joe wondered if he was ill. "Is something wrong?" he asked, sitting down.

Dorsey moved his coffee cup around the table, rattling the saucer. "Remember I told you I had a friend, a reporter in Milwaukee?"

"The man you asked about the Moses?"

Dorsey nodded. "Right. All he told me then was the funny stuff—the girls and gambling debts. But that was it." He held up a piece of paper. "I just got another letter, and my friend tells me Kleinschmidt's been busy this winter."

Suddenly, Joe's heart was pounding in his chest. "Doing what?"

Dorsey drank some coffee and looked toward the door. He ran his hand through his short brown hair. "I think maybe I misjudged this guy." He winced in embarrassment, then continued. "Kleinschmidt's been giving speeches about the Jews. Says you're going to take over Wisconsin and turn it into a synagogue. And there was a piece in one of the Milwaukee papers about a crazy wedding at New Zion."

Joe remembered the stranger taking notes at Rebecca's wedding and wondered how many articles he had written. "I saw it," he said.

"This stuff goes over big in Milwaukee," Dorsey said. "Lots of Germans there. Anyway, Kleinschmidt's been raising money. My friend says the way this guy is, once he sees it's working, he'll keep on until the money dries up."

Milwaukee was all the way across the state, but suddenly Joe felt vulnerable. "What will he do with it?"

Dorsey shrugged. "We know he's got a big household to support. But the word is he's got bodyguards, too. Lots of them."

"A private army?" Joe said. Kleinschmidt's group sounded like the Black Hundred, mercenaries who would do anything for money and hated Jews.

Dorsey nodded. "You could call it that. They ride around in purple-and-green robes." He raised his eyebrows. "Purple because they're soldiers of God, and green because they like money." He smiled apologetically. "Sorry. I know it ain't funny, but most people treat this guy as a joke. Sometimes his crew starts fights, but mostly the Moses gets up, makes his speech, and they collect and ride away. Anyway, they're heading this way." Dorsey held up the letter. "I'm printing a story about the Moses based on this. Just to let folks know what they're in for."

"You could lose your business," Joe said.

"There ain't much to lose. If things don't get better, I'll go broke in a year anyway. Maybe this will sell some papers." He got up and stretched. "I've got to get back to the office. Stay and eat. I'll see you later."

But Joe had little appetite. America was a contradictory country. Land was free, food available, and the people open-hearted, but it also harbored Kleinschmidt and his anti-Semites. In Russia, Joe had known he would never own land, never be able to live outside the pale or enter a profession. America allowed him to hope for the world and then immediately put everything in jeopardy.

He sighed. Then he remembered his letter. The note was brief:

> Arrive Milwaukee Road February 19.
> Cahan

twenty-three

Joe arrived at the station to find that the train had come and gone, but Cahan was nowhere to be found. All week he had been anticipating the editor's visit, wondering what he had done wrong, why Cahan had decided without warning to travel a thousand miles to see him. Joe assumed it was something important. A man like Cahan, with responsibilities, couldn't just leave on a whim. Who would take care of the *Forward*? Yet despite his anxiety, Joe found the days dragging by in his eagerness to see his employer. And now he had lost the editor in the wilds of Wisconsin.

Cursing himself, Joe rushed in and out of the small waiting room and was about to ask the ticket taker if he had seen a man of Cahan's description when he saw the editor striding purposefully up Main Street. Cahan was wearing a black suit with a high white collar and pince-nez, but no hat, despite the biting cold. Joe ran out the door, waving his arms. "Mr. Cahan! I'm sorry, I was late. I was afraid you'd be lost."

The editor smiled thinly. "You weren't late, Joseph. The train was early." He pulled out a heavy gold pocket watch. "10:15," he said. "We should just be arriving." He snapped the watch shut and looked around. "It doesn't matter. I was interested in seeing the town. Usually, there isn't so much brick."

"Brick?"

"Yes," Cahan said. "The buildings." Now he gestured vaguely toward the shops. "It's unusual to see brick in the territories. Generally, the buildings are constructed of wood or, as you said in your letter, mud. Of course, here in Wisconsin you also see sandstone, or sometimes they call it Lannonstone. And in Milwaukee, that milk-white brick. It's known as the Cream City, I believe."

"I didn't know you'd been to Wisconsin," Joe said. He had hoped there would be one area at least in which his knowledge surpassed the editor's, but he now realized he had hardly noticed the buildings in town.

"I did some reading before I came," Cahan said.

Joe ducked his head, afraid the editor would start criticizing his dispatches for their lack of architectural detail. But Cahan dropped the subject as quickly as he had taken it up. He squeezed Joe's shoulder warmly. "You've grown," he said, and without waiting for a response, asked, "Where can we get a cup of tea?"

When they were seated inside the cafe, Cahan brought up Kleinschmidt. "Is this man really dangerous or just *meshuggah*?"

"I don't know," Joe said. "My friend who edits the local newspaper thinks he's harmless, a publicity seeker. But I worry about the townspeople."

"Have you had trouble with them before?"

"None. They act as if we're not even here, except when we come to town for supplies. Then they're friendly. Occasionally, we've had to borrow a plow or a horse, but we've always repaid our debts promptly, with interest."

"Then what are you afraid of?"

"I don't know," Joe said. "That's what worries me most. In Russia, we had many enemies, but no surprises. Even the pogroms weren't unexpected; usually, we were warned. Here, everyone talks about freedom—and it's true, I've never felt so free. I come and go as I like, travel where I want, do what I please. But there's something deep and violent I don't understand about America. Everyone carries guns, and it's only a matter of time before one goes off."

"You're speaking metaphorically?"

"Not entirely."

Cahan closed his eyes to concentrate. Then he opened them and drank his tea. "It's good to be cautious, Joseph, but what does your uncle say?"

"He's not worried. He says he's been here twenty years and has better things to waste his anger on."

"And what does Mr. Liberty think of all this?" Cahan asked.

"He wants to debate Kleinschmidt."

For the first time since Joe had known him, he heard Cahan laugh. It was a rich, full baritone that echoed through the room. He slapped the table and tears came to his eyes. "Excellent," Cahan said when he could speak. "Wonderful, really. Now I can see why you worry."

Joe didn't understand the editor's reaction. "Why is it so wonderful?" he said, annoyed.

"Because it is so typical—typical, that is, of a certain kind of Russian. They always want to debate, whether or not anyone wants to listen. The Cossacks could be in the street, and they would argue about which door would provide the best escape route. Are you sure this man isn't Jewish?"

Joe shook his head. "But he's serious about the debate. He thinks the people would reject Kleinschmidt if they knew more about us."

"Probably the opposite is true. The less they know, the better. But with luck, the town will ignore him." Now he looked at Joe. "And whose side are you on? What is your position? Or have you only worried and not thought? I make fun of Liberty, but at least he has decided on a course of action. That's something."

Cahan had a knack for knocking Joe off balance. But the editor was right. He hadn't really considered who was right or wrong. His instinctive reaction to conflict had always been to run. It hadn't occurred to him that there was anything he could do about it. "I suppose I've been too busy to think about that," Joe said.

"And rightly so," Cahan said. "But you are threatened, or if not that, at least aware of a potential threat. As one of the community's leaders, you should be thinking over your strategy. America is not Russia—you're right about that. We have more freedom, and so do our enemies. Kleinschmidt may not even be fully aware of what he's doing or where he's going. Still, whether he means to or not, he might set a series of events in motion that could destroy you."

Joe hadn't thought of himself as a leader before. Instinctively, he wanted to protest the editor's description of his responsibilities. Everything was happening so quickly—Cahan hadn't been in Gays Mills an hour—but he sensed Cahan was right. He had to start considering these things. "I think Mr. Kleinschmidt knows very well what he's doing," Joe said. "I think people have tended to underrate him."

Cahan seemed impressed. "Interesting. And you're obviously in a better position than I to make that judgment." He drained his cup and checked his watch again. "You say it's five miles to New Zion?"

This caught Joe by surprise. "I reserved a room at the hotel," he said quickly. "And a wagon for tomorrow."

But Cahan was scornful of such luxuries. "Who do you think you're entertaining—Rothschild? I'll stay where you stay, eat what you eat. And if you walk back and forth to town, then why shouldn't I?"

Joe looked at the editor in his woolen suit and hard leather shoes and remembered the day he had arrived in Gays Mills. Then he thought of the drafty loft in which he slept with ten others. But Cahan looked determined. "As you like," he said.

In the next week, Cahan studied every aspect of the community. He visited the forest with Abe, helped prepare meals in the kitchen, inspected the now barren garden, and showed great interest in the small canning operation. Though the soft white farmer's cheese was unfamiliar to him, he ate it with relish and spent an afternoon churning butter in a wooden barrel. His energy made Joe feel inadequate.

Morris Held, despite his angry declamations, was respectful, almost bashful, when he approached Cahan, and happy as a child when the editor remembered him. At night, Cahan sat with Shmuel, Abe, and the others in the common room and encouraged them to tell stories of life in the West, which he jotted down in small, precise handwriting in a little black notebook. One mild day, he asked permission to join Lizzie's exercise class and later pronounced the idea of women's fitness "advanced and worthy of emulation."

"Wouldn't you like to talk to Mr. Liberty?" Joe asked. The leader would be too proud to request an audience, but Joe knew him well enough to know that Liberty would feel slighted if he weren't included in Cahan's visit in some way.

Cahan demurred. "I see him at every meal. That's enough. If the leadership is sound, the people will show it in their everyday lives," he said. "But I am curious about this Dr. Briggs everyone speaks of."

"The phrenologist?" Joe said. "You don't want to see Mr. Liberty, but you wish to have your head examined?"

"Perhaps this is what I most need," Cahan said. "Could you arrange it?"

Reluctantly, Joe took Cahan to the tent that served as Briggs's office and examining room. He hadn't seen much of the doctor since their argument over Annuta, but he heard from him frequently, as dispatches were delivered to the office by the God-men daily. Briggs's messages were brief, often consisting only of page numbers from a book Joe should read, or copy for the *Investigator.*

Most recently, he had developed an interest in Mesmer, and though Joe could make no sense of it, Liberty had ordered him to print an article in which Briggs explained that animal magnetism was "based on the existence of some magnetic force, an external, visible agent that permeates the universe. Phreno-magnetism" the doctor continued,

> is the science of exciting the organs by means of animal magnetism and consists in the magnetizer passing his hands from the top of the head down the patient's face and arms, shaking them at each pass to shake off the diseased magnetism. The author has cured and been cured of headache, toothache, and neuralgia and other aches and pains by this means and urges all afflicted by such or other disorders to contact him at once through the offices of this journal.

Despite the scientific jargon, Joe didn't trust the doctor, and he was relieved that Cahan was along to act as a buffer. Briggs met them at the entrance and, beaming, offered Cahan his hand. "The esteemed editor and literary man," he announced, as if he were introducing Cahan at a banquet. "It is an honor, sir. I am J. G. Briggs. Please, come in."

Briggs swept his hand toward the entryway, and though it was unnecessary, Cahan ducked his head as he entered the tent. Once inside, Cahan straightened and returned Briggs's greeting. Joe had often wondered how Briggs and the God-men could live in tents through the bitter winter, but now he saw that the doctor's accommodations, though not luxurious, were superior to his own. Oriental rugs covered the dirt floor and hung from the lodge poles, providing both color and insulation from the wind. Low camp beds lined one wall, and in the middle of the room sat a wooden table covered with papers where Briggs had apparently been working.

A plaster skull with the various phrenological organs defined in red and numbered in a careful script stood on a pedestal atop a bookshelf. Joe moved closer to examine the skull and admire the leather bindings, but Briggs's library was not for the generalist. Joe recognized *Fowler on Matrimony,* but the others were new to him. He thought Liberty would approve of *Amativeness, or Evils and Remedies of Excessive and Perverted Sexuality.* In addition, there were bound collections of *The Water Cure Journal* and the *Yearbook* of the New York Hydropathic Institute. Looking around, Joe was impressed. Perhaps he had not given the doctor his due.

Cahan sat in an upholstered chair and Briggs faced him. "I must confess, Dr. Briggs, that I am somewhat surprised to find a man of science in the wilderness."

Briggs was wary, suspecting irony, but then he decided to take Cahan's remark as a compliment. Smiling broadly, he said, "Of course, your friend Mr. Abrams provides intellectual companionship, but I assume you are referring to my work. I only wish I could take credit for introducing Phreno-magnetism to the frontier, sir."

"You mean there are others such as yourself in this region?" Cahan said.

Briggs laughed and stroked his beard. "Not in Gays Mills, certainly, and, of course, the major establishments of the science are in the East, in Washington, New York, and London. But Wisconsin has a proud tradition in phrenology. Even fifty years ago, this territory was second only to Ohio on the subscription rolls of *The American Phrenological Journal.* And it was on a visit to Janesville that Orson Fowler himself first conceived the idea of his famous Octagon Building."

Cahan's eyes lit up at this, and Joe thought he and Briggs would confine the rest of their discussion to architecture, but the editor only said, "I see."

As they talked, two of the God-men entered and took up positions behind Joe. Though they said nothing, Joe felt trapped in the airless tent. Yet Cahan seemed perfectly at ease. "I understand you are from Oneida," he said. "Shortly after I arrived in America, I was able to tour the factory and Mansion House. I was very impressed."

Briggs was visibly moved by this. Rather than reply, he brushed his hand across his eyes and nodded without speaking.

"I must say, however, that I fail to see much resemblance between that colony and this, despite your observations in the *Investigator.*"

Sorrow vanished from Briggs's expression. He looked alert, even crafty, as he replied. "I've always been blessed with an optimistic turn of mind," he said.

"Of course," Cahan said. "Why else would you be here in the frozen winter? I wonder about your impression of the other members of the community?"

Joe decided it was a chess game, with Cahan probing and Briggs on the defensive. It occurred to him that no one else had thought to question the doctor's motives, not even Liberty. Now Joe understood what Cahan was after. If Briggs was so important, with such a distinguished lineage, why *had* he come? Liberty had been blinded by his own sense of self-importance and the money Briggs could provide. The others, well, the others hadn't bothered to wonder. People came and went on the frontier all the time. You couldn't afford to get excited about the latest arrival. Besides, the comrades reasoned, if they had come, why wouldn't others? To question Briggs would ultimately be to question themselves, and few of them were secure enough to hazard that. Cahan was under no such limitation. Looking at New Zion from the outside, he could ask the obvious question—perhaps the most relevant one of all.

"I'm not sure what you mean," Briggs said.

"I'm informed that you've examined a number of the people here."

"Some thirty-five have come voluntarily to learn how they may better exercise the faculties that God has given them but which now lie dormant. Of course, they also wish to modify those traits that are less advantageous."

"No curiosity seekers?" Cahan persisted.

"If so, they leave my office persuaded of the scientific basis of our work. Frankly, sir, I'm surprised that a man of your learning would raise the question. Surely you've read of Fowler's experiments in which he palpated the organ of Devotion and the subject lifted his hands to the Lord in prayer, or touched the organ of Combativeness only to see those prayerful hands turned into fists?" Briggs raised his eyebrows, but Cahan didn't respond.

"The great men of our age, from Ralph Waldo Emerson and Thoreau to senators and presidents, have consented to phrenological examination and testified as to its validity. Indeed, the analysis of Mr. Poe might be of particular interest to a literary man." Briggs seemed about to continue with other examples, but then thought better of it and sat back, apparently satisfied that he had made his case.

Cahan tilted his head slightly to the right and rested it on his fingers. "I was only wondering about the other comrades," he said. "Not presidents and poets."

Briggs seemed to gain confidence from this, becoming conspiratorial now. "As you know, they are unusual. Progressive, idealistic, willing to sacrifice all for their convictions. Taken together, an excellent group for research purposes." He pursed his lips. "Of course, I'm reluctant to generalize, since my work has only begun."

Cahan nodded. "Then you plan to stay on for some time?"

"As long as I am needed," Briggs said. "As long, that is, as I can contribute in some way to the community."

Cahan rose suddenly and offered Briggs his hand. "I understand that you're a busy man, Dr. Briggs. I'll take no more of your time."

Caught by surprise, Briggs raised his arms in protest, and Joe felt rather than heard the God-men move behind him. "Before you leave, Mr. Cahan, I wonder if you'd consent to a brief examination?" Cahan saw the God-men blocking the entrance but did not seem intimidated. "I am always interested in the heads of distinguished men," Briggs explained smoothly. "It is a contribution to the science of intellect."

Cahan looked quickly at Joe, but before Joe could react, he had submitted to Briggs's request. "If you wish," he said simply. "Will it take long?"

"A few minutes." Briggs pointed to a chair. One of the God-men brought a basin of water, and the doctor washed his hands. Then the other man wrapped a soiled sheet around Cahan's shoulders while Briggs took a position behind his chair. Initially, Briggs did nothing except observe the editor's shoulders and neck, first from the front and then the back. He stood in a crouching position, bent at the waist so he could better examine the line of Cahan's chin and the angle of his neck and back.

"In those with inflamed animal propensities, we often see massive muscular development here," he said meditatively, touching the base of Cahan's skull gently. "Of course, yours is most refined—perhaps, if anything, a bit underdeveloped."

Now Briggs moved around to the front of the editor's chair and placed his hands on Cahan's temples. "Are you married, Mr. Cahan?"

"Shouldn't you tell me?" Cahan said.

Briggs smiled. "I only wondered because of the absence of amatory development. Of course, I could be mistaken. Often we see more in children."

Cahan was not drawn in. "Are you sure you've found the proper gland?"

"I could not be mistaken in this. My specialty is marriage counseling."

"Then could you tell me whether you mean sexual love or simply love."

"I was not speaking of love, Mr. Cahan. Only marriage."

Cahan settled back into silence and Briggs continued his examination. He radiated his fingers forward from the base of the skull to the hairline and then back past Cahan's ears, exploring the moon of his forehead delicately, tracing lightly over the eyes before parting Cahan's hair and looking closely at the sickly whiteness of his scalp. Finally, the doctor stepped back and took a book off his desk. He opened it and showed Cahan a picture of Poe. "You recognize the poet, of course," he said in a melancholy voice. "A brilliant man whose flame was extinguished prematurely. The embodiment of the nervous temperament. The dark eyes, haunted by . . . what? We'll never know, Mr. Cahan. But we can sense just by looking at his picture the excitability of the artist in the overdeveloped areas of Sublimity, Ideality, and Imitation, not to mention the Amativeness we spoke of before, which almost drove him mad."

"Are you suggesting I have something in common with Mr. Poe?" Cahan asked. "I wish I could be so fortunate, at least as far as his poetry is concerned. But I understood you to say I was deficient in this area."

Briggs laughed, enjoying Cahan's challenge, playing with him. "Not really. Though we are all perhaps secret madmen?"

"You speak for yourself then," Cahan said sharply. "I am perfectly sane."

Briggs's small eyes glowed with anger. "What are you saying, sir?"

"It is you who should be plain," Cahan replied. "What is your real mission here, Dr. Briggs? Why should a follower of Dr. Noyes have traveled five hundred miles to encamp in an obscure gathering of Jews and Russian immigrants?"

Joe thought Briggs would reply, but the doctor checked himself and withdrew instead into a sly smile. "Is it your place to interrogate me, Mr. Cahan?"

"Why not? I consented to your examination."

Now the God-men moved behind Cahan, and Joe waited for Briggs to give the signal that would bring them down upon him, but inexplicably, Briggs relaxed, the set grin replaced by a lazy smile. Cahan had shaken him momentarily, but then Briggs had remembered: it was his tent, his commune; Cahan was the outsider.

"You did submit," Briggs drawled, "and I thank you for it, Mr. Cahan. But I was really only curious. You see, sir, I am one of the curiosity seekers you spoke of earlier. Scientific curiosity, that is. Thank you for indulging me in that."

Cahan grunted and threw off the dirty sheet. He nodded to Joe and walked to the entrance of the tent, with Briggs close behind. As they paused at the entrance, Briggs looked appraisingly at Joe. "One day I would also like to examine Mr. Abrams," he said to Cahan.

To Joe's relief, the editor offered no encouragement. He shook Briggs's hand, then turned and walked slowly away. Joe followed, feeling the hard eyes of Briggs and the god-men on his back all the way to New Zion. Cahan said nothing until they reached the door of the dining hall. Then he stopped and looked seriously at Joe. "Liberty is harmless," he said. "But I would watch that man, Joseph."

twenty-four

"So," Cahan said. They were outside the station, waiting for his train. Cahan's collar was askew and there was dried mud on his Astrakhan coat, but Joe had never seen the editor looking more cheerful.

"Did you enjoy your visit?" Joe was cold and his feet were wet. Cahan had insisted on walking along the river to observe the Kickapoo. He was a great observer and made Joe feel he had seen nothing during his time in Wisconsin.

Cahan nodded vigorously. "It is good to get out of New York. Too few of us do, and so they are able to keep us penned up like cattle in their filthy tenements. A journalist should see the world. And I'm always happy to have a story."

"A story?" Joe was surprised that Cahan had found anything worth writing about.

"Oh, yes," the editor said. "I learned something about agriculture, the Midwest, even communism and phrenology. It should make up at least two or three columns. Well worth the trip. I must confess, however, that it is not what I thought it would be when I was going to Am Olam meetings in Brooklyn twenty years ago."

"How is it different?"

"It's real. Like most young men, I was a dreamer. I imagined people living together in perfect harmony with no problems. But that wouldn't be nearly as interesting as this, and I'd have nothing to write about, would I?"

Joe smiled. "I suppose not."

Cahan clapped him on the shoulder. "Good, I've taught you something. But now it is time to get back. I have a paper to run."

Cahan's beaming enthusiasm discouraged Joe. He felt tired all the time, it seemed, yet Cahan, who was a much older man, couldn't get enough of life in the wilderness. "What did you think of Mr. Liberty?" He had persuaded the editor to see Liberty, and the two men had spent an hour together on the last day of his visit.

"A tragic man," Cahan said. "He has vision, of course, but I think it must be corrected. I only wonder if it isn't a bit late for that."

"You agree with my uncle?"

"Shmuel and Liberty have more in common than either would like to admit. No, I don't agree or disagree with Shmuel. But I understand him. I also understand Liberty. It is hard to be an idealist, Joseph; that is one burden I don't have to contend with." He hesitated, then said decisively, "It is a community question. Let the comrades decide who is right. But don't forget about Briggs."

Joe heard the train whistle in the distance. "What do you mean?"

"It is as though you are all waiting for Liberty or Shmuel or Briggs or even this Moses to do something." Cahan smiled and poked Joe's chest. "But you have the power—the people do. Why wait for someone else to change your lives? Take action! Perhaps neither Shmuel nor Liberty should lead?"

"Who, then? Morris Held?"

Cahan's heavy-lidded eyes were expressive. "Why ask me? You are all young people in a new land, why not look for new leadership? But I say no more. It's your decision. Choose among yourselves. Just don't be so afraid to be wrong."

Joe knew he was too cautious, too willing to let others take the lead. Yet it was hard not to be aware of the pitfalls. "I'll try," he said.

Cahan nodded approvingly. "And remember that if you are strong within yourselves, no outside force will be able to destroy you." To Joe's surprise, Cahan clenched his fists and gritted his teeth. "Be strong, Joseph. Individuals among you are strong. But as a group, you wander to and fro like Talmudists, hearing all sides and discussing everything, fearful of nothing so much as making up your minds."

Joe didn't feel strong, but now the editor took him in his arms and gave him a bear hug. "I talk too much. It is a disease exacerbated by age. I think I know everything. You are good people, I know that. And you are growing into a real mensch before my eyes, Joseph. I envy you."

"Me?" It seemed incredible that Cahan would envy anyone.

"Yes, you. I wish I had done as you have when I was young. I wish I hadn't been fearful. Yours is a great adventure. I have confidence in you."

The train was at the station, steam billowing from it like fog, enveloping them. Joe wanted to hold onto Cahan, to keep him there. The editor's confidence made him feel he could do all things. But two ancient men appeared with metal carts carrying baggage, and the waiting passengers prepared to board. "I'll write," Joe said.

"Of course," the editor replied. "That's what I pay you for. But I will write you as well." He looked seriously at Joe, his dark eyes warm. "And you will think about what I said, about the new leadership?"

"Yes," Joe said, not certain exactly what it was he was agreeing to.

Cahan squeezed Joe's shoulder and turned to board the train. Joe stood on the siding, watching as the brick-red cars moved past, first sedately, then gathering speed. He remained with his hand uplifted in farewell until only small puffs of smoke rising above the trees and soiling the sky were visible in the distance.

It was early, and there was work to do, but Joe felt no inclination to return to New Zion. It was as if he and not Cahan were on a journey, for he felt curiously free and anonymous. The straight metal tracks leading off to the horizon, the piles of luggage and perishable goods that lined the platform, all made him feel part of some great continuing adventure. He stood at the siding for a few minutes, reluctant to give up his fantasy, then he walked down to the cafe.

Through Dorsey, Joe had become familiar with many of the merchants in town and now felt at ease in the restaurant. By working on the paper, he had come to know the essential rituals of the people in a new way—the morning gathering to drink coffee and discuss the weather, the different groups that congregated at the lunch and dinner hours. And because he had never been in such close contact with gentiles, he found himself strangely absorbed and moved by the progress of their lives in print. He read the birth notices with hope and the obituaries with a regret that occasionally approached despair. For him, the newspaper took the place of literature and religion now, the essential terseness and brevity of its agate type serving actually to increase the power of the events it recorded.

He had been seated only a moment when Dorsey burst into the cafe and rushed over to the table, red-faced and out of breath. "Look at this," he said, thrusting a poster at Joe. Badly printed on cheap paper was the announcement:

MOSES RETURNS
CITY HALL
8 P.M.

Joe rested his head on his crossed arms. "Oh, God," he said. "He came back after all." Then he raised his head to look at Dorsey. "Are you surprised?"

"I haven't had time to think about it. I've been busy." Dorsey pulled a newspaper from his pocket and smoothed it on the table. "This is the new issue."

Joe read the headline—"MOSES OR JUDAS???"—and looked questioningly at Dorsey. "Read it," the editor said. He seemed giddy with excitement, and this worried Joe. He shrugged and unfolded the paper.

> Reports reaching correspondents of this journal indicate that Jacob Kleinschmidt, also known as the "Moses of the Menomonee," has been involved in various illicit activities in Milwaukee and Chicago and may, in fact, have been in prison in those cities. According to eyewitnesses, Kleinschmidt lives in a sumptuous mansion outside of Milwaukee, paid for with contributions to his crusades in the state. In addition, Kleinschmidt is said to have several common-law wives and to be involved in gambling and prostitution in the Metropolis. "The Moses," who visited Gays Mills last autumn, is said to be planning another appearance in town this evening at City Hall at 8 P.M.

Joe put down the paper and sat back. "Has anyone else seen this?"

"Not a soul. It won't go on sale for an hour."

"Good," Joe said. "Then there's time to destroy the whole edition. Say there's no news this week if anyone asks." His decisiveness surprised him.

Dorsey looked crestfallen. "I thought you'd be happy that someone's sticking up for you. It's all true. I spent the last week checking that story. I didn't even print everything, just the things I knew were fact."

Joe nodded. "I appreciate that. But people won't believe this; they won't want to believe it. And then you'll suffer."

"You mean you'll suffer." Dorsey was quiet. Then, "I don't care. It would be worse for that fool to come here without people knowing about his brothels back in Milwaukee."

"That would be bad," Joe said. "You're right about that. But there are worse things." He looked at his friend again, sorry that he had offended him. It took courage to defend New Zion in his newspaper, and now he was telling him to destroy the edition. But it didn't really matter. Joe knew his arguments would have little effect. Dorsey was a friend, but he was also a journalist. Like Cahan, he had a story, and now that it was in print, Dorsey would never suppress it. "Go ahead, then," he said finally. "Print everything. Maybe no one will read it."

Dorsey smiled broadly. "They'd better," he said. "I hate to be ignored."

By seven, every seat in the small auditorium in City Hall was taken. People stood against the wall and sat hunched on the proscenium at the front, leaving only a blond circle of stage around the podium for the Moses and his entourage. "Curiosity seekers," Dorsey told Joe. "Nothing else to do on a cold night. Let's go upstairs. You can't see anything from back here."

Joe nodded assent, but the crowd worried him. Outside, people pushed against one another in the muddy street, and there was a sullen, grudging quality that he hadn't noticed in the townspeople before. All afternoon, he and Dorsey had heard rumors. The Moses would be late, or he wouldn't appear at all; then, he would appear, but not tonight. He had been held up in La Crosse. Perhaps later in the week. Now, though no one had actually seen Kleinschmidt, the faithful had packed the small brick building to wait. Such devotion was impressive, whatever the cause.

When they found seats in the balcony, Dorsey began writing in his notebook. He seemed engrossed in his thoughts and disinclined to talk. Joe was too distracted to write. He stared intensely at the stage, willing the Moses not to appear, the Moses not to appear, the program never to start. When eight o'clock came and went and nothing happened, he looked upward, offering thanks for the miracle. Still no one moved.

Relieved, Joe relaxed and remembered the ancient shul in Russia where his family had gone to worship. It had been smaller than City Hall, but the crowding was the same. On the High Holy Days, it smelled of damp wool and the bad breath of a hundred fasts. Never observant at home, in America Joe had fallen even further away from Judaism. He hadn't even gone to synagogue on Yom Kippur. This wouldn't have been so bad in itself; after all, he didn't know where to go. There were Jews in Milwaukee and Minneapolis, but could there be a synagogue in La Crosse? In Russia, the faithful traveled for days to pray with a favored rabbi, but here things were different. Perhaps God would forgive his laxity. What disturbed Joe more was that he had lost the habit of penitence, of self-examination. Had he less to regret here? Had he committed fewer sins, or become spiritually pure? It was more nearly the opposite.

"Who's that?" Dorsey said, pulling Joe from his reverie. "Where?" Joe followed Dorsey's pointing finger to the floor, where Edward Liberty had suddenly appeared, accompanied by Lizzie and a handful of comrades. Their entrance was noticed only by a few townspeople seated toward the back of the hall. And when Liberty remained standing quietly by himself, they lost interest and turned away.

"It's Edward Liberty," Joe said at last.

"Who's the girl?"

"His daughter. The others are also from our community."

Dorsey nodded and resumed writing. As Joe watched Lizzie, he heard the dim beating of a drum outside and down the street. Slowly, it grew louder as the drummer moved closer and finally climbed the stairs to the hall. Joe felt his heart beating like a metronome in time to Kleinschmidt's procession.

There was a commotion in the back of the room as the drummer made his way inside. Though at first there seemed to be no room, a narrow aisle somehow appeared, and the parade approached the stage at a stately pace. Joe recognized the drummer, but his checked vest had been replaced by a purple cloak with a green cross running down the back. The beat was the same, however, resonating through the hall. Kleinschmidt followed three steps behind, accompanied by ten acolytes, all in uniform. They marched down the aisle and then made a complete circuit of the room before finally ascending the stage. Neither Crazy Dog nor the girl was there, but Joe assumed they were nearby.

Suddenly the drum ceased, and silence became a potent force in the crowded hall, eerie and impressive. Kleinschmidt stood alone, facing the crowd. He seemed taller, nearly majestic, his ears fringed by white hair. Dressed in a purple caftan and carrying a scepter, he looked like a bishop come to bless the multitudes.

"My friends," he said at last in the deceptively soft yet powerful voice Joe remembered from the preceding fall. "I did not plan to be among you again so soon. It is still winter, the season in which we keep to our homes for warmth and succor. But Satan knows no season and his enemies cannot wait for favorable weather." Kleinschmidt had a solemn expression on his face. Now he pulled a newspaper from his tunic. "No doubt many of you are familiar with this journal. It is published here in Gays Mills, and it would surprise me if the perpetrator of its lies were not in this very room tonight." Dorsey winked at Joe, pleased to be recognized.

But Dorsey's satisfaction was temporary. Now the Moses pursed his lips, causing his dewlaps to quiver and his face to turn pink. Joe could see he was working himself up to a crescendo of outrage, but then Kleinschmidt exhaled loudly and seemed to compose himself. "This article is libelous, probably actionable in a court of law, but it would be wrong to suppose that our good editor is the source of this vicious slander. No, my friends, he is nothing more than its tawdry vessel, the sewer through which such slime is flushed untreated into a Christian society. Such a man is incapable of developing and expressing original ideas, no matter how vile."

Kleinschmidt paused and looked down at the audience, as if examining them for signs of doubt. Joe was surprised he had even seen the paper. It had only been on the streets a few hours, and Kleinschmidt, by all reports, had been in La Crosse. If anything, someone might have shown it to him minutes before the speech, and, despite himself, Joe was impressed with Kleinschmidt's spontaneity. Should the Moses be serious about destroying New Zion, he would be a formidable enemy.

"Sadly, the truth is much more disturbing than that," Kleinschmidt continued. "For if it were only that a small-town editor, frustrated with the meager success he has found in the world, was reduced to attacking someone more influential than he, who would care?" Kleinschmidt shrugged his shoulders to show the extent of his disdain for Dorsey. "If that were the case, I would attribute it to envy and wish the poor man whatever peace he could find in the time remaining to him here on Earth. Such a person merits only pity, not our anger. Indeed, if such were the case, I would not even be here tonight." Kleinschmidt paused, seemingly distraught by what he had to tell these good people. "Unfortunately, as I said, our editor is the mere manservant of others far more dangerous than he. And while he is only a conduit for their pernicious theories, it is in his power to do untold damage just the same."

Dorsey seemed to shrink into the collar of his shirt during this speech, and Joe felt sorry for him. It was one thing to be a crusading journalist, or even to be punished for it, but being publicly dismissed by a consummate actor of Kleinschmidt's ability was humiliating. He patted his friend on the arm, but Dorsey didn't look over.

"Well, then," Kleinschmidt continued. "Who are these others? What is this cabal? Indulge me, my friends, while I trace for you the serpentine trail of this blasphemy to its ineluctable source." He drank from a glass of water and then looked into the crowd again. Finding no challenges, he resumed his speech.

"A few months ago, the first vile whispers surfaced in an obscure socialist newspaper in Chicago whose editorial stance is virulently anti-Christian and whose writers actually exalt their truculence. These same charges eventually found their way into the yellow press of Milwaukee, a city that has never been known for its virtue. Finally, embroidered with still more imaginative calumnies and accompanied by a squadron of half-truths to give the appearance of legitimacy, this story has appeared in your newspaper."

Kleinschmidt looked down at the floor and seemed to pull an imaginary thread from his robe. When he turned back, his face was clouded with concern. He seemed to be in pain. "I asked myself why such lies should be given currency in the press and then find a public among sick minds all across this great state. It makes one despair of mankind. But despair is not my habit, and so I thrust despondency aside and vowed to go abroad to clear my name and fight the agents of Satan."

Now he held the *Beacon-Call* aloft. "The entire publication is barely four pages in length, hardly enough space to mention all the good people who have been married, blessed with children, or passed on to a better life in the preceding week. Not enough, one would think, for news of the big city." Kleinschmidt shook his head in bemusement. "Well, folks, the fact is, your editor has an assistant. You might ask why the editor of a four-page scandal sheet would need help, or what this assistant might do." Joe felt his ears burn as he realized the abuse would not be limited to Dorsey.

Kleinschmidt shook his head, as if the whole sordid business were simply too much for a Christian to comprehend. "Unfortunately," he said, "this assistant has plenty to do. You see, he is only recently arrived from Russia. He is a member of that godless community of anarchists that squat like rodents just outside your town, living lives that can only be imagined by decent folks like yourselves."

There was a rumble in the audience, and Kleinschmidt ducked his head, a small smile on his face, ingenuous as a small boy in a candy store. But before he could continue, Joe heard a familiar voice ring from the back of the hall, just below the balcony where he sat. "Liar! Malfeasant!" Liberty yelled, his high-pitched voice tight with anger. "Blasphemer! Why don't you tell the truth about your whoremongering and white slaving? Is it the fault of socialism that you've taken the hard-earned dollars of the working men and women who come to hear you and put them to work in the flesh markets of Chicago?"

Kleinschmidt didn't appear upset by this outburst, merely puzzled. He squinted into the darkness of the hall until he located his antagonist. Then he smiled again, though more slowly this time, as if he were counting his teeth with his tongue. "The Devil has many disguises, my friends," he began, but got no further.

"Liar!" Liberty screamed, and started for the stage, displacing the faithful as he went until someone grabbed his coattail and pulled him back with several men on top of him, fists flailing.

"Hold, hold, my friends," Kleinschmidt called out. "He can do us no harm." But Liberty had introduced uncertainty into the room, and now chaos reigned as men swung wildly at each other and the din of a hundred voices drowned out the speaker. Still, the locus of it all was Liberty, and in their eagerness to get at him, men leapt over chairs and hurdled children. For a moment, Liberty gained his feet again, but then Joe saw three men in purple and green wrestling him to the floor.

Dorsey was absorbed in the battle, so Joe fought his way to the main floor alone, looking not for the leader, who was beyond help, but for Lizzie, who had disappeared in the melee. Everything was a muddle; the hall was a sea of waving arms, and the noise was deafening. It was impossible even to see the stage, for those who weren't fighting on the floor now stood on chairs. Working his way slowly along the wall, Joe looked down the cluttered aisles until finally he found Lizzie crouched in a ball, hands wrapped tightly around her head.

"Come," he shouted. "Let's get out of here."

"Yosl," she said gratefully. "Where did you come from?"

"The balcony. I got here early."

"I told him not to come," Lizzie said. "But he's so stubborn; finally, you just give in." She was crying, her voice a murmur of despair.

"I know," Joe said, putting his hands under her arms to lift her. "But come. He'll be all right." She clung to him, and he felt her soft flesh; in the midst of everything else, that was what seemed most real.

"I'm just so tired," Lizzie said.

Joe held her by the elbows and guided her. Together they made their way, slowly at first, along the wall to the stage door. But as they were about to go outside, Joe paused. He could see Kleinschmidt, just five feet away and up the stairs, having a hurried conference with his lieutenants, his caftan held daintily in one hand above the dusty stage. Behind him, the crowd had reformed around Liberty, who was now, miraculously, on his feet, his blond-gray mane clearly visible as he gesticulated toward Kleinschmidt. The leader was indomitable, Joe decided, and led Lizzie outside.

They walked to the *Beacon-Call* office, where Dorsey was already hard at work. "Great story," he said as they came in. "Nothing like it since I've been here." Then he stopped. "Who's the lady?" He smiled at Lizzie.

"This is my friend Elzbeta," Joe said. "I've told you about her. Lizzie, I'd like you to meet Bryan Dorsey."

Dorsey bowed slightly. At first, Joe thought he was mocking them, but then he saw Dorsey was perfectly sincere and resented his manners. It would never have occurred to him to bow to Lizzie. But she seemed to like it and gave Dorsey her arm as she stepped further into the office. Bryan offered her a seat next to the coal stove. "Could I get you some tea?" he asked.

"Thank you," Lizzie said, blushing slightly.

It was too much. For months Joe had tried to accommodate her, to be what Lizzie wanted him to be—a communist and freethinker. Now all it took was Dorsey's fine manners to show that what she really wanted was tea and fine conversation in the parlor. He looked into the street, where people were beginning to congregate. At least they had disrupted Kleinschmidt's rally, he thought.

Then, without warning, he heard hoofbeats, and two riders dressed in green carrying burning torches scattered the passersby and charged up the street. When they reached the *Beacon-Call,* they pulled up sharply, causing the animals to rear crazily, and held their torches at eye level, the glow reflecting in the store windows across the way.

The fire mesmerized Joe. Though he saw the men's eyes wildly searching out the building as they headed up the boardwalk, he was unable to move. He was transfixed by the spectacle, watching the orange flames darting against the night sky, insensitive to his own danger. He thought the horses walked in a strangely sedate fashion, delicately picking up their hooves and replacing them on the wooden sidewalk. Then he realized that they were coming for him—coming straight at him, in fact—and in this moment it occurred to him to warn the others, but there wasn't time. Joe reached out his arm in protest and felt, rather than heard, himself cry out. Then there was a loud crash as the window shattered and his head exploded in light.

Later, he decided he had been unconscious for only a few minutes, but it seemed like days. He had dreamt of Cossacks storming his home again and again, but this time there was no escape. They had followed him to Wisconsin, and now he must die like the rest. When he tried to rise to fight them, something held him back. Then he felt Lizzie's cool hands on his forehead and heard her soft voice. She cradled his head in her lap and bathed his face with a wet rag.

"Come, Yosl," she said softly. "Wake up, they're gone now."

"The Cossacks?"

"They are all gone. You're all right. Can you sit up?"

Joe struggled to his knees. He felt as if knives had been forced into his eyes and temples and driven out through the back of his skull. Papers were strewn everywhere and glass glittered on the floor of the shop. The press had practically been dismantled by the raiders. "My God," he said. "Did they ride their horses in here?"

Lizzie nodded. "Right over you. You're lucky you weren't killed. How do you feel?"

Joe tried to stand but the room began to move, so he sat back down. "I'm alive," he said. This was surprising and comforting. "Where's Bryan?"

"He went after them."

"Fool. He'll be killed."

"Maybe," Lizzie said, and then she laughed. "Actually, they seemed afraid. He found an ax somewhere and started waving it over his head and screaming. They thought he was mad. It was quite frightening. After all, I'd just met the man."

"Quite a mensch, isn't he?"

Lizzie stopped smiling. "What do you mean, Yosl?"

"Not only does he have beautiful manners and serve you tea, but he chased the hoodlums out of his shop with an ax while I lay unconscious."

Lizzie looked amused. "Why, Yosl, here you've nearly been trampled to death, and all you can think about is being jealous."

"Don't underrate jealousy," Joe said. "It started the Trojan War." He shook his head. "Anyway, why should I care? It's just that with your advanced ideas, I wouldn't have expected you to be attracted to an Irish newspaperman like Dorsey."

"I thought he was your friend. Anyway, what's wrong with the Irish?"

"Nothing," Joe said. "That's not what I meant." But what had he meant? Every time he opened his mouth around Lizzie, he seemed to make a fool of himself.

She took his hand in hers and kissed it. "He was nice to me, that's all. I was worried about Father and he was sympathetic. Is that such a crime?"

"I suppose not," Joe said. His head still hurt, but the furniture had stopped revolving.

Lizzie moved closer, her fair hair white in the streetlights, her skin like ivory. She put her arm around him and leaned on his shoulder. "You would have gone after them, too, if you hadn't been unconscious," she said.

"No, I wouldn't," Joe said. "I'm not as crazy as Dorsey. Getting run over is more in character."

After a moment, she said, "Oh, Yosl, what's going to happen to us?"

Joe had begun to doze off. "What do you mean?" he said sleepily.

"Don't you ever think about it? I mean, I'll stay here with Father, for now. But I don't want to spend the rest of my life at New Zion, do you?"

Joe hadn't thought about it for months. In Russia, he had dreamed of coming to America. He had never imagined being unhappy in such a place; it hadn't seemed possible. And now that he was here, he was too busy to dream. But was he happy? He didn't really know. "I suppose not," he said warily.

"What were you interested in studying?"

"Studying?" Joe was surprised by the question. His mind moved slowly, unable to adjust to sudden changes.

"In Russia. At the university."

It took enormous effort for him to call up the image of the study house, the books he had read, his life in Minsk. It seemed impossible amidst the wrecked office of the *Beacon-Call.* He worked his mind around to the question. "I told you. Many things. My father wanted me to become an agronomist, to go to Palestine."

"Yes, to be a great man. You did tell me. But what did you want, Yosl?"

She seemed totally absorbed by the question, oblivious to the ruined print shop, the commotion in the streets, the threat to their lives. It was as if Kleinschmidt's men had never broken in. Dorsey didn't exist and neither did Liberty. Drawing closer, Joe lowered his voice as if he were revealing a confidence.

"I used to imagine I'd study medicine," he said. "There was a young man from our village who went off to attend the Sorbonne in Paris. He was seventeen when he left, five years older than I, but he never came back. Someone said he came to America after he graduated, but I never knew where. Even though I hardly knew him, I used to think of joining him in practice. But that was very foolish."

"Maybe not," Lizzie said. "Couldn't you go to university here?"

"Sometimes I think it would be possible," Joe said. "At other times, not. I'd have to improve my English, and where would I get the money?"

"You'd find a way, Yosl. You're very clever."

"I?" Joe was so pleased, he didn't mind his headache. He hesitated for a moment. "It's funny, I met a man, right here in Gays Mills the other day."

"A man?" Lizzie said, not understanding the connection.

"Yes, not much older than I. But he told me the same thing—that I should go to university in Madison and not waste my time on the commune. That I would find a way to do it. He asked me to call on him if I ever go."

Lizzie's eyes were warm. "In Madison, you would become a doctor?"

Joe looked around the shop, wondering where Dorsey had gone. It was an odd time to have such a conversation, but he was glad they were alone. Chaos seemed to breed intimacy. And though it was illogical, he suddenly felt optimistic. Pulling himself decisively to his feet, he walked to the window and looked out into the night.

"Yes," he announced with authority. Then he qualified it. "If I leave, then perhaps there I will become a doctor."

twenty-five

Community meetings began at seven, but though it was nearly eight, people were still milling about looking for seats. Shmuel and Morris Held sat on the right with a small group of supporters while Edward Liberty stood alone at the front of the room, waiting, as always, for the comrades to recognize his authority and sit down.

"Poor Father," Lizzie whispered to Joe. "He doesn't understand that things have changed."

Joe nodded, but he wasn't thinking of Liberty. That afternoon, Dorsey had told him that Kleinschmidt supposedly had pledged to organize a militia that would rid Gays Mills of the scourge of New Zion, though Bryan couldn't say whether the rumor was true or not. "Then why tell me," Joe had snapped at him.

"I thought you'd be interested," the editor said. "I just report the news. Someone else said it, so it's news. Whether it's true or not is something else again."

"But you'll print it?"

"I'll report that someone claims this is so, and if I can, I'll find out whether it's true. You know you don't find truth in newspapers, Joe. That's for higher minds than ours. Philosophers and poets. We just tell people what's happening in the world."

Dorsey's insouciance irritated Joe, but he admired his friend's courage. Bryan hadn't caught up with Kleinschmidt's men, but he had spent half the night trying to put together an issue of the paper on the broken press. "Anyway, I'd be ready for them if I was you," Dorsey said as he left.

Word of the riot had spread quickly, and many of the comrades worried that pogroms would follow. Some had already packed their bags. Liberty, who had expected to return to a hero's welcome, found open hostility instead and was bewildered by the general anxiety. "Don't they see that I revealed that fellow for the fraud he is?" he asked plaintively when he met Joe in the office.

"They think you brought attention on us," Joe said. "As long as we stayed out of the way and attended to our own business, no one minded. But now we're vulnerable." He was surprised by his tone of voice. He wouldn't have imagined he was capable of instructing the leader. Without his being aware of it, the balance in their relationship had shifted.

"Did minding their own business help your parents?" Liberty asked.

"Of course not. But your appearance last night didn't stop Kleinschmidt and his thugs from destroying the *Beacon-Call* office."

"At least I stood up for our principles," Liberty replied, his thin shoulders hunched against the cold. He would wear no coat, and his lips were blue.

"Yes," Joe admitted. "And I respect you for it. That doesn't change the fact that Kleinschmidt's support is growing. We'd have no way of stopping him if he did actually organize an army and come out here."

"What about your friend at the newspaper?"

"He's stubborn. Kleinschmidt's men destroyed his press, so now he's trying to put out an edition on a hand-operated machine. You know how hard that is."

Liberty ran his hand through his hair, looking thoughtful. "So. Now the world will end, is that it?"

"Some of the comrades think so—or their part of it, at least. You have to understand that this has already happened to them once. When you've been destroyed, it becomes easier to believe it could happen again. To them, security is more important than principle."

"Yes," Liberty said. "But a leader's responsibility is to lead. It's nothing to prevail during peaceful times. It's only during a crisis that we are really tested."

They had left it at that. Liberty would assert himself, and the comrades would follow, as they always had. But tonight's gathering was rudderless; the room itself seemed to surge first in one direction and then the other as people moved about or left and then re-entered from another door. At last, Joe walked to the front of the hall and stood next to Liberty. He picked up a piece of firewood and beat it against the wall three times and then three again, calling for quiet, until at last, the crowd faced forward, unsure what to make of this usurpation of power.

Joe nodded to Liberty, signaling him to begin, as Briggs and two God-men appeared in the doorway. "Go ahead," Joe said, ignoring them. He started to return to his seat, but the aisle had closed, so he remained standing at the leader's side.

Liberty cleared his throat. "Thank you, Joseph." Then he turned to the congregation. "We are here to discuss a threat to our community," he began. But immediately Morris Held was on his feet, his thin body shaking with indignation.

"Haven't you said enough already?" Held shouted. "Who asked you to go to town and start a riot? There's a threat all right—the threat is you!"

A loud murmur of assent rose. Held remained standing, his finger pointed dramatically at Liberty. When there was relative quiet, Liberty tried again. "I went to Gays Mills as an individual," he said, "not as your representative. Certainly, I started nothing; it was, in fact, the opposite. They attacked me. Don't be deceived—Jacob Kleinschmidt's feelings toward New Zion predated his visit."

"We always got along fine before," Held persisted. "Now they got an army coming out to destroy us."

Before the crowd could react, Briggs's baritone filled the room. "Perhaps we are unfair to Mr. Kleinschmidt," he said. "After all, we've not heard him out; we don't really know what he intends, or if he intends anything. All we have are the reports of a socialist newspaper in Milwaukee. Why not give the man a chance."

"A chance to do what?" Joe said, surprised by the power of his voice. "Kill us, take over what we have worked to build?" His hands were shaking, but his voice was fierce. "Comrades, permit me. I have seen this before—not here, surely, but in my village in Russia. As the enemy grows stronger, the Jews sit and argue."

He knew he was only repeating what Cahan had told him earlier, but now he realized that it was true. "You may not agree with Mr. Liberty; I'm not sure I do. But no one can question his commitment to our community, and he's right about this Moses: Kleinschmidt has intended to destroy us for months and has made no secret of that. We ignore him at our own peril."

"You would say that," Briggs replied. "Liberty is your mentor."

Joe looked over at the doctor, fat and confident, eyes bulging in his red face, and felt only contempt for him. "I'm an individual," Joe said. "I have my own thoughts, my own ideas. And I make my own decisions. Can you say the same?"

"Explain yourself, boy," Briggs said angrily. He tried to rise, but the arms of his chair held him in place.

"Who was it that informed Kleinschmidt of our existence in the first place?" Joe cried. "Who sent him a copy of our newspaper? I know it wasn't any of us—I sent the papers out myself. I know the list of subscribers. Who caused a libelous article about New Zion to be published in Milwaukee, and who then placed an advertisement in the Gays Mills *Beacon-Call* announcing Kleinschmidt's most recent visit? The editor says the person bore a remarkable resemblance to you, Dr. Briggs."

There was an uproar in the room as people turned to face the phrenologist, whose face and neck had turned a deep purple. "Blasphemy," he cried out over the crowd's noise. "Lies and distortions."

"Very well," Joe said, holding up his hands for silence. "Then tell us the truth; it may be a new experience for you. Why did you really come here? And why do you undermine Mr. Liberty, who listened patiently to your nonsense and then welcomed you as a brother? I would be very interested in answers to these questions."

The crowd quieted, awaiting Briggs's response, but the doctor said nothing. With difficulty, he rose from his chair and stood glowering at Joe. Then, abruptly, he turned and left the hall with the God-men behind him.

An uneasy silence followed, but there were no protests. Joe was amazed at how little it had taken to finally drive Briggs out. He had thought the doctor's large following would bring the house down when he made his charges, but no one had said anything. The comrades sat looking at him obediently, expecting him to tell them what to do. Before, they had been sitting in disparate groups; now, though no one had moved, they seemed to radiate out from Joe as from the epicenter of the room. He felt taller, older, in control. "With luck," he said, "he will leave us forever. But whether he does or not, we must make plans." For what, he wasn't sure, but he didn't say so.

Held had regained his composure. "We need new leadership, that much is clear," he said.

Joe looked to see Liberty's reaction, but the leader seemed shrunken and ineffective. Held was right; Liberty couldn't lead them any longer. "Are you nominating yourself, then, Mo?"

"No, not me," Held said quickly. "I nominate Shmuel."

"The name of Sam Abrams has been put in nomination," Joe said, realizing with some surprise that he had taken charge of the meeting. The sound of his voice pleased him; he liked the formality of expression, and the slight echo that rang through the room when he spoke. Perhaps he would be a lawyer rather than a doctor, and spend his life arguing cases in court.

Lizzie stood and waited to be recognized. "There has been too much bitterness in the community already," she said. "And Father has had his part in that. But is this the time to change leaders? We are on the defensive, threatened by forces from outside. Can we afford to experiment when we are in such danger?"

Abe's deep voice boomed from the back of the room. "We've always been in danger, Sister. If you were older or a Jew, you'd understand that. We live under the constant threat of exile or death; it is bred into us, part of the milk we suck from our mothers' breasts. We eat each meal knowing it may be our last. This is not ideal, of course, but it is all we have ever known. I don't share my friend's opinion of your father. Liberty is a good man and has worked hard. He has his own ideas, but who among us would persecute a man for that? Still, there is no denying that without a mandate from the community, he has brought this Kleinschmidt down upon us."

Before anyone could respond, Liberty was on his feet. "I did nothing," he screamed. "The man *came* to Gays Mills intending to destroy us, don't you see that?"

Calmly, Abe stood to face Liberty across the crowded room. "Fair enough," he said. "But who supported him before last night? We've been here for years, buying from the stores in Gays Mills, causing no trouble. By attacking him, you made him sympathetic, and the people showed that when they jumped you. Mo is right," Abe said decisively.

Liberty wasn't finished. He shook his fist at Abe. "I've given my life to this movement," he said. "I have starved and worked harder than any man for its success. I won't step aside now. I won't resign." He swiveled around, his nervous eyes scanning the crowd for signs of support, but no one spoke. Some looked away, avoiding him. At last, he turned and walked to the door. Then he held out his hand in Lizzie's direction. For a moment, she hesitated.

"Come, Elzbeta," Liberty said. "We're not wanted here." Lizzie nodded her head obediently, and together they left the meeting.

There was a charged silence in the vacuum created by Liberty's departure. He hadn't resigned, but he had gone, which amounted to the same thing. Finally, Joe spoke. "Are there other nominations?"

For a moment there was nothing, and Joe wondered if Liberty had, by leaving, stolen the meeting's momentum, upstaged them all again. Then Abe said, "I nominate Joseph Abrams to lead us through this difficult time."

There was an audible gasp in the hall, followed by a sigh, as if a door had been closed. The comrades turned to question one another, craning their necks to look first at Joe and then at his uncle. Joe was speechless. Flattered by Abe's proposal, he nevertheless felt presumptuous opposing Shmuel. He imagined the discussion that might go on among the comrades if he were not there.

"He is young," a comrade would observe.

"We need the energy of youth at times like these," his friend would answer.

"But he has no experience!"

"Experience," the first would say with disdain. "Look where experience has led us. Perhaps we need innocence."

"But he is Shmuel's nephew."

"Exactly. That is the genius of it. For he is also Liberty's secretary and his daughter's lover."

"Ah, then you would compromise, comrade? I prefer passion."

"Why not, then, passionate compromise?"

"Is such a thing possible?"

"That is what we shall see."

Now, as if understanding the awkwardness of Joe's position, Shmuel stepped forward. "Is there a second?" he said in a hoarse voice.

"I second the nomination." Joe turned to see Annuta standing, her face flushed, eyes shining.

"Good," Shmuel said. "Then we must have discussion of the nominations. Before you start, however, let me say that I'm withdrawing my name. I prefer to support my nephew, Joseph Abrams."

There was considerable nodding and talking, though Joe wondered what discussion there would be now that his was the only name in nomination. Then Ben Levis, Rebecca's husband, stood to speak. Pale and attenuated, Ben had never spoken before, but now, despite a slight stammer, he was determined to oppose Joe.

"I have nothing against Joseph Abrams personally," he began. "Nor his uncle, and certainly not Mr. Liberty. But I do not like the way Dr. Briggs has been treated tonight. In the months he has been here, most of you have visited his tent for consultations, and many have profited from them. The fact that he may have known or corresponded with this Kleinschmidt is of far less importance than the good he has done among us. Both my wife and I have received important advice from Dr. Briggs, with the result that we are now expecting a child, a gift from God. Therefore, I nominate J. G. Briggs to lead our community."

There was tumult in the hall. Shmuel, Held, and Abe were talking furiously among themselves, but Joe couldn't make out what they were saying. Finally, Abe rose and waited for the furor to subside. He twisted his gray fringe of beard like a rabbi and stared fixedly at the ceiling, as if waiting for it to open and God to appear. When he began to speak, his eyes remained focused on the rafters, as if he were working his way through a difficult passage in a commentary. "Are we committed to self-destruction?" he asked. "Is there truly no other way for us? Even when we say we are no longer Jews but communists, we suffer from the same paralysis. We are as intent on argument as scholars in a study house. I don't say Dr. Briggs is evil—let God decide that. I wouldn't even say he has done nothing of value here; those who have consulted him would know better than I. If, as my young friend says, he and his wife have been helped, then I'm satisfied that Dr. Briggs's stay among us has been good for New Zion.

"But this is not the issue. Whether or not Briggs has done good in the past, it is clear that he has chosen to ally himself with Jacob Kleinschmidt, a man whose purpose is to destroy us. Therefore, our choice is simple: do we participate in our own ruin, or shall we fight the invaders? I can assure you that this peril will no more disappear than did the Black Hundred. But the result need not be the same. This is a new land; let us show a new determination to resist. I vote for Joseph."

Before there could be further discussion, Shmuel said, "Abe's right. I vote for Yosl. We need new blood, and he seldom agrees with me about anything, which should recommend him to some of you."

Like a huge wave, hands rose across the hall, and in the end it was all but unanimous, with only Ben and Rebecca sitting alone in angry silence. Yet even an hour later, sitting alone with Lizzie, Joe remained stunned.

"Are you the new leader, then?" she asked.

Joe nodded, and Lizzie had thrown her arms around him. "I had to leave with Father," she whispered. "He's so disappointed. He feels he is in disgrace."

"Of course," Joe said, with a confidence he didn't really understand. "Where is he? I'll go speak to him."

"Not now." Lizzie smiled again. "I want to be with you now."

Joe nodded. "It's a good thing you left. I think Morris was going to nominate you."

"Perhaps we could rule together?"

"I would be honored," Joe said. "It's absurd, really. I know nothing about agriculture. Nothing."

"That doesn't matter."

"But this is an agricultural commune."

"Exactly. If they'd wanted a farmer, they would have elected Yitzhak or Schlomo. We need someone who can unite us. You have friends in town, you speak and write English, and the other comrades like you. You're the perfect leader, Yosl."

"Of course, you might be prejudiced. In fact, I hope you are."

Lizzie smiled, her teeth white and beautiful. "It's only that I've had the opportunity to better appreciate your fine qualities."

Joe shook his head again at the strangeness of it all. "I wonder where Briggs has gone. His tents have disappeared. He always wanted to examine the two of us," Joe said wistfully. "To see if we were compatible, he said. But I think he was really interested in you."

Lizzie shivered. Then she kissed Joe. "Do you need more proof?"

Joe look at her and felt enormously fortunate. Leaders needed luck as much as wisdom. "It is enough," he said. "More than enough."

twenty-six

"So now you're a politician, just like Herzl." Dorsey was smiling, having fun with Joe. "It's not enough to report the news, you want to make it?"

"I'm not a politician," Joe said. He settled back in his chair and enjoyed the warmth of the fire after his walk from New Zion. "Anyway, who would want to publish anything about a community as small and insignificant as ours?"

Dorsey was reading proof for the latest edition, which was headlined "MOSES'S MARAUDERS WRECK PRESS!" He looked at Joe with new respect. "That's what all the best ones say—'Who me? Nothing interesting about me.' I underestimated you, Joseph. I apologize. You should have a bigger job."

Joe laughed. "This is enough for me. But you know what I mean. We're just a small group out in the wilderness. What's so important about that?"

Dorsey shrugged. "Ask your boss, Cahan. The Milwaukee papers might even be interested, since it involves Kleinschmidt. Watch out, or you'll get famous."

"God forbid. That's what got us into trouble in the first place."

"You mean the newsletter?"

Joe felt uncomfortable criticizing Liberty in Dorsey's presence. Perhaps he was becoming a politician. "That and other things," he said vaguely.

In the street, Kleinschmidt's men stood in groups along the boardwalk. They looked oddly ceremonial in their gowns, as if they were on their way to a banquet. Joe wondered if they shouldn't have less formal robes for everyday wear. What did they put on when they chopped wood or carried water? "What are they waiting for?" he asked.

"Who knows," Dorsey said. "Maybe reinforcements. The way Kleinschmidt talks, he must think you've got an army out there."

"Some army. Thirty-five men armed with axes and spades. The rest, women and children. We have ten knives and five guns, but almost no ammunition. That's our entire arsenal, Bryan."

Dorsey whistled softly. "I won't print it. Just hope they don't come."

"I heard Kleinschmidt called another meeting for tonight," Joe said.

Dorsey nodded. "The talk is he wants to go out to New Zion from there."

Joe looked out at the street. The men were lounging in the winter sun, oblivious to him. A woman walked by, swinging a straw shopping basket, averting her eyes from the loafers. A wagon passed. It was all so maddeningly ordinary. Yet Joe knew that even as some people lay dying, others were going quietly about their business, drinking coffee, arguing over trifles. That was the way of the world. Even God didn't demand that all suffer simultaneously. "At least it'll be dark," he said.

"Yes," Dorsey said. "You've got that going for you."

Joe walked the length of the town looking for Lizzie. They'd come together and agreed to meet for lunch, but she was nowhere to be found. It didn't matter; he was glad for the solitude. He had to plan now that others were relying on him to foil Kleinschmidt. He wondered what he could learn from Liberty's mistakes.

A crowd had gathered at the end of Main Street. For lack of anything better to do, Joe joined them. They were all looking intently at the river, and it was only after someone pointed it out that Joe realized the boat jetty had disappeared.

"It's still rising," a man said. "Two feet since yesterday."

"Rising?" Joe said.

"The river, man. It's been high since January, and now it's flooding."

How could one be unaware of something as catastrophic as a flood? Joe had always imagined huge tidal waves overwhelming buildings, washing out cities, driving people in terror-stricken masses before the rampaging waters. Something cataclysmic, biblical, in its impact. But this seemed gentle; no one could possibly have been overrun by the lapping river at his feet. It was only when he noticed the absence of familiar landmarks that he realized the man was right. While they had been worrying about Kleinschmidt, the Kickapoo had silently invaded their lives, and now the town was in danger. Looking back at the buildings on Main Street, Joe saw what he had missed before: the brown mud stains of previous years' floods at various heights on the walls. "What will you do?"

The man's eyes crinkled with amusement, as if he were talking to a child. "Why, build dikes, of course, hold it back best we can. What would you do?" Then, as he seemed to be an official of some sort, he turned to the others standing around them. "How many men have I got here to work?"

A few hands went up; others turned to examine the water, trying to determine the seriousness of the flood. "I can offer thirty-five hard workers," Joe said.

The man turned sharply, as if he thought he were being mocked. "All as big as you, mister?"

"Some bigger, some smaller. All good, hard workers."

The man squinted at the gray sky, hands on hips. Then he looked back at Joe. "Who the hell are you, anyway?"

"Joseph Abrams. I'm the leader of the New Zion community."

"The Russians," the man said to himself. "And you say you have thirty-five men out there?"

"With women to cook for them and the others," Joe said.

Now the man smiled broadly and extended his hand. "Welcome to you, then, Mr. Abrams. I'm Tom Jensen. For what it's worth, I'm mayor of this mess."

Shmuel was unenthusiastic. Joe found him in the kitchen, kneading flour. "What's the matter with you, Yosl?" he said, wiping his hands on his apron. "This Cossack's about to ride out here and murder everyone, and suddenly you want to do a *mitzva?* We've got to figure out how to protect ourselves. Let the people in town worry about the goddamned flood."

"That's exactly what I'm trying to do," Joe said. "We can't fight the Moses—not now, not yet. What chance would we have with a few spades and hoes?"

"At least we wouldn't humiliate ourselves," Held put in.

"What's so humiliating about helping our neighbors? Anyway, the Moses can't recruit men to invade us if they're all digging trenches and building dikes."

"The boy's right," Abe said. "All that education wasn't wasted. Besides, the people are less likely to turn on us if we help save their homes."

"That's what the *maskils* thought, and look what happened to them," Shmuel said. "After they spent years organizing and starving in the villages, the peasants couldn't find enough Jewish throats to slit."

"This isn't Russia, Sam."

"So you say," Shmuel intoned glumly. "So you say."

Joe prepared to leave. "Stay here if you like, Uncle. I'm going to town."

"I'd prefer not to die alone," Shmuel said, shouldering his pack. "Being young and idealistic is no crime. But you'll learn not to expect gratitude from the people you help. Meanwhile, you're my nephew, and this family will stay together."

From his post behind the dry goods store, Joe could feel the panic that gripped the town. He continued to stack flour sacks filled with sand on the growing wall, but it was only when he looked to his left and saw large maples sticking out of the brown water that he truly realized the seriousness of the situation. The water was now a mere ten feet from the Main Street buildings, and merchants were piling their goods on wagons or carrying them to second-floor living quarters. Boys in boats floated past, yelling to one another, excited by the danger, while women cooked soup over open fires that had been laid in the street. Up and down the row of laborers, comrades stood next to townspeople, filling bags and adding to the dikes. With satisfaction, Joe noted that his people were indistinguishable from the Americans in the spreading darkness.

Shmuel's predictions hadn't come true. The townspeople had accepted them eagerly and with enthusiasm. There had been neither repercussions nor hostility. There wasn't time. When he turned back to his work, Joe saw Dorsey had joined him.

"No sign of the Moses," he said. "I've been all over town. He was in a suite at the hotel, but they say he checked out and took his gang with him."

Joe nodded. He wasn't yet confident, but he felt better than before. If Kleinschmidt did come, at least they'd be less vulnerable here than if they were all clustered together at the commune. Still, he doubted the Moses had gone. Unsuperstitious about most things, Joe still felt Kleinschmidt's malevolent presence. And even if he had decided to take his men and ride away, it was always best to plan for the worst.

In a sense, Joe wanted the Moses to attack; he wanted the challenge, the experience. He had always walked away from fights before, but now he was eager for battle. His plan wasn't foolproof, but at least they had taken the offensive. Instead of sitting out in the country and waiting, they had come to meet the enemy. If they escaped this crisis, they would be better prepared for others in the future.

The first rider thundered into town around eight. Joe was drinking tea with Lizzie when he appeared, dressed in green and carrying a blazing torch. Then, abruptly, riders were everywhere, surrounding the workers with fire, forcing everyone to stop and gaze at the spectacle. In the darkness, it was impossible to tell Jew from gentile; all were covered with mud and exhausted from their labors. Mesmerized, the townspeople dropped their tools to stare.

Kleinschmidt rode to the head of the column, resplendent in a purple cloak and headdress and riding an enormous white stallion. "People of Gays Mills," he cried out, raising his torch. "We want only the anarchists who have cleverly insinuated themselves among you."

Joe calculated their chances. The Moses had perhaps twenty men, not an overwhelming number. But they were mounted and armed. No doubt they were also experienced fighters, recruited for that purpose. The comrades were strong but untrained. They would fight with more passion than skill.

"Step back and let the vermin reveal themselves," Kleinschmidt roared.

A few men shuffled in place, but before anyone could move, Tom Jensen was at the front, tall and blond, his face red with anger. "Mister," he yelled. "I haven't got time for this nonsense, and neither do my men. We're trying to save our homes and businesses from a flood, and you're all decked up for a fancy dress ball, scaring people. These Russians came here to help us while you were drinking wine in the hotel. Now, you want to fight so bad, you come on down and fight me." Jensen raised a large fist and shook the bridle of Kleinschmidt's horse so hard the stallion reared, almost throwing the Moses into the street.

The townspeople closed ranks behind Jensen now. "People of Gays Mills," Kleinschmidt began again. "Do not be intimidated—" But he got no further before Jensen grabbed his torch and waved it in the horse's face. Terrified, the animal reared again, throwing the Moses into the mud, where Jensen towered over him.

"I told you once," the mayor said. "And this is the last time. Either you and your boys leave, or I'll throw you in jail to think it over."

Several of Kleinschmidt's men went to their leader's aid, and finally he stood shakily on his feet, his caftan covered in mud, his headdress gone. Pale with anger, the Moses looked for his horse, but the animal had disappeared. He glanced at the mayor with hatred before climbing up behind one of his lieutenants. From this height, he was able to regain some of his dignity. "I will return," he said haughtily.

"Sure you will," Jensen said. "After the work's all done. That's your style. Come on, men, show's over." And he walked away, leaving Kleinschmidt looking foolish in his mud-stained cloak. Now Joe saw that Dr. Briggs was among Kleinschmidt's band. He raised his hand in a mock salute to the phrenologist, but Briggs's eyes were set on the horizon. At a signal from the Moses, the men circled their horses and rode out of town.

Joe watched them go. Somehow, the hurried retreat left him feeling unfulfilled; things had been resolved too easily, without enough struggle. But this feeling was quickly replaced by relief. Lizzie put her arm around his shoulders. Her hair was held in place by a red kerchief, and her face was streaked with dirt. Except for her blue eyes, Joe thought, she almost looked Jewish.

"At least that's over," she said.

"We'll be seeing them again." Despite Jensen's courage in turning Kleinschmidt back, Joe knew there were people in town who supported the Moses. The flood had given them time to prepare a better defense, that was all.

"For now, then," Lizzie said. "Why can't we relax and feel victorious for a day or two?"

"Victorious?" Joe said quizzically. Was this the way great warriors felt after battle? "Who have we defeated? Who have we even fought?"

"You fought with your mind, Joseph. That's just as important."

Joe wasn't so sure. This was the way Jews had always comforted themselves: "We were thoughtful, more serious. We didn't resort to violence to solve problems." But they had learned that conflict was inevitable and that their enemies were unimpressed by their wisdom. "In a way, we did," he said finally. "Thanks to Jensen. Next time we may not be as fortunate. But for now, all we have to worry about is the flood."

twenty-seven

The water rose another foot during the night. By noon it was six inches higher. From the loft of the *Beacon-Call* office, where he had slept, Joe could see the river spreading across the foot of Main Street, a brown blot clear to the horizon, encircling the tiny houses and stores. As smaller communities upriver had flooded, people had gravitated to Gays Mills, where hundreds were now camped in City Hall and the Methodist church. Periodically, rafts floated by, outfitted with makeshift tents for shelter, fishing lines and smoke from cooking fires trailing in their wake.

All night, people had manned the dikes, trying in vain to restrain the river, pulling back and then resetting their lines ten feet behind, only to retreat again, inevitably, doomed soldiers in a natural war. The Kickapoo lolled lazily against the wooden walls of the buildings, large and arrogant in its effluence, disdainful of the pitiful efforts of the townspeople to hold it within its banks. Now the junk of a dozen townships floated half submerged on its dirty surface as the river made its way leisurely through the town like a Saturday-morning shopper.

"Coffee?" Dorsey called out from below.

Joe shook his head, then was aware of a sudden, responsive movement as Lizzie retreated further beneath the blankets.

Dorsey appeared at the top of the ladder and winked at Joe. "Shy, ain't she?" He put two clay mugs on the floor. "It's okay, miss, I'll go back downstairs."

Lizzie lifted the covers now. They had never spent the night together before, and Joe hadn't known what to expect. But the disarray of her hair and red sleep spots on her cheek and forehead made her even more attractive. She took the coffee cup in both hands and shivered slightly. "I wonder where Father is," she said.

They had left Liberty and a few others to watch the commune. Since Joe had become leader, he had seen little of his mentor, though as far as he knew, Liberty bore him no ill will. In fact, he had seemed relieved that the community had not elected Shmuel in his stead. They were both busy, Joe told himself. He would make it up with Mr. Liberty later. "Are you worried?"

"Not exactly. Father can take care of himself. I'm just used to seeing him in the morning. It feels funny to be alone."

"You're not alone," Joe reminded her, but he knew what she meant. He remembered his mother bent over the morning fire, his father in his undershirt, drinking coffee, and wondered when he would stop missing them. "Do you want to go back?"

Lizzie looked annoyed. "Of course not. We've got to help these people. Come on." She stood up, naked and beautiful in the bright light. Then she noticed him. "Stop looking at me that way, Yosl. We don't have time."

The street was full of rearing horses, wagons mired in mud, and crying children. Joe and Lizzie walked to City Hall, where Annuta and Rebecca were serving oatmeal from a large cauldron to an unending line of refugees. Sitting at one of the wooden tables was Edward Liberty, writing in a small notebook.

"Father," Lizzie cried. "I thought you were at home."

Liberty looked up and smiled. "I was, until the water came inside my cabin. Then I thought it would be prudent to leave. Ben and Rebecca were kind enough to accompany me."

"What are you writing?" Joe asked.

"Just something for the next issue of the *Investigator*. I am still editor, aren't I?" Liberty's pale gray eyes were neutral, but it was a real question.

"Of course."

Liberty nodded. "Well, then, it's about our recent encounter with the Moses. Did you know he paid us a visit last night?"

"At New Zion? But they were here, in town," Lizzie said.

"Must have been after that, or before. Doesn't matter."

"What did they do?" Liberty's mysterious good humor annoyed Joe.

"Do? Oh, nothing really. They rode around waving their ridiculous firebrands but succeeded only in burning their robes. They threw one or two torches our way, but with the flood, the last thing we were worried about was fire. Some younger men went to confront them, but they had gone. Cowards, as I always suspected."

Liberty looked at Joe and licked his lips. "I can't see why everyone was so concerned. We drove them off with a handful of men."

"Father, that's wonderful," Lizzie said.

"I was quite pleased," Liberty admitted. "Especially considering all that was said about my inadequacies as a leader."

Joe felt defensive, as if driving Kleinschmidt off and holding the commune was Liberty's way of undermining him, but he knew this was absurd. "Perhaps the comrades made a mistake," he said. "I wouldn't stand in your way."

"No, no," Liberty said, waving him away. "I am perfectly content as I am, Joseph. It's a job for a younger man."

Now Annuta appeared at Joe's side. "Here. You must eat, Yosl." She handed him a bowl of cereal. There seemed to be no guile in her, no resentment of Lizzie or of his prolonged absence. Her brown eyes were warm and liquid, her smile sincere. He followed her to a table.

"You're very kind," Joe said when seated.

"That's what you always say."

"Only because it's true."

Annuta shrugged and smiled again, embarrassed by praise. "You can't stay up all night working and then forget to eat. You'll get sick."

Joe watched Lizzie and her father walk off toward the hotel. He sipped the gruel and watched Annuta work. She could have been one of his sisters, grown up now, with her kerchief and dark eyes. He had never minded their attention, and he was grateful now for hers.

Dorsey joined him a minute later. "Who's the girl?"

"Annuta? She lives with us at New Zion."

"An embarrassment of riches." He looked at Joe critically. "Tell me, Abrams. You're an ordinary enough fellow—not tall, not short, not bad looking, but certainly not handsome. Yet you have two beautiful women following you around."

Joe smiled. "A leader must know his comrades," he said. "You can understand that, can't you, Bryan?"

"Sure," Dorsey said wistfully. "I just wish they'd look at me the way they look at you, that's all."

Joe was about to answer when the bell on the old fire engine started clanging again, calling for a new shift of men. Without finishing his oatmeal, he grabbed his jacket and ran off to pile sandbags.

The water peaked the next morning. By nightfall the river had fallen back nearly to its banks, and the townspeople moved their furniture back into their homes. After three days of cleaning, it was as if the flood had never occurred, and Kleinschmidt was only a bad memory.

There was only one significant change. Liberty made no move to reoccupy his shack, preferring instead to sleep in the second-floor bunkhouse with the other men. After a respectful waiting period, Joe moved in, and nothing was said by either man.

twenty-eight

The day is different from the night. Each morning, the comrades are waiting when you open your door; in the evening, you sleep alone in your room without the comforting nightsounds of your friends' breathing to lull you. Having always followed—first your father, then the melamed at cheder, the professors at university, and finally Liberty—you are now expected to lead. The habit of a lifetime is difficult to break.

You try. You understand that others are depending on you to tell them where to go, and you surprise yourself by knowing. This assumed certainty becomes narcotic; the confidence of others makes you even more self-assured. Though you have only recently begun shaving, you start cultivating a beard, hirsute wisdom being better than none, and at times, you wonder if there is anything you don't know, anything you can't do. Then you remember who you are and feel embarrassed.

And even as the comrades have raised you above them, you find that this new height distances you from your old friends. It is awkward now to visit with your uncle, for it is he whose rightful place you have taken. You wonder whether to join the group in his shack in the evenings, and then chastise yourself for wondering. You go and feel Shmuel's mixed pride and sadness, and leave early and return alone to your room, resenting the loneliness that has settled upon you.

At midnight, without warning, Lizzie comes, and you make love with quiet determination, neither speaking until later, when you sit in candlelight and drink tea. Without agreeing to it, you do not acknowledge each other otherwise; you are even more discreet than before, and you wonder who you are protecting. In silence, the visits become even more intense and private.

You wake early and watch as the sky turns pink, then red-orange. You drink your tea and think about the day. You wonder if things will continue like this—and whether you want them to. You know it is important to plan, but you don't know what you are planning for. You try to remember the Talmud, to imagine what the rabbis would have said, but your mind has become willfully irreligious.

Alone in the early morning, you feel a quiet pride in your accomplishment, in the changes in your life, and you think then that it is worth the loneliness, the isolation. That it is better this way. Necessary, perhaps even desirable. It is better to lead than to follow, better to take responsibility than to passively accept what life offers you. Better. Then, after sitting alone all night, you open your door to the first comrade, and the day begins.

twenty-nine

He was working when there was a knock at the door and Lizzie stuck her head inside. "There's a man out here who wants to see you," she said. "A new man."

"Send him to my uncle," Joe replied. He had reorganized the group, giving Shmuel responsibility for recent arrivals.

"I told him that already, but he insists. He says he knows you."

"That's ridiculous," Joe started to say, but thought better of it. What if Cahan had refused to see him? "Send him in, then." Joe continued to study his papers.

"I have come to join the revolution." Joe recognized the hoarse voice and looked up to see Hayim Goldman. Then they were in each other's arms, performing a kind of dance in place. Finally, they stood apart, grasping each other's forearms.

"How in God's name did you find me?" Joe asked. "I meant to write, but there was never time."

"Find *you*?" Goldman's eyebrows arched in surprise. "That was no problem. You are now a famous man, Yosl. Everybody knows about you and this place." He gestured vaguely outside. "Even in Hamburg, I read your letters in the *Forward*. I asked myself, 'What is so wonderful that I'm staying here?' The answer was, "Nothing." So I came to America, and Mr. Cahan told me what Wisconsin was."

"You mean where?"

"Both. To tell you the truth, I had no idea what I was going to find here. I couldn't even imagine such a place. But I wanted to see you." He squeezed Joe's arm. Then he slapped his forehead. "Ach, I forgot. He gave me this for you."

Joe placed the envelope on the desk. "That can wait. Tell me about yourself. I thought you were going to stay in your friend's wonderful house."

"I stayed long enough, believe me. Look!" Hayim stepped back, hands on his hips. He looked healthier to Joe. The creases in his face were gone; his color was restored. He wore an expensive suit and carried a beaver hat.

"You look wonderful," Joe said. "Like a rich man. A lawyer or a doctor."

"Exactly," Hayim said. "For a year I ate well, slept in a feather bed with soft pillows, and lived like a gentile. All white bread and sausages. The trouble was I felt like an impostor. I didn't deserve all that, or even want it. I was always afraid I would be found out and sent back to prison in Russia."

"Who would find you out?"

Hayim shrugged. "I don't know. Myself, maybe. Anyway, when I read of your community, I decided to come. In Russia, revolution is a foolish dream. In America, perhaps it is possible. After all, you've already had one."

Now Joe noticed Lizzie standing awkwardly in the doorway. "You must meet my friend, Elzbeta Liberty," he said. "Without her, I'm nothing here."

Goldman bent over Lizzie's hand. "Enchanté," he said, and Lizzie blushed. He winked at Joe. "A beautiful girl."

"You're having visions," Lizzie said. "You must be hungry."

"Smart, too," Goldman said approvingly. Then, to Lizzie, "I could eat." But he made no move to leave.

Joe broke the stalemate between them. "Take Hayim over and introduce him to my uncle. I'll meet you in a few minutes."

Goldman looked hurt at being dismissed, then shrugged ironically. "So many responsibilities for one so young," he said, and followed Lizzie out of the room.

When they had gone, Joe opened Cahan's letter and spread it on the desk, enjoying the sensation of resistance, as if the paper's starchy creases were a measure of the editor's personality. Then he began to read.

Dear Joseph,

I must admit that when I urged you to demand more of your leaders, I did not expect you to become one yourself. You are very young to hold such a post, but then I came to the *Forward* at an even earlier age, so I am in no position to object, even if I were disposed to do so, which I am not. *Mazel tov!* I hope your new office suits you, that you do justice to it, and that the result is that the community prospers under your leadership. I believe it will.

Now, I have less pleasant news to pass along. On my return from Wisconsin, I took it upon myself to conduct a private investigation of your Moses and our friend Dr. Briggs. From what I have learned, they are associated with a loose confederacy of anti-Semitic and racist organizations calling itself the White Christian Legion. That they are not very Christian in their treatment of Jews and others has given rise to the belief among some that they are similar to the Black Hundred and must be dealt with in a similar fashion. But they are not really the same at all.

Exaggeration cannot help us fight our enemies, though it is certainly understandable. The Legion is viewed with disdain by many—if not most—Americans who know of its existence and has been more often harassed than assisted by the government. The Legion's size is a matter of conjecture, but this should not lead us to take it lightly. At best, Kleinschmidt and his followers will attempt to arouse the citizenry against you, break your windows, and destroy what property they can. At worst, these people are capable of all the depredations of a lynch mob.

Our friend Hayim believes they are part of what he calls the International War Against the Jews. He has historical reasons for feeling as he does, and I understand them. But I hope you will have a more reasoned view, a more moderate one, and take appropriate action. That the American government does not support the Legion does not mean that you will receive assistance in your battle. America prides itself on its many freedoms. Among these is the freedom to campaign openly against those who would destroy you. Thus the Legion is also free to vilify the Jews, impugn us in the minds of our gentile neighbors, and encourage fear and misunderstanding.

I will not presume to advise you in this, but I did want you to know about it. Again, *mazel tov,* Joseph. You are my best pupil and as close to a son as I shall ever come. Be strong, but more important, be wise.

Cahan

thirty

"Patzer," Shmuel roared. He took a long swallow of cider and passed the jar across the table to Hayim Goldman.

Joe looked hopelessly at the chessboard. His mind had wandered, and now he saw clearly the trap Shmuel had created for him. It was checkmate in two moves, or at best three. Joe had hit upon the idea of having Goldman room with his uncle, and the two men had become inseparable. But though his guilt about Shmuel had eased, Joe's chess game had not improved, despite his nightly visits. He looked over at Goldman.

"I see you've developed a taste for my uncle's cider, Hayim."

Goldman smiled. "Shmuel is my *lehrer.* From him, I will perhaps learn to be an American."

"You've chosen an unusual model."

"Ah, yes. But original," Goldman said.

"Quit delaying, Nephew," Shmuel interrupted. "Make your move."

Joe raised his hands in resignation. "I have no move and you know it. I resign." He turned a pawn over on the board.

"A leader should never admit defeat, Yosl," Goldman said disapprovingly.

"I'm not much of a leader," Joe said. "I have no program. I'm no visionary; I don't inspire people or have a philosophy. I'm a realist, that's all."

"In a place like this, that's not so bad," Shmuel growled.

"Thank you, Uncle. That's the nicest thing you've said to me in weeks."

Shmuel laughed and raised his glass just as Bryan Dorsey came in the door. "Trust an Irishman to find the liquor," he said.

Bryan smiled and took off his hat. "My people wouldn't call this liquor," he replied.

"There's something to that," Shmuel said, and poured Dorsey a cup.

Since meeting Annuta, Dorsey had become a regular visitor to the commune, and though Joe knew he had no right to screen Annuta's suitors, he found he resented Dorsey's attentiveness. He felt protective and on occasion had stationed himself in the same room with the couple as an uninvited chaperon.

Hayim, who knew nothing of this, had taken an interest in the romance. "And how is the young lady this evening?" he asked.

"Annuta's fine," Dorsey said quickly, attempting to change the subject. "I came to show you this." He took a piece of paper from his pocket and handed it to Joe. It was a yellow handbill:

DR. J. G. BRIGGS, Specialist in the
Arts of Phrenology and Hydropathy,
late of the communities of Oneida and
New Zion, now of Milwaukee, offers his services
IN CONSULTATION
May 15–17
Hotel Kickapoo
Gays Mills
ALL ARE WELCOME

Shmuel read the handbill and spat into the dirt. "The old fraud must be short of money again," he said. "Where did you find this?"

"They were put up overnight. No one knows who posted them."

"At least it doesn't mention the Moses," Joe said.

"That doesn't mean anything," said Dorsey. "Briggs could be an advance scout."

"Scout what? He lived here for three months. He knows everything there is to know."

"Perhaps we are making things more complicated than they are," Hayim said. "Maybe this man has gained a following, and now he wants to capitalize on it."

"The trouble is his following is here, among the comrades," Joe said.

"There's nothing to be done about that, Nephew. We can't stop Briggs from coming to Gays Mills, and we've already thrown him out of the community."

Joe sighed. "I don't even want to try to stop him," he said. "Anyway, it would be impossible to keep such news from the others."

"They already know about Briggs," Dorsey said. "Ben and Rebecca are planning a reunion in town."

"Wonderful," Joe replied. "And what does Annuta say?" He wondered how widespread the phrenologist's following was.

"She loves her sister, but she's not a convert, if that's what you mean."

Joe remembered that Ben had argued against him and nominated Briggs as leader. "I don't think Ben is really disloyal," he said mildly.

"That's the problem," Shmuel said. "Save us from our friends, and we can take care of our enemies. Everything that goes wrong will be traced to Briggs's departure, and then he becomes the answer to the world's troubles."

"You're going too far, Uncle."

"Ach," Shmuel said, and walked to the window to look into the snow.

"You're both right," Dorsey broke in. "Since Ben thinks Briggs saved his marriage and therefore his life, he believes in him. And because Ben is a good man, others will listen."

"Don't they see that Briggs is Kleinschmidt's ally, that they rode together, for God's sake?"

Dorsey shrugged. "I'm only a visitor here and have no right to advise you, but Briggs says neither of them meant any harm, that they were only exercising their rights of free speech."

"And the torches were for light," Shmuel growled. "Believe that, and you'll believe anything."

Hayim seemed nervous. His voice was high and thin in the small room. "I am, as you all know, a foreigner, a newcomer both to America and New Zion. My friend Abe Cahan has told me how little I know about America, and no doubt he is right. But I remember Russia very well. In the '80s and '90s, when I was a young man, I heard conversations like this among my revolutionary friends." Hayim hesitated, his dark eyes darting from one side of the room to the other, taking everyone in. He licked his lips and turned to Joe. "Yosl, I have never given you advice, and perhaps because of that, you have thrived. But if you think this Kleinschmidt is a threat, *do* something. Even if you're wrong, it will be better than standing by."

"Fine," Shmuel snapped. "We all agree something should be done. But what? That's the question."

"Yosl is the leader, Shmuel," Hayim said. "Let him decide."

Shmuel started to answer, then thought better of it and turned again to the window, his huge back a retort. Joe studied the handbill in the dim light. The print was smudged and swam before his eyes. "Today is the ninth. Dr. Briggs will be among us in less than a week. Perhaps I will arrange for a consultation then."

"A consultation," Shmuel said, turning back to face the group. "Are you crazy?"

"Perhaps. If so, it's time I saw an expert about it. Dr. Briggs always claimed he had a special interest in my head."

thirty-one

Joe and Dorsey sat watching the steady flow of people marching up the steps of the hotel. "Where do they all hear about it?" Dorsey asked.

"Perhaps they read your paper."

"If that were it, I'd have subscribers coming into the office instead of you. Anyway, how many heads can there be in a town this size?"

Joe said nothing. He didn't really blame Dorsey for Briggs's success, but he felt frustrated. Maybe it was only the novelty of phrenology during a long winter, he told himself. Whatever the reason, Briggs had already announced an extension of his stay, and there was even talk about his establishing a permanent office in Gays Mills. Joe looked gloomily out the glazed window. Dorsey had rebuilt the press and replaced some of the glass, but a cardboard reminder of Kleinschmidt's visit remained.

"If it were just Briggs, I wouldn't mind," Joe said, wondering if this was true. "But I'm afraid before long we'll be seeing the Moses again."

"You handled him the last time."

"I had the assistance of a flood," Joe said.

"Sure, but you're jumping to conclusions. Briggs is out for himself."

"What of it?"

"So he comes in here, reads some heads, sells his pamphlets, and makes some money. Where's the harm in that?"

Joe just smiled and shook his head ruefully. It was impossible for him to think of Briggs as a benign capitalist. He knew the doctor was more sinister than that.

"I was over there," Dorsey put in now.

"For an examination? I thought you were a journalist."

"I am. This is news, isn't it?" Dorsey seemed insulted by the insinuation that he had been taken in. "Sure, I went to see the doctor yesterday morning."

"Don't keep me in suspense," Joe said, surprised to find he was a little jealous that Dorsey had gotten there first.

"Well, I had a complete analysis," Dorsey said. "He says I have high intelligence because of my forehead. And I thought I was just going bald. Briggs says my brain's so hot it's burning the hair right off my head, from the inside out—what do you think of that?"

Joe was amused in spite of himself. "He actually told you this?"

"Would I lie?" Dorsey said in mock indignation. "But that's not all. He said I should have sex more often, that it might cool me off."

"He made quite an impression on you."

"Sure. Who'd argue with that advice? Then I read his book—well, it's not actually his." He held up a copy of Orson Fowler's treatise.

Joe turned a few pages idly. There were diagrams of the head and scalp from various angles, as well as instructions for self-examination. He handed the book back to Dorsey and said, "I guess I'd better get over there myself. If he's got you talking this nonsense, God knows what the others must think."

Dorsey waved good-bye beatifically. "Just keep an open mind," he said.

The Hotel Kickapoo had been built twenty years before by an entrepreneur from Boston who envisioned the river as a western version of the Ohio. With a steady stream of traders traveling north and south, Gays Mills would become a mercantile hub, and all those merchants would need a place to stay, a hotel as grand as the town's future. As the years went by and the number of new settlers declined rather than increased, however, the man became discouraged. Eventually, he sold out and left town. Still, the Kickapoo remained, a faded relic of his grandiose dream.

The hotel faced the river, with a large verandah and broad steps leading down to the shore. Inside, there remained one of the original crystal chandeliers and an elaborately tiled floor with marble staircases leading to the mezzanine, which hung over the lobby like the prow of a ship. Joe walked around the building, eschewing the small back entrance on Main Street that most visitors used, to enter from the river, as the hotel's founder had intended.

Inside, people moved back and forth from the restaurant to the public rooms. Briggs was occupying the mezzanine, and when Joe climbed the stairs, two of the God-men blocked his way. They were dressed innocuously enough in brown suits and lacked some of the naked fierceness that Joe remembered from their days at New Zion. "I'd like to see Dr. Briggs," he said.

"He's busy," the first God-man replied.

"I can wait."

The man shrugged his powerful shoulders and pointed to a hard-backed chair overlooking the lobby. Before long, Ben came out of the suite.

"Nice to see you, Ben," Joe said, offering his hand.

Ben ignored the gesture. He was wearing a black suit and had greased his hair to part it on the right side. Now he looked more like a businessman than a yeshiva boy. "What do you want?" Ben said.

"I saw the placards, so I came. It said everyone was invited."

"Of course," Ben snapped. "We'd just like to avoid trouble."

"So would I, but I have my doubts about Dr. Briggs."

"You were the one who threw him out."

"Actually, that's not true. No one forced him to go; he left of his own free will in the dead of night."

"Yes, after you humiliated him," Ben said.

"You flatter me. How could I possibly outwit a man like Dr. Briggs who has studied at university and traveled widely?"

Ben thought this over for a moment, his face tight and pale. He looked unhappy, and Joe felt sympathetic. It couldn't be easy, being caught in the middle like this. It occurred to him that if they'd met in Russia, they might have been friends. Ben was from Odessa and had also been a student. They even looked somewhat alike. "I don't know," Ben said finally.

"What's there to worry about? What can I possibly do, after all? I'm alone."

Without answering, Ben rose and left Joe sitting in the lobby. After half an hour, the door opened again and one of the God-men motioned him inside. The curtains were drawn, and much of the paraphernalia Joe remembered from Cahan's visit was spread around the examining room. The only thing he didn't recognize was a huge water tank that squatted against one wall. Joe wondered if Briggs had branched out and now performed baptisms. The doctor sat behind a gilt writing table in a starched white shirt and stiff collar. His tight black waistcoat caused the shirt to billow out in front slightly, and his fat hands were clasped in front of him, like a dead man's. A black swallowtail coat hung on the chair.

This time Briggs eschewed the elaborate courtesies of their last encounter. Fixing Joe with a steely glare, he said, "To what do we owe this visit, Mr. Abrams? I'm a busy man."

Joe shrugged his shoulders to relieve tension. He felt the God-men staring at his back and was determined not to be intimidated. Ben was nowhere to be seen. "Is it a crime to want to see the man who has drawn most of Gays Mills to his door?"

Briggs was unmoved by this flattery. "You're not here for a consultation, and I neither need nor desire your good wishes. Had you wished to see me professionally, you might have done so during those wretched months when I was in residence in your community."

Joe nodded. "I'm sorry for your discomfort. We can't afford the luxuries you have here." He looked around the room and then back at Briggs. "But you're right. I didn't come to be examined."

"Why, then?"

"I hardly know myself, Dr. Briggs. I suppose I hoped our talking might help to avoid more of the kind of trouble we had in February."

"Which you brought on yourself."

"Interesting," Joe said. "And how did we do this, exactly? By wishing to live as best we could, on our own land, bothering no one?"

"You are socialists."

Joe wondered if the man was joking, but Briggs's face was solemn as stone. "That's true; most of us are. As far as I know, this is no crime. But why should this have resulted in Mr. Kleinschmidt's crusade against us? What have we done to you?"

"Nothing, except offend the laws of God, man, and common decency."

"You make me feel powerful. How did we accomplish all these things?"

Briggs took a deep breath and rose from his seat to stalk the room. "I don't wish to indulge in a theological discussion, Mr. Abrams. Despite your youth and humble appearance, you are clever, and with your friend from the newspaper, capable of turning truth into falsehood with no help from me."

"Of course, that's not why I came," Joe said quickly.

"Perhaps not. I feel no need to explain myself to you, but since you ask, and appear sincere, I will say your disavowal of the Almighty in your charter was one thing. Also, you allowed promiscuity and fornication to flourish." Briggs pointed a meaty finger at Joe. "I am told you have personal knowledge of these matters."

Joe's cheeks were hot. He hadn't expected Briggs to be puritanical. "Weren't you the one with the interest in nudity? I would have expected you to respect the privacy of others."

Joe expected to be thrown out, but Briggs only smiled slyly. "Philosophers are accustomed to being misinterpreted by laymen," he said. "And as far as privacy is concerned, it is only sacred if it affects no one else. If the moral laxity of a few is permitted to invade and infect the surrounding mass, then such things cease to be private any longer."

Joe nodded. "I wasn't aware that our sins, whatever they are, had threatened Milwaukee. After all, that's a distance of over a hundred miles."

"Dr. Kleinschmidt perceives his ministry as extending far beyond the state's eastern region. As you know, much of his work has been among the savages. Our mission is to meet the Devil wherever he may appear, and in whatever guise."

Briggs walked to the window, pulled back the curtain, and looked briefly into the street. But he made no signal. His skin looked gray and dead in the fading light of dusk. "You see how it is then, Mr. Abrams?"

Joe felt uncomfortable. The room was overheated, and he imagined the God-men at his shoulder while Briggs stared hungrily at him, his eyes wide as a reptile's. "Not exactly. I don't see your part in all this—why you came all the way from Ohio to spy on us, why you're here now."

"J. G. Briggs is no spy," the doctor thundered. "Nothing I did was deceitful or misleading."

"Everything you said was. The trouble is, Mr. Liberty believed you. You told him you were a positivist, and all the time you were working for Kleinschmidt."

"I'm not on trial here, young man," Briggs said. "You would do well to remember that. But I'm curious, did you have any real purpose in coming here today—other than slander, I mean?"

"Yes," Joe said quietly. "I wanted to save some lives, if possible. But I have a question for you. Do you really come from Oneida?"

Briggs's booming laugh filled the room. He slapped his knee and howled until tears came to his eyes. The God-men, not knowing what to make of this, entered in hesitantly, and even Joe was unable to stifle a smile. Now Briggs wiped his eyes with a handkerchief and blew his nose. "Anything else, Abrams?"

Joe stood now, close enough to smell the onions on Briggs's breath. "Yes, Doctor. I want to warn you that we won't sit idly and watch you destroy what it has taken years to build. New Zion is more than a place for us to live; it's a dream that others have died for. We're willing to die, too, if necessary. But we have other friends in this community, as you discovered last time, people who know the true nature of our life. You speak of slander, but you're the slanderer, not I."

To Joe's surprise, Briggs seemed to take this seriously. "I will pass on your message to my colleagues, Mr. Abrams. Your very words." He nodded at the God-men, who took hold of Joe and guided him into the empty lobby.

Outside, Joe looked around and saw nothing. The door had closed behind him, but he had the distinct feeling he was being watched. When he reached the door, he turned to see Ben, tall and dark, leaning on the rail of the mezzanine. Joe raised his hand, but Ben didn't respond, and finally, he let his arm fall limply to his side and pushed out the door toward the river.

Book Four

For the Lord thy God is a
devouring fire, a jealous God . . .

—Deuteronomy 4:24

thirty-two

Dear Mr. Cahan,

I write out of relief and sadness—relief that the things we most fear haven't yet occurred, sadness because we live in their shadow. This is unfortunate, because, were it not for outsiders, we would be happier than ever.

The furor over our change in leadership has subsided. We have additional acres under cultivation, and we continue to produce our own milk, cheese, and bread. As a result of last winter's rebellion, our women now share more equally in the community than ever before—one, indeed, shows a particular talent for carpentry, while another makes periodic trips to town, having apprenticed herself to a friendly stonemason. Though some of the men grumble about having to bake and sew, for the most part, the revolution has been congenial.

My complaint, if I have one, has little to do with New Zion. It's true that Morris Held and a few others see me as a conciliator—I'm guilty as charged—but they don't bother me. In fact, I would miss Held if he were to suddenly disappear. He is necessary as a goad, my compass as I travel.

What concerns me is something else altogether: the occasional feeling I have that pleasant—and even important—as

New Zion is, it's not enough, at least not for me. Worse, I have no right to feel this way. I didn't intend to spend my life as a farmer, a politician, or even a journalist. Perhaps I had nothing concrete in mind, but certainly these weren't my goals. I'm not a gifted orator, though my comrades have chosen me to lead them. I find myself questioning their choice.

I came to America in search of adventure; it was to be a voyage into the unknown. I've grown and changed in my time here, I know that. And it would be a mistake to say our life is without excitement, but routine is what we strive for, and I find it is the problems that interest me, that make me feel alive. When things go well, I feel useless, even bored. I want to be at greater personal risk, and this knowledge makes me feel disloyal to my comrades and unworthy of their trust. Perhaps I will travel west in search of gold or, as my uncle advises, go to university. I know I sound very young, and, of course, I am. I may change my mind tomorrow.

Assuming, that is, we continue to avoid extinction. Kleinschmidt has been quiet for months, but it is an ominous silence. Your counsel, as usual, in these and all other matters would be greatly appreciated by

Your friend and employee,
Joseph Abrams

Joe sealed the letter and leaned back in his chair. The malaise he had described troubled him more than he had been able to convey. It was mysterious, even physical in the cloudy feeling he had many mornings which kept him in bed, unable to think clearly. He didn't understand it—and didn't want to understand. He only wished it would disappear. He was about to return to the papers he had been working on when the door opened and Hayim Goldman entered, his face red with anger.

"Have you seen the newspaper, then?"

"Not yet." Liberty didn't clear his copy with Joe, and since becoming leader, he hadn't spent much time on the *Investigator.* "Is something wrong?"

"Something besides the *meshuggah* articles on vegetarianism and the power of long division to heal the world, you mean? To me, the whole journal is the work of a madman."

Joe relaxed. Hayim had thrown himself into the work of the commune and now protested daily some aspect of its operation. "Yes, Hayim, something besides that. Mr. Liberty has advanced ideas, and he's entitled to them."

Hayim looked mildly ill. "Advancing toward what, is the question we must ask," he said, and held up his hand. "No, Yosl, please. No lectures about freedom of expression, no arguments. This is not what I've come about."

"Not the newspaper?"

"Yes, the newspaper. God in heaven, what else?"

"Then I don't understand."

Hayim pulled a copy of the *Investigator* from his pocket and placed it before Joe. "Yes, the newspaper, but not the *mishegoss.* This." His finger rested on a black box centered on the first page.

"Someone died?"

"Go ahead. Read it."

A CHALLENGE

> Followers of the so-called Moses of the Menomonee, whose given name we are told is Jacob Kleinschmidt, were disappointed in February when their assault on the New Zion community was repulsed by a handful of men, women, and children. Most of the membership was away, occupied with fighting the flooding Kickapoo River in Gays Mills. Since Herr Kleinschmidt had gone to the trouble of installing a spy, a nudist named J. G. Briggs, in the community, such a defeat must have been particularly galling.
>
> Properly, however, such disputes should not be resolved by thugs carrying torches on horseback, or even by the forces of nature. As man alone among God's creatures possesses the faculty of Reason, we should consider open discussion of all issues a Sacred Responsibility. Accordingly, I challenge the aforementioned Kleinschmidt to a debate, to be held at a mutually agreeable location at the earliest possible time.

> Failure to respond to this invitation will only reinforce what many already suspect—that Herr Kleinschmidt's ideas do not extend beyond the indiscriminate use of violence to intimidate those smaller and weaker than himself.
>
> — Edward Liberty, Editor

"Has this been mailed?"

"Unfortunately, yes," Goldman said, shaking his head. "But no one here has seen it. Apparently, Mr. Liberty was trying to keep his debate a secret from the comrades who will pay for it."

Joe looked at the older man. He seemed to have aged since entering the room. His lower lip trembled slightly. Fear sometimes masqueraded as outrage. "The damage has been done, then, though I suspect Kleinschmidt would have returned even if we hadn't invited him."

"That's not the point, Yosl," Hayim said harshly. "It's also not the point whether you are the lover of Liberty's daughter, though it is a badly kept secret."

"Perhaps, then, Hayim, you'll tell me what the point of all this is?"

Goldman began pacing the room in order to pace the room. His small body was stiff with indignation, his face rigid. "This newspaper is not Liberty's private hobby; it is the organ of the community."

"He started it."

"With our money. And even if he did, that doesn't make it his. He must represent all of us."

"I agree," Joe said quickly. But he knew consensus was impossible. "Still, how many editors can a four-page paper have, and how many of the comrades really care? When I was working on the *Investigator,* only Liberty and Briggs ever contributed, though anyone else was free to do so."

"That doesn't matter. They aren't writers. The question is how many of them want this Kleinschmidt among us again?"

Joe couldn't argue the point. "You're right. I agree that he shouldn't have published his challenge. But he has; it's already out in the world. What can we do?"

Goldman looked solemn. "First, this should be discussed by the entire community. We should decide if there will be a debate and, if so, who will represent us. Certainly, it should not be Liberty."

"I would hope to avoid any debate," Joe said.

"How, after this?" Hayim said, slamming his fist on the desk. "How can we turn away now without looking like cowards? I'll tell you, Yosl, in Russia, we may have been fools, but we were smart enough not to invite the Cossacks to come into our villages and murder us. I demand you remove Liberty from the editorship."

"I don't have the power to do that."

"Then the community must."

For reasons he didn't completely understand, Joe was not as upset as he thought he should have been, considering his previous involvement with Liberty and his relationship with Lizzie. Still, he felt an obligation to try to mollify Hayim. "It's all Liberty has left, Hayim. Why take it away when the damage has already been done? Why humiliate the man?"

"Because even a moron can be dangerous," Hayim said.

He was right. They couldn't allow Liberty unlimited license, not so long as what he did affected the rest of the community. And there was no doubt that he should have informed them of his challenge. Joe stood and walked around the desk until he was facing Hayim. Then he put both hands on Goldman's skinny shoulders and squeezed. "I will call a meeting, old friend," he said. "But I dislike what we're about to do. I'm sorry this has angered you."

"I'm not angry, Yosl; I'm scared. If you were older, you'd be scared, too."

thirty-three

They had been making love, their legs tangled amidst the bedclothes, their arms wrapped tightly around each other, still remembering passion. Now Lizzie slept on his chest while Joe, awake, thinking, lay immobile. As they had grown more expert at lovemaking, his involvement had grown less intense. At times, he felt like a skilled technician, hoping through manipulation to achieve ecstasy, a cry in the night. And while there was satisfaction in this, it was that of the competent craftsman, not the passionate artist. He'd never again felt the complete release and euphoria of that first time in the forest, when this was all new and he'd had no idea what he was doing.

Often, after sex, he became despondent, thinking of death and decay, projecting himself ten or twenty years into the future and wondering if Lizzie would still be beside him. In the weak light of the moon, he looked at her sleeping peacefully, her face soft as a child's, her legs carelessly spread, exposing the blond ruff of her crotch, still damp from love. He pulled off the blanket and went outside to urinate. When he returned, she was awake, her eyes red-rimmed and anxious.

"I thought you had gone away."

"Where would I go? This is my cabin." He climbed back into bed, shivering from the night.

"I don't know," she said, drawing close again. "To Annuta."

Joe laughed. "She's not interested in me anymore. Ben's trying to marry her off, if Dorsey doesn't get there first."

"It's not reassuring to say she's not interested, Yosl. What about you?"

Her insight bothered Joe. She was too smart to fool much longer, and what would he do then to cover his growing indifference? "I have worries of my own," he said vaguely.

"I'm sorry I worry you."

"That's not what I meant," Joe said quickly, feeling guilty because she was right. He wondered how he had given it away. Sometimes when they made love, it was Annuta's slim brown body that he thought of at the moment of climax, but he had never said anything, never even mentioned her name. "I was only thinking about the community meeting," he said.

Lizzie got up and began making tea on the small stove. She wore one of Joe's shirts for warmth. As he watched her, his doubts began to fade. It was insane to question his feelings for her.

"What about it?" Lizzie said.

"Some of the comrades are upset with Mr. Liberty." Despite his involvement with Lizzie, Joe's relationship with her father remained formal.

"Someone's always upset with Father."

Joe nodded. "This time I think it's more serious."

She handed him a mug and arched her eyebrows in a question.

"Because of the last issue of the newsletter," Joe explained.

Lizzie laughed harshly. "Because he challenged that madman? They're upset about *that?* You saw what happened the last time Father tried to debate him."

"That wasn't planned, though God knows it was bad enough. This time he's speaking for the whole community through the newsletter, inviting trouble. They're afraid it will bring Kleinschmidt back with his men."

Lizzie sat cross-legged on the bed and drank her tea. Then she looked up. "What's really bothering you, Yosl? It can't be this. You knew Kleinschmidt would return. Father didn't have to invite him. After all, no one did the first time. And Dr. Briggs was out here for months without anything coming of it."

Joe took a deep breath. Lizzie was used to controversy; she'd grown up with it. It wasn't so easy for him. "I'm afraid the comrades will take the newsletter away from Mr. Liberty. I'm grateful for all he's done to help me, but your father was wrong in this. I have responsibilities to the others. After all, I'm supposed to be their leader." He didn't mention their relationship, but it hung between them in the night.

Lizzie looked as if she were about to laugh. "You can't be serious, Yosl. Father started the paper. It was his idea and he does all the work. Now suddenly the community is full of literary critics?"

Joe didn't mention his own efforts on the *Investigator.* "It's true that he works hard, but we all pay for it. The community owns the press."

Lizzie nodded, but when she looked up from her tea, he was surprised to see that her eyes were filled with tears. "He thinks of it as his, Yosl. They took away his office; they humiliated him. He does no harm writing his editorials; no one reads the newsletter anyway."

Joe took her in his arms. "I thought it was harmless, too. But that's how Kleinschmidt learned about us—and others will, too. Words are never harmless; we just act as if they were."

Lizzie wiped her eyes on the blanket and sat up, covering her breasts with the shirt. "Will you stop them?"

Joe felt trapped between Hayim and Lizzie, drawn to each but ultimately responsible to neither. "I can't. Don't you see what a position I'm in?"

"That's what leaders are for," Lizzie said sharply. "It would take courage to defend Father, Yosl, I know that. I'm asking you to show some courage."

"It's not that simple."

"It is to me," Lizzie said. She started to dress while Joe watched silently. He felt he should try to dissuade her, but to his surprise, he didn't want to. It was her decision. "Where are you going?"

"Where I belong," she said. "To Father."

"When will I see you again?"

"That's up to you, Yosl. You must choose."

"Even if I disagree with your father? What if I think the comrades are right and that he should give up the paper?"

She stood fully dressed before him, her eyes sad in the early morning light. "I'll be at the meeting," she said, and walked out the door.

Joe surveyed the fields in the fading dusk as the hall began to fill. Outside, everything seemed fresh, abundant, and healthy. The corn was already knee-high in the common garden, and the raw wood of several new buildings stood out in the background. Jews could endure misfortune, he thought. They always had. The question was whether or not they could survive prosperity.

Hayim, Shmuel, and Morris Held were huddled together, while Ben, thin and austere, sat opposite them with his small group of supporters. Liberty and Lizzie were alone near the door. Joe felt exhausted and the meeting hadn't even begun.

"Can an outsider attend?"

Joe turned to see Bryan Dorsey, dressed more formally than usual in coat and tie. "You're hardly an outsider. You spend practically as much time here as I do."

"Ah, well, that's a thing of the past now," Dorsey said.

"Annuta?" Joe was surprised.

"To tell the truth, there wasn't much hope to begin with. But the lady has made herself clear, so now there's no hope at all."

"I'm sorry to hear it," Joe said. And now that Bryan was no longer a rival, he did feel sympathy for him.

"Yes, well," Dorsey said, suddenly embarrassed by his revelations. "What about this meeting, then?"

"Are you going to write about us?" Joe said.

"Of course not. I'm just an interested member of the community. I did hear something I think you'd like to know, though." Dorsey leaned close and cupped his hand around Joe's ear. "The Moses is on his way back."

Kleinschmidt's quick response surprised Joe. The papers had only been mailed the previous week. "To answer Liberty?"

"Who knows? He says your sinning brought on the flood, though, that it was a sign from God."

"Good thing we helped clean up, then. The rabbis would probably agree."

"I suppose they would at that," Dorsey said, grinning. "I'd better find a seat." He tapped Joe on the shoulder and melted into the crowd.

The comrades churned in the room, agitated and intense tonight. Insularity was so much a part of their lives that it was almost unconscious, like a facial tic or nervous cough. They all lived with the knowledge of a hostile world, but usually they were able to ignore it. When had worrying about the Tsar done the Jews any good? The rabbis had always taught them to look after themselves and let the rest alone. Now that they were no longer religious, but democrats in a new land, however, they were unsure how to act. In America, their self-absorption would be seen as clannishness, exclusivity, almost an abdication of the franchise. Not understanding the new rules, and unable to put aside the instincts of oppression, the comrades were at a disadvantage. Democracy could hurt them badly, and there would be no rabbinical court to instruct them should they make the wrong decision.

Joe waited for silence, but he wasn't as patient as Liberty. When a majority seemed to have found seats, he rapped his knuckles against the lectern three times and began. "Brothers and sisters," he shouted, and waited for the others to face him. He tried again. "Brothers and sisters, I was asked to call this meeting to discuss the *Positivist Investigator.*" The din subsided somewhat. Joe continued. "As most of you know, a letter challenging Jacob Kleinschmidt to debate was recently published in its pages. The question is what, if anything, should be done?"

"Liberty should be fired," Morris Held shouted, but his response was so automatic that the others hardly noticed.

"That possibility has been mentioned," Joe said quickly. "But it seems to me there are two separate questions: first, what to do about the debate; second, if a mistake has been made, how to avoid such problems in the future."

Whenever Abe Rosenfeld addressed the group, his deep voice seemed to cloak the room in reasonableness. Now he stood and looked around for a moment before speaking. "Mr. Chairman," he began. "Comrades. You all know where I stand. I came here to be a farmer, not a politician. Anything that takes away from that, I'm against. I've never been close to Edward Liberty. I'm not a vegetarian and I missed his lessons in mathematics. As I said, that's not my interest. As far as I'm concerned, his positivism is a lot of nonsense, but harmless. Let people believe what they want if it doesn't hurt anyone else. Even his newspaper I didn't object to, because by and large, he's been a good leader and the community prospered under him. Finally, let us admit it, he works as hard as any man or woman in New Zion. He is, in his way, a man of courage and principle. We'd be foolish to deny that."

Joe felt grateful to Abe and ashamed of himself. Why hadn't he thought to say these things himself before setting the shape of the discussion about the newsletter? So the man had made a mistake. Who among them hadn't? And didn't the good things he had done outweigh the bad? Lizzie had been right and he hadn't seen it. Thank God there were others with more experience. But Abe wasn't finished.

"So. Liberty is a man of principle and we should admire this. At least, I do. But this debate he proposes is not mere foolishness; it could be devastating to our community. What's the point of trying to explain our life to the people of Gays Mills? Who are we trying to convince, and what would we be trying to convince them of? Jews have never recruited converts, and there is no reason to do so now. I believe there should be no debate. We can inform Kleinschmidt of this and, if necessary, apologize for the challenge. Then we must give Mr. Liberty new responsibilities that recognize his gifts. You can say I have my head in the sand, but I think the less the goyim know about us, the better. Thank you."

Ben was dressed in a black suit, and his steel-framed glasses reflected the candles in the hall. "Comrades," he began in a voice so low Joe had to strain to hear. "My dissatisfaction with the direction our community has taken is well known. Our current leader is a newcomer, very nearly our most recent arrival, and our present predicament is due, I believe, to his lack of experience."

"Joe didn't write that challenge, comrade," Shmuel interrupted in a loud voice. "Next you will blame him for the heat of the summer sun."

Ben looked hurt and hesitated, but Rebecca patted him on the arm, and after a moment, he continued. "When Mr. Liberty was our leader, we had no threats from the outside world; we lived in peace with our neighbors. Now that we have come to know better some of the people of Gays Mills—I notice the editor of their newspaper is here tonight—we are in constant peril. Perhaps our leader is too anxious to become an American. I agree with Abe that we came here as farmers, and farmers we should remain. But I disagree with his conclusions. Change our leadership and restore Mr. Liberty to the position of honor he deserves!"

He tried to hide his hands under his coat as he spoke, Ben was literally shaking with emotion. Though Joe knew he should feel defensive, instead he was nostalgic, charmed by his adversary. For the passion of Ben's speech, the earnestness of his expression, even his threadbare clothes and ragged beard, reminded Joe of nothing so much as the days in Minsk when he and the others would argue long into the night about fine points of philosophy.

And, realizing this, Joe knew Ben would never give in, any more than he would have yielded on a point in Spinoza. For Ben was a *maskil,* and the Jewish students were always the first to arrogate opinions on these matters to themselves. Prior to the Enlightenment movement, who had ever heard of Jews in universities or the professions? Even the rabbis had been against it, and for ninety-five percent of the Jewish population, education had remained an impossible dream. And ironically, those students who finally made their way to Minsk or Odessa or Yehupetz or one of the other universities were not, by and large, sons of the *negidim,* the intelligentsia. Those people sent their children to France or Germany to become assimilated like Heine or Marx. Joe's classmates were from the shtetl or ghetto. Their fathers were tailors, shoemakers, and carpenters. The Jewish students had been the hope of the future, the means by which their fathers survived their daily lives. Despite this, or perhaps because of it, the students were avowedly idealistic and impractical. Against their parents' wishes, they would go off to the city and live in garrets with their friends, dividing a piece of herring ten different ways and, every two weeks, perhaps a small piece of meat. "Hallelujah," they would say to each other, "We are students, intellectuals. Our lives will be different." Joe remembered it well.

Of course, now their lives were different, unimaginably so, but Ben's speech made Joe wistful. He wanted to live buried in his books again, unconcerned about the outside world. He wished to be unsophisticated, naive, but this was impossible. He had made his choice. He smiled slightly at Ben and said, "Thank you, comrade." Then to the group: "Ben has suggested a change in leadership. Is there further discussion, a second to his motion?"

"Mr. President?" Hayim stood, his clothes rumpled, his hair in disarray, and nodded his head, as if agreeing with himself about something. "My friends," he said. "You say you are no longer Jewish, and it is true. Since I have been here, no one has thought to light the candles or, God forbid, say a prayer. So *mazel tov,* you're not religious. But whatever you say, you remain Jews in one important respect: you are determined to commit suicide through argument and petty disagreement."

An undercurrent of disapproval ran through the room, but Joe raised his hand for silence. "Hayim has the floor. Each of us has the right to speak his mind."

"Thank you, Mr. President." Hayim bowed in Joe's direction. "Now, then, since I am the one responsible for this meeting, I should like to make clear my reasons for calling it. I have proposed that Edward Liberty be removed from his position as editor of our newspaper. Why? Not because I disagree with him about politics or religion, though I do. Every man is welcome to his beliefs. This is why we left Russia and came to America. And not because I dislike Mr. Liberty personally. I hardly know him, but he has always been courteous to me. No, I oppose Mr. Liberty only because I believe he acted irresponsibly and selfishly in challenging this goniff Moses, and because he has already elected himself to represent all of us in this debate."

"Who should debate, then?" Ben said. "You?"

Hayim smiled benignly. "My English isn't so good yet, my young friend. But at least you are beginning to understand the question. What Mr. Liberty writes about positivism or whether he eats meat or wants a woman, this is nothing to me. But when he invites a man who leads an army of barbarians to come and visit, this does affect me, and this I must protest. Who is our leader is not the question we have to be concerned with now. If we don't survive, that won't matter. What we must decide is what to do since Mr. Liberty has challenged Kleinschmidt. Thank you very much."

Hayim stood for a moment, swaying slightly from side to side, then he made a quick little bow and sat down. There was nervous silence in the room. People looked at their shoes, or away, avoiding each other's eyes. It never hurt to bring up survival, Joe thought. It was always on their minds anyway. He found it hard to accept as real the parallel of Kleinschmidt's ragged crew and the carefully selected killers of the Tsar's Black Hundred, but that was no reason to take the Moses lightly.

"Is there further discussion?" he asked.

Shmuel rose now, his huge body seeming to crowd everyone in the hall. "Mr. President, I move that Edward Liberty be replaced as editor of the newsletter by a committee to be democratically chosen by the comrades of New Zion."

Morris Held quickly seconded. Joe looked at Liberty, who had as yet said nothing in his own defense. For a moment, he thought Lizzie had been deputized to speak, but her father put his hand on her shoulder and she remained silent. Under the circumstances, Joe felt compelled to say something in Liberty's behalf.

"I have listened to both sides," he said, "and think there is much to what Hayim and Abe have said. We can't afford to ignore a threat to our community. But I'm not convinced that Mr. Liberty's challenge has significantly increased the danger in which we find ourselves." He nodded at Dorsey. "I'm told that Kleinschmidt had already decided to return to Gays Mills before the *Investigator* was in print, that indeed he may be among us already. The debate could be a further irritant, but I don't believe it would cause the Moses to come among us any more than staying silent would have resulted in his remaining away. This is nonsensical thinking. The man has his own plan, and we are only a part of it, probably not an important part. This doesn't change the fact that Mr. Liberty was wrong, but he has served us long and well, and he deserves forgiveness and another chance."

Held said, "He's had enough chances." And there was no further discussion, no one else rose to defend Liberty. The vote was nearly unanimous, and before they had finished counting, Annuta called out.

"Mr. President?"

Joe recognized her.

"Though we have decided now to change editors, I wish to express my personal gratitude to Mr. Liberty and thank him for the many hours, days, and weeks he has spent working on our newsletter. We should remember that it was his idea to tell the world that we are here. There would be no *Investigator* without him."

Joe was about to put this in the form of a motion when he looked over and saw that Lizzie and her father were gone.

thirty-four

He needed to work, to sweat, to contribute in some concrete way to the community. He knew that what he was doing was valuable, but all the same, he often felt irrelevant. Without him, the fields were tilled, the trees cut down, bread baked, and meals prepared. Being leader was easier than he would have thought, and this made him feel guilty. When he sat in the dining room in the evening and saw the others with their sweat-stained clothes and thickly callused hands, he felt counterfeit and wondered what he had done to deserve the food on his plate.

The laundry was situated in a lean-to near the river. The wood was blackened by smoke, and as he drew closer, Joe saw there was a fire burning in a kind of wooden bowl erected atop a small platform. Alarmed, he cried out, "Fire, fire!" which brought a harsh laugh from a wizened old woman whom he now saw behind the platform. Though she looked vaguely familiar, Joe had never spoken to her. It surprised him that there should still be members of the community he hadn't met. It made him feel new again.

"I hope there's a fire," she said. "We'll never get any soap otherwise." Now she laughed and extended her hand. "I'm Sarah, and you're our leader, though I don't know what you're doing here. Am I being replaced?"

Joe's mind was still on the fire. "No, no. I just thought I'd come and help out if I could," he said. "The problem is I obviously have no idea what you're doing." Then he pointed at the bowl. "What is that?" he asked.

Sarah reached up with a wooden pike to rearrange the ashes. "That's our hopper," she said. "And it's not a bad one, either."

Joe looked carefully at the platform. He had never devoted much thought to where his clean clothes came from, never had any idea what was involved. Now he saw it differently, with a pride of accomplishment that he wouldn't have imagined he could have felt. The hopper was constructed of rived clapboards set upright on a base of raw boards. The tops of the clapboards were held in place by a frame with posts at either end. A large bowl of straw lay in the bottom, and beneath that were the smoldering ashes. "What does it do?" Joe asked.

"Do?" Sarah laughed. "It's what we do with it that counts. Climb up and see for yourself." She offered her hand, but Joe declined and clambered up on his own. Once atop the platform, he could see into the straw depression. It was much deeper than he'd imagined. There had apparently been many fires before.

Now Sarah handed him a bucket of water. "Pour it down in there," she directed, and Joe complied. Almost immediately, she was back with another and then still another until Joe had poured enough water into the bowl to produce a choking blend of fire and smoke that made his eyes tear. He stood back to wipe them with his shirtsleeve, but Sarah was unconcerned. She climbed up and peered into the hopper herself. The smoke seemed to have no effect on her.

"I guess it's about ready," was all she said. Sarah was tall and rangy, and Joe couldn't even guess her age. Her skin was dry and wrinkled, but she had a girl's waist and moved around the hopper as if she had been doing such things all her life. Her gray-blond hair was covered by a blue kerchief, and she didn't look like the other Jews. But she didn't seem exactly like a Russian, either.

Now she climbed back down and disappeared beneath the platform. Joe followed and saw a large bucket half filled with drippings from the hopper. The enclosure was small, and an acrid smell radiated from the bucket, causing him to cover his eyes and nose and retreat outside. Sarah stayed to stir the mess around with a wooden paddle before finally emerging herself.

"What's that?" Joe asked, wiping his eyes with a handkerchief.

"Lye," Sarah said simply. "Not as good as we made back home, but here we don't have a good stove and we're burning pine instead of hickory." She sniffed the air. "If it's good lye, you can float an egg in it, but we can't afford to waste food, so I guess it's good enough."

Joe had wanted to work, and all he'd done so far was douse a fire. Still, he was fascinated by this process. "What is it for?" he asked.

"Is there anything you do know, Leader?" Sarah smiled good-naturedly, and to show she was joking, patted him on the shoulder. "We make our own soap, right? Well, to make soap, you've got to have lye. So we make that, too. It takes a while, but one thing we've got plenty of is time."

Joe's mother and sisters had always done the laundry. He had never thought about where they got soap. It had simply been there, and he didn't think they had made it themselves. Could America be more backward than Russia? "I've never made soap," he said carefully.

"Most men haven't—women either, unless they come here. Here, we make everything." Sarah was rooting around in the back of the lean-to, and now she beckoned Joe to help her. In the corner was an enormous iron kettle that they proceeded to drag out into the sunshine, placing it atop a pile of dry wood that Sarah set afire. The kettle was filled with grease, and before long, it was bubbling around the edges. Then Joe poured in the bucket of lye and stood back. Sarah brought a straight-back chair and sat next to the cauldron, standing up to peer in every so often. Occasionally, she would stir the grease and lye with her ladle. After an hour, she rose and looked into the pot for a long time. Then she stood, hands on hips, and sniffed the air again. "I guess that's enough," she said.

"Enough what?"

"Take it off the fire," she ordered, and disappeared in the direction of the river. When she returned, she had two buckets of water, which she poured into another wooden trough. Then she began scooping the liquid soap from the kettle into the trough. Joe found a shovel in the lean-to and helped her until she called a halt. Then Sarah got down on her knees and skimmed her fingers delicately over the surface, stopping frequently to smell them until finally she was satisfied. "Get the cover." She pointed at the platform. Joe found a wooden plank that seemed about the right size and brought it. He covered the trough and awaited further instructions.

When Sarah remained silent, he asked, "What do we do now?"

"Nothing," she said. "If we had some salt or a little rosin, we could put it in and make hard bars, but we mostly use soft soap here. It's good enough. In a day or so, it'll be ready."

Joe spent the rest of the afternoon hauling water from the river to boil for washing. Using a washboard and a stiff brush, Sarah attacked the pile of shirts, dresses, and overalls relentlessly, rubbing in soap and then scouring the stains again and again. Afterward, she rinsed the clothes, and Joe hung them from branches or spread them over bushes to dry in the sun. Sarah said little during all this, but the work was companionable and she seemed friendly. At last, Joe asked her how long she'd been at New Zion. "Oh, it seems like my whole life," she said. "But I guess only three years. I came with my husband, and when he went off in the spring, I stayed, but don't ask me why."

Joe nodded. Everyone seemed to have been dropped here, though not necessarily against their wishes. Only Liberty had been inspired by conviction; the others all seemed to have followed someone, flotsam on the American plains. "Did you live in other communes before this?"

"Oh, child," Sarah said. "I grew up in places like this. My parents were Shakers until my mother got pregnant and they were thrown out for breaking the celibacy rule. We made a stop at Oneida, and then my dad had his own place for a while back in Connecticut. America is full of idealists. Everyone thinks they can do better than the next man, and they spend their whole lives finding out they can't. We were even Mormons for a while, but that didn't last."

Joe wanted to ask why but held back. "I didn't know there were any Americans here," he said.

"Aren't, except me," Sarah said. "And the only reason I'm here is my husband. He came from Russia with Sam and the rest. It seemed like a real adventure at the time to marry a Jew. I had never seen anyone with sidelocks before. I kind of liked that, the hair growing vertically. Now I'm probably a better Jew than he is, which isn't saying much."

She seemed wistful, resting her arms on the limb of a tree and relaxing her shoulders. But then her face became resolute. "That Aaron. He was fine until he took to reading the newspapers. Next thing you know, he doesn't believe in marriage anymore. He's off to save the world, all because of Cahan and those others."

"What did Mr. Cahan have to do with it?"

"When he was here, he was talking about socialism and got the comrades all fired up. Before that, we were just going to be farmers and not worry about the rest of the world." Her voice softened. "But I guess that's all right. Where would we be if no one thought this world was worth saving?" She smiled maternally and put her arm around Joe. "You must be hungry. Why don't you go eat, and I'll finish up here."

With the return of good weather, Joe resumed his walks, though now he seldom went toward Gays Mills, preferring to strike out in unfamiliar directions. He needed time alone to think. Sometimes he would sleep in the woods, using the thick grass as his mattress, and imagine the future. Often, he read Whitman:

Stop this day and night with me and you shall
possess the origin of all poems,
You shall possess the good of the earth and sun,
(there are millions of suns left,)
You shall no longer take things at second or
third hand, nor look through the eyes
of the dead, nor feed on the spectres
in books,
You shall not look through my eyes either, nor
take things from me,
You shall listen to all sides and filter them
from your self.

The poet made him feel new, as if his brain had been strained through freshly cut grass and his eyes washed with springwater. When he returned to New Zion, he would find he had hardly been missed. Yet no one resented his absences; in fact, their good will settled over him like a blanket. He must be doing something right, then, however it seemed.

As he was returning from one of these excursions along the riverbank, he came around a bend to see Annuta bathing in the Kickapoo. It was sudden and there was no question of hiding or turning back; she was looking straight at him, almost as if the meeting had been planned. Joe started to apologize, but Annuta held up her hand. "Never mind, Yosl," she said. "What have I to hide from you?"

Her logic was so disarming that Joe said nothing. Annuta rose from the water and walked naked to the riverbank, where she leisurely dried herself with a towel. She seemed taller now, more assured. Her long hair fell in a single braid to her buttocks, which were round but without fat. Her breasts were heavier, and there was a muscular firmness to her body that he imagined had come from the exercise class. She looked up and seemed amused. "Do I pass inspection, Mr. President?"

Against his will, Joe felt himself grow hard and tried to change the subject. "I was just out for a walk," he said lamely.

Annuta dried her legs and slipped into her skirt. Her bare breasts gleamed in the morning light like a wet nurse's fresh from suck. They swayed as she moved. "And where did you go? Your walks are of great interest in the community."

"Up there," Joe gestured aimlessly. What was the matter with the girl, acting this way? He'd never thought of her as being provocative. Of course, he'd come upon her, but what was she doing here alone? "Along the river, toward the bluffs."

Fully dressed now, Annuta came and sat next to Joe on the grass. She smelled fresh and sweet. After sleeping in his clothes, Joe was aware of his own odor and moved away discreetly, but she moved with him. "Do I make you nervous?"

She did, but Joe didn't want to admit it. He didn't know what to make of aggressive women, and there was no other kind in New Zion. "It's not your fault," he said. "It's just that you're very beautiful this morning."

She seemed charmed by his embarrassment. "Have I changed?"

"That isn't what I meant," he said.

"Why should my looks, whatever they are, bother you, anyway?"

"Perhaps because I haven't treated you well before."

Annuta laughed. "Now you feel bad because you'd like to treat me that way again, and then leave me alone? Perhaps I'm stronger than you think, Yosl."

"Perhaps," Joe said, and smiled. Her joking put him at ease. "You've changed, Annuta. I'm serious about that. A year ago you would have run away like a frightened rabbit if I'd come across you bathing. Now you walk in front of me nude and feel no shame. And the other night when you spoke in the meeting, that was the first time I've heard you say anything in public. You're different, that's all."

Annuta nodded. "I was afraid. Everyone seemed older, wiser, and better educated. Now I'm more confident. Ben and Rebecca helped. So did you. And Lizzie."

"Lizzie?"

"Yes, but not in the way you think. We aren't good friends; we hardly ever talk. But I learned from her about work, about myself. Without meaning to, she taught me how to live. When she said women must do other work besides baking and cooking, at first I thought no, but then I saw she was right. And when she spoke out against her father, I thought perhaps I would say something someday, too. You see?"

Annuta's eyes were bright, and she was so eager for approval that Joe was touched. "She's never had a better student," he said. Annuta had absorbed Lizzie's strength and determination and combined it with beauty and calm good judgment with a remarkable result.

"What did Lizzie think of the meeting?" Annuta asked, changing the subject. Joe had tried to forget it.

"She blames me for everything."

"Well, you could have stopped it," Annuta said reasonably.

"I'm not a dictator. This is a democracy. If a comrade wants to call a meeting, who am I to stand in his way?"

"Yes, but your support of Mr. Liberty would have persuaded the others."

"Maybe," Joe said. He knew she was right—and that Lizzie was, too. "The problem was I agreed with Hayim. No one can be allowed to endanger the community. I'm grateful to Mr. Liberty for many things. He helped me when I came here, and I know he believed in what he was doing, but in this case he acted irresponsibly."

Annuta put her hand on Joe's arm and squeezed. Her eyes were dark and warm. "So now you have lost Lizzie because of your beliefs?"

"I don't know," Joe said. "I respect her loyalty to her father, but I'm not heartbroken. It surprises me, but I'm not."

"Perhaps you've changed, too, Yosl?"

Now Joe looked frankly at Annuta, enjoying her clear dark eyes and tan skin, the long brown hair she had coiled around her neck and shoulders like a rich woman's boa. The candor in her expression was new, and he thought how impossible it would have been in Russia. In Kiev they would not have been allowed even to meet alone, much less walk in the woods. Here, she was free to bathe in a wild river instead of a *mikva* and return his looks without shame. They could make love and discuss philosophy without the help of a *shadchen* or rabbi. The two of them were enough. It made Joe feel impossibly free.

Even realizing this, however, Joe held his tongue. In the past year, he had learned to say less and feel more. He could imagine what Shmuel would say: "Again, Yosl? You fall in love like other people catch cold!" So this time he decided to reveal nothing until he was sure, not only of her but of himself. Finally, they arose from the grass. Annuta put her arm in his, and they started back to New Zion. It was only later, when he was back in his room, that Joe realized they hadn't made love, or even kissed. It had all been so chaste, and yet he was profoundly moved.

From a distance, everything looked as it had when he left. The garden, overrun with tall stalks of corn and lined with small puffs of cabbage and kale, stood to his left, while smoke rose from the chimney of the kitchen, signaling the noon meal. People moved back and forth leisurely but not without purpose. A sense of routine permeated the large central lawn between the buildings. Then Joe saw Hayim rushing toward him. "Yosl, where have you been?" Hayim looked accusingly at Annuta.

"Upriver. I left last night and slept outside. What's the matter?"

Hayim looked at him as if he were a half-wit. "We've been searching for you all morning. Why didn't you tell anyone? You're supposed to be our leader."

Hayim's insistence annoyed Joe. To him, everything was a crisis. Joe felt completely peripheral to the commune unless something was wrong. Then they were all over him. "I remember, Hayim. But what's so important, what happened?"

"Liberty has left. This morning. He took the press with him, claimed he had bought it. Then he left."

"Gone?" Joe was astonished. "But where would he go?"

Hayim raised his slight shoulders in resignation. "Who tells me? You leave like a thief in the night. Then Liberty. One morning I'll wake up and the whole community will have vanished like a dream. I'll tell you this, the others are upset. Some were ready to go along with him, including your brother-in-law, young lady."

"Ben?" Annuta said.

Hayim nodded. "And your sister, too. They stayed behind in the end, thank God, and it was just Liberty and his daughter who deserted us. Took a wagon, too, for their belongings. But they said they'd send it back."

Annuta disengaged herself. "I must talk to Becky," she said, and ran off.

Joe looked up at the clear blue summer sky and regretted that his life couldn't be as flawless. Just ten minutes ago, it had seemed possible. He patted Hayim on the shoulder. "Thanks for telling me, and I'm sorry I was away when you needed me. I'll see you at lunch."

On his desk was an envelope, addressed in Lizzie's hand. For a moment he sat weighing it in his palm, still smelling Annuta on his clothes. Then he slit it open with his fingernail.

Dear Yosl,

By now you know I have gone away with Father and will not be back. I hope you will not blame yourself too much or come after us. I don't really think you will, but a part of me wishes you would make some extravagant gesture—I feel there is so little romance left in our love now. Father is, of course, furious with you for not supporting him and with the others for taking away his newspaper. I am not—I hardly think it matters to the world whether or not the *Investigator* continues. But I hate to see him suffer, as he has already undergone so much pain in his life. I know you will not see this, but in his way, Father is a great man. He deserves better.

He talks of going to London, where most of the other positivists are, or perhaps back to Russia. I hope we return to New York, but for now, we'll wait in Gays Mills for friends to send money. Father is quite incoherent, but I am sure he is harmless. In time, he will recover, but it is an awful burden to feel oneself inspired by a deity, natural or supernatural, and this is his world.

What I regret most in all this, though, is leaving you. Finally, we managed to love each other, and for a time it was so good for each of us. I know I should think such love is bourgeois, but the truth is I don't. I will always remember our time together, and in a way, I will always love you.

Marry Annuta, but think well of

Your Friend,
Elzbeta Liberty

Joe sat quietly for a quarter of an hour, his eyes unfocused, staring at the wooden wall of his cabin, thinking of Lizzie and the last time they had made love. It was in this room, not three feet from the chair where he sat. Her warmth invaded the cabin, and the knowledge of his loss made him shiver with regret. In that moment, he did want to go to Gays Mills and take her away from Liberty.

Not to bring her back to New Zion, though. He knew that would be impossible. They would have to go somewhere else. Colorado, perhaps, or maybe just across the state to Madison. Even as he considered this, however, he realized Lizzie was right. He was too sensible for impulsive gestures, and she would never leave her father. Which made him wonder if he really loved her, or if this swell of emotion was just guilt. It was all too complex; the waves of experience and sensation braided together like an immense challah, yet the effect was not sweet but sour. He had made a mess of things with Liberty, who had befriended him, and he had convinced Lizzie to love him and then turned cold. The pity of it was that he had no idea where he had gone wrong, nor what he should have done differently.

There was a soft knock and Ben entered. For a moment he stood at the door, squinting behind his silver-rimmed spectacles in the dim light, his long arms slack, elbows turned out as if he were prepared to run. He was collarless, dressed in black, with a vest hanging loose around his body. His face was as colorless as ice.

"Yes, Ben, I'm over here."

Ben jumped slightly and turned in Joe's direction. Then he straightened his shoulders and came to stand in front of the desk. "You've heard about Mr. Liberty?" His voice was scratchy, hoarse, as if it carried a great burden of emotion.

"I also heard you nearly left with them. I'm glad you didn't. We need you here." It was the truth. Their leaving might have brought the community down.

Ben relaxed perceptibly, and Joe offered him tea. Then they sat across from each other with their hot cups, companionable if not friendly. "Funny," Joe said. "If we had stayed in Russia, we might have been plotting a revolution together."

Ben seemed put off by this. "I was never political," he said. "I might have been a Zionist, but never a revolutionary. If I hadn't come here, I would have gone to Palestine. I always knew I would leave Russia."

"How could you know?" Joe said. "For centuries, our people lived there—not well, but well enough to stay alive. Who could have predicted such an exodus? We lived through an extraordinary historical moment. Who would have thought the progress of the Pahlen Commission would be put aside during the '80s and '90s, that the Tsar would hire gangsters to destroy whole communities?"

Joe felt excited by ideas, by controversy, but Ben seemed bored. "What you say is true, Yosl. But it had little to do with me. Pogroms were what I grew up with, what I expected. That's not why I left. I joined Am Olam because it was agricultural, not political. I just liked the idea of spending my life with mud on my boots. My only quarrel with the Tsar was that he wouldn't let Jews be farmers."

Joe nodded slowly. He understood the Jewish dream of land. "So why come here? Why America?"

"Palestine is a land of bondage. How can a Jew be free there? But this isn't why I came to see you," Ben said, breaking the easy mood of nostalgia that had settled upon them. "Mr. Liberty has left, but I don't think he's gone for good."

"I thought he was traveling to London," Joe said. He gestured toward the desk. "Lizzie left a note."

Ben shook his head vehemently. "Not until he destroys New Zion."

"Why would he do that, assuming he could?"

"When we first came here," Ben said, "he was only recently arrived. Elzbeta hadn't yet joined him. Many nights we would sit together and talk, and in time we became friendly. One thing he used to say is that constant struggle is necessary for change to occur. I asked him what he meant." Now Ben turned to Joe. "I admired him, you see, and wanted to learn all I could."

Joe nodded. He understood this. Encouraged, Ben continued. "It would be better, Mr. Liberty said, for the commune to fail, for all its members to perish, than to stray from his principles. The lesson wasn't just for us here, but for the world, he said. He was always ready to quarrel violently with those who disagreed, and he'd evict them if he could. Many left, but Liberty saw this unwillingness to compromise as positive. He said it was creative tension and would make us stronger."

"Yet you believed in him."

"Yes," Ben said. "I couldn't imagine disagreeing with Mr. Liberty. The idea still frightens me. I thought he was a great man."

"And now?"

Ben looked at the floor. "Even great men make mistakes."

Ben looked away, and Joe waited a moment before continuing. He knew that for Ben, coming to him with this information represented a kind of surrender.

"What puzzles me," Joe said, "is that he seemed to have become more accommodating in the time I knew him. More accepting."

"It's true. I noticed it, too," Ben said. "I believe Elzbeta made the difference. She could disagree and he would listen. But when he lost the newspaper, he became as suspicious as before, seeing enemies everywhere. That's why I refused to go with him. He said we would return and set the community on its proper course. But I'm tired of fighting, and New Zion is my home."

Joe sighed. "And now you believe he'll try to take over the community single-handedly?"

Ben shrugged. "It's not in him to simply disappear. Perhaps he will find others."

"Who?" Then in an instant, Joe understood what Ben was getting at. "Kleinschmidt," he said, answering his own question. "My God."

"He didn't say so," Ben added quickly. "But Mr. Liberty would join anyone, stop at nothing, if he felt the end justified it." He looked down at the floor and said softly, "And I know Dr. Briggs is returning to Gays Mills."

Joe's knees cracked as he stood and walked to the window. "Is everyone against us?" he asked the room. Then he turned to look at

Ben. This man had turned his back on two mentors out of loyalty to the commune, despite his feelings about the direction Joe had taken it in. He put his hand on Ben's shoulder, "Thank you," Joe said, "for telling me. I know what this meant for you."

"I loved Mr. Liberty," Ben said. "He was the only father I've had since leaving Russia. But New Zion is more important than any man. It was my duty to tell you."

thirty-five

The wind was dry and from the west. Joe's tongue felt as if it had been dragged in the dirt all the way from Nebraska. He swallowed, trying to locate some saliva from the nether regions of his throat, but the roof of his mouth was as rough as sandpaper. He scanned the railroad tracks but saw nothing except a cloud of gnats hanging expectantly in the air, waiting, as he was, for the morning mail train.

It had been dry since the flood, but no one had been concerned until the end of June. Now they were calling it the worst drought in ten years. It seemed to Joe that Wisconsin was a land of extremes: either there was too much water or none at all; the summer sun burned the corn, and in winter the cold made their lives miserable. He asked his uncle if the weather was ever temperate. "Remember that nice stretch we had in May?" Shmuel said. "The trees were just turning and the sun was warm?"

"It lasted two days, Uncle."

Shmuel nodded. "That was spring."

Now even that short period was but a fond memory. The heat was unremitting, and the dirty ribbon of the Kickapoo had shrunk to a trickle incapable of floating leaves. The vegetables in the community garden had shriveled into brown cones and the men returned to work in the forest, knowing that if the crops failed, they would need to sell wood to survive. The cows' teats, like the river, had dried up, and there was no milk, no cheese. As in the days when Mr. Liberty was their leader, the comrades made their meals of graham crackers and dirty water. But now they lacked the spiritual underpinning he had provided. There were only hardships, no rewards. With nothing to do in the evening, the comrades sat inert in their sweaty despair. Joe felt responsible. He knew they'd be better off solving mathematical problems and chanting positivist slogans than cursing the weather.

Now he walked across the platform, looking for shade. He was alone this morning except for the stationmaster, a small man who busied himself with a luggage cart that needed a wheel. Looking up the tracks, Joe imagined he was about to set off on a journey, to San Francisco or New York, the direction didn't matter, as long as it was away from Wisconsin. He would start over again, working in an office or perhaps back at the *Forward* with Cahan. There he could rededicate himself to the ideals he had believed in when he arrived in America. Anyway, it would be different, better.

In the distance, he heard the train, and as it grew closer, his fantasy faded to reality. The engine drew only four cars, from which the exhausted passengers hung, their faces charcoal gray with soot. The train sighed to a stop alongside the platform, pausing only long enough to unload a few tired parcels and the canvas mailbags onto a wagon before pulling away again, until only a dusty curtain of cinders indicated it had ever been there. Joe watched it recede in the distance. Then he pulled his shirt off his back and followed the wagon to the post office to pick up his mail.

Main Street was empty and the hotel shimmered in the morning sun like a mirage. It looked preposterous now, with its welcoming dock extending out over the dry, cracked dirt of the riverbed. Without thinking, Joe turned into the *Beacon-Call* office after half a block. For a moment he was blind in the darkness, but then he saw Bryan Dorsey sitting in the back, waving a large fan that carried an advertisement for a La Crosse funeral parlor. "Hot enough for you?" Bryan said, indicating a chair next to him.

"Where'd you get the fan?"

"Side benefit of my business." Then he smiled. "You don't think taking it compromises me, do you?"

"Not unless funeral homes are in the news."

"Someone dies every day," Bryan said. "Probably every hour, somewhere." He pulled his shirt away from his skin. Perspiration glowed on his forehead. "What brings you to town, or is this just a social call?"

Joe looked around. The press had been repaired, and there was little evidence of the previous winter's destruction. Bryan had put his life back together. "I was wondering if you'd seen Mr. Liberty? We've heard nothing since he left."

"No news is good news," Dorsey said. "Actually, though, I have. And his beautiful daughter, too. Who, incidentally, is looking better than ever since she bought some new clothes. A dress in royal blue I noticed particularly. Sets off her hair nicely and brings out the color in her eyes."

"It sounds like you've been studying her closely."

"Part of the job," Dorsey said, and smiled. "Society page. Keeping my ear to the ground and all that."

"Sure," Joe said. "But what about Mr. Liberty? I suppose you've had the same watch on him?"

"Not exactly. Not much to watch, to tell the truth. From what I hear, he just stays in his room over to the hotel, even to eat. Seems to be waiting for something, but don't ask me what. Want a drink?" He produced a bottle of whiskey from beneath his chair, and it occurred to Joe that Dorsey was drunk.

"No thanks," he said, rising from his chair. "I think I'll take a walk."

"Looking for blue dresses?" the editor said, then raised his hand in a salute. "No offense, now, Joe. You know that."

Joe smiled. "Maybe I'll stop back and we can have dinner. It's been a long time since we've talked."

"Do that," Dorsey said, and returned to his bottle.

Outside, Joe hesitated briefly, uncertain what to do. He stopped at the general store, then walked the length of Main Street twice. Finally, he went to the hotel and asked for Mr. Liberty's room. He climbed to the third floor until at last he stood in front of the door, feeling the heat pressing against him. He breathed deeply and smelled dust. Then he knocked.

Inside, a chair scraped on the floor, and Joe heard the rustle of what might have been bedclothes. It seemed unlikely that he would still be in bed. Yet when the door opened, Joe saw not Edward Liberty but Lizzie.

"What a surprise, Yosl," she said. But she didn't seem especially surprised. Perhaps she'd been expecting him all along. "Come in."

She was wearing the blue dress, but Dorsey's description hadn't done it justice. The fabric fit tightly in the bodice and clung to Lizzie's hips before opening into a modified train that just brushed the floor. Her hair was diaphanous, backlit by the windows and bleached white by the sun, and her eyes were brilliant, clear and blue. Joe swallowed, ashamed of his dusty overalls and scuffed boots in front of this elegant lady. He tried to speak, but his voice was an unrecognizable croak. Lizzie rescued him. She took his arm and pulled him gently toward her. "Come," she said.

Joe smelled perfume—some exotic spice, he guessed—but the room was violent with light, and there was practically no furniture. She offered him water, and he took the glass gratefully, drained it and then another. Then he said, "I was looking for your father."

"We have adjoining rooms," Lizzie said, gesturing toward an open door. "Unfortunately, Father has left for the day."

Joe started to ask where he'd gone, but thought better of it. He stood awkwardly with the water glass in his hand, having no reason to stay but not wanting to leave. "I appreciated your letter," he said stiffly.

Spots of red appeared over Lizzie's cheekbones. "You do understand, don't you, Yosl? I had to go. I couldn't desert Father."

"Of course," Joe said, not understanding anything. A beautiful young girl, supposedly in love, leaves to follow her father, a man who cares less for people than for mathematics. This made sense? Liberty was a man of principle, Joe would grant him that. But he was also selfish and vain. "I understand," he repeated dully.

"You didn't really love me, anyway," Lizzie said.

"Who says so?" Joe felt betrayed. It bothered him that she knew.

"I saw how you looked at the other girls. Did you think I was blind?"

Was it that obvious? Joe had looked indeed, at all of them, even the married women, their breasts round and full of milk, their blouses damp over their nipples where babies hadn't sucked them dry. And not just at this. He'd also noticed their faces and arms, ruddy from the sun, their solid, muscular rumps barely camouflaged by the tentlike dresses they wore. The women of New Zion were constantly bent over and coy, Joe thought, in their way of flashing a few centimeters of white skin as they moved by. Even their smell—a fruity ripeness—aroused him. But he had never done anything imprudent. His manner was always shy and respectful, and he'd thought his voyeurism had been well hidden.

"Where is the crime in watching?" he said now.

"No crime," Lizzie said. "But we all knew. The other girls liked it. When we exercised, they'd tease me, threaten to kidnap you and take you to the riverbank."

"Well, you were always against ownership; you said we were free."

"Don't be silly," Lizzie said archly. "Ideally, but people are selfish."

Suddenly she sounded reasonable, and Joe wondered when the change had occurred. "I had no idea I was so popular," he said. "It seems unfair, considering the shortage of women. The men have to go off to Milwaukee or Chicago to find wives."

Lizzie laughed scornfully. "Most of them will have to go farther than that. Either they're old and fat, like your uncle, or young and foolish, like Ben. All they can talk about is politics."

"I didn't know you were so romantic. Most of the men learned what they know from your father."

"Let them marry him, then," Lizzie said. "Anyway, we agreed you were the best man available. But don't let it go to your head."

"I can't help it," Joe said. "I'm pleased." He shook his head in wonder.

Lizzie looked at him, her eyes sad. "Father won't be back until later," she said. "But I was serious, Yosl. I'm leaving."

"Yes," Joe said. "I know." He pulled her to him until he could rest his head against her hip, feeling her warmth on his forehead. "You're leaving, I know that. But for now, for an hour, we'll be together again, the way we used to be."

Lizzie's face was intent as they made love. Their bodies were slick, as if they'd been greased, and slapped together like seals. Soon the sheets were soaked through to the mattress, but Lizzie was insatiable, pulling him to her until he ached and then arousing him again with her mouth. She rolled over on top, her body like a furnace, wet and more familiar than Annuta's, her legs muscular and elastic with desire. Finally, they slept, the sheets cool and refreshing in the hot room, and when Joe awoke, the sun was slanting through the window. He felt sore, but euphoric.

Lizzie was at the washstand, running a cloth over her nude body and between her legs. The motion, innocent as it was, made Joe hard again, but the pain was too much. He wrapped the sheet around his waist and rolled onto his stomach. Still silent, he admired her slim waist and firm behind until she turned to see him staring at her. "You must leave," she said. "Father will be back."

"I can't move."

"You have to," Lizzie said sensibly. "That's his bed."

Joe looked at the stained sheets and imagined Liberty coming in and finding them this way. "I'll manage," he said.

Then they stood at the door, facing each other. He noticed slight blue smudges under her eyes, a small stain on her dress, imperfections he would take away with him. This was the moment he would remember, but he could think of little to say.

"Will I see you again?" Lizzie asked.

"I thought you were going away."

"Yes. To Kansas. Father has friends from one of the other communes." She smiled slightly. "It's terribly hot and dry there, but Father has his hopes."

Joe envied Liberty his convictions, and his hold on Lizzie. "He was always an optimist."

Lizzie flashed a radiant smile. She seemed both embarrassed and proud. "Yes, isn't it all ridiculous? My God, what a way to spend my life, following a madman around from place to place all over America. You know, he still plans to return triumphantly to Russia one day." She nodded at the foolishness of it all. Then, as an afterthought, "They are progressive about women."

"In Russia?"

"No. Kansas. I think there's even a woman mayor."

"But women can't vote."

"In Kansas they can."

They stood talking about other things, prolonging the time before he would leave for good. Joe imagined Lizzie on the stump, giving speeches. It wouldn't be so different from New Zion. "So you'll go into politics?"

"I don't think so, but why should men always run everything? I'm sure women couldn't make a greater mess of the world than you have."

"I have only ruined a small part of the world," Joe said. "But I agree with you. What does your father think?"

"He's a strong supporter of women's rights."

Then there was nothing more to say. They held hands silently in the dusty hall, turning shyly from one another. Still redolent of love and sweat, they talked of justice and women's suffrage. "I'll miss you, Elzbeta." Joe said so softly that he wondered if she had heard it. Then he caressed the small blue vein that pulsed beneath the translucent skin of her forehead. He kissed her chastely on each cheek and on the lips. "I'll miss you forever."

"I know," Lizzie said, nodding. Then, just before the door closed, the whisper of wood against carpet loud in the empty corridor, he heard, or thought he heard her say, "Forget me. Marry Annuta."

thirty-six

They set out at ten for the Indian camp. While the others complained about the weather, Shmuel said, he did something about it. He drank cider in his cabin. Having run out, however, he had decided to replenish his supply, and Joe had agreed to keep him company. He felt guilty for not having shown more interest in the Indians and thought he could write Cahan about the trip. When they left, there was a slight breeze, but by noon Shmuel was laboring, and they stopped to rest. There was nothing to drink, so Joe chewed grass, imagining moisture in it.

"You look tired, Yosl," Shmuel said.

Joe had thought he was asleep. "Yes, but I have no right to be. I work very hard every day at doing nothing."

"What else is there to do?" Shmuel said. He sat up and wiped his forehead with a handkerchief. "Why don't you start another newspaper, but without all that positivist *mishegoss*?"

"When Mr. Liberty left, he took our treasury, also the press. The comrades wouldn't appreciate my spending what little money is left on such things."

"To hell with them," Shmuel said. "Who knows what they want?"

Joe smiled. He appreciated Shmuel more now, appreciated his judgment. "The truth is they deserve a better leader," Joe said. "Someone like Ben."

"That nudnick? He couldn't lead prayers on shabbos."

"You, then, or Abe, or even Held. I don't care. Whatever you say about Mr. Liberty, he inspired some of the people. I can't even inspire myself. At least when he was here, I had a function. Now, there's no correspondence and no paper to edit."

"You sound like you miss the crazy fool. Or is it just his daughter?"

"Both of them," Joe said honestly. "But mostly, I miss the way I felt then, the sense of purpose I had."

"You're getting old, or at least you sound old. Just remember, Yosl, it's a long, hot summer. Everyone feels useless."

"This is more than that, Uncle."

Shmuel lay back in the weeds and breathed sonorously, but he wasn't asleep. "Suppose you're right. I don't agree, but suppose you are as incompetent as you think you are. The fact is you're the only one the community can agree on right now. Unless you want to split us up the middle, you have to stay on as leader—there's no other choice. Anyway, what else would you rather do, run after more *shikses*?"

Joe ignored this. "I might go to university. Father wanted me to be an educated man, not a farmer."

Shmuel nodded. "A fine idea. But you can't study for nothing. And while you're studying, how will you eat?"

"I have a little money from the *Forward*. I'd get a job. And I met a man, a Russian, who told me poor students can get loans to pay their fees."

Shmuel got up and they started walking again. "What about the Moses?"

"Should I ask his permission, too?"

Shmuel laughed and cuffed Joe on the head. "I have an idea what he'd say, but that isn't what I meant."

"What then? We haven't heard of him in weeks."

"And also nothing from Briggs and nothing from Liberty. This doesn't strike you as strange?"

"It strikes me as fortunate, Uncle, something we should be thankful for, not question." He didn't want to tell Shmuel about his meeting with Lizzie.

"You're right. Praise God. But after the winter and spring, it seems odd that they'd all disappear at once. I don't trust such coincidences."

"Perhaps they've forgotten us and gone on to more worthy projects."

Shmuel snorted and looked up at the sun. "Liberty, I know, is a man who is unable to forget. And I have a feeling that the Moses is similarly afflicted."

Joe remembered Ben's saying the same thing. When his uncle and Ben agreed on a point, Joe had learned to pay attention. "So you think they're working together?"

"Who knows, but I don't trust them. You want to do something, why don't you start getting ready?"

"For what? We don't know what's going to happen."

"Exactly. If we did, it would take no brains to prepare for it."

The Indian village came into sight, and a few mangy dogs ran to meet them, nipping at their heels and then mounting their legs until Shmuel drove them off with his walking stick.

"You're right," Joe said. "I was only thinking of myself. I'll stay until this business with the Moses is finished. But after that, I must go."

"If there's anything left of New Zion after that."

"Yes," Joe agreed. "If there is."

It seemed to Joe that no one in the chief's tent had moved since their last visit. It had been winter then, and now the summer heat lay on them like a blanket, but the group of Indians hunched around the fire appeared not to have noticed the change in seasons. They sat in their heavy blankets, staring vacantly at the carcass of dog or wild pig turning slowly on the spit. Shmuel had disappeared, so Joe squeezed between two braves who neither granted him room nor seemed to resent the space he created. Yet despite the familiarity of the tent, beneath the smoke and fetid smell, something was different. Joe squinted in the light and then he saw it—his jacket, the one he had lost in Gays Mills to the drunken Indian. That fierce killer of women and children, the murderous savage saved by the Moses, was sitting beside him in the tent, pie-eyed on jimson weed, wild hemp, and the harsh cider that was the cash crop of his people.

Excited and fearful, Joe looked at the Indian out of the corner of his eye, then turned back quickly to the fire. Just as he had been amazed at Crazy Dog's transformation from a hopeless drunk to a renegade brave at Kleinschmidt's rally, so now was he shocked anew by the Indian's condition. Smashed veins crisscrossed his broken nose, and his eyes were bloodshot and overlaid with yellow bags of pus. Though his arms were muscular, a loose fringe of flesh belted his waist, and his color was a sickly gray. Kleinschmidt had called Crazy Dog a Menomonee warrior, a fierce killer whose fury had only been stanched by the power of Christ. But these people were Blackfeet, and they'd fought no one in years.

Joe drank when the leather mug of cider was passed to him, though he said nothing. He was perplexed by the Indian's presence but didn't know how to approach him. Finally, he whispered, "Crazy Dog, can you hear me?"

The Indian didn't move. Now he appeared to be asleep, and his eyelids flickered spasmodically in a dream. Amazed by his own bravery, Joe nudged him slightly, and the Indian swayed but remained silent. Joe didn't want to draw the attention of the rest of the tribe, but he was determined to engage the Indian. "I saw you with Kleinschmidt," he hissed. "The Moses. In Gays Mills." Still no response. Finally, in desperation, he tugged the sleeve of the Indian's jacket. "You're wearing my coat."

Now Crazy Dog turned slowly, majestically. The small bags of fat undulated on his eyeballs like butter as he regarded Joe dully. "What?"

"This is my jacket," Joe said. "I found you lying in the street and covered you with it. Then I saw you in the park with the Moses. Later on, I mean."

The Indian nodded imperceptibly. "Who are you?"

"Joseph Abrams. I came here with my uncle to buy cider."

"Fat Sam. Your uncle is Fat Sam, the Jew man?"

Joe smiled involuntarily. He wondered if Shmuel knew what they called him. He nodded. "Fat Sam's my uncle."

The Indian grunted and turned back to the fire. But Joe wasn't satisfied. "Crazy Dog," he said again.

This time the Indian looked annoyed, and another transformation occurred. Now his features seemed sharper, clearer, and his speech wasn't slurred. "Look, my name isn't Crazy Dog. And I'm no Menomonee or I wouldn't be here, would I? That's just something Kleinschmidt dreamed up. Call me Antonio."

"Antonio?" Joe didn't know much about the Blackfeet, but he was pretty sure this wasn't a tribal name.

"My father was half-Italian. He came here, knocked up my mother, and disappeared. But she was always sentimental about it, so I got his name."

Joe looked carefully at the Indian to see if he was telling the truth. He looked like the others, but Joe supposed the black hair and dark skin could also be Mediterranean. What did he know? It was possible. "Antonio," he repeated.

"Tony, if you like that better. Doesn't matter to me. Anyway, no more Crazy Dog, all right?"

"Fine," Joe nodded. "How did you meet Kleinschmidt, anyway?"

Antonio shrugged. "Friend of a friend. I was in Milwaukee working at a stable near the river, and a man comes in one day looking for an Indian."

"Any Indian?"

"Happens all the time. Someone's opening a store or having a party, and they want a savage around for some color. Anyway, next thing I know, I'm undressed, wearing all this makeup, dancing onstage. I was drunk, but to tell the truth, I kind of liked it, scaring the people, getting them mad. Around here, the girls could always kick my ass. It was good to feel mean for a change."

"You mean you never killed anyone?"

Antonio looked contemptuous. "How long you been in this country? Any Indian that actually touched—I mean *touched*—a white woman, they'd hang him by his balls from the hotel balcony at noon. I'm a drunk, but I'm not stupid."

"And Kleinschmidt knows this?"

"He wouldn't want me around if I was really dangerous. But I'll admit the first time he used Crazy Dog in a speech—we were up in Kewaunee—I almost pissed in my pants. I thought I was going to get lynched, and I almost did. Some guy started coming after me until his friends pulled him back. After that, I asked them to take the raping and killing out of the act, but the word was out. The papers printed it, and then it was no use."

Antonio talked about Kleinschmidt's organization as if it were a vaudeville troupe, traveling around, making money, hurting no one. He wondered if New Zion even entered the Indian's mind. "So you went along with it?"

"What could I do? Who'd believe some Indian greaseball against the Moses of the Menomonee?"

"I see your point," Joe said. They both drank from a circulating gourd, and Antonio took a deep draw from a smoldering clay pipe, holding the smoke in his lungs before coughing and exhaling. Out of courtesy, Joe waited until he caught his breath. Finally, Antonio seemed to have recovered. "Why do you do it?" Joe asked. "Why humiliate yourself this way?"

"Money," Antonio said simply. "It's better than shoveling horse shit at the stable. And like I said, it's not all bad, scaring white people. I spent a lot of years being scared of them, of you."

Joe had not thought of himself as an oppressor before—or even as white—but Antonio had a point. The Indians were America's Jews, and American cavalry troops were no less marauders from the Indians' point of view than the Black Hundred had been from his. He changed the subject. "Why aren't you with the Moses now?"

Antonio looked surprised. "I am. He's in La Crosse, but we only work once or twice a week. In between, he lets me come back here. He figures I'd only get in trouble up there." Antonio looked thoughtful now. "Bastard's probably right."

So Kleinschmidt was in the area. Immediately, Joe became suspicious. He wasn't scared, not yet, but he wanted to know more. Antonio took another drag on the pipe and passed it to Joe. Anxious to preserve the bond between them, Joe put the wet stem in his mouth and sucked the acrid smoke into his lungs, holding it until tears came to his eyes and his cheeks seemed about to burn. Then he exhaled gratefully and surprised himself by not coughing.

"Not bad," Antonio said and clapped him on the back. "I never seen a Jew smoke before."

"Not Fat Sam?"

"Is he here?" Antonio looked around, but his head was swimming. "Fat Sam's got a weakness for cider and women, but he never comes into the tent."

Joe waited until he was sure he could speak. "Is Kleinschmidt coming back to Gays Mills?"

The Indian nodded. "Watch out." The words were soft but sharp in the dim light, and now the easy conversational tone was displaced by a subtle tension.

Joe was leaning forward so intently that his neck cramped, and he shook it to relieve the tightness. "For what?"

Antonio looked around, but none of the other Indians had moved. What would they care anyway, Joe wondered. "Fat Sam and my uncle are friends; that's the only reason I'm telling you," Antonio said. "That and the coat. Personally, I don't give a shit if you all kill each other."

"We don't want to kill anyone," Joe said. "Who wants to kill us?"

"No one, yet," Antonio said. "Just watch out, like I said. It's easy to think Kleinschmidt's crazy—all that Moses crap, and the robes—but don't let that make you overconfident. There are important people behind him."

"The White Christian Legion?"

Antonio was impressed. "How'd you know about that?"

"We have our own spies," Joe said, and smiled. In one sense, he had an advantage: he'd always taken Kleinschmidt seriously, even when others hadn't. "I just don't understand why they're after us—sixty people out in the country."

Antonio nodded. "I don't really see it either. But Kleinschmidt got a little crazy after the flood. Before that, we'd go out and do a show and wait for the money to roll in. When we got low, we'd go out again. And that was it. The only reason we went to Gays Mills in the first place was that they were sick of us everywhere else. We needed something new, and someone told him about the Jews. He just stuck New Zion in at the last minute because he didn't know what else to say. You couldn't scare a baby with stories about these sacks of shit." He gestured to the others around the fire, and Joe had to admit they didn't look very fierce.

"It was an accident, then," Joe said softly.

"You could say that. But after the flood, like I said, he changed. Now he doesn't want to go around and do shows anymore. He doesn't want the women or the booze; he's a new man. He closes up the big house in Mukwonago and spends all his time traveling by himself. He buys guns, talks to these nuts from Chicago, I don't know what all. All he talks about is how he's going to go back and get the Jews. Crazy stuff. Then, just when he was beginning to quiet down, one comes to us."

"One of us?"

"He said so. Tall, yellow hair, but old?"

"Mr. Liberty," Joe said.

"That's it. So him and Kleinschmidt sit and talk, a long time, all afternoon, maybe. After, they bring in the head reader and talk some more."

"Dr. Briggs."

"That's the one. The three of them talk all one day, and then they have dinner and go on some more. Next thing I know, the whole Milwaukee operation is over, closed down, and we're going to La Crosse, which is okay with me—I get to see my people. But now, in between shows, Kleinschmidt ain't happy like he used to be. He wears that goddamned cape all the time, even when there's no reason for it, and there's guns all over the place. One guy blew his big toe off by mistake, and I figured I could be next. So I came down here. Like I said, watch out."

Joe took another drag from the pipe and watched the fire. He was aware of a tickling sensation over his eyes, as if his forehead were set in drying mud. He wondered if he could move. "When?" he whispered. Antonio said nothing, and Joe wondered if he'd gone too far. Antonio was gazing into the fire, a new serenity on his face. Joe had the eerie impression that the others were listening, though no one had moved. Finally, Joe rose to his knees with difficulty and shook his head. He wanted to tell Shmuel, and it was a long walk home. He thought Antonio was too far gone to say much more.

"Next week, maybe sooner," the Indian muttered, his voice a hoarse growl. Joe put his hand on Antonio's shoulder and leaned forward in the gloom. The Indian's eyes were glassy. Around them, the others seemed no more than bunches of cloth piled around the ceremonial fire.

"Thank you, friend," Joe said. But Antonio gave no sign of having heard.

Shmuel was disgruntled when Joe found him in a smaller tent well on his way to incoherence. He was with two half-dressed Indian girls who were pulling playfully at his trousers. "Take one," he said. "But for God's sake, leave me alone."

"No, Uncle, we must leave. Kleinschmidt is coming back with Mr. Liberty and Briggs. We have to warn the others."

Shmuel looked up with more interest. "Who says so?"

"It doesn't matter. Come." Joe grabbed an arm, but the Indian girls refused to let go. Shmuel seemed pleased to be the object of such competition.

"It matters to me," Shmuel said. "Who told you this nonsense?"

"An Indian who lives here. He's part of Kleinschmidt's group. He says his uncle's the chief, and he calls you Fat Sam."

Shmuel laughed, the sound loose and liquid in his throat. "Fat Sam, how do you like that, Nephew? Well," he said, shaking his head violently. "When is this calamity supposed to occur?"

"I don't know. Antonio didn't, either. Next week, maybe."

Shmuel looked at Joe with the tolerance reserved for lunatics and children. Then he shook his head again. "Nephew, despite appearances, I'm a man who abhors waste. I've paid these ladies for their time, and I intend to enjoy my investment to the fullest. You're welcome to share them with me, but don't ask me to leave. Anyway, what difference does it make? From what you say, we can choose either to be killed now or later. I prefer later."

"How much later?"

"An hour or two?" Shmuel smiled now. "Are you weakening, Nephew?"

The idea of sharing women with his uncle was so foreign to Joe that he couldn't make sense of what he was feeling. He knew it was wrong, but despite this, he felt himself becoming aroused. "I suppose an hour or two won't make any difference," he said.

"Ha," Shmuel said, and pulled him to the ground. "Here, Yosl, drink. In a few minutes, you won't think about a thing. And that might do you some good."

As they walked back to New Zion, Joe told his uncle what Antonio had said. He didn't want to talk about the girls; he felt guilty for having enjoyed himself. But Shmuel showed little interest. The older man breathed heavily, tired from the day's exertions and the fast pace they were keeping. Two heavy leather bags of cider swayed from his neck, as if he were a dray horse, and sweat gleamed on his forehead. "If we go, we go," Shmuel had said. "But there's no special virtue in dying sober."

The sun was sinking, but the sky remained a perfect cerulean blue. Intermittently, Joe smelled smoke, but looking, he saw no huts, no sign of human habitation. But then he noticed the row of maple and birch trees that lined their path. Here and there, a branch or cluster of dry leaves smoldered like smudge pots, sparks rising from the trees like fireflies, carried by the wind from limb to limb.

"Uncle, there's a fire," Joe said, feeling foolish for pointing out the obvious. Shmuel was unconcerned. He kept walking, head down, sweat darkening his shirt and dripping onto his pants.

"Uncle," Joe said again.

Shmuel stopped, plainly annoyed. "Look, you made me cut short my stay at the camp for no reason. Now you announce what is plain to anyone with eyes in his head—that there are fires along our way. Must we also act to save these trees?"

"That isn't what I meant," Joe said. "What if the fire spreads?"

"Then we shall all be cinders by morning—and probably the better for it. But why worry about things you can't help?" Shmuel stopped, and lowered his bags to the road. "See here, Yosl," he said. "Hunters and Indians are always in the woods and on the river, looking for game. At night, they build huge fires to keep the animals away, and in the morning, they leave without putting them out. The Indians think they would offend the gods if they did otherwise; the farmers have no excuse. In a dry year, the sky is always full of fire and smoke, with the woods glowing everywhere. I've seen immense forests incinerated in a matter of hours. Yes, it's true, don't look at me like that. This is our life; this is what we must accept if we're going to live here."

"I didn't mean to doubt you."

"Good. You may be the leader of the community, but you're still my nephew, and I'm responsible for you, God help us."

As Shmuel talked, Joe noticed the sky growing darker. All around them there was an eerie silence. The sounds of birds calling to one another, usually omnipresent, were replaced by crackling sounds and occasional loud pops as branches exploded in flames. Now, Joe noticed a small peninsula of fire moving fluidly along the dry grass at the base of the trees, measuring their progress along the path.

"Look there," he said.

"What of it?" Shmuel grunted irritably. "I don't worry about a grass fire. I've seen them move over the ground like lightning, faster than this." He snapped his fingers in Joe's face. "It's forest fires you worry about, and here there are only a few trees. The wind will take this past us in a moment, wait and see."

As if in response, the wind picked up, blowing sparks across the road, until Joe and Shmuel were walking through a blazing gauntlet of fire, even as burning branches from the trees overhead dropped to temporarily block their way. Now the wind blew the flames higher until the wall of smoke and cinders made it nearly impossible to see. Joe's nostrils were on fire, and his throat ached when he tried to breathe. Panic settled over him like a blanket. His eyes were tearing and his lungs throbbed. "I'm burning up," he said.

Shmuel took a flask of cider from his pack and doused his handkerchief. "Here," he said. "Cover your face with this."

"But it's alcohol. We'll go up like torches."

"It's all we have," Shmuel said roughly, pushing the rag into Joe's hand.

They huddled together in the center of the road, the fire so close that Joe expected his clothes to ignite at any moment. "Go for the river," Shmuel said.

"How?" The Kickapoo was two hundred yards away, through the fire, and Joe couldn't see five feet.

"If we can get out of this circle of fire, we'll be all right," Shmuel shouted. "It's better than burning to death in the middle of the road." He pointed to the charred limb of an ash tree in Joe's path. "Grab that branch!" he ordered.

Joe wrapped his kerchief around his arm and hand and picked it up. "Now what?"

Shmuel was holding a spruce bough with its needles burned off. "Hold it in front of you and beat the flames," he said, putting his head down. Then he started flailing at the fire—left, right, then directly in front of him. Joe followed in his uncle's wake, inheriting an instant of fresh air with each step. He did his best to imitate Shmuel's motions, but the smoke blinded him. Tears were hot on his singed cheeks, and his feet were burning from the cinders underfoot. Still, he kept going, swinging his branch like a sword and breathing shallowly into the cider-soaked rag.

Then they were past it, and the brisk wind cooled them instead of fanning the fire. Shmuel's eyebrows were charred and white ash coated Joe's body, but they were safe, while behind them, the fire continued to burn in a tight circle. The countryside was quiet. Perhaps Shmuel had been right: maybe the fire would burn itself out without affecting any of the settlements. Joe stood looking at his uncle, surprised that they were still alive but too shaken to be happy.

"Should we get water?" Joe asked at last, pointing to the fire.

"Where? The river is little more than a puddle."

"But can we just assume it will die on its own?"

"No. We'll go back and cover all the buildings with wet blankets and put buckets every few feet around the grounds. Then we'll pray, since none of that would stop a real fire."

They started to walk again, smelling cinders all the way home. Just as they were about to turn in at New Zion, Joe stopped. "Uncle," he said. "Were you scared back there?"

Shmuel looked at him and smiled. "I would have to be crazy if I wasn't scared. I'll be dead soon enough, after all. At my age you come to understand this. But it's over now. Forget it."

They wet down the buildings and slept with damp rags on their faces and buckets next to their beds. But even after the fire had passed them by, Joe couldn't expunge the image of a black cloud, rising high as an office building, threatening all of them. For days afterward, he was spitting out ashes.

thirty-seven

Joe watched his uncle work. Shmuel breathed loudly as he dug, his shovel rooting deep into the dry red soil. Then he deposited the dirt where he had thrown the rest, his head barely visible over the accumulated mound. Now he stopped to drink from the flask and wipe his face with a large blue handkerchief. Joe looked right and left at the haphazard network of trenches that cut across the field, some narrow, others, like Shmuel's, broad and deep. It looked rough, but it would be enough to break a horse's leg in the dark—or a man's, if he weren't careful.

"Excellent work, Uncle," Joe said. "Everyone should do as well."

Shmuel grunted. "For all the good it will do. What if they come by the road, as any sensible person would, instead of across the field?"

Joe was carrying a water bucket and held the ladle out for Shmuel to drink from. "They probably will," Joe said. "That's the easiest part of the plan. With all the rocks on the bluff, it'll be easy to create a small landslide and block it. Then we'll run the trenches from the river up to the road. Where else could they go?"

Abe came over for a drink and put his arm on Joe's shoulder, but Shmuel wasn't finished. "You could step over some of these trenches," he said. "You think the Moses won't see that?"

Abe laughed. "Give the boy some credit, Shmuel. It's a good plan.

Of course, if you knew the trenches were there, it would be easy to avoid them. But that's our advantage: we know the land and they don't."

"A regular Judah Maccabee," Shmuel said. "It's our only advantage."

Joe continued examining Shmuel's trench. "You're right, Uncle," he said. "And it isn't much. We can surprise them and we know the territory. But some will get to the camp anyway, and they have guns. For that matter, they could use the river as a highway, if they only knew it. The water is low enough."

"Very good," Shmuel said. "For once you agree with me. We have no more weapons now than last time. So how can we fight this Christian Legion?"

"I've been thinking," Joe said carefully. "Perhaps we could start a fire?"

"You want to invite them to dinner?"

Joe smiled. "No, but if the wind is right, we could create a wall of smoke that would drive them back more effectively than rifles would."

Shmuel was impressed. "Who'd have guessed you'd be such a strategist, Yosl? But what of the town? Gays Mills. It would be destroyed."

"Better them than us," Abe said bitterly. "What have we asked, except that they let us live in peace?"

"But it's not the town that opposes us, Abe," Shmuel said. "Just this Moses."

"No?" Abe said. "I was there this morning, and you'd think the circus was coming. It was like a holiday—crowds in the street, children skipping along, signs in the shop windows saying 'Welcome Moses.' Even the newspaper had a big headline: 'Moses Returns.' You say it's not the townspeople, but who shelters Kleinschmidt and who profits from his crusades against us? For the merchants, it's a wonderful opportunity. The girls flirt. It's like an occupying army."

"They're not against us, Abe, not the people," Shmuel said. "We've been shopping there for too long; they know us."

"Oh, they're willing to take our money," Abe said. "But we keep to ourselves most of the time, and we don't patronize the saloons or the hotel. We're different, Sam—surely you can see that, feel it. Well, they know it, too, so don't be surprised if some of your friends join with this Moses. Want a little evening entertainment? Go and watch the annihilation of the godless Jews. Mark my words."

"You agree with this nonsense, Yosl?" Shmuel asked.

Joe was impressed by Abe's anger. Usually he was quiet, reserved. "I've been to town, too, Uncle. And Abe's right. I don't want to kill anyone, but we have to defend ourselves. Besides, we're desperate. Do you have any other ideas?"

Shmuel looked into his trench and shook his head. "No. But I hope our work will be sufficient to hold them here."

"I hope so, too," Joe said. "And they may not come at all."

Shmuel shook his head grimly. "They'll come," he said. "Liberty will make sure of that."

Night came gradually in the summer, first a slight diminution of light, a new angle as the sun cut horizontally across the fields, turning everything golden. Then the actual, subtle darkening as the shade trees extended their influence, casting shadows between them and the buildings. And finally the soft lamps appeared inside and seemed to bring evening ever more quickly, like the falling of a curtain over the town. By nine, all was black except for the moon, full and orange, hanging large and ominous in the sky.

"So where are they?" Dorsey asked. Sweat dotted his forehead and he licked his lips nervously.

They were in front of City Hall, to the left of the platform that had been erected for the evening's rally. Joe tilted his head slightly and sniffed the air. He still smelled cinders. "The posters said 8:30. Maybe he's waiting for a larger audience."

Perhaps forty people stood in the dusty square, a disappointing crowd, Joe thought, especially considering the publicity Kleinschmidt's visit had received.

"They're scared," Dorsey said. "They think he's serious this time."

"Why should that bother anyone else? We're the ones he's after."

"Once someone starts shooting, it's easy for innocent people to get in the way. And Kleinschmidt didn't choose his men for their good judgment. If they start raising hell out there at New Zion, they're likely to continue on into town afterward."

Afterward. Dorsey's casual observation made Joe cold. Where would he be then—perhaps dead in a ditch, or, if he were lucky, only wounded? How many comrades would be lost, and what of New Zion itself? "They should have thought of that before they invited him," he said.

"No one invited anyone, Joe," Dorsey said sharply. "Unless it was Liberty with that goddamned newsletter. And you can't blame people for coming out to look. Hell, you're here, ain't you?"

"I have to be here," Joe said. But he knew Dorsey was right. It was natural for people to be curious. He'd learned that if he'd learned anything. No one was anxious to share the troubles of others, and you couldn't expect them to. He went over the plan again in his mind. To his surprise, Ben had offered his help. Once Liberty's alliance with the Moses had become known, he'd lost the support of the comrades. Joe and Ben had come to town together, and Ben had stationed himself across the square. Once it became clear that Kleinschmidt was going to attack New Zion, Joe would signal Ben, who would ride cross-country to warn the others.

Joe figured the Moses would be delayed for a few minutes getting organized, and then there was the roadblock. With luck, Kleinschmidt would be too impatient to try to dismantle it. Then the comrades would hope to fight on fairly equal terms in the darkness, despite their lack of weapons. The women and children had all been moved to the forest. They had planned what could be planned; there was nothing left to do. But Joe still felt pressure in his chest. He exhaled loudly.

"Nervous?" But before Joe could answer, Bryan pointed up the street. "There they are now," he whispered.

Suddenly the square was bright as day. His way lit by thirty men with torches, Jacob Kleinschmidt approached on horseback, circling the square grandly with his entourage before finally dismounting. He ascended the stage, accompanied, as usual, by his drummer, beating out the cadence as masked men in caftans took positions in front of the platform. The audience moved closer together, closing ranks now in front of the Moses, but their number hadn't increased significantly.

Joe studied Kleinschmidt. He thought the Moses looked more reserved than angry tonight, almost somber. Perhaps he was thinking of what lay ahead. Now Joe noticed that Kleinschmidt's retinue included Edward Liberty, who stood diffidently to the right of the stage, his eyes staring out blankly over the crowd in the direction of New Zion. Liberty wasn't wearing a green cloak like the others, but Joe wasn't reassured. He seemed totally self-contained, unaffected by noise of the proceedings, though ostensibly part of them. On the other side of Liberty, Briggs and several of the God-men stood laughing among themselves as if they were at a party. The idea that some would find the anticipation of violence stimulating frightened Joe. What chance did he and the comrades have against these fanatics?

Now the drummer was silent and Kleinschmidt stepped forward. "People of Gays Mills," he shouted, not bothering to wait for the crowd to settle. "When last I was here, you were imperiled by a treacherous flood that threatened to carry away what had taken a lifetime to build. Now, only four months later, you are once again in crisis, fighting the most prolonged drought in recent memory. Corn shrivels in your fields and the air is sulphurous with dust. The river that raged last February is so low it cannot carry boats downstream. The cows will no longer give the milk that allows you to produce the cheese for which your valley is justifiably famous.

"Why, you might ask yourselves, has all this happened to us? We're ordinary people. We work hard and pray to our God at night. We live good, clean lives. So why must we cover our little children's mouths with damp rags in order for them to draw breath? Some of you have left already, gone to friends and relatives who are not so afflicted; others are preparing to go. Gays Mills could become a ghost town, peopled only by the memory of the courageous pioneers who cleared the fields, braved the wilds, fought the Indians, and made this fine village what it is today."

Kleinschmidt paused for a moment to let this apocalyptic vision sink in, turning first in one direction, then the other, like a Chasid at prayer. Then he stepped forward again, his right arm raised in the air. "Well, there is a reason," he thundered out, causing his listeners to look at each other in surprise. "And I know what it is. It's as plain as the sun in the sky," Kleinschmidt shouted. "The Lord *wants* Gays Mills to suffer, and that's a fact."

Kleinschmidt stood, hands on hips, his cheeks as fat as a pouter pigeon's, challenging his audience to doubt him, but they were with him now, tense where they had been lethargic, eager to receive the True Word and angry that it should have taken this long to arrive. "And why?" Kleinschmidt said in a hoarse whisper that nevertheless carried over the square. "Why should the Lord want good folks who have worked and slaved all their lives to build something fine here on the prairie, folks who are the very image and soul of America, why should He want such people to suffer?"

Kleinschmidt shook his head as if the question were deeply troubling. "I asked myself that very question. I prayed to God, and he gave me the answer."

Kleinschmidt poised himself and pointed dramatically in the direction of New Zion. "There, friends, there is the reason for your troubles. The socialistic, atheistic commune that has the audacity to call itself New Zion. Rid your community of that cancer, and your river will fill, your fields will be green, and your cows will give milk. It's that simple."

Now the mood of the crowd seemed to shift. There was no questioning, no debate or discussion. Even the horses were eager to go, throwing their heads from side to side and snorting through their bridles. Joe worked his way around to the far left of the stage and locked eyes with Ben. It was still possible nothing would happen, he thought, but unlikely. In any case, it was best to be prepared, even if the assault never came. He nodded his head, and Ben was running to his horse.

"What was that?" Dorsey asked. He had watched the whole thing, but Kleinschmidt was speaking again, and Joe didn't answer.

"Now, you might say the Lord has more important things to do than pay attention to a few itinerant Hebrews who are sinners but who, after all, amount to little. Yes, you might say that. There are more important things in the world than these heathens, more pernicious threats. But as we know from the Sacred Book, nothing is too small for the Lord's attention. Who can say that these apparently natural calamities—this flood, the drought—were not caused by the Master, He who knows all and sees everything? Who can say that you aren't suffering for sins against Him?"

Kleinschmidt's forehead was crosshatched with wrinkles, and his body was tensed like a fighter's. "And so it came to me: the Jews must go. Rid this land of them and we are free! And then I knew I must come, that it was my duty, as it was Moses's before me, to warn you of an even greater tragedy if we fail to act now."

Joe was struck by the irony of Moses's arousing the people against the Jews, inciting the people in the name of God to attack His Chosen People. But now the Moses dropped theatrically to his knees and began to pray, eyes closed tight, his lips moving silently. For a moment, there was quiet in the open square, then someone shouted "How?" from the back. Kleinschmidt didn't move, so others took it up, at first sporadically, throwing the word back and forth across the street like a ball until so many were calling out that it became rhythmic, resounding through the small square like a locomotive. "How, how, how," the crowd chanted, while Kleinschmidt, deep in prayer, knelt on the stage, his face gleaming with perspiration. Finally, he rose to his feet and raised his arms. "How, how, how," continued echoing through the square.

"How, indeed?" Kleinschmidt said, and the chant started again, but lower this time, like a chorus beneath his voice. Kleinschmidt orchestrated the crowd, waving his arms like a conductor and then bringing them down. "How?" he asked again. "I say, by showing God we understand and accept His holy decree, His sacred mission." "How, how, how," rose again, but this time Kleinschmidt was ready. Raising a rifle overhead, he screamed, "By driving these Hebrew anarchists, the Antichrist, out for good, by reclaiming the land for decent Christian people, that's how."

This was greeted by howls of acclamation, and then the chant was back again, louder than before but accompanied this time by a contrapuntal response: "How, how . . . kill the Jews. How, how . . . kill the Jews."

Joe had seen enough. He was running now, with Dorsey keeping pace alongside. Behind him he heard gunfire, and turning, he saw horses rearing and sparks of fire rising in the night air. When he reached his horse, he said to Dorsey, "There's no point in your coming. It's not your fight."

"That's not the way you talked before. Are Jews the only ones against prejudice and bigotry?"

Joe mounted his horse as the animal canted to the right. "Do what you want, then. I don't have time to argue."

"Then shut up," Dorsey said, and climbed up behind him.

"Why do you want to be killed by these maniacs?"

"I'm a reporter," Dorsey said.

"That's a lousy reason to die," Joe said, and kicked the horse in the ribs. The animal bolted, almost throwing both of them before Joe got hold of the reins and steered for the Kickapoo.

By the time Joe and Bryan reached New Zion, the lights from Kleinschmidt's torches were visible in the distance, but there was no panic among the comrades. Dressed in black, their faces smudged with cork, they moved back and forth across the clearing in cadres of four or five. Each group had been assigned a position and equipped with whatever weapons were available. Joe hoped to force Kleinschmidt's men from their horses and then draw them into the clearing, where the comrades would attack in sequence from different directions. In a small area, rifles would be less effective because there wouldn't be time to set and aim. And in the dark, familiarity with the terrain could be crucial. Whether this would be enough to overcome the disadvantage in numbers was uncertain, but it was their only hope.

Ben approached, his face flushed and sweating from his ride. "They've hit the barricade," he said. His eyes were tearing in the strong wind. "They should be coming any minute."

Joe nodded. "Have everyone stay down until they pass the trenches, assuming they do. Some should be on foot by then. Then come around behind them. They'll probably go for the buildings, assuming we're all sitting inside reading anarchist tracts and discussing philosophy."

Ben smiled. "Anything else?"

"You've taken care of the rest. You're a soldier."

"They were your ideas," Ben said. "I only followed instructions."

Joe patted him on the back. "At New Zion, that's not such a small thing. Now, go to your position."

Dorsey was leaning against a large elm tree. "Thoughtful of the Moses to wave those torches around like that," he said. "Otherwise, you might not know where he is all the time."

Joe hefted an ax in his hand, testing the weight. He felt strong, and something like love for the people hiding in the long grass. "I don't think it ever occurred to him that Jews might fight back."

"Well, your people don't exactly have a history as great warriors."

"Read your Bible," Joe said grimly. The night, the proximity of the river, the howls of Kleinschmidt's army, all took him back to Russia, to the pogrom when he had run for cover, eager to save himself. He thought of his parents, dead in the street, and the wolves in the forest waiting for their meal. This time he would hide, but he wouldn't run. He inhaled deeply, smelling smoke and death, and surprised himself by not being afraid. They had a plan—he had one—and they believed in it. That was enough. Joe took his place behind the smooth trunk of a huge cottonwood and waited.

Out in the field, the bright lights of the torches looked oddly festive, like paper lanterns at a party. There were perhaps forty of them, and now they drew into a circle, gathering around Kleinschmidt for directions, Joe supposed. The lights looked like gaily colored birds, and from the safety of his hiding place, it was difficult to remember what they represented, why these people had come. Then the torches spread into a line across the field and started advancing slowly toward the commune.

Initially, they moved slowly, hesitantly, then the horses picked up speed, galloping now, until suddenly, only ten or twenty yards from the spot where Joe stood, all of them seemed to collapse at once, like a tower of cards at a carnival game. Shouts of anger and pain carried over the field and then the anguished cries of the crippled horses. The animals had done nothing, he thought, why should they have to suffer?

The trenches had accomplished their purpose, and it took time for the Moses to regroup. Joe heard men shouting curses and guns firing wildly. But then they attacked in earnest, the men howling like banshees now, furious at having been tricked, shooting indiscriminately at the dim outlines of buildings, trees, the sky.

In a moment, they were in the clearing, their cloaks ripped, headdresses askew. Rifles and pistols held high, they milled around uncertainly, looking for victims, heedless of resistance, but before they could analyze the situation, Ben's cadre burst out of hiding and was upon them. Kleinschmidt wheeled around to meet the challenge, but no sooner had he done so than Abe Rosenfeld, huge and angry, led Morris Held and a few others into battle. Abe was swinging a long scythe that Joe had watched him sharpen that afternoon, and in seconds dark patches of blood stained a half dozen caftans brown. Held, incongruously helmeted in a milk bucket with eye slits cut into it, darted back and forth behind and beneath Abe, jabbing the attackers with a long wooden pike fashioned from a hoe handle.

"Pull back, pull back," Kleinschmidt yelled, firing his rifle wildly.

A few men obeyed, but it was hard to distinguish lines in the darkness, to tell who was enemy or friend. At such close distances, their shots were as likely to hit their own men as the comrades.

Joe and his group were supposed to charge next, but before they could move, he heard an angry yell to his left and saw Shmuel, immense in a white tallis held on his head by a braided Blackfoot headband. Beneath the robe, Joe could see the leather straps of tefillim tied around both arms. Shmuel had prepared for battle as if he were going to shul.

"For Zion," Shmuel bellowed now, swinging a sharpened ax blade, and in the moment before he raised his hand to lead his group into the clearing, Joe wondered if this was sacrilege or merely a prayer for a new and violent land.

Then they were all fighting together, dust rising around them like ether as the green cloaks tried to retreat toward the trenches, the only escape left in the face of the comrades' furious opposition. Rifles, burnt-out torches, and bloodied bodies littered the ground, and it occurred to Joe that if there were ever another battle, they would at least be better armed.

As Kleinschmidt fell back, Abe and Shmuel led the comrades after him. Choking on dust in their wake, Joe felt euphoric, victorious. Each cough was a battle cry. He was running, following a green hulk, when he heard his uncle shout, "Yosl, watch behind you." He turned quickly to his right and ran into a rifle butt. For an instant everything seemed clear, illuminated by pain. The dust was replaced by a brilliant red flame in the center of his forehead. Then everything went black.

Joe awoke under a tree, disoriented, his feet halfway up the trunk. His first impulse was to take inventory, to make sure everything was intact. His arms and legs seemed fine, but his head felt like an overripe melon—enormous, and soft on top. Somewhere, something was leaking, and when he took his hand away, it was covered with blood. Joe's initial reaction was not fear but confusion. Then it all came back to him—the ambush, the battle, and Kleinschmidt's retreat. The calm that surrounded him seemed eerie. He wondered if he was dead, if this was the afterlife.

Slowly he sat up. The brisk night air was revivifying, and his vision began to clear in stages. It seemed surprising that his eyes were open, that he wasn't dead. He didn't see the other men; Dorsey and Shmuel were gone. To his right, near the main building, he noticed lights and movement. He imagined that Annuta and the other women had returned to restore order to the camp. Soon there would be a victory celebration with squash pies and latkes. Perhaps Shmuel would offer up some of his cider as an anesthetic. They were warriors returned from the fight, Joe thought with some satisfaction, though no one else had as yet come home. They had protected their land, their homes, their women, and they had actually won. It was a miracle. For a handful of yeshiva boys and aging radicals to turn back a gang like Kleinschmidt's, armed with rifles on horseback, there was no other word for it. A miracle.

Then, slowly, Joe realized that something was wrong. No one had come to his aid, though that meant little. They would be busy cleaning things up, cooking, doing what had to be done. What bothered him was that the glow of lights seemed to be growing stronger as he sat in his stupor. There were only a few oil lamps in the settlement. How could they have bought more in only a few hours?

Then, abruptly, he understood. The crowd he had imagined standing before him in the clearing was only two or three men running from hut to hut, carrying burning torches, setting the buildings afire. With difficulty he stood and staggered toward the dining hall, waving his arms.

"Stop," he croaked in a weak, unrecognizable voice. "Uncle," he called, but Shmuel was nowhere in sight. He was confused. Kleinschmidt had been beaten, humiliated, so who, then, was trying to burn down their community?

Joe wheeled around, looking for his weapon, but the ax had disappeared. He grabbed a rock and walked unsteadily toward the burning shacks. Sparks danced overhead and the wind carried them aloft to set new fires in the hayloft and high grass that surrounded New Zion. Joe turned around, wondering where everyone had gone. Then he heard a gun go off very close to his head and saw Edward Liberty astride a tall black horse, waving a rifle overhead as he rode toward him. Liberty's eyes were wild in the firelight and a gleeful smile played across his broad face.

"My gift to you, comrade," he screamed as he passed Joe, firing again. Joe fell to the ground and rolled against a tree. Where had Liberty come from? How had he gotten through their lines? Circling, Liberty charged past Joe again, sweeping low this time to scream, "We followed you up the river, comrade. Very clever, yes? But then I know the area well." Then he rode off, shooting into the sky.

The God-men were also mounted and coming at him. Joe ran for cover just as Liberty fired again, this time in earnest. The bullet kicked up dust to his right, and Joe knew they would corner him like an animal if he didn't get out of the open and find a hiding place. His head ached but his vision was clear. In the darkness, they wouldn't be able to see him if he moved away from the light.

Liberty was turning his horse in a circle, but this time he moved too close to the fire, and the animal reared high on his hind legs as his master took aim. Like a circus act, horse and rider pirouetted around until at last the horse, arching his back, staggered into an overhanging branch and knocked Liberty to the ground. For a moment, he seemed only dazed, about to rise to his feet. He shouted, "Freedom! Victory!" at the top of his lungs, and then he fell back, unconscious.

Watching from the brush, Joe wondered where the God-men had gone. Suddenly the clearing was quiet, though New Zion continued to burn. The fire had skipped over the buildings, and, where it was aided by the wind, Joe could see it running free, like a gigantic red wave, toward Gays Mills. Shaking off his fatigue, he started after it to warn Shmuel and the others.

Annuta was coming toward him, her face white as milk in the dull red glow of the fire. "Yosl, you're bleeding," she said. "Let me bandage your head."

"No," he said vaguely, but then he sat, too exhausted to argue. In the distance he saw the women coming out of the forest, their small shapes stopping every so often to look cautiously at what was left of their homes. Joe thought of the fire racing toward Gays Mills, and it occurred to him that few of the townspeople had joined with the Moses in the end. At least, he hadn't seen them. Perhaps he hadn't given them enough credit, had assumed that America was more like Russia that it was.

Now Bryan Dorsey appeared, looking more like a ghost than a

man, his coat dusted with ashes. Joe reached out a hand. "Bryan, you're all right. Thank God."

Dorsey appeared stunned. "The whole town will be destroyed," he said dully. "I've never seen anything like it. With the wind, they won't have a chance."

He shook his head and turned to leave. Joe rose with his bandage only half wrapped. "I'll go with you," he said.

Annuta protested, "But what can we do, Yosl?"

The buildings of the commune continued to burn. "We can fight the fire."

"But what about our own dead, our homes?"

Joe looked around him. Women were ministering to the lifeless shapes on the ground. "It's too late for us," he said.

thirty-eight

The large bell in the Lutheran church was clanging furiously, though no one was in the belfry pulling the ropes. The air was full of sand, white ash, and cinders, and Joe's eyes and nostrils burned. He began to tie the horse's reins, then changed his mind. Better to give the animal a chance to live if he couldn't get back.

Main Street was jammed with wagons filled with chairs, rugs, and other furniture, and people milled helplessly about, their eyes glazed with terror, but saying nothing. That was what was most surprising: the silence, and over it the wail of the wind and the smell of fire.

At the north end of town, men were working frantically, their heads and mouths covered with wet handkerchiefs, digging trenches and felling what trees remained standing. For the moment, the wind had reversed, and fire rose up against it like a huge scarlet building, a plume of sparks and cinders suspended in the air.

Joe found Tom Jensen clearing away underbrush, his blond hair black with ashes. His eyebrows were already singed off. "This is a hell of a job you've gotten us," he shouted.

"We had nothing to do with it," Joe said. "It was Kleinschmidt."

Jensen spat at Joe's feet. "Kleinschmidt never would have come here if it wasn't for you—you know that as well as I do."

Joe looked at the young mayor in astonishment. "You didn't talk that way when my people were saving your homes and stores from the flood."

"We have floods every year," Jensen said, but his tone softened.

"Can I help?" Joe said finally. "There's no point in arguing."

Jensen measured him carefully, then pushed a shovel at him. "Why not? If we're going to burn, you might as well, too. We haven't got enough water to keep those buildings wet, and it wouldn't do any good anyway. All we can hope is that the wind don't turn back again. If it does, all the water in the world won't help."

In an hour they cleared a twenty-yard strip of dirt around the town's edge. The wind had shifted again, blowing southeast now and causing the fire to jump the Kickapoo, setting the cottonwoods on the other side ablaze. Joe's throat was raw from breathing soot, and he'd lost track of Annuta and Dorsey.

There was nothing more to do on the north end, so he worked his way toward the river, but before he could reach it, he saw a man trying to steal his horse. He shouted, but his voice was lost in the wind, so he threw a rock at the thief, hitting the horse instead. Now the man turned, and Joe saw Dr. Briggs holding a gun.

"That's my horse," Joe said stupidly.

Briggs smiled ironically. "Now, comrade, you know we have no personal property. Each to each, according to his needs, eh? Get out of my way." He waved the gun in Joe's direction.

But Joe stood his ground. There was noise all around, but they seemed alone. Briggs could shoot him in the street, and it would cause no excitement. Still, it was satisfying to see Briggs obviously in retreat. "We defeated you," Joe said.

Briggs shrugged. "I got what I came for," he said.

"What do you mean?" Joe said. "Kleinschmidt's finished. After this, everyone will know him for what he is."

"You're probably right," Briggs said. "But that doesn't matter to me."

"But you work for Kleinschmidt," Joe said, frustrated by Briggs's nonchalance, the sneer on his fat face.

The doctor smiled broadly. "You're such a smart boy, Abrams, always studying, writing. But you still don't see how it is, do you?"

Joe knew he should head for the river, that this was no time to debate. But Briggs annoyed him. "How what is?"

"I don't work for Kleinschmidt," Briggs said, waggling the gun in Joe's direction. "Maybe he works for me, but it doesn't really matter now. Anyway, what can you say for yourself? Last I saw, your place was burning up."

Joe felt like a fool. Suddenly, it was obvious that Briggs had been using all of them—Kleinschmidt, Liberty, even Ben and the other comrades. And while Joe had never trusted the phrenologist, he hadn't even suspected his true motives. He was furious and went for Briggs, but the doctor stepped nimbly out of the way and grazed Joe's temple with the butt of his revolver. When Joe came to, Briggs was on the horse, towering over him. He thought the doctor would shoot, but instead Briggs leaned down to shout over the din.

"Good luck, comrade. You'll need it. And if you live, I'd have a good phrenologist take a look at your head." Then he laughed and rode off toward the river.

Joe sat waiting for the fog to clear. Then he got to his feet and walked slowly back to the trenches. Jensen was nowhere to be found, and there were only a few men talking among themselves in a desultory way. But then the wind turned again, this time blowing the fire directly into their faces with a force so strong that there wasn't time to sound the alert. The heat was like a blast furnace sucking up air. Joe dropped back instinctively and raised his hands to cover his eyes. The water wagon was in front of the dry goods store, and now two men started pumping frantically.

Momentarily, the fire was thwarted by the trenches and piles of dirt in its path, but soon the wind carried sparks over the cleared area and rained them on the dry wooden roofs lining the street. Like small torches, the cinders fell everywhere, and soon the general store was in flames. Then the post office went up like waste paper in a grate, and the small homes that flanked the commercial buildings began to catch fire one by one, like spokes in a wheel.

"Fall back, fall back," someone yelled as the men flailed helplessly at the burning buildings with their axes. Then the tall, graceful elms were afire, and overhead Joe saw the trees like huge constellations burning brilliantly in the night sky.

Step by step they retreated in a ragged line down Main Street, the water wagon an anchor between them. They stopped frequently to douse themselves with water or throw dirt at the flames, trying always to fight the natural impulse to give in to fear and run. Joe's vision was blurred by tears and his cheeks throbbed; now it felt as if an enormous ball of hot cotton had lodged in his throat, but there was nothing that could be done about it. The fire advanced inexorably but leisurely, stopping periodically to venture down a side street or alley before returning to its primary task. Joe knew he would soon be swallowed up as casually as the stores and homes had been, but he continued to throw water at the flames anyway, to fight for his life.

Behind him, he heard the shrieks of frightened women and children and wondered where Annuta had gone. Now that Briggs had taken the horse, they had no means of escape from the inferno, but he wanted to be with her, to help her if he could. On his right, the *Beacon-Call* office was empty, but as they passed the livery, he heard, incredibly, the bass voice of Jacob Kleinschmidt speaking from the stage that had been erected just hours before.

Bareheaded, his robe in tatters, the Moses stood alone, no drummer or bodyguards with him now, ranting at the terrified masses fleeing toward the river. "Oh, yes, oh, yes," he screamed. "The end is nigh—the fires of iniquity burn bright; our sins are being repaired by the Lord and we will pay for our immorality, we will see for ourselves the fires of the Apocalypse."

But Kleinschmidt might as well have been talking to himself. He stared blindly into the holocaust, shaking his fists at the people in the street and the burning buildings. "Vengeance is mine, saith the Lord," he shouted as a large branch fell, narrowly missing him. "Vengeance is mine." The branch landed on the back of the stage, where it set the dry wood ablaze.

Joe started to mount the stage, but Jensen appeared from nowhere to pull him back down. "Don't be a damned fool any more than you are already. It's not your job to save that jackass's life."

Joe stood down, remembering what Briggs had said. He'd always thought Kleinschmidt was cynical, a manipulator, but he had been wrong. It turned out the Moses was a true believer, crazy perhaps, but sincere. Now the fire danced around his outstretched arms, illuminating the Moses's sweating face. He raised his fist again as flames climbed up his caftan and screamed, "Vengeance is mine," as the stage collapsed in flames, burying him in burning timbers.

But there was no time to rescue him and probably no point, anyway. They were barely twenty-five feet from the Kickapoo with the town in flames before them. The river was crowded with women, children, and animals. Furniture floated in the water as wagons capsized and people took shelter beneath them. Jensen called the small group of men together in the lee of the hotel, a few feet from the landing.

"Nothing more we can do," he said, "except maybe save ourselves. The hotel and the mill are brick and ought to last longer than the rest. Downstream, the river gets a little wider, a little rougher. You might try to move some of the women down there if you can, but it's so crowded now, it's going to be hard without someone drowning. I don't know if it's better to drown or burn. You choose. Watch yourselves." He shook hands all around, and then the men scattered without speaking.

The banks of the river were lined with people as far as Joe could see. The burning trees on the east side of the Kickapoo blocked any escape in that direction, and downriver the houses on the bank were burning already. If the river had been wider, their chances would have been better. As it was, so much burning debris was falling into the water that it looked like an oil dump. He rubbed his eyes and was suddenly paralyzed by pain. Dumbly, he staggered into the water, not caring where he was going, his head aching from his wound, his arms numb with fatigue.

"Yosl, here," Annuta called, and then she was with him, dousing his shoulders, caressing him, kissing his burning eyes. She was an angel, he thought as he collapsed into her arms. Then they squatted as best they could in the shallow river as Annuta continued to pour muddy water over Joe's burning back and shoulders. She tore off a piece of her dress and tied it around his face, partially covering his eyes, and he pressed his face to her breasts so hard that he could hear her heart pounding.

They stayed in the shadow of the mill, which had remained standing, its contents on fire but its brick walls strong against the flames. It occurred to Joe that they'd be killed if the walls collapsed, but he was too tired to move, nearly too exhausted to stand, to keep his head above water. Although upriver the Kickapoo was nearly dry, in the natural basin that bordered the town, enough water had accumulated to power a modest current. A cow swam past with a child on its back, holding onto its horns. Then a woman appeared next to Joe, clutching a bundle to her bosom. When she looked into the wrap, however, it was empty. "Daniel," she shrieked. "My baby." She looked despairingly at the roiling water, but no one seemed to hear, and then the woman was gone, carried downstream with the cow and the baby.

Throughout the night, Joe and Annuta remained on their knees holding each other, too exhausted to speak but alive. Toward dawn, he felt his legs cramp and feared he would be pulled under by paralysis. His body wracked by spasms, he rose and started stumbling blindly toward shore, only to hear Annuta cry out, "Yosl, stop! You're on fire again."

She pulled him back into the water, where he sprawled full length in the river. His arms and legs jerked convulsively, setting up new currents in the river, and still the fire blazed on. Where buildings had stood, a solid wall of flames now rose imperiously on every side, and below the wail of the wind he heard a hundred people wailing piteously in the night.

A young woman sat to Joe's right. Her clothes had been burned away, and red sores covered her back and arms. "Truly, it is the end of the world now," she said dully. "Yes, this is the Apocalypse upon us. It is the end at last."

thirty-nine

They came out of the river when dawn was well established in the sky. The heat was still intense, but it was no longer necessary to sprinkle one another constantly. Joe and Annuta threw themselves on the ground, and immediately he started shivering uncontrollably. The rag had fallen from his eyes, and all around he could see only destruction: the burned husks of buildings, the charred stumps of trees, lifeless bloated bodies floating among the debris in the water. There was an odd, high-pitched keening coming from somewhere behind him, but he lacked the strength to investigate. Somehow Annuta found a dry blanket, which she wrapped around them. Then Joe took her in his arms and wept.

At ten o'clock, wagons started arriving from La Crosse. Food and clothing had been donated by one of the churches, and two large tents were erected in the park, now the only shelter in town. Joe's eyes had begun to cause him acute pain, burning like coals. They were nearly swollen shut, like puffballs of charred skin.

"More dead than alive, ain't you?" said the doctor who examined him. A nurse bandaged his head while the doctor swabbed his eyes with a solution that stung but finally eased the pain. "Good thing you washed them out during the night," the doctor said. "Fella over against the wall had his burned right out. You got off lucky."

"Thank God," Joe said.

"You might start there," the doctor said.

Joe slept through the night and into the next day, unable to differentiate between nightmares and dreams. His parents appeared, but they seemed sad, lost, and when he tried to talk to his mother, she didn't respond. Then Cahan and Liberty came in, arguing about the true nature of socialism. Lizzie and Annuta were together at his bedside, but when he reached out, it was only the cool hands of Annuta that he felt, and then he was as profoundly grateful for the reality as he had been for the dream.

The procession continued. Hayim Goldman looked down at him and shook his head in dismay; Rabbi Isaacson appeared with Jacob Kleinschmidt, but the Moses had shed his green robes and was instead wearing a yarmulke and black capote. Finally, the delirium passed and Joe was alone, neither awake nor asleep, aware only of indistinct noises around him that he couldn't identify. He had survived again, though he wasn't sure why. Life was either a gift or a curse, he didn't know which. They would be the eternal people for at least a while longer.

After a time, he opened his eyes, expecting to see Annuta. But Dorsey was sitting in the chair instead. "You're alive," was all Joe could think of to say.

"Through no fault of my own. The fire outran me, skipped right over the trench I was in like a kid in the park, and by the time I got to town, there was no way past the flames. I spent the night at New Zion."

Joe nodded. He was more comfortable when he closed his eyes. "And how are the comrades?" In the uproar of the fire, he had forgotten all about the battle with the Moses.

For a moment, Dorsey said nothing. Then, "Your uncle's dead. He took a bullet; it must have been the only thing those lunatics hit all night. But he was a big target."

The salt of his tears made Joe gasp with pain, but it was right that he should suffer. What right did he have to live when everyone else in his family had died? He thought of Shmuel, tall and profane, arguing with him at the Indian village barely a week before, of the way he had saved his life during the brush fire. Fat Sam, Antonio had called him, but now Shmuel was a martyr, like Isaac, a hero. Perhaps he would have liked that; maybe it was what he had wanted all along, but Joe didn't think so. Shmuel had wanted to live in peace, but peace was impossible for him to find.

"And the others?" he said at last.

Dorsey seemed relieved. "They made out surprisingly well. There are some burned buildings and some split heads, but your friends are rebuilding, wearing their bandages like battle ribbons."

"Which is what they are."

Dorsey laughed. "If you say so. I'll tell you now, I wouldn't have bet a dime on your chances."

"You fought with us."

Dorsey was embarrassed by this. "When was the last time Ireland won a war?" he said. "Besides, I couldn't have you think all Christians were against you."

"I never thought so, Bryan. You could have been killed as easily as Shmuel, as any of us. You did a brave thing."

Dorsey looked at the ground and said nothing. He seemed to associate compliments with lying, as if he had been brought up to distrust praise. Finally, he said, "Will you stay on here?"

"I think I've had enough of the frontier," Joe said. "I'm not much of a leader anyway, and I'm a terrible farmer. I was never made for this place, interesting as it is. I came here only because of my uncle, and now he's gone."

"Back to New York then, to the *Forward*?"

"I'm no journalist either. Cahan used to complain that I got so involved in peoples' problems that the paper would never get written. No, I think I'll go to the university in Madison, if they'll have me. My father wanted me to become an educated man." With difficulty, Joe raised himself to an elbow. "What about you?"

"My shop's ruined, the second time this year," Dorsey said. "I guess I could rebuild, but I don't know if it's worth it. There ain't much left of the town, and the last thing they'll need right away is a paper."

"Maybe your friend in Milwaukee can find you a job?"

Dorsey didn't seem enthusiastic. "Maybe, but when you've been in charge of something, even a sheet as small as mine, it's hard to go back to working for someone else." He rose and offered his hand. "It's been good knowing you, Joe."

"I'll see you again, won't I?"

Dorsey smiled. “Sure, but there’s someone else waiting.”

Joe fell back on the pillows and closed his eyes. Annuta. He was glad; he’d had enough visitors for one day. He heard her come in, but she said nothing. Finally, he opened his eyes and saw Lizzie instead. She had been crying, and Joe realized he’d never expected to see her again, despite the dream. “What are you doing here?” he said, and immediately regretted his abruptness. “Not that I’m not happy to see you,” he added lamely.

She nodded. “It’s all right. I heard about the fire and had to make sure you were all right. I was in La Crosse. They said it destroyed everything.”

Suddenly, Joe remembered Liberty lying unconscious in the clearing, but couldn’t bring himself to ask the question. Lizzie anticipated him. “Father was lucky,” she said. “They took him to the hospital in La Crosse this morning.”

Joe nodded. “I’m glad to hear it,” he said. He was. He’d never wished Liberty harm. But he was surprised Lizzie wasn’t with him. “What will you do now?”

Lizzie’s eyes filled with tears. “I came to tell you something, Yosl. I wanted to before, but I couldn’t; now it doesn’t matter, except to me.”

Joe wondered if she was going to propose marriage. He was too exhausted to think about his feelings—if he even felt anything anymore. She crushed her handkerchief in her hands, arms trembling, then she looked up, resolute. “It’s about Father,” she said, struggling for words. She opened her mouth, but there was no sound. Joe waited. Finally, she got it out. “He’s not my father,” she said simply.

Joe wondered if he had understood her correctly, if perhaps there was some problem with language. “What, then?”

“He’s my husband,” Lizzie said. And then, since Joe could say nothing, she continued in a rush of words. “Edward and my father were friends. They started a commune together in Missouri. I was only thirteen, but I loved Edward and admired him; I still do. He had been married before and his wife did run off—that much of what I told you was true. Now he was alone, and he needed someone, even a girl as young as I was. That winter my father died, and then I was alone, too. It seemed like a natural thing to do, but we knew others wouldn’t understand, so when we came here, we said he was my father. It didn’t matter before you came.”

Joe said nothing, but already he was adjusting his view of things, because she was right. It did seem natural; in a way it made sense. Now he understood why she couldn't leave Liberty, even though she was a grown woman. But he and Lizzie had been lovers. He didn't understand that. Joe looked at her seriously. "I thought you were in love with me."

Lizzie dried her eyes and blew her nose. "I was. That was the problem. Edward didn't mind my being with others because there was nothing like that between us, but I'd never gotten emotionally involved with anyone else before, never cared for another man. We talked about telling you the truth, but it always seemed too complicated."

Complicated. That was the least of it. He felt deceived, duped, a fool, though he knew Liberty was the cuckold. Anger burned behind his left eye, but Joe couldn't find the words to express what he felt. And he wondered what Lizzie was getting at, anyway. Did she expect him to come live with them? It seemed impossible, and besides, now there was Annuta. Suddenly he appreciated her more than ever. He wanted to see her, to tell her, before she escaped. But Lizzie was in the way, as usual. He couldn't look at her without doubting himself. At last, he said, "Yes, I can see that." Then there was an awkward silence between them.

Finally, Lizzie got to her feet. She leaned over and brushed his forehead with her lips. "Good-bye, then, Yosl," she said.

Joe looked up, his eyes tearing now. He tried to raise his hand in salute but lacked the strength. Then she was gone. "Good-bye," he whispered to the empty tent.

forty

Suddenly, you are a famous man. Dorsey sold the story of the battle with Kleinschmidt and the fire to his friend's paper in Milwaukee, and reporters have been talking to you ever since. More important, donations have poured in, not just from Wisconsin or the Midwest but from all over the country and even Europe. A wagonload of lumber arrived from St. Paul, along with workmen to help rebuild New Zion, and food comes daily from Madison and Milwaukee. Then Cahan rewrote Dorsey's story under the headline "The Maccabees of Wisconsin," and now you must find an investment advisor.

Still too weak to work, you are amused by all this, but soon you've had enough. Annuta guards the door, and you give interviews to no one. Each afternoon, you take her arm and walk tentatively to the river, where you sit for an hour and talk quietly. You feel that the efforts to restore what was should be satisfying, but the scars of the past are too painful. You prefer the river, for it is always new, always moving.

In time, you return to New Zion to survey the work that has been done. There is a new dining hall and a beautiful library with books sent from New York. A dormitory is being built in the woods, and the laundry has been torn down for a stable. Suddenly, there are five more horses and workers in for the summer to help with the garden and other chores. It strikes you that the commune now looks as you had imagined it would when you came over from Russia. Then you remember the price of this success, and you know it wasn't worth it.

Gays Mills is rebuilding, too. The publicity surrounding the conflagration of New Zion has benefited them as well, and Tom Jensen has asked you to serve on the town council. You tell him you're too weak, and eventually they select Ben in your place. You are weak, but the truth is you feel your life here is over.

During the long slow afternoons, you think, oddly, of the Moses, and wonder if he and the rabbis were right, if this devastation could possibly have come from God, and whether, now, He has caused New Zion to be reborn like the phoenix. You find yourself asking if there was a reason for the suffering, for your uncle's death. And the town is bustling, people have returned; it has even rained, ending the long drought.

You still have not spoken to Annuta, and the more time goes by, the harder it seems. So much is assumed, so little is said. You are together, but as before, she is your nurse, and you wonder how to make the subtle transition to lover, or even wife. And you find yourself afraid that she'll turn away once she knows your true intentions. You know Lizzie is gone—with Liberty to Kansas, as she had said—but you wonder if she has gone far enough—if she could—and what Annuta will say about that. At times, the words seem to bubble in your mouth like milk, but when you try to speak, nothing comes out, and you settle back into comfortable routine. She works on her sewing pattern; you read your book. Time goes by.

forty-one

July 27, 1906

Dear Mr. Cahan,

Since you know of our recent troubles, there is no need to inform you further. My uncle, Shmuel Abramovitz, is dead after having fought gallantly on our behalf. I am only glad that Shmuel's efforts were ultimately in a victorious cause and that we had a minyan and a rabbi to sing Kaddish for him.

My purpose in writing is twofold: I want to ask that you look after my friend Hayim Goldman, who has decided to leave Wisconsin and return to New York, and I am resigning my position as correspondent on *The Forward.* It has been a great honor as well as a pleasure to work for you, but I'm leaving New Zion and doubt my further adventures will be of any interest to your readers.

I'm pleased to report that the work of New Zion is continuing under new leadership. Ben is taking my place, and thanks to the donations of our many friends all over the world, our future is now secure for the first time.

As for myself, I plan to devote my time to the corporeal needs of mankind rather than the spiritual ones. If I can understand the body, perhaps in time I will glimpse the soul.

I'm grateful for your help and friendship and hope in some way the dispatches sent from this office have justified your faith in me. You have, sir, my prayers for your continued success, though I know you neither want nor need them, as well as my very best wishes.

Sincerely,
Joseph Abrams

There was a knock on the door as Joe sealed the letter, and he looked up to see Hayim Goldman standing there. "Here, I've just written Cahan about you."

Hayim folded the letter and put it in his pocket. "I don't read other people's mail," he said. "But don't worry about me. I can take care of myself."

"I never doubted it," Joe said. "After all, you found your way here."

"And a good thing I did," Hayim said.

"Then why leave? Ben wants you to stay on. Why not make New Zion your home?"

Hayim seemed touched by this but shook his head vigorously. "No, this country isn't for me, just as it wasn't really the right place for Shmuel. That was his trouble, even if he didn't understand it. We're still Europeans," he said sadly, "too old for a new country." Then he seemed to brighten. "But in New York I will find others who are similarly crippled, perhaps even a woman to take care of me in my old age."

It was the first time Joe had heard Hayim mention a woman other than his wife. "You sound almost cheerful," he said.

"Why not? I don't fear death, and there may be more awaiting me than I expected." He looked out at the comrades working. Raw wood and noise was everywhere. "This was my Gomel, Yosl," Hayim said quietly. "Here, we met the barbarians and I fought like a mensch. It doesn't erase my shame at what happened before—nothing could do that—but somehow I survived this catastrophe, and for the first time I feel free to live again, to be a man like other men. My wife and child are still dead, but I no longer feel they are on my shoulders, that laughing would be a crime. God knows why, but that is the fact. It is time to go back."

They embraced at the door, and then Hayim was gone, his quick, jerky walk taking him across the clearing, past the dining hall, and toward Gays Mills without a backward glance. Joe looked around. The unnatural neatness of the office saddened him. He had put his few belongings in a rucksack and the desk was clear, a soft patina of dust already softening the wood. He was about to leave when he thought of Shmuel and Liberty and regretted their rivalry. He had spent hours with each of them, and now both were gone. All that remained of his time at New Zion was this small pack and the letter he'd just written. It didn't seem like enough.

He closed the door and stood for a moment in the sunlight. Then he walked first to the kitchen and then to the river, looking for Annuta. The Kickapoo was high and fast, and he found her just below the rapids. They were only a few yards from the spot where Liberty had married Ben and Rebecca. As he was about to speak, she turned around but didn't seem surprised to see him packed to leave. She moved slightly, as if inviting him to join her, and then they sat on the grass, shy, like new lovers, and Joe remembered the first time they'd met, how she had cried in the loft of the old dining hall. And how, later, he'd hurt her and lacked the courage to ease her pain. He remembered the night of the battle, when she had insisted on coming to Gays Mills and then stayed all night with him in the river, washing his eyes repeatedly with water. What was most remarkable was that she had never asked for anything in return, and now he understood that he couldn't possibly leave without her.

"I came—" he began.

"I know," Annuta interrupted. "You're leaving. I heard from Ben." She spoke rapidly, as if it were something she wanted to get over.

Joe nodded. He wanted to continue speaking but couldn't frame the words properly. He felt he should apologize, but now that seemed inappropriate. It was too late for apologies or for thanks. They were what they were to each other. He looked at her. Dark hair framed her face and her skin was fresh and golden in the morning light. Now it occurred to him again that she might not be willing to leave, that she might have changed her mind and fallen out of love with him. The thought made him shiver. "My eyes are much better," he said weakly. "Now I think I should use them for something worthwhile."

"More worthwhile than our work here at New Zion?"

"Of course not," Joe said, embarrassed. "What I meant was that I've never really been at home here. I'm not a farmer like Ben."

Annuta nodded. "I see," was all she said.

"What will you do, Annuta?" Joe said. The idiotic question made him blush, but he couldn't help himself.

She looked at him directly for a moment, her eyes flashing with anger. Then she looked upstream. "Becky wants me to stay," she said.

Joe wanted to reach out, to hold her, but she seemed cold now, withdrawn. Then he remembered Whitman, the man Cahan said would teach him about America.

"Camerado," he said softly,

"I give you my hand!
I give you my love more precious than money,
I give you myself
. . . .

Will you give me yourself?
Will you come travel with me?
Shall we stick by each other as long as we live?"

Annuta smiled at him, pleased and surprised. Then she reached for his hand. "I want to be more than your comrade, Yosl. I've had enough of that."

A surge of happiness moved through his chest. "Then be my wife," he said. "Please."

She put her arms around him, and he held her tight beneath the noise of the rapids. In that moment he felt the essential mixture of joy and happiness he knew he had been searching for. Painful as it had been, he had grown; he had become a man, capable of going out on his own and living a life with her. Together, they rose from the grass and started arm-in-arm for the commune. There was an announcement to make to the others, it was already midmorning, and they had a long way to go.